GUARDIANS OF THE FOREST

LEOFRIC, A KNIGHT who has been raised to fear
the dark forest of Loren since birth, is plunged
into that strange realm when he is drawn into
a plot to avert a magical disaster of cataclysmic
proportions. Joined by the ferocious wood elf
Kyarno, they must avert a plot by the
monstrous beastmen to corrupt the land with
their Chaotic influence. As the forces of magic
run wild, can wood elves and humans put
aside their differences for long enough to
defeat the evil forces of Chaos?

A WARHAMMER NOVEL

GUARDIANS OF THE FOREST

Graham McNeill

For the real Helene du Reyne. Once in a while, right in the middle of an ordinary life, love gives us a fairy tale.

A BLACK LIBRARY PUBLICATION

First published in Great Britain in 2005 by
BL Publishing,
Games Workshop Ltd.,
Willow Road, Nottingham,
NG7 2WS, UK

10 9 8 7 6 5 4 3 2 1

Cover illustration by Jeff Johnson
Map by Nuala Kinrade.

A CIP record for this book is available from the British Library.

ISBN 13: 978 1 84416 235 2
ISBN 10: 1 84416 235 4

Distributed in the US by Simon & Schuster
1230 Avenue of the Americas, New York, NY 10020.

Printed and bound in Great Britain by
Bookmarque, Surrey, UK.

See the Black Library on the Internet at
www.blacklibrary.com

Find out more about Games Workshop
and the world of Warhammer at
www.games-workshop.com

THIS IS A DARK age, a bloody age, an age of daemons and of sorcery. It is an age of battle and death, and of the world's ending. Amidst all of the fire, flame and fury it is a time, too, of mighty heroes, of bold deeds and great courage.

AT THE HEART of the Old World sprawls the Empire, the largest and most powerful of the human realms. Known for its engineers, sorcerers, traders and soldiers, it is a land of great mountains, mighty rivers, dark forests and vast cities. And from his throne in Altdorf reigns the Emperor Karl-Franz, sacred descendant of the founder of these lands, Sigmar, and wielder of his magical warhammer.

BUT THESE ARE far from civilised times. Across the length and breadth of the Old World, from the knightly palaces of Bretonnia to ice-bound Kislev in the far north, come rumblings of war. In the towering World's Edge Mountains, the orc tribes are gathering for another assault. Bandits and renegades harry the wild southern lands of the Border Princes. There are rumours of rat-things, the skaven, emerging from the sewers and swamps across the land. And from the northern wildernesses there is the ever-present threat of Chaos, of daemons and beastmen corrupted by the foul powers of the Dark Gods. As the time of battle draws ever nearer, the Empire needs heroes like never before.

30 miles

the wild heath

DARRAVON

GREY MOUNTAINS

the northern sentinels

X Battle of the deathliness

Tower of the eternal wood

hills of the dead

glade of the lost

upper drannafar

waterfall palace of the naiad court

chasm glade of berthir seun

vaults of winter

spyre of the skull lords

crag halls of findol

council of branch

feast halls of the wardance

deep forests

halls of anagreth

mirror pools

greenskin monolith of anchip

glade of eternal moonlight

glade of woe

THE EMPIRE

BRETONNIA

altdorf · talabheim · nuln · corak · norn · carak zor · parravon · athel loren · quenelles · marienburg · bad spa sterno

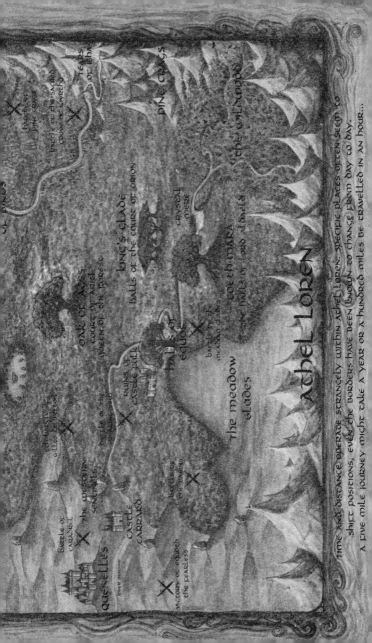

'I shall wolfe your flesh and snap your bones,
Skrind your folk and burne their homes.
For mocking ked to dare my rage,
Your jibe it traps me like a cage.
The unclaimed ones must dread my kinde,
Can never squander fear behind.'

PROLOGUE
Season of the Beast

THE BEAST AT the centre of the cave dreamed of blood, blood and war, civilisations torn down and entire populations gorged upon by the children of Chaos. Flames and the coming of the End Times consumed its every thought, order overturned and the rule of the Dark Gods absolute.

Its massive, shaggy form shifted position, its cloven hooves rippling the rock as though it sat upon glistening mud. Curling horns sprouted from its bestial skull, protruding from a ripped and stained leather mask behind which two bovine eyes glimmered with dark malice. A web of skulls was woven into the shaggy mane that ran the length of its twisted spine, the jaws opening and closing in silent screams of anguish.

The monster clutched a gnarled and twisted staff in one massive fist, its substance slithering and insubstantial, as though the beast's flesh merged with the dark

11

wood. It traced patterns and lines in the fluid matter of the cavern floor, ever more chaotic and irregular as they overlapped and spiralled.

Clouds of stinking vapour gusted from its snorting nostrils, twisting and swirling in the air before being absorbed by the fabric of the walls. The rock glistened with a dank dew of moisture, dancing images of war and death burning in its depths, reflections of the twisted thoughts of the shaggy beast that drooled thick ropes of animal saliva.

Humans called it the Shadow-Gave, while the elves knew it as Cyanathair and in the dwarf tongue it was called Gor-Dunn.

The fires of war burned in its eyes and it could feel the approach of its children, the true inheritors of the world. It could sense the breath of Chaos within them, the boon of change and mutation that marked them out as the chosen of the gods. Three came, the mightiest beasts of their herds, fierce and proud, filled with power and drawn towards this dank, icy cave to seek approval from the gods that theirs was the right to rule this gathering of warherds.

It turned a rheumy eye towards the cave mouth as the weak autumn light was blocked off by the three supplicants. It saw they were tall and broad, with great, corded muscles beneath dark, matted fur, each the master of a great warherd. All three carried crude weapons: heavy iron axes or thick, blade-studded clubs, though in truth any one of them could fight as well with horn, tooth or claw. One stood on thick, goat-like legs, its shaggy head crowned with a mass of bronze-tipped antlers and a thick mane of bright orange fur. Another stamped iron-shod hooves, its rump elongated like that of a horse, though its skin was scaled and bronze. Dark spines grew from its back and an extra set of arms sprouted from beneath its armpits.

But greatest of all the Beastlords was a massive, bull-headed creature with dark, bloodstained fur, its hide scarred by decades of killing and battle. Thick, hooked chains looped across its chest and it wore spiked shoulder guards crudely fashioned from the breastplates of those it had slaughtered. It carried a massive, double-headed axe, its blades rusted, but with a potent magical aura surrounding them.

The beast in the cave let out a single bray, guttural and wet, and the three supplicants advanced towards it, their steps halting and unsure, though none wished to show weakness before the others. To do so would be to die.

The Shadow-Gave felt the breath of the gods sluicing through its body in a torrent of power and exhaled it as a noxious cloud of dark, writhing mist. The mist pulsed with the essence of the north, growing and billowing outwards to envelop the three who had come to stand in its presence.

Instantaneously, the creature with bronzed antlers collapsed, roaring in agony as its body was gifted with the power of the gods and thrashing limbs and grasping, thorned pseudopods erupted from its fluid flesh. The other two backed away from the howling creature spawned from the Shadow-Gave's gifts and awaited their fate at the hands of the magical mist.

Both were enveloped by the miasmic cloud of sorcerous power and the Shadow-Gave felt their will and ambition war with the power of change that seared through their veins. The bronze-skinned centaur creature reared up on its hind legs, the dark spines on its back mutating into rippling tentacles with snapping jaws. It lunged towards the Shadow-Gave with a shriek of bestial fury, but a massive, clawed hand dragged it back, the huge bull-headed monster slashing its axe through the writhing creature's midsection. Dark ichor sprayed from the wound, hot and stinking, and the Beastlord cried out as its matted fur burned where the blood spattered then ran in rivulets down its fanged, bovine features, scarring pale grooves in its face.

Its flesh darkened, taking on the bronze hue of the beast it had just killed and its breath smoked with the heat of a furnace. It let out a mighty bellow, the very walls of the cave cracking at its din, and the Shadow-Gave nodded in acceptance as the writhing black mist dispersed and faded from sight.

The massive beastman let out a great, snorting breath, its hide now dark and scaled, its horned head scarred and burnt, but its flickering, multi-coloured eyes shone with purpose and power. It raised its axe in a brief salute to the shaggy, horned creature at the centre of the cave and ripped one of the chains from its armour, plunging a barbed hook into the screaming flesh of the thrashing creature that had first succumbed to the Shadow-Gave's magic.

Without further ado, the Beastlord turned and marched from the darkness of the cave, leading the snapping, howling spawn by the thick chain looped around a muscled forearm. Its thoughts crystallised as it left the dank confines of the Shadow-Gave's lair, feeling the breath of cold air from the mouth of the passage-way.

It stepped into the cold light of day, feeling its eyes burn with its purity, and grunted in satisfaction as it saw the gathered warherds. Hundreds of twisted bestial creatures awaited the return of their leaders, braying

minotaurs, growling beastmen, stamping centaur creatures and all manner of things so blessed by the touch
of the Dark Gods that any resemblance to the beasts of
this world had long since vanished.

As great a herd as it was, the Beastlord knew that
many of these beasts would not survive the winter, too
malnourished and too weak to hunt what they needed
to survive. The resurgence of the rat-things in the high
peaks had driven them from their hunting grounds and
down the northern flanks of the mountains.

The herds had bemoaned their fate, but the Beastlord
now saw this for what it truly was – a sign from the
gods.

Now it was time to descend to the lands of men and
feed once more.

The Beastlord led its chained spawn towards the monstrous host, revelling in their howls and snorts of
abasement – the touch of the Shadow-Gave was upon it
and all the beasts could see its favour. They gathered
around the Beastlord, raising their bellowing voices in
praise of the Dark Gods as it marched through the herd.

Far below, the Beastlord could see a massive, sprawling expanse of forest, a patchwork of browns, greens
and golds, nestling at the foot of tall, snow-capped
peaks of grey rock.

With his newly enhanced flesh he could smell the
rank stench of earth magic emanating from the forest
and see the dimming power that radiated from its heart
as winter closed in.

The Beastlord raised its axe and led the warherd
towards the forest.

BOOK ONE
Autumn's Dying Fire

'The beastmen, the children of Chaos and Long Night, are our sworn enemies. They fight us for our right to exist in the woodlands and forests, and have always, and will always, seek to claim and corrupt Athel Loren for themselves. These are your enemies, child. Know them well, and keep your bow always ready.'

CHAPTER ONE

LEOFRIC COULD FEEL the tension in the men-at-arms around him as they rode through the cold, autumn morning, sensing it in their stiff, awkward movements and strained conversation. He felt apprehension too, but hid it beneath an aloof exterior. It would not do to show nervousness to the lower orders and it would only serve to unsettle his men more were they to sense their lord's unease.

The day was cold and Leofric could feel the coming winter in the sharpness of the air and see it in the golden leaves of the few trees they had passed. The further east through the dukedom of Quenelles he and his soldiers rode, the more scattered patches of snow he saw, the little-used roadway unnaturally dotted in crisp white with drifting clouds of icy mist clinging to the muddy ground.

Thirty nervous-looking peasant men-at-arms rode behind him, their yellow surcoats bright and stark against the dreary landscape. A cold wind blew off the mountains far to the south, their soaring dark peaks cloaked in shawls of snow and despite the thick, woollen undergarments Leofric wore and the padded jerkin beneath his magnificent plate armour, he could still feel the coming cold deep in his bones.

'How far is it to the forest now?' said a voice beside him.

Leofric reined in his tall grey gelding and twisted in the saddle to smile at his wife, Helene, who was riding side-saddle on a slender bay mare. She wore a long gown of red velvet and was wrapped in a thick cloak of bearskin from a great beast Leofric himself had slain with a single lance thrust while on the hunt. Tousled blonde hair spilled around her shoulders and despite her smile, a worry line just above the bridge of her nose spoke to Leofric of her unease.

'Not far now, my dear,' answered Leofric, raising the visor of his helmet. 'Lady willing, perhaps another mile or so.'

Helene nodded and shivered beneath her cloak.

'Are you cold?' asked Leofric, guiding his horse alongside his wife's and detaching his long wolf-pelt cloak from his carved, silver pauldrons.

'No, I'm fine,' she answered. 'It's not the cold. It's… well, you know what it is.'

Leofric nodded. He too could instinctively feel the forest's fey presence on the air, a ghostly, feathery sensation down his spine as though a thousand eyes were spying upon him. His instincts had always served him well as a warrior and he fought the urge to draw the broad-bladed sword that hung at his waist.

'Don't worry,' said Leofric, patting a canvas sack that hung from his saddle, 'once we reach the waystone, it will only be a matter of hours before we are on our way back to the castle and our son. I will have Maixent prepare a hot bath for you and we will all eat roast venison before a roaring fire in the grand hall, then the three of us shall fall asleep together.'

'That sounds heavenly,' agreed Helene. 'I just hope little Beren isn't giving old Maixent too much trouble. You know what he's like when we're not with him.'

'If he is, he'll soon regret it,' said Leofric, remembering the punishments meted out to him at the hands of the castle's sharp-tempered chamberlain. 'It will teach him the virtue of discipline.'

'He's only three, Leofric.'

'A boy is never too young to learn the duties and responsibilities of a knight of Bretonnia,' said Leofric sternly.

Helene stood in the wide footrest of her sidesaddle to kiss her husband and said, 'You're adorable when you're being all serious.'

Leofric Carrard was a tall man, powerfully muscled from long years of wielding a long lance and wearing heavy plate armour into battle. He carried himself like the warrior he was, confident, brave and noble – every inch a knight of Bretonnia. A dark moustache and a triangular wisp of beard below his bottom lip were his only concession to vanity, and his clear green eyes were like chips of emerald set in an angular, regal face that plainly wore the cares of his twenty-five years.

Another horse drew near and a heavyset man with a long beard halted his mount in a splash of mud. He wore a yellow surcoat over a jerkin of studded leather armour, a domed sallet helmet and carried a long, iron-tipped spear. He was accompanied by a similarly dressed figure, a young boy of no more than thirteen summers who carried a tall banner pole. Atop the banner, a fringed pennant of gold depicting a scarlet unicorn rampant below a bejewelled crown snapped in the wind – the banner of Leofric Carrard, lord and master of these lands.

'My lord–' began the heavyset man, respectfully touching the brim of his helmet.

'What is it, Baudel?' said Leofric.

'Begging your pardon, my lord, but we had best not be dawdling here,' explained Baudel, Leofric's chief man-at-arms. 'Best we don't get caught out in the open this close to the forest folk's realm. This time of year it ain't good to be outside.'

'It's never a good time to be outside according to you, Baudel,' pointed out Leofric.

'Aye, nor it is, my lord,' said Baudel, nodding to the east. 'Leastwise not near Athel Loren, anyway.'

'Don't speak that name, Baudel,' chided Helene. 'They say the faerie folk can hear when mortals name their land and are much vexed by how ugly it sounds from our mouths.'

'Begging your pardon, milady,' apologised Baudel. 'I meant nothing by it.'

'You're right though, Baudel,' agreed Leofric, looking into the lifeless grey skies, 'best to be done with this and away before night falls. Prithard of Carcassonne sends word of beastman warbands in his lands – the damn things are everywhere now.'

'My lord!' scoffed Baudel. 'The Distressed is always sending word of such things. He worries when he has nothing to worry about!'

'True,' agreed Leofric, 'but this time I think he might not be crying wolf. I have had similar correspondence from Anthelme and Raynor, men not known for their scare-mongering.'

'All the more reason to be away from here sooner rather than later.'

Leofric nodded, saying, 'And I wish to be near that damned forest not one second longer than I have to be.'

'Hush, Leofric,' said Helene. 'Don't say such things.'

'I'm sorry, my love. I apologise for such language, but you know…'

'Yes,' said Helene, reaching out to lay a hand on Leofric's vambrace. 'I know.'

Leofric patted his wife's hand and gave her a forced smile before snapping down the visor of his helmet and raking back his spurs.

'Ride on!' he yelled, setting off along the road that led towards Athel Loren.

A LOW MIST closed in around the riders, deadening sound and imparting a ghostly quality to the soldiers that followed Leofric as he rode ever eastwards. The road, which had never been more than an overgrown mud track, little travelled and little cared for, petered out to nothing more than a flattened earthen line, barely distinguishable from the rest of the landscape.

The lands of Bretonnia were rich and fertile, the soil dark and fecund, its landscape tilled by the peasants, its sweeping plains of the dukedoms open and green. Unlike the thickly forested realm of the Empire far to the north over the Grey Mountains that embraced the new sciences of alchemy, astrology and engineering, the realm of Bretonnia kept to the ancient ways of chivalric conduct. The beloved King Leoncoeur maintained the codes of behaviour set down by King Louis

.over a thousand years ago and held by the grail monks in the Chapel of Bastonne.

By such martial codes of honour did the knights of Bretonnia uphold their honour and defend their king's lands. To be a knight of Bretonnia was to be a warrior of great skill, noble bearing and virtuous heart, a paragon of all that was honourable.

Leofric felt his right hand slip from the emblazoned reins of his horse and grasp the hilt of his sword as he crested the misty summit of a low rise and saw a dark line of green and gold on the horizon.

Athel Loren...

For centuries this forest had lived in the dreams and nightmares of the Bretonnian people. Even from here, Leofric could feel the power that lay within the dark depths of the forest, a drowsy, dreaming energy that clawed its way into the landscape like the roots of a tree. Dark oaks stood like sentinels at the forest edge, their branches high and leafy, a mixture of greens and russet browns.

Cold mists hugged the ground leading towards the forest, a wild, scrubby heath of unkempt grasses and thorns with stagnant pools of water and lumpen, snow-covered mounds of earth. Here and there, Leofric could see a rusted sword blade, spear point or arrowhead and the occasional bleached whiteness of bone.

No matter how many times he had come to enact the traditional family ritual, the sight of this ancient battle-field always unsettled him, as though restless spirits of the dead still haunted this bleak landscape.

'It's not like I imagined it to be,' said Helene, her voice just a little too shrill.

'No?'

'No, it's... it's, well, I don't know, but I thought it would look different. Given what you've told me I expected something more... unnatural.'

'Trust me, my dear,' said Leofric, 'there is nothing natural about this place.'

'I don't like it though,' said Helene, pulling her cloak tighter about herself. 'It feels like death here.'

'Aye,' agreed Leofric, 'it is a place of darkness.'

'What are those?' asked Helene, pointing to the raised mounds of earth and stone.

Riding alongside Leofric's wife, Baudel said, 'They say that those mounds are burial cairns, raised by the first tribes of men to come this way.'

'Really?' asked Helene, ignoring Leofric's disapproving gaze. 'What else do they say?'

'Well,' continued Baudel, warming to his theme. 'My old da used to tell us that an evil necromancer once raised the dead from their tombs and tried to destroy Athel Loren itself.'

'I know that story!' nodded Helene. 'His army entered the forest and was never seen again. Do you know what happened?'

'It was the forest, milady,' said Baudel, lowering his voice theatrically. 'My old da said that it was the forest what came alive and destroyed his skeleton army.'

'Hush, Baudel!' snapped Leofric. 'Do not be filling my wife's head with such nonsense. If this necromancer existed at all, then no doubt he was killed by the elves of the forest. That's what they are good at, killing and stealing what is not theirs!'

'Sorry, my lord,' said Baudel, suitably chastened.

'Oh, come now, husband, surely it's just a story,' said Helene.

Leofric stopped and turned his horse to face his wife, his face drawn and serious. He shook his head and said, 'Helene, I love you with all my heart, but you are from Lyonesse, not Quenelles.'

'What has that to do with anything?'

'It means you have not grown up in the shadow of the faerie forest, not had to lock and bolt your doors on certain nights to be sure that elven princelings do not come and steal away your children. You have never had to spend days with every gate and shutter drawn as the wild hunt thunders through the sky, killing everything in its path. Trust me on this, we will find no welcome here.'

Helene opened her mouth to let fly a witty riposte, but saw a familiar look she had come to know all too well in her husband's eyes and the quip died in her throat. She nodded and said, 'Then let us be about our business.'

Leofric nodded curtly and turned his horse back towards the forest. The mist thinned as they drew near the forest's edge and he saw the familiar sight of the waystone within the passing of an hour. It reared up atop a flowering mound of grass, its smooth grey surface carved and painted with symbols and spirals, meaningless to him, but which nevertheless raised the hairs on the back of his neck.

He looked left and right, knowing that there were other stones spread evenly along the edge of the forest, but unable to see them due to the clammy mist that the sun seemed unable to burn away.

The knight guided his horse into a hollow depression in the earth with an icy pool at its base and a low cluster of rocks and bushes gathered around its ragged circumference. The top of the looming waystone was still visible, but the majority of its unsettling form was hidden from sight by the lay of the land.

'Halt!' he shouted as he reached the base of the hollow, dragging on his reins and bringing his horse to a halt. He rose in his stirrup and swung his leg over the fine saddle, its leather the colour of polished mahogany. As he dismounted, he saw that the tasselled ends of the yellow and scarlet caparison were muddy and stained, but it couldn't be helped. The gelding was named Taschen, standing seventeen hands high with wide shoulders and powerful muscles that could carry his armoured weight into battle without effort. King Leoncoeur himself had presented the magnificent animal to Leofric after he had saved the king's life during the charge against the daemon prince at Middenheim...

Leofric pushed the thought away, unwilling to relive the terrible memories of the horrific days defending the great northern city of the Empire from the traitor knight Archaon.

He handed Taschen's reins to his squire, a lad whose name he hadn't bothered to learn after his previous squire, Lauder, had died screaming with a beastman's spear in his gut.

The rest of his soldiers drew up in a circle around their lord, dismounting and walking their horses before brushing them down and loosening their girths. Compared to Leofric's steed, the men-at-arms' mounts were poor specimens indeed, and did not bear any heraldic devices or caparison, their riders' lowborn status prohibiting them from doing so.

Leofric marched over to his wife's horse, the reddish brown coat of which was silky and well cared for. He reached up and helped her dismount gracefully from

the saddle, smiling as she hitched up her long red robes
to avoid the worst of the autumnal mud.

'I warned you that your dress would get muddy,' he
said gently.

'And I told you that I didn't care,' she said with a
smile. 'I've grown tired of this gown anyway. My ladies
tell me that red is very passé for this time of year and
that you should be buying me something in lavender
next season.'

'Oh they do, do they?' said Leofric. 'Then the peasantry must work harder next year to pay for it.'

'Indeed they shall,' said Helene and they laughed, not
noticing the pained looks on the men-at-arms' faces at
their overheard conversation.

Leofric turned from Helene and removed the canvas
sack from his saddle, shouting orders to his men and
directing them to the ice-covered pool at the base of the
hollow. The men began breaking the thinner ice at the
edge of the pool with the butts of their spears, taking it
in turns to lead the horses to drink.

Leofric and Helene's horses drank their fill first as was
only right and proper.

The knight of Quenelles moved to the far side of the
icy pool as his squire struggled to lift a gilt-edged reliquary adorned with woodcuts from the back of his dray
horse and carried it over towards Leofric.

'Set it down there,' ordered Leofric, pointing to a flat
rock before him and drawing his sword, a magnificent
blade as long as the butt of a lance and fully three fingers wide. Though it was stronger than steel, the sword
weighed less than the wooden swords the peasants
trained with and could cut through armour with lethal
ease. Its blade was silver steel and shone as though captured starlight had somehow been trapped in its

forging. The sword had been touched by the Lady of the Lake herself many centuries ago and had been passed down the line of Carrard since time before memory. Leofric knew that it was a great honour to bear such a blessed weapon and that when he could no longer carry out his duty to defend his lands and people, he would pass it to Beren, his only son and heir.

Leofric's squire gently set down the reliquary before his master. The box was crafted from young saplings hewn from the Forest of Chalons and carved with stirring scenes that told of the heroic battles of Gilles le Breton, legendary founder of Bretonnia.

Atop the box, an image of the Lady of the Lake, goddess of the Bretonnians, was picked out in silver and rendered with swirling golden tresses. Leofric dropped to his knees as his squire closed his unworthy eyes and opened the winged doors of the reliquary.

The insides of the reliquary were painted with scenes of wondrous lakes and pools of reflective water, with the image of a breathtakingly beautiful woman rising from the depths. A deep cushion of sumptuous red velvet sat within the reliquary, together with the broken hilt of a sword and a faded scrap of cloth, its golden edges frayed and torn.

Leofric closed his eyes, feeling the peace of the Lady's presence wash over him at the sight of such holy relics: the faerie flag, a scrap of shimmering material supposedly torn from the cloak of an elven princeling by Leofric's great grandfather after he chased him from Castle Carrard, and the hilt of a Carrard sword that had cut down the orc warlord, Skargor of the Massif Orcal.

Leofric reached out and ran his gauntleted fingers along the broken hilt and folded cloth as he began his prayers to the Lady.

'Lady, bless me your humble servant, grant me the strength to confront those who ignore the wisdom and beauty of your holy light. You, whose bounty is with me all the days of my life, grant the lands I defend in your name the peace that this appeasement might bring…'

As LEOFRIC BEGAN his prayers to the Lady, Helene sat upon a rock at the edge of the cold pool, gathering her skirts beneath her to make it marginally less uncomfortable. She felt a coldness here, and not just the coldness of the coming winter – something deeper chilled her. She looked back over her shoulder, seeing the gently swaying treetops of Athel Loren and the very tip of the tall waystone that marked the edge of the elven realm.

Strange that the forest did not grow beyond the stones. Idly, Helene wondered why, but then put the thought from her mind as Baudel approached with a pewter plate laden with cuts of cold beef, apples and a wedge of pungent cheese.

'Some lunch, milady?'

'No thank you, Baudel,' she said. 'I'm not really feeling hungry at the moment.'

'I'd ask you to reconsider, milady. It'll be a good few hours before we get back to the castle. Nice cheese, fresh beef to keep you going till then?'

'Very well, Baudel,' said Helene, accepting the plate.

Baudel turned to leave, but Helene looked over at Leofric with a concerned expression and said, 'Sit with me awhile. I want to talk.'

'Milady,' nodded the man-at-arms and sat on a nearby rock, his spear still held upright.

'Baudel, does Leofric seem different to you?'

'I'm not sure I follow, milady,' replied Baudel, guardedly.

'Yes you do,' said Helene. 'Ever since he came back from the Empire and the battles against the northern tribes I've felt a distance between us. You were there too, Baudel, does he seem changed… after the war, I mean?'

'War changes a man, milady.'

'I know that, Baudel, I'm not some milkmaid from Brionne. He's gone off to fight before, but he's never come back like this.'

'Like what?'

'Withdrawn and unwilling to talk about what happened.'

Baudel sighed and glanced over the pool at Leofric who was still kneeling before the Carrard reliquary, deep in his prayers. 'It wouldn't be right, me speaking out of turn about my lord and master, milady.'

'It's all right, I give you leave to speak your mind.'

'I appreciate that, milady, but it still wouldn't be right.'

Seeing the defensive look in the man-at-arms's eyes, Helene nodded and said, 'Very well, Baudel, your loyalty to your master is commendable.'

'Thank you, milady.'

'If you won't tell me what happened, at least tell me of Middenheim, it sounds like a magnificent place.'

'Aye,' nodded Baudel, 'it's grand all right, you've never seen nothing like it, milady, perched on top of a great big rock they call the Ulricsberg, higher than the lighthouse of l'Anguille by a long ways. To look at it you'd think nothing could take it, not man, not monster or nothing. But them northmen had wizards, dragons and other flyin' things that tore the place up with fire and magic, and they damn near won.'

'But they didn't, did they,' stated Helene.

'No, they didn't, but it was a close run thing, let me tell you,' said Baudel, darkly. 'The king himself led a hundred knights in the charge that faced a great daemon lord. Leofric rode in that charge and only the king and a handful of his knights rode out from that battle and... and you're a clever one aren't you, milady, getting me to spill my guts like that.'

Helene shrugged, realising that she would get no more from Baudel this day. She nibbled on a cut of meat and broke off a piece of cheese.

'It was devious of me wasn't it?' she admitted with a smile.

'Downright cunning,' agreed Baudel, rising from his seat.

'One last thing before you go,' said Helene.

'Yes?' asked Baudel, warily.

'Why can't I hear any birds or animals here? It's all very quiet apart from us.'

'The forest sleeps milady. It's waiting, just waiting for spring. As for the animals, well I think that perhaps they're all getting ready to sleep away the winter.'

'Yes, that must be it, Baudel. Thank you.'

'You're most welcome, milady,' said the man-at-arms, making an extravagant bow before turning and making his way back down to the pool where the rest of the soldiers looked to their mounts or ate hunks of hard bread moistened by a thin gruel.

Helene watched him go, frowning and cursing herself for being too obvious. Baudel might be a peasant, but he was cleverer than most and had seen through her, admittedly clumsy, gambit.

She shivered again, feeling a crawling sensation up her spine and the ghostly caress of something unseen. Nothing stirred the air or broke the unnatural silence around her, save the hushed conversations of Leofric's soldiers. The cold was seeping through her furs and she wished to be away from this place, back in the castle with little Beren clutched close to her as she read him tales of heroic knights who slew evil dragons.

She missed her little boy and hoped that this strange ritual of the Carrard family would not take too long.

Helene still didn't understand the full significance of the ritual Leofric was here to perform, something to do with planting a seedling before the waystone and making an offering to the faerie folk.

Apparently, the practice had begun eighty years ago when family legend told that a much loved ancestor of Leofric's had been taken by the elves as a young boy and had never been seen again. Carrards had been coming to the edge of Athel Loren every five years since then to enact its quaint traditions.

She knew that Leofric begrudged such entreaties to the elven realm, though understood that he would never think of leaving the ritual unperformed, as such a stain upon the family honour would be unthinkable to a knight of Bretonnia.

As she watched her husband pray, she smiled, feeling the love she had for him as a contented warmth in her heart. She remembered the sun-drenched tilting fields outside Couronne where she had first met Leofric, picturing the dashing young knight errant with his scarlet unicorn pennant streaming from his lance as he unhorsed Chilfroy of Artois, a feat none of the gathered knights and dukes ever expected to see in their lifetimes.

Leofric had had the pick of the ladies that day, all wishing him to carry their favour upon his lance, but he had knelt before her, Helene du Reyne, sweat-streaked hair plastered across his forehead and a mischievous grin creasing his face.

'It would honour me greatly if you would consent to grant me your favour,' he'd said.

'Why should I do such a thing?' she had replied, straining for a regal aloofness.

'Lady, I have unhorsed my opponent in the glory of the joust!' he said. 'None other than the Duke of Artois himself. I am the greatest warrior here!'

'You are arrogant, young man, and have not the humility of a knight.'

'It is not arrogance if it is the truth,' he had pointed out.

'How do I know that for sure?'

'Tell me how I may prove it to you, my lady, for I love you and would ride to every corner of Bretonnia if you would but grant me a kiss.'

'Only the corners of Bretonnia? Is that all?'

'Not at all, I would ride to far Araby and drag back the greatest sultan were you to look favourably my way.'

'Just to Araby?' she had teased.

'Only to begin with,' he had continued with a smile. 'Then I would sail to the far jungles of Lustria and bring back the treasures of the heathen gods if you might consent to speak my name.'

'Impressive.'

'I'm only just getting started,' he said. 'I've the rest of the world to travel yet!'

Deciding she had teased him enough, Helene had laughed and handed him a silken blue scarf, edged in white lace, and said, 'Here, you may carry my favour, sir knight. Win me this tourney and I might let you attempt to make me happy…'

'I shall, my lady! I will unhorse every man here if it will make you happy!'

And he had. Leofric had defeated every knight at the tournament before courting her as diligently and as wonderfully as any young woman could want. They were wed in the grail chapel in Quenelles a year later, and ten months after that, Helene had borne Leofric a strong son, whom they had named Beren, after one of the heroic Companions of Gilles.

Beren was so like his father, proud and with the haughty arrogance of noble youth. Though since Leofric had come back from the Errantry Wars in the north, a knight errant no more, but a knight of the realm, he had lost much of his former boisterousness.

Such was only to be expected, for a knight of the realm was tempered in battle, the fiery impetuosity of a knight errant moulded into a dutiful warrior.

But there was more to it than that. Helene knew her husband well enough to know that something more terrible than a bloody charge had happened in the war that had engulfed the Empire.

What had turned her fiery husband into a melancholy warrior who saw the cloud rather than the silver lining, the rain, not the nourished crops?

She finished the last of the beef and cheese and set down the plate on the rock beside her, feeling a shiver ripple its way along her spine.

'Colder than a Mousillon night,' she whispered to herself, as the sound of a soft, mournful weeping drifted on the air from above.

Helene twisted around, wondering if she had perhaps imagined the sound when it came again… a barely audible sobbing that tugged at her maternal heart. Unbidden tears welled in the corners of her eyes as she listened to the unseen mourner, the sound reaching deep inside her and touching something primal in her very soul as she realised that the sobs were those of a child.

She rose from the rock and turned her gaze towards the forest.

The sound of the weeping child came again, beguiling and wistful, and, without conscious thought, Helene began walking towards the edge of the hollow. She glanced over her shoulder, seeing the yellow-surcoated men-at-arms gathered at the base of the hollow while Leofric continued his prayers.

She considered bringing the unearthly sound to the attention of her husband and his soldiers, but even before the thought was fully formed it was plucked from her head and vanished like morning mist, replaced with an insistent, urgent need to find the crying child.

Helene climbed from the hollow, the full majesty of the forest stretching out before her. The thick trunks of the mighty trees seemed to lean towards her, their branches sad with leaves of autumn gold. Leaves lay thick and still about the trees' roots and blew in a soft wind that whistled between the branches like an ancient lament.

Coils of greenish mist crept from the treeline, but Helene ignored them, her attention fixed on the sight of a young girl child kneeling at the edge of the woods, clad only in an ankle-length nightgown of pale cream. The child's back was to her, and Helene's heart went out to the child, whose long black hair fell about her shoulders and reached almost to the ground.

'Oh, my dear…' wept Helene as she saw the distraught condition of the child, feet stained green with grass, and twigs and branches caught in her hair.

Was this what had happened to Leofric's ancestor? Had he been snatched as a child and left to die on this bleak moorland before the great forest of Athel Loren? Was this one of those poor unfortunate children taken by the elves, never to be seen again?

Helene took a step forward, hearing the jingle of trace and whinny of horses from behind her, and the thought of fetching help once again came to her.

The little girl let out a grief-stricken sob and all desires, except that of aiding this poor, wretched child, were banished from her thoughts.

'Hello? Child, can you hear me?' asked Helene, taking yet more steps forward, feeling a growing fear settle in her belly with each mist-wreathed footfall. Dim lights flickered at the periphery of her vision and she had the fleeting impression of haunting melodies of aching loss from far away.

The child did not reply and though Helene tried to stop herself, she felt her arm reaching towards the young girl and said, 'Please…'

Her hand closed on the girl's shoulder and Helene sobbed in terror, feeling the softness of her flesh as a mulchy wetness.

The child's dark-haired head slowly turned to face her, and Helene whimpered in terror as she saw that this was no innocent child, but a thing of horror.

In an instant, the blackness of the girl's hair thinned, becoming a whipping tangle of thorned barbs, her face a haggard crone's, full of heartless spite and wicked malice. The nightgown sloughed from the thing's body, its greenish skin transforming into lashing wood, its fingers stretching into razored talons.

The creature of the forest leapt upon Helene with snapping fangs and slashing claws that ripped and bit and tore.

Helene screamed and screamed as pain and blood filled her senses.

CHAPTER TWO

THE SCREAM TORE through the morning air, its tone reaching deep inside every man gathered in the hollow. Leofric surged to his feet, spinning his sword in his grip so as to hold it before him. Instantly, he saw that Helene was not in sight and that a soft greenish mist gathered at the lip of the hollow.

'Helene!' he yelled, running for his horse.

The men-at-arms stood transfixed in fear by the green glow at the top of the hollow, coils of mist slithering down towards them. Another wailing scream, anguished and terrible, echoed from beyond the hollow and the spell was broken, soldiers running for horses and gathering their weapons.

Leofric lifted his foot into the stirrup and hauled himself into his saddle, raking his spurs viciously back and driving his mount onwards. A terrible fear gripped him, hot and urgent in his belly, as he once again shouted

.Helene's name. Behind him, his squire struggled to catch up, the gold and red of Leofric's banner waving crazily in the air.

The greenish mist sparkled with light and Leofric muttered a prayer of protection to the Lady as he rode Taschen into its glittering depths. Hidden, spiteful laughter whipped around him, together with something that sounded like the musical tinkling of an icy wind-chime.

'Come on, damn you!' he yelled, looking over his shoulder to ensure that his men-at-arms were following. 'Your lady is in peril! Make haste!'

His sword shone with a spectral light, its blade cutting through the mist with ease as Leofric felt the ground level out beneath his horse. Ahead, he could faintly see the dark outline of the forest's edge, the gnarled trunks of the oaks seeming to close ranks as he charged towards the source of the screams.

'Helene!' he shouted, circling his horse and riding up and down the length of the treeline. 'Helene! Can you hear me?'

Leofric heard the muffled thump of hoof beats and turned as he saw Baudel and the men-at-arms riding towards him.

'Spread out!' yelled Leofric. 'Ride along the forest's edge and do not stop until you find her!'

Baudel nodded, but before any of the soldiers could begin the search, another scream sounded, this time beyond the trees, echoing from inside the forest. Leofric turned his horse once more and felt his flesh chill as he saw a splash of fresh blood on a tree trunk.

'Oh no…' he whispered. 'The forest has her.'

'Wait, my lord!' shouted Baudel as Leofric rode his horse towards the dark, mist-wreathed trees. 'We can't go in there.'

'We have to,' cried Leofric. 'In the name of the Lady, I order you to follow me!'

The soldiers milled in fearful uncertainty, their duty to their master warring with their lifelong dread of the faerie folk's realm. Sparkling laughter, rich with the promise of dark amusement, rippled through the mist, and the horses stamped their hooves in fear, eyes wide and ears pressed flat against their skulls.

Leofric snarled in anger and jabbed his spurs into his mount's flanks, riding into Athel Loren.

Behind him he could hear Baudel shouting, 'Come on, men! Lady Carrard needs us and you're just going to let her die? Call yourselves men of Bretonnia, you're no better than bloody dogs! Move!'

Belittled into action, the majority of the men-at-arms followed Baudel as he rode after Leofric, but some did not, dragging the reins of their beasts and riding away, tears of shame and fear burning their eyes.

Leofric charged heedlessly through the forest, seeing a flash of a scarlet gown ahead, his horse plunging deeper into the forest as he cried out Helene's name once more.

'Baudel!' he shouted, pointing with his sword. 'Left! Go left!'

There was no reply and Leofric angrily twisted in his saddle, ready to berate his soldiers, but his mouth snapped shut as he saw that he was alone. Dimly, he could see the shadowy forms of horsemen riding beyond the dark lines of the trees, ghostly and indistinct. Laughter and a hissing rustle of leaves in a strong wind sounded and Leofric spun his horse searching for the source of the noise.

Again he saw the flash of scarlet and urged his mount towards it. He rode through the trees, emerging into a glade with a fallen tree at its centre, resting atop a cloven rock. The ground was churned with hoof prints and a broken spear lay in the mud.

'Helene!' shouted Leofric, once more catching sight of her red gown and pushing his mount onwards. He leapt his horse over a growth of thorns, landing on a worn path, and charged around a spur of dark evergreens before emerging into another glade, similar to the previous one.

No… not similar, he realised, seeing the same fallen tree and cloven rock, identical. How could he have circled back on himself? More hoof beats sounded and he heard a scream, a man's, then a gurgling cry of pain.

The noise of rustling leaves grew louder and louder, as though a storm whipped through the forest, but Leofric could see nothing.

'Helene! Where are you?'

His fury and fear growing by the second, Leofric rode from the glade once more, leaving by a different path, as he heard the sounds of battle from ahead. Briars snatched at him as he rode past, tearing his caparison, branches seeming to close in and block his passage, but he slashed and hacked with his sword and the way was opened.

He rode into another clearing, thankfully a different one from before, in time to see two of his men-at-arms snatched from their saddles by unseen assailants, dragged into the deep undergrowth behind them.

Leofric charged forwards, shouting, 'Come out and show yourselves, damn it! Fight with honour!'

The undergrowth shook with terrible violence and one of his men-at-arms crawled from the greenery, his face a mask of blood and terror. Something green and icy-white rose up behind the soldier and Leofric cried out as he saw the gnarled, hag's face atop a writhing branch-like form of moss, weeds and wood. Slashing fingers struck at the man, who screamed in agony as he was torn to shreds.

Leofric charged forwards, swinging his sword in a downward arc towards the hag's face. His sword struck the centre of her skull, but fast as quicksilver, the crone of wood came apart, her outline blurring as the branches and leaves reknit themselves once more.

Leofric turned to strike another blow, but something landed with a malicious cackle on the back of his horse, slashing at his armour with grasping talons. The rank stench of winter moss assailed him, the rich wetness of the cold earth. Lank hair, like that of a corpse, spattered his armour.

He gagged and hammered his elbow back, hearing the crack of splitting wood as another creature of branches and pallid green flesh erupted from the under-growth.

His horse reared and struck out as it had been trained to do, its iron-shod hooves smashing into the creature before it with the crack of splintering wood. The creature burst apart in a flurry of leaves and mud, and the sickly smell of wood sap filled Leofric's senses.

'Get off me!' he yelled, hammering his elbow back once more and crying out as he felt razor-sharp talons slide between the gaps in his armour and pierce the mail below. Blood streamed down his leg as he reversed the grip on his sword and hammered the point back-wards through the gap between his arm and body, feeling it slide into wet, mulchy flesh.

His assailant screeched in rage, tumbling from the back of his horse as he saw Baudel ride into the clear-ing, with his men-at-arms behind him. He could see the fear on their faces, but could not spare them any words as he wheeled his horse to face his fallen attacker.

The thing of branches sprang through the air, its haggard face full of spite, and Leofric swung his sword in a great upwards sweep that hacked it in two as it leapt. It exploded in a green mist of sap, wood and leaves, a dazzling ball of light whipping from its remains and flashing into the trees.

Leofric raised the visor of his helmet and shouted, 'Baudel! Any sign of my wife?'

'No!' called back Baudel. 'We have to get out of here. I don't know how many men we've lost already!'

'No! I won't leave without her,' roared Leofric. 'Come on, she can't be far.'

Without waiting to see if his men followed, Leofric rode off once more, desperation surging in his veins. He charged wildly into the forest's depths, the cackling laughter of the woodland hags following him at every turn. Darting lights spun and looped through the high branches of the trees and sparkling mists wove in and out of his path.

Leofric wanted to weep in frustration as the forest closed in around him. Where was she? He could no longer tell which way was which...

Again he saw a flash of red and pushed his lathered mount onwards once more. He thundered down the overgrown path, emerging into a clearing with a familiar fallen tree and boulder.

'Lady, no!' he wept. 'Please, please, no!'

He slumped over the neck of his horse, his hope that he might find Helene growing fainter by the minute. What chance did he have when the very forest conspired against him?

Angrily he pushed such despairing thoughts from his mind. Was he not a knight of Bretonnia, sworn to uphold the traditions of chivalry? A knight never gave up, never despaired and never abandoned a damsel in distress.

He straightened in the saddle as Baudel and six other riders finally caught up with him. All of them bore the scars of battle and their yellow surcoats were stained with blood and dirt. Fear was writ large on every face and their desire to flee the forest was plain. His banner still flew, but the lad who bore it wept in terror.

'Spread out into a line!' ordered Leofric. 'We'll quarter this area of the forest.'

'My lord, it's no use,' said Baudel. 'It's impossible, the trees confound us at every turn!'

'I know,' snapped Leofric, 'but what choice do we have?'

'We can live,' said Baudel, pointing to a patch of clear sunlight beyond the trees that plainly led back to the heath before the forest.

'No, we stay,' stated Leofric. 'I won't leave her.'

Baudel nodded and said, 'Then we stay too.'

Even as the words left his throat, the light of the sky was snatched away as the branches of the trees closed in. Leofric readied his sword as the cackling of the woodland creatures grew from all around them, the crack of branches weaving themselves into new and terrible forms and the frenzied rustling of leaves growing louder with every passing second.

'Ride!' shouted Leofric as the creatures attacked once more.

Monsters of branch and root rose up from the ground, weaving from the trunks of the trees with an unearthly green light. With thick, ridged skin of hardened bark and malicious black eyes, they tore at the Bretonnians with implacable fury. Leofric chopped his sword through the branch-like limb of one of the creatures, the timber cracking from its body in a spray of sweet sap.

It screamed in rage, its other arm slamming into his breastplate with a solid thump and Leofric grunted in pain, feeling as if he'd been hit by a thunderous lance impact. He reeled back in the saddle, dragging on the reins to prevent himself from being unhorsed and brought his sword back in a deadly reverse stroke that took the forest creature's head off.

He rounded on the other creatures in time to see his standard fall, the young lad lifted from his saddle with a scream of terror. Long, stabbing talons plunged into his chest, dragging his body high into the trees with a deathly wail.

Leofric rode forwards and caught the falling banner, wedging its base into the stirrup cup normally used to hold the butt of his lance.

'Carrard!' he yelled as the ground beneath him writhed with life. His horse sidestepped nimbly as roots and creepers surged upwards, grasping and clawing with thorny appendages.

Another man was dragged down, his body obscured by dancing lights that spun around him with capering laughter. Shifting forms spun through the lights: imps, daemons and tiny, ghostly knights. Baudel rode through the mass of branch creatures, stabbing with his spear and screaming obscenities at his foes.

Leofric urged his horse onwards, riding towards Baudel's aid as a whipping branch leapt at him, striking the visor of his helmet with a ringing hammer blow.

Starbursts exploded around him and he felt the banner slip from his fingers as he fought to stay conscious. His head rang with the impact and he could taste blood, but he gritted his teeth and held on. He couldn't see properly, his visor had been buckled inwards by the blow, so he snapped it upwards.

Something dropped from above him with a high, skirling laugh and he felt moist, clawed hands tearing at him. Straddling his horse's neck before him was a creature of pallid green flesh, its features running like wax, changing from a maiden of unearthly beauty to a hideous, wrinkled hag and back again in a heartbeat. She was laughing, but there was nothing but hate and bitterness in the icy sound.

Leofric slammed his helmet into the hag's face, and her laughter turned to a squeal of rage as she toppled from his horse, but by then it was already too late. Baudel fell from his horse, his belly torn open and emptying its contents across the forest floor, his eyes glazed and dead.

'No!' shouted Leofric as slashing branches pummelled him and he felt himself pitched from his saddle, landing in an ungainly heap across the fallen tree. He cried out as he felt at least one rib crack and rolled onto the wet ground, fighting through the pain.

'Forgive me, Helene,' he hissed. 'I failed you…'

A flash of colour caught his eye and he reached out with a bloodstained gauntlet to grasp a silken scarf of blue, edged in white lace that lay on the forest floor.

'Helene…'

Leofric snarled in anger, snatching up Helene's scarf and tucking it inside his gauntlet, before pushing himself to his feet as a dozen or more of the fell forest creatures emerged from the wood, capering, malicious crones and blank-faced tree wraiths surrounded by clouds of swirling lights. His horse whinnied in fear and cantered over to him, its nostrils wide and flaring in fear.

He pushed himself painfully to his feet, hot agony flaring in his side where his ribs were cracked. Blood streamed down his leg and he felt nauseous and dizzy from his head wound.

'I am Leofric Carrard! A knight of the realm and warrior of Bretonnia!' he shouted defiantly, 'and if you damned forest creatures want me dead then you're about to find out how a knight of Bretonnia meets his end!'

He raised his sword in salute until the quillons were level with his chin and kissed the blade.

'For Quenelles, the king and the Lady!' he roared.

But before he took a single step, the forest creatures hissed and pulled back from a growing light that slipped effortlessly through the forest. Its course was towards this thrice-cursed glade and Leofric felt a surge of hope flare as he saw the faint outline of a glowing woman in the depths of the light.

Was this the Lady of the Lake come to save him?

The spiteful forest beasts retreated from the light, but as the stranger drew closer Leofric saw that this woman was not the Lady, but must surely be elfkind. She moved effortlessly through the woodland, the branches and roots of the forest parting before her and easing her passage towards him.

She wore a long robe of spun gold and elven runes, weaving streamers of pale blue and green billowing around her as though in the grip of an invisible wind. Her hair was the colour of molten copper, teased into braided tresses above her tapered ears with silver pins and woven with feathers and gemstones. She turned her large, almond-shaped eyes on Leofric and he could feel a great and terrible power in the elf witch.

She carried a long staff of woven twigs with a carven eye at its top and the creatures of the forest backed away from her. Despite the obvious power of the elf sorcerer, the forest wraiths were not cowed, their spite and anger plain at being denied their kill for now.

Behind the elf, Leofric could see the outlines of a great many figures, but each time he tried to focus on one, it blended back into the forest, leaving him unsure of what he was seeing. Was that the curve of a bow, the glint of sunlight on an arrowhead?

So that was it… they were going to kill him themselves. Trust an elf to want to finish the job.

Though it railed against his code of chivalric conduct to attack a woman, he knew that this was no ordinary woman, this was an immortal elf with the terrible power of magic at her command. He pulled out Helene's scarf, the very same favour she had given him on the tilting fields of Couronne, and wrapped it around the hilt of his sword.

Leofric screamed in loss and rage and charged the elf woman, pain and anguish lending his limbs fresh strength. The elf didn't move, the creatures of the forest surging forwards as he charged.

Tears blurred his vision as his sword slashed towards the elf's head.

Dazzling sparks of cold fire leapt from a resounding impact and Leofric shook his head clear of the blinding light to see that his blow had been intercepted by another blade – a blade the colour of moonlight, its length curved in a long, leaf shape and etched with intricate, spiralling patterns.

His gaze travelled the length of the exquisitely crafted weapon, past the intertwined leaves of its silver quillons towards the gauntleted hand that held it.

Leofric felt a prickling sensation of magic and wrenched his eyes from the blade to the warrior who bore it, seeing a magnificent figure riding a steed with a mane the colour of fire, clad head to foot in a suit of heavy plate armour, fluted and chased in the manner of a Bretonnian knight. In his other hand, the knight carried a banner of rippling cream silk, emblazoned with a heraldic device Leofric did not recognise, a scaled dragon of pale jade set atop the image of a flowering oak.

The knight's armour was old, ancient even, and heavily damaged. A series of parallel grooves carved a path diagonally down the knight's breastplate and his vambrace and cuirass were browned as though burned by some corrosive substance. Pieces of the knight's armour were also mismatched, the helmet was a design Leofric had never seen before, and the pauldrons had clearly been repaired many times.

But for all that, there was a terrifyingly potent aura of power surrounding the knight, a faint, yet unmistakable haze of something unseen. The green eyes behind the helmet's visor blazed with some internal wychfire and though they spoke eloquently of great power, Leofric sensed no evil in them, only an aching sadness and purity.

And what manner of knight rode a steed such as this one? The knight sat atop a destrier with a remarkable coat of purest white, but whose mane was a fiery bronze, like captured flames rippling from the wonderful beast's neck. Its limbs were elegant and muscular, sculpted as though from marble.

Leofric knew the qualities of a fine steed as well as the next knight, and while the Bretonnian warhorse was a creature of rare power and endurance, this was an elven steed, a beast of savage beauty, strength and grace.

Was this knight…? Could he be…?

A Grail Knight, one of the virtuous few who had long quested for the grail, driven ever onwards by visions of the Lady of the Lake to seek for her chalice in far-off lands, to vanquish evil, to aid the needy and forever prove his virtuous heart in the heat of battle. If this knight was such a warrior, then he had supped from the grail; blessed beyond all men and honoured with a life of service to the Lady.

A Grail Knight... A saint amongst men, a warrior beyond compare who had slain great monsters, fought in wars beyond number, vanquished the most dreaded of foes and who had been granted powers beyond the ken of mere mortals.

Leofric opened his mouth to speak, but the mounted knight shook his head.

He stumbled as a wave of dizziness threatened to overcome him and the creatures of the forest closed, scenting their prey's weakness.

Without seeming to give his mount a signal, the strangely clad knight interposed himself between Leofric and the hissing hag-creatures, and their lashing, branch-woven forms retreated before him.

Leofric supported himself on the fallen tree, watching the power and authority that the warrior commanded. It seemed to him that a shimmering golden aura surrounded the knight, but Leofric could not be sure, his vision blurring as blood loss and pain conspired to rob him of his strength.

'We are not your enemies, sir knight,' said a melodic voice at his ear and he cried out in surprise. The elf witch was at his side, a cadre of fey-featured elves behind her with long recurved bows carried lightly at their sides. Though the forest floor was thick with dry leaves, they had made no sound as they approached.

Clad in a mixture of russets and greens, their clothing was perfectly chosen to blend with the colours of the forest, and they carried scabbarded swords belted at their sides. The elves regarded him with expressions of faint disdain.

Each had feathers and braids woven into their long hair, held in place by leather circlets and the pale skin of their heart-shaped faces was almost translucent, painted with curling tattoos.

Leofric tried to raise his sword, but its normally lightweight blade felt as though it weighed as much as a greatsword.

'No...' he whispered, dropping to his knees. 'Helene!'

The elf witch glanced over at the hulking form of the Grail Knight who said, 'We are too late again?' His voice was rich and deep, yet filled with pain.

'We are,' nodded the elf. 'But we may yet–'

'Spare me your platitudes,' said the knight, turning his horse and riding away. 'I have heard them all before.'

'When will we see you again?' the elf sorceress called after the knight's retreating form.

'You already know the answer to that, Naieth,' replied the knight, disappearing into the forest without another word.

Leofric watched the exchange with dazed incomprehension, feeling his limbs fill with a strange lethargy as the elf sorceress returned her careworn gaze upon him once more. The elven archers surrounded her, their bows drawn and grey-fletched arrows nocked to the strings.

Her voice was musical and lilting, with a haunting edge to it as she spoke to him, the words running like honey through his head.

'Leofric, I bid you welcome to the woodland realm of Athel Loren,' she said. 'My name is Naieth and I have been waiting for you for a very long time.'

CHAPTER THREE

CRYSTAL FOAM SPRAYED the air, cascading over glistening rocks from high above, the roaring of the tumbling waterfall drowning out the cries of distant eagles and the calls of wolves as they padded through the evening. The waterfall cut a deep groove through the rocks above and fell in lazy arcs to the foaming pool in the centre of the clearing below, where two figures lay naked in each other's arms and two elven steeds roamed its edges.

Morvhen Éadaoin held her lover, Kyarno Daelanu, tightly, relishing the hard, alabaster smoothness of his skin against her own. Both elves were long limbed and graceful, with a languid suppleness to their movements as they made love by the water's edge. A mist of fine water sheened their bodies as they moved against one another until at last Kyarno gave out a long sigh and rolled from her, a contented smile creasing his boyish features.

He lay back, curling an arm behind his head as she lay close to him, enjoying the light of evening as it spilled like molten gold over the treetops. Darting lights flitted between the trees and bobbed like fireflies across the surface of the churning water, dancing in the air with gleeful abandon.

Morvhen draped an arm around Kyarno's chest and whispered, 'That was wonderful…'

'Yes,' agreed Kyarno. 'I'm no expert, but it looked like you were enjoying it.'

'Oh, I think you're an expert, my love,' smiled Morvhen, sliding on top of Kyarno to straddle him and leaning down to kiss him.

They made love once more, finally lying side-by-side as the sun dipped below the treetops and soft moonlight spilled into the glade. Distant songs could be heard from the trees, carried on warm winds from the north.

Morvhen ran her hand across Kyarno's smooth, hairless chest and teased the wet locks of his braided, chestnut hair around her fingers, leaning up to kiss his chin. His features were hard and angular, as though carved from stone, though there was a softness to his dark eyes that most folk missed, simply seeing the arrogant, troublesome youth many considered him to be. Spiralling tattoos looped across his chest and neck, winding in coiled snake patterns on the hard muscles of his shoulders.

Even in repose, she could feel the buried tension in Kyarno, a tension that nothing she could do could quite dissipate. As a lover, Kyarno was tender and giving, though she knew that there was a part of him that she still had not reached.

'So much for having me back to Coeth-Mara before nightfall…' said Morvhen.

Kyarno smiled and ran a hand through Morvhen's lustrous, dark hair, kissing the top of her head.

'Not my fault,' he protested.

'No? How so?' laughed Morvhen. 'I seem to recall it was you who wanted to stop at the Crystal Mere for "a rest".'

'True, but then I wasn't the one who suggested we go for a swim, was I?'

'Tell that to my father,' said Morvhen, instantly regretting the words as she felt him tense up beneath her fingers.

'Would he listen?' snapped Kyarno. 'Or would he send the Hound of Winter to cast me from Coeth-Mara once again?'

'I'm sorry,' said Morvhen, rising up on her elbow to look into the eyes of her lover. 'Forget I mentioned him.'

'How can I?' said Kyarno. 'His disapproval hangs over everything we have like a shadow, Morvhen. You know as well as I that he will never accept me.'

'No,' agreed Morvhen sadly. 'But things can change.'

'How?'

'I don't know, but there must always be hope. Don't judge my father too harshly, he has a duty to his kin-band, and–'

'And I'm not part of that, I know,' said Kyarno bitterly. 'I am nothing but a troublemaker and that's that.'

Morvhen sighed and reached up to run her hand across Kyarno's brow, feeling the anger and bitterness he carried as a poison that ran through him as surely as the blood in his veins. She kissed the clenched line of his jaw and ran her hand through his hair, slowly easing his anger with gentle caresses and feathered kisses.

The moon rose higher in the night sky and Morvhen could feel Kyarno's anger recede, giving way to the love she knew he felt for her. Sadness touched her as she realised that he was right, her father would never accept Kyarno the way he was now – there was a reckless wildness to him that sat ill with the lord of the elven halls of Coeth-Mara. Lord Aldaeld of the Éadaoin kinband had a sacred duty to protect his people and the forest of Athel Loren, and Kyarno was not a part of that, as much as she could see he desperately wanted to be.

Darting spites flitted overhead, like laughing shooting stars against the darkness of the night sky, and the two lay in silence for a while before Kyarno broke the uncomfortable silence.

'I'm sorry,' he said at last. 'I didn't mean to get angry at you.'

'Hush…' whispered Morvhen. 'Let's not allow it spoil this night, it's too beautiful for harsh words.'

'No, *you* are too beautiful for harsh words,' said Kyarno, cupping Morvhen's face and looking into her sapphire eyes and taking in the graceful curve of her jaw. 'I know what others think of me, and they are right to, but when I am with you… I feel a stillness, I am at peace. I want that feeling to stay.'

'I know, I know,' whispered Morvhen, holding him tightly, knowing that his wishes were as dreams, fleeting and insubstantial, though she had not the heart to tell him.

'Did you see what Naieth and the Waywatchers brought in earlier?' she asked, quickly changing the subject. 'A human.'

'Yes,' nodded Kyarno. 'Though why she brought him to Coeth-Mara is beyond me. She brings more woe upon the Asrai than even I do.'

Morvhen said nothing, knowing the source of Kyarno's rancour towards Naieth.

'Why did they not just kill him and be done with it?' continued Kyarno. 'The human entered our forest and the Waywatchers should have slain him.'

'Kill him? Oh, come now… it's just one human, what possible harm could he do?'

'You don't understand,' said Kyarno. 'Where one comes, others will follow, it's their way.'

'Maybe, but this was one of the horse-warriors from the lands to the west and they don't often come this way. Just think of what far-off lands he might have travelled to, what strange things he could have seen!'

'Why do you care?' asked Kyarno. 'What is there beyond Athel Loren but enemies? No, far better that we have nothing to do with the humans.'

Morvhen sat up, stretching like a cat and running her hands through her hair, tying it back into a long ponytail with a leather cord.

'So you're not the least bit curious why she brought him back?'

Kyarno shook his head. 'No. And neither should you be. Your father won't allow you to associate with a human.'

Morvhen laughed and gave him a pointed stare, 'Just like he didn't allow me to associate with you, and we all know how much attention I paid to that.'

'That's different,' said Kyarno. 'Aldaeld doesn't like me, but he hates humans.'

Morvhen shrugged, tucking her leg beneath her body and smoothly rising to her feet. She began gathering up her long ochre dress and doeskin boots, her body drying in the warm breeze as Kyarno collected his clothes and bow.

'Well, I for one will speak to the human, learn of his lands and his life,' said Morvhen, slipping on her dress and pulling on her boots. 'I want to hear of his adventures in far-off realms against monsters and the armies of the Dark Gods! I want to know of lands with high mountains, deep blue seas and endless deserts. Can you imagine a desert? A landscape without trees or greenery that stretches out beyond the horizon and never ends.'

'Sounds horrible,' said Kyarno. 'Why would you ever want to go to such a place?'

'Oh, I don't want to go to a desert, but I wish to know everything about it.'

'Be careful what you wish for, Morvhen,' cautioned Kyarno, pulling on his clothes and beckoning his horse to him. He sheathed his bow in an oiled, leather case and buckled on his sword belt as his steed nuzzled him. 'You may not like what you hear.'

Morvhen laughed at Kyarno's seriousness and leapt lightly to the back of her horse, its rump painted with spiralling patterns and its tail woven with garlands of leaves.

She twisted her fingers into its silvered mane and said, 'We should get back to Coeth-Mara. The Hound of Winter will be going out of his mind looking for me before my father finds out I'm not there.'

Kyarno nodded, a gloomy expression settling on his features once more at the mention of his uncle and the prospect of return to Coeth-Mara. He vaulted onto the back of his horse, riding alongside Morvhen and leaned close to kiss her. She could feel the heat of his skin as his hand slipped around her neck, drawing her close until their lips met.

They kissed long and tenderly until Kyarno reluctantly pulled back, still with his hand resting at the nape of her neck. He rested his forehead on hers and said, 'When will I see you again?'

Morvhen started to speak, when a strident voice from the edge of the clearing shouted, 'You won't! I'll have your hide first!'

Kyarno groaned and turned to see Cairbre, the Hound of Winter and champion of Lord Aldaeld Éadaoin, ride into the glade. The warrior of the Eternal Guard wore armour of banded gold, with a grey cloak of feathers and leaves worn draped over one shoulder. His bronze helmet was conical and ridged, its sheen bright and polished.

Carried lightly in one hand was a thin-hafted spear, both ends bearing long, leaf-shaped blades of pearlescent white that were rich with etched spirals and grooves.

'Cairbre, Kyarno was just about to escort me back to Coeth-Mara,' said Morvhen, as the Hound of Winter walked his horse towards her, his face a mask of controlled anger beneath his bronze helmet.

'He shouldn't be here with you, my lady, you know that,' said Cairbre, without looking at Kyarno. 'How can I protect you if you insist on behaving like this? Your father was clear about your liaisons with my nephew. Why is he with you?'

'I am right here, uncle, you can ask me yourself,' growled Kyarno.

Cairbre's spear was a pale blur and Kyarno was pitched from the saddle as the flat of one of the blades smashed into the side of his head. He sailed through the air, twisting to land lightly on his feet with an arrow nocked to his bow and a murderous anger in his eyes.

'Kyarno, no!' shouted Morvhen, but Cairbre shook his head.

'Damn you, uncle, I'll put an arrow through your throat!' shouted Kyarno.

'Don't be foolish, boy, even you are not that stupid,' said Cairbre.

Kyarno and Cairbre locked eyes and Morvhen could easily see the familial bond in both their features. But where the Hound of Winter was tempered by battle and age, Kyarno's face still carried all the fires and foibles of youth.

'Stop this foolishness!' she cried, her voice laden with all the noble authority of her lineage. 'There will be no blood spilt this day. Cairbre, take me back to Coeth-Mara, I wish to return to the halls of my father.'

'As you wish, my lady,' nodded Cairbre, turning away from his nephew.

As Cairbre led her horse towards the edge of the glade, Kyarno lowered his bow. Morvhen saw the fire dim in his eyes, his anger replaced by sadness. She wanted to go to him, to say something hopeful, but knew that Cairbre would never allow it. The Hound of Winter may have tutored her since she was a child, but he was still her father's champion, first and foremost.

As they reached the edge of the clearing, Cairbre turned his horse and shouted back to Kyarno. 'You too should head back to Coeth-Mara, boy. Lord Aldaeld desires to speak with you.'

'He does?' replied Kyarno, warily. 'Why?'

'Don't be stupid, boy,' said Cairbre, seeing the defiance in Kyarno's eyes, 'you know better than to disobey such a command. Make your way to your lord's hall. Now.'

'And if I don't?'

'Then I'll drag you there myself,' stated Cairbre.

Kyarno swung onto the back of his horse and said, 'One day you will push me too far, old one.'

The Hound of Winter did not answer, but Morvhen saw the disappointment in his eyes as Kyarno yelled and pulled on his steed's mane, riding hard and plunging into the darkness of the forest.

THE WARM DUSK of the forest closed in around Morvhen and Cairbre, fluttering spites in the shape of glittering butterflies lighting their way as they flew alongside the horses. A gentle breeze blew from the west, carrying smoky, aromatic scents and the sounds of life, and Morvhen felt the invigorating heartbeat of the forest in her blood as she rode once more beneath its russet canopy.

As they rode from the glade towards the settlement of Coeth-Mara, Morvhen rounded on Cairbre, her anger rising as she saw his grim exterior assert itself once more.

'Must you always be so harsh on him?' she said. 'He has gone through so much.'

'I know,' said Cairbre. 'I was there when the beasts killed his family, remember? But the boy brings trouble on his own head, my lady.'

'Do you hate Kyarno?' asked Morvhen.

'Hate him?' exclaimed Cairbre, turning to face her. 'No, of course I do not hate him. He is my kinsman and I love him, but there is a madness to him that I do not understand.'

'Have you ever *really* tried?'

'Believe me, I have, but every time we speak we argue, as though he sees my every word as an insult. As much as I wish to, I cannot reach the boy and I am too old to change my ways now.'

Seeing a rare moment of vulnerability in the warrior, Morvhen reached out and placed her hand on the metal of Cairbre's bronze vambrace and said, 'His heart is true, Hound of Winter, trust to that.'

'I know,' said Cairbre sadly, 'I see courage and the seeds of greatness within him and know that he could become a fine warrior. But he takes after his father in too many ways and I fear that will be the undoing of him and anyone close to him.'

'Come now, Cairbre. Surely you're exaggerating?'

'You think so? What about his theft of the Laithu kinband's steeds from their stable glades? That foolishness may cost your father dear and I do not wish to see you caught up in his reckless folly.'

'He released the Laithu steeds almost as soon as he stole them,' pointed out Morvhen. 'He only took them to prove that he could.'

'That is not the point,' replied Cairbre. 'Valas Laithu is not quick to forgive an insult done to his kinband. He will demand recompense.'

Morvhen nodded, remembering the last time she had met Valas Laithu and his odious sons: a gathering of kinbands at the King's Glade sixty years ago. She had not liked him then and had no reason to suppose he had changed any in the intervening years.

'Valas is a snake,' said Morvhen.

'Aye, he is,' agreed Cairbre, 'but a powerful one, and that is another reason why you must not remove yourself from my protection. The forest is a dangerous place at this time of year, and if something were to happen to you, Lord Aldaeld would have my life. And that of Kyarno. You know this, yet still you defy his wishes.'

'I am not a child any more, Cairbre,' said Morvhen. 'You taught me to shoot and to fight. I can take care of myself.'

Cairbre chuckled. 'Of that I have no doubt, but I have sworn to protect the Éadaoin kinband as well as Athel Loren, and the Hound of Winter does not forswear such an oath.'

Morvhen nodded, grateful to have such a faithful protector as Cairbre, and they rode on in silence through the secret paths known only to the Eternal Guard, before eventually reaching the glittering lights and warmth that were the elven halls of Coeth-Mara. Its beauty never failed to captivate Morvhen and she rode into the settlement with a light in her heart.

'Home...' she said.

GOLDEN LIGHT LIKE HONEY.
Silken voices like a symphony of maidens.
The sensation of floating, as though in a dream.
Leofric felt at peace, his limbs relaxed and light-weight, his body cured of all its hurts. He smiled dreamily to himself, the singsong voices spinning in his head like dancers, coyly flitting from understanding as he tried to concentrate on what was being said.

Flickering lights fluttered before his eyes, though he could feel they were still shut. Tiny, shrill laughter seemed to come from the lights and slowly he opened his gummed eyes, squinting against the brightness.

A trio of hazy green lights hovered in the air above him, insubstantial wings flickering behind them and giggling faces swimming in each one's depths. The distant voices grew louder as he rose from sleep to wakefulness, their meaning still a mystery to him, but their ethereal beauty beyond question.

The green lights spun away from him, squealing in fright as his eyes opened.

Above him he could see the slender branches of several trees, their boughs curving gracefully to form a leafy, arched roof, through which he could see the cool, pale blue of the sky. He pushed himself upright on his elbows, his head still groggy as though he had drunk too much wine. He was lying on a bed of golden leaves nestled between the roots of a mighty oak. A silken sheet of golden cloth covered him and from its soft, almost liquid touch on his skin, he could feel he was naked beneath it.

A low partition of woven branches and impossibly graceful saplings offered him some privacy, though not from the laughing lights that bobbed and wove in the air above him. He heard distant music carried on the fragrant air, its lilting melodies both beguiling and terrible, and smelled a mouth-watering aroma of nearby cooking.

He lifted a hand to his head, trying to remember how he had come to this place, wherever this place actually was…

Memories struggled through the cloudy mists of recall, but they remained frustratingly out of reach. The flickering lights darted down from the roof to hover before him again, and though he knew he should be wary of such things, he felt nothing but a faint amusement at their impish behaviour. One transformed into a ghostly image of a tiny knight on horseback, another a flitting butterfly. The third swooped and dived between them, daring them to chase it as they zipped around his head.

He laughed, the sound sending the creatures rushing back to the safety of the roof as he saw two tall women glide into view from around the partition of saplings. As they drew near, he saw they did not glide, but walked with such effortless grace that it seemed they barely touched the ground they walked upon.

Leofric felt his jaw hang open at their beauty, their forms slender and exquisite. Clad in ankle-length, crimson dresses, the women had long, fine-boned features with alabaster skin, pale and smooth like a doll's. Their eyes were oval and dark, their hair bound up in coiled, leaf-bound tresses above their gracefully curved, pointed ears.

Something in their appearance tugged at the cords of memory, but such thoughts evaporated as they smiled hesitantly at him, and his heart broke to see such beauty in that simple gesture.

'What…' he said. 'Where…'

His heart lurched as he realised he looked upon the features of elves, the faerie folk, the woodland creatures. The lords and ladies of the wood. His heart hammered in his chest, fear and dread warring with the allure and beauty of the elven maids before him.

One carried a bowl of crystal water and a wooden platter of fruit and bread, the second a bundle of what appeared to be neatly folded clothes. The food was offered to him and he gratefully snatched a handful of berries, wolfing them down as he suddenly felt a fierce hunger.

He had taken several mouthfuls, the juice of the berries staining his chin, when he noticed a tiny disdainful curl to the elf maid's mouth.

'I'm sorry,' he said, wiping the juice from his face. 'My manners have deserted me.'

The elf maid tilted her head curiously to one side, glancing at her companion who set down the clothes beside him, clearly not understanding his words. She spoke a few words in a language Leofric did not know, but could have listened to for hours, such was its lyrical splendour.

The other shook her head, reaching out to pull the silken sheet from him and Leofric was seized by a sudden fear as she touched his skin. He held himself immobile, trying not to imagine what manner of enchantment the touch of the fey folk might put upon him.

Her fingers were long and dexterous, questing beneath the sheet to his hip, and despite himself he could not help but be aroused by her touch. Fighting to hide his embarrassment, he reached out to remove her hand. Fast as quicksilver, her hand was withdrawn before he could touch her and she backed away from him, her umber eyes wide and fearful.

'Don't touch me,' he said, grunting in pain as he felt stitches pull tight across his hip and he shifted position to better conceal his shame. The pain cut through the fog of his awakening and his smothered memories, and he moaned in fear as he remembered the battle with the forest creatures; he and his men-at-arms blundering like blind men through the forest searching for...

'Helene!' he cried, fear and loss tearing at him as the full weight of remembrance surged into his mind. He remembered the pallid, hag-faced forest wraiths that tore his men apart and the awful screams of his squire as the tree creature had stabbed him with fingers like long daggers.

'Helene!' he said once again, pushing himself away from the fearful elf maids. They backed away, quickly disappearing from sight behind the screen of slender, curved branches.

Tears of loss streamed down his face as he realised he had lost Helene, lost her to the damned forest of dark magicks. Hot anger flared at the thought of another of the Carrard line taken by Athel Loren and he cast his eyes around this place looking for a weapon, anything with which to strike back at the evil creatures that had taken his beloved.

Leofric threw off the sheet and staggered to his feet, swaying as he realised how weak he still was. Sweet Lady, they had taken everything from him! Helene...

He dropped to his knees as grief swamped him and he wept bitter tears as the enormity of his loss threatened to crush him in its grip. Leofric howled his pain to the skies, beating his fists against the thick roots of the oak, scattering his bed of leaves and cursing all the gods of the world. The green lights that fluttered around him, dropped towards him, their giggling faces now drawn into fearful grimaces and fanged, skeletal grins.

He collapsed against the thick trunk of the great oak, his warrior's anger brimming over and submerging his grief for the moment. He turned, dizzy and weak, and batted away the lights, shouting, 'Get away from me, damn you!'

They buzzed away from him, a kaleidoscope of colours flashing through their insubstantial bodies, angrily hissing at him as they grew horns and claws of light.

He ignored them and gathered up the clothes the elf maids had left him, tugging on a pair of soft, buckskin trousers and a thin overshirt of cream silk.

Leofric wiped the tears from his eyes and ran his hands through his shoulder-length black hair, taking deep breaths and gathering his strength. He had no idea where in the forest he was, but was damned if he would meekly face whatever fate the elves had in store for him. The elf maids had long since fled and he was in no doubt as to the fact that they would even now be seeking help.

Fighting to keep his grief at bay, he moved swiftly around the saplings the elf maids had disappeared behind and found himself in a wide chamber of curved walls crafted from gently swaying branches and leaves. The floor was an elegant weave of thin branches and coloured stone that formed a graceful mosaic. Through gaps in the wall, he saw flashes of other figures and the verdant green of the forest.

The irritating floating balls of light still followed him, darting in with shrill shrieks and whipping around his head as he limped towards a leaf-shaped archway that looked as though it offered the best chance of escape.

He had taken only a few steps, keeping one hand pressed to his hip, the other batting away the troublesome spites that continued to pester him, when two warriors in segmented golden armour over rugged brown troos stepped through the arch. Both wore long grey cloaks and open helmets of fluted bronze, with elaborate patterns etched into the metal. Each bore a pair of curved daggers at his side and a quiver of arrows slung at his shoulder.

'Ah... I wondered when someone like you would show up,' grunted Leofric as they each drew one of their long, slender bladed daggers. Leofric knew full well that unarmed and unarmoured, he would be killed if he fought these elves, but his grief drove him onwards and he lunged at the nearest as they warily approached him.

The elf nimbly sidestepped his clumsy attack, moving with a liquid grace that amazed Leofric with its speed. He could see amusement on their narrow, alien faces and he furiously attacked again, launching a thunderous right hook at one of the elves. Again his blow was dodged and Leofric knew he would never be able to strike these warriors. In the King's Errantry War, he had been privileged to witness Kislevite *Droyaska* fight in battle, swordsmen who could move with incredible speed, but this was something else entirely, the elves displayed a rapidity that bordered on prescience.

'Stand still, damn you!' he roared, missing with yet another punch and feeling his already weakened constitution falter. He dropped to one knee, his breathing hoarse and ragged, blood seeping from the torn stitches on his hip.

After a pause, the two elves reached down to drag him to his feet. It was the moment Leofric had been waiting for and he snapped his head back, slamming it into the face of one of the elves as he leaned down. The elf staggered back, blood streaming from his broken nose and Leofric spun, snatching the remaining dagger from the scabbard at his hip. He slashed at the second warrior, who leapt aside, only barely avoiding having his belly opened.

'Ha! Not so tough when your prey has a weapon, eh?'

Leofric turned to the stunned elf and kicked him between the legs, dropping him to the floor with a grunt of pain.

But before he could deliver the killing blow, a silver-white blade swept out from behind him and plucked the blade from his hand, sending it spinning across the room. Leofric turned in time to see another elf warrior, similarly attired to the others, but with a silver hound engraved upon his armour. He was older, with an implacable coldness to his eyes, and carried a spinning spear with two shimmering white blades.

The spear slashed towards his legs, its bladed edge turning at the last minute and the haft hooking his legs out from under him. Leofric crashed to the floor, the breath whooshing from his lungs as he hit the ground. He struggled to rise, but saw the elf with the cold eyes standing over him, the two-bladed spear aimed squarely at his throat.

'Do not move, human,' said the warrior, his voice redolent with age and threat. 'I am Cairbre, the Hound of Winter, and I will kill you if you so much as touch one of my warriors again.'

Leofric's eyes darted between the tip of the spear, its lethal point a hair's breadth from his Adam's apple, and the furious features of the elf. He saw an icy resolve in his face, and knew that were he to move in any way that displeased this Cairbre, the spear would be instantly rammed through his throat.

Leofric nodded, the movement almost imperceptible thanks to the blade at his neck.

'I would kill you now, but Naieth wishes you alive,' said Cairbre.

'Who?'

'The Prophetess.'

'The witch?' sneered Leofric, remembering the female elf that had appeared to him in the forest. 'What could an elf witch have to tell me that I would want to hear?'

'Your future,' said Cairbre, touching the cold blade to his neck. 'Or, more precisely, whether you have one.'

CHAPTER FOUR

FANGS SNAPPED SHUT on the iron plates of the Beastlord's armour, breaking on the thick metal as the wolf-headed monster slashed at its bronzed flanks with sharp talons. The Beastlord rolled, using its superior weight to pin its opponent, but before it could snap the neck of the challenger, the wolf-creature squirmed free of its grip and savagely tore at its flesh in a flurry of tooth and claw.

Blood the colour of liquid bronze splashed the glistening rocks and the Beastlord hammered its gauntleted fist into the challenger's face. Fangs snapped and spittle flew in the rain-lashed air as the combatants snarled and roared and pummelled one another in a frenzy of blows. The Beastlord lowered its head and rammed a ridged horn into the wolf's belly, tearing upwards with a powerful twist of its thickly ridged neck muscles.

The wolf-monster howled and leapt back, pressing a clawed hand to its torn side, desperation clear in its wide eyes as the Beastlord's monstrous spawn slithered after it, a multitude of snapping, tentacled mouths and grasping, clawed pseudopods. The Beastlord growled, hauling on the spawn's chain and pulling it away.

It could destroy this upstart beast without the help of its ever-hungry spawn.

Howls and brays surrounded the combatants: monsters with bestial faces marked by the favour of the gods stamping in the mud washed down from the peaks. The snarling challenger howled, thick saliva spattering its grey, blood-spattered fur. The Beastlord answered with its own roar of challenge, hefting its massive axe and awaiting its opponent's charge.

The wolf-creature leapt towards it, clawed arms reaching for its throat, but the Beastlord sidestepped and hammered the axe into the rival beast's midriff, hacking the creature in two in a spray of dark blood. The shorn halves dropped to the rocky shale of the mountainside, the remains twitching feebly as it died, and the warherd roared its approval of the kill.

The Beastlord kicked the upper torso of the creature it had just killed over onto its back and hammered the axe into the wolf-creature's chest. It dropped to one knee, reaching down and placing its thick fingers into the great wound, then heaving the beast's chest open with a loud crack of splintering bone.

It reached into the exposed chest cavity and tore out the challenger's heart, rising to hold its axe and the gory organ high above its horned head for its followers to see. The Beastlord bellowed in triumph as the rest of the warherd saw the fate of the beast that had questioned its right to lead. It lowered the heart and swallowed the hot, dripping meat with one throaty gulp.

The meaning of the gesture was clear: defy me and die.

The nearest creatures, red-furred centaurs with long spears, backed away from the Beastlord, their heads bowed in supplication. Others let out a series of ululating cries in its honour, their loyalty assured... at least until another challenger arose.

Such challenges made no sense to the Beastlord. None could doubt the blessings the gods had bestowed upon it, nor the favour they displayed by allowing it to stand in the presence of the Master of Skulls and live. The reasons for such behaviour were a mystery, but it did not let such trivial thoughts distract it from its duty. If other challengers arose it would fight them and it would kill them.

The Beastlord turned from the carcass, allowing the scavengers to gather around the corpse and tear fresh meat from its body with great bites. Warm meat was a rarity and none were about to let such a morsel go uneaten. The weakest members of the herd had already been slaughtered for their flesh, but the Beastlord knew that he would need fresh meat if he hoped to keep the herd together, favour of the gods or not.

The mountains were becoming less steep now that they had descended from the summits, the jagged black rock of the highest peaks giving way to the mossy, scrubby shale and powdered scree of the lower slopes. Their goal was now almost within their reach. Three times had the warherd rested since the Beastlord gathered it beneath its rule, the creatures' loyalty maintained through fear and displays of sheer brutality.

Below, the forest had gone from a greenish brown stain on the landscape to an undulating swathe of greenery that offended the Beastlord's altered eyes. Tendrils of rain-soaked mist and dangerous magic snaked upwards from the vast expanse of forest below, trickling into the mountains like rivulets from a cracked dam. The Beastlord could feel the power stinging its flesh through its iron-hard hooves, though the power was weak and unfocussed. With its newly gifted senses, it could feel the glacial heartbeat of the woodland realm ahead of it, the rank purity filling its heart with the urge to destroy.

Warm rain fell in dreary sheets from the corpse-grey sky, washing down the misty mountain in foaming waterfalls of silt and dark earth. The herd followed the Beastlord, its braying filling them with purpose and power; the Children of Chaos were its to command. The sacred task appointed to the Beastlord by the Master of Skulls now became clear as its gaze was drawn to a dark shape, barely visible as more than a tall, black shadow through the clammy mist.

With a clarity it should not have possessed, the Beastlord saw the task appointed to it by the gods and roared in affirmation as the herd devoured the latest challenger.

KYARNO LOOSED AN arrow, a second nocked to his bow almost before the fletching of the first had passed his bowstave. A third followed the second and then a fourth. He pressed his left knee against Eiderath's flanks, guiding his steed a winding course through the trees as he sent arrow after arrow thumping into the bole of a long-dead ash tree.

His frustration grew with every arrow he loosed, picturing Cairbre's face on the bole until at last his doeskin quiver was empty and he halted Eiderath with a gentle pressure of his knees. He vaulted from the back of his steed, a light sweat coating his chest and a pleasant burning sensation in his arms from hours spent practising with his bow.

The bow was finely crafted from soft yew, a perfect six-foot stave offered directly from the trunk with the bark, sapwood and reddish, nut-brown heartwood intact. Kyarno had made an offering to the tree, seeking its permission to make use of its body and the tree had consented to grant him a portion of its precious wood.

Taking the stave, thick with grain lines, he had placed it in the fast-flowing and pure waters of the forest river until the sap and resin were washed out before beginning the long process of crafting such an elegant weapon. He had taken no less care with his arrows, each finely wrought and deadly, crafted with a skill that would make the finest human fletcher's work look shoddy and amateurish.

He loosened the bowstring from the end of the bow, allowing the stave to relax, and placed the weapon on an oiled leather cloth. He wiped the back of his hand across his forehead and gathered up his arrows, not one having failed to find its mark in the wood of the dead tree.

Though his anger at Cairbre was great, he knew there was no sense in angering the forest around him with his own woes. The creatures and spirits of the forest were restless and agitated, more so than was usual for this time of year, when, traditionally, the forest slowly slid into a quiet period of slumber.

As he sheathed the last arrow, he cupped his right fist in his left palm and bowed to the tree.

'Thank you, brother,' he whispered, 'for allowing me to hone my skills to better protect your living brethren and the forest that shelters me.'

He hung the quiver from a branch next to Eiderath, rubbing a hand down the magnificent animal's lathered chest. Taking out a brush, Kyarno rubbed the horse's silver flanks down and said, 'And thank you, my friend. As ever you are my companion in all things.'

Eiderath whinnied, nuzzling him gently before Kyarno moved towards the small, gurgling stream that meandered its way along the edge of the glade. Stripping off, he waded into the knee-deep stream and lay down, allowing the icy waters to cleanse the sweat from his body and massage the tension from his shoulders and arms.

As the waters rushed over his flesh, he angrily recalled his meeting with Lord Aldaeld the previous evening. Though he had travelled back through the shadow paths of the forest, it had still taken him the best part of three hours to reach the warmth and safety of Coeth-Mara.

The towering oaks that formed the great, arched processional were wreathed in the ghostly light of flitting spites, their capricious laughter echoing from the boughs high above as he made his way towards the halls of Lord Aldaeld Éadaoin.

Grey-cloaked Eternal Guard with their twin-bladed spears parted to allow him access to the great hall. Its magnificence was wasted on Kyarno, who had seen it many times, though usually only briefly before once again being banished from its glory.

The lord of the Éadaoin kinband was flanked by more of his Eternal Guard, seated before them upon a throne of pale wood sung from the roots of the hall's trees. His cloak of leaves and feathers was swept over his shoulders, revealing his bare chest, slender yet powerful and covered with looped tattoos of dragons and winged serpents.

A longsword with a flaring, leaf-shaped blade lay across his lap, its pommel glowing with a faint green light and the blade an exquisite blue steel.

Cairbre paced the hall like a caged wolf, having obviously returned some time ago via the paths known only to his warriors and the wild and dangerous wardancers.

'Kyarno,' began Aldaeld, 'Cairbre tells me you have been with my daughter once again.'

Kyarno shot a venomous look towards the Hound of Winter, but said nothing, knowing it would do no good to deny the accusation.

'Is that true?' demanded Aldaeld.

'Yes,' nodded Kyarno, defiantly meeting the lord of the Éadaoin kinband's eyes.

'Even though I forbade you to do so?'

'Even though,' agreed Kyarno.

'You are a troublemaker, Daelanu, and you would be gone from my lands forever, but for the counsel of your uncle.'

Kyarno gave Cairbre another look, puzzled as to why he should speak on his behalf.

'I am not to be banished?'

Lord Aldaeld shook his head. 'No, though my every instinct is to hurl you to Valas Laithu and be done with you.'

'Valas Laithu is coming to Coeth-Mara?' asked Kyarno, a cold dread settling in his belly. 'Why?'

'You know fine well why,' said Aldaeld. 'He and his sons will be here for the Winter Feast and though I do not know what season he carries in his heart, I do not think it will be summer.'

'What are you going to do?'

'I will keep my own counsel on that, stripling,' growled Aldaeld, and Kyarno bristled at being branded so. 'But your uncle seems to think that you may yet earn your place in my kinband by more than an accident of birth. It is now time for you to prove him right.'

Now Kyarno understood. Lord Aldaeld had some menial task that Cairbre had volunteered him for and he felt his resentment flare once more.

'What would you have me do?' he said at last.

'Naieth has need of you,' said Lord Aldaeld. 'She brings a human amongst us and though he should be dead, she believes he may yet be of use to us.'

'What use could a human be to the kindreds of the forest?'

'That is for her to know,' said Aldaeld, and Kyarno caught the elven lord's irritation at his ignorance of the Prophetess's motives. 'But you will attend upon her come the morn.'

'It demeans an elf to nursemaid a human, my lord,' protested Kyarno.

Lord Aldaeld nodded. 'Indeed it does, but I do not offer this task to you as a choice, Kyarno Daelanu. You will do this duty or I will hand you over to Valas Laithu.'

Faced with such a destiny, Kyarno knew that he had no choice but to agree and bowed curtly, saying, 'Then I will do as you bid, my lord,' before striding from the hall with his head held high.

His anger had not dimmed with his distance from Coeth-Mara, rather it had swelled until he felt his hatred for this human grow like a weed within his heart. Trust his uncle to have convinced Aldaeld to curse him with such a duty; the aged warrior hated him and seemed to bend his every effort to seeing Kyarno humiliated.

As the first rays of dawn had spilled over the treetops, he had ridden hard into the forest to take out his frustrations with some archery, though, in truth, it had done little to ease his bitterness.

He leaned his head back into the stream, holding his breath and letting the water cover his face. Its chill touch numbed his skin and he surrendered to the cold, staying beneath the water until his lungs were on fire before finally sitting bolt upright in a wash of cold water and heaving breaths.

'One of these days you'll not come up in time and I'll have to drag your body back to Coeth-Mara,' said a voice.

Kyarno shook his head free of water and smiled humourlessly at the newcomer, 'And tell me, Tarean Stormcrow, who would mourn for Kyarno Daelanu?'

'Well, no one, obviously,' said Tarean, brightly, 'after all, you're nothing but an inconvenience to us.'

'Is that so?' said Kyarno, not bothering to conceal his hostility and climbing from the stream to pull on his clothes.

'Almost certainly,' nodded Tarean, stroking Kyarno's steed's mane. 'Though Morvhen seems to like you, so perhaps you should think of her the next time you play your dangerous games.'

Kyarno shrugged on his overshirt, warily watching Tarean as he strolled around the glade, reading the tracks of where he had been training.

Tarean Stormcrow was tall and physically resembled him, in that they were the same age and shared the same lithe, supple physique common to most of the Glade Riders of the Éadaoin kinband, but his features had an easy confidence to them that Kyarno knew his did not. Tarean's golden hair was held in place by a silver circlet, upon which was set a sapphire gem and his clothes spoke of an elf not given to living alone in the forest. A long-bladed sword was buckled at his waist, and he carried a short, recurved bow slung over one shoulder.

Kyarno knew that Tarean's appearance was deceptive, for though he might look as though he were more at home in the comfortable confines of Coeth-Mara, he had fought many battles to defend Athel Loren against intruders.

'You use that bow well, Kyarno and that steed of yours is a fine beast.'

'His name is Eiderath, and he is the finest steed I have ever ridden,' agreed Kyarno.

'Better even than those of the Laithu kinband?' laughed Tarean.

'Ah…' said Kyarno, 'then that is what this is about.'

'What?' replied Tarean. 'Can't I offer a friendly word without there being an ulterior motive?'

'You and I are not friends, Tarean,' said Kyarno, gathering up his bow and sheathing it over Eiderath's back. 'You are Lord Aldaeld's herald and kin to him.'

'And that precludes us from being friends?'

'Say what it is you are here to say and be gone,' said Kyarno. 'I do not wish your company.'

Tarean sighed and said, 'Your words are needlessly barbed, Kyarno Daelanu. I offer you friendship, but you do not see it.'

'I need no friends,' snapped Kyarno.

'You are wrong,' said Tarean, grasping Kyarno's arm. 'We all need friends, now, in these dark times more than ever.'

Kyarno shrugged off Tarean's grip and swung onto Eiderath's back. 'And you would be my friend?'

'I would, yes,' said Tarean, offering his hand with a grin, 'though Isha alone knows why, you're a hard one to like.'

'You mock me!' spat Kyarno.

'No,' said Tarean, 'I was merely making a poor jest and if I offended you, then I am sorry. If you wish me to go then I will go, but you are right, I do have a message for you.'

'What is it then?'

'Lord Aldaeld bids me command you that it is time for you to fulfil your duty to your kinband and take the human to the Crystal Mere.'

'To nanny a human,' cursed Kyarno. 'He mocks me in all things.'

Tarean shook his head. 'No, Lord Aldaeld honours you with this charge. See this duty for what it is and you will see no slight in its issue.'

'What good can it possibly do to have a human within Athel Loren? They are nothing but firestarters and fellers of trees. They are not to be trusted.'

'For what it is worth, I agree with you, my friend, but Lord Aldaeld has made his desire in this matter plain.'

'Then Kyarno the troublemaker will see it done,' said Kyarno bitterly.

Tarean shook his head and said, 'I feel sorry for you, Kyarno, you could be part of this kinband, but you won't let yourself.'

'I don't need your pity, Tarean,' said Kyarno, digging his heels into Eiderath's flanks and riding away, leaving Lord Aldaeld's herald alone in the glade.

LEOFRIC WATCHED THE elf named Cairbre as he spoke quietly with the two who had prevented him from leaving this place. Their voices were clear and song-like, but Leofric knew not to put his faith in such false beauty. Though the words were unknown to him, it was no leap of imagination to surmise they were speaking of him and whatever terrible fate they had in mind for him.

As the adrenaline of his brief fight with the elves wore off, the pain of loss returned to him as he pictured Helene's smiling face, her laugh and her beauty. He had sat on the shaped stump of a tree and wept as the sunlight dappling in from overhead changed from the strong, clear light of dawn to the soft, warmth of midmorning.

What was left to him now that Helene was gone? Assuming he was able to escape this place, how would he tell Beren?

Leofric felt hollow, as though his spirit, so nearly crushed on the east causeway of Middenheim, had now been shattered into a thousand pieces. The dark shadow that had settled upon his soul since facing the lord of daemons and the rout at the hands of the Lord of the End Times once more threatened to swallow him completely.

He heard the sound of voices once more, the rich tones of the males accompanied by the soft, feminine lilt of a woman's voice. For the briefest moment, his soul was soothed by the sweet, musical sound, before he reminded himself that this was the beguiling voice of an elf and therefore not to be trusted.

His fists clenched as he saw the hawk-faced elf-witch who he had seen in the forest enter the chamber of branches, her movements as graceful as those of the young elf-maids that had attended him earlier. She wore the same dress of spun gold and carried her staff of intertwined branches, her hair still bound in an elaborate headpiece of leaves, pins and feathers. A faint corona of light surrounded her and Leofric could sense the unwholesome aftertaste of faerie magic.

'Good day, Leofric,' said the elf-witch. 'My name is Naieth. Do you recall me from our meeting in the forest?'

'You are a witch,' spat Leofric.

'Your kind have called me worse than that before now,' said Naieth without apparent offence. 'But that is unimportant. What *is* important is that you listen to me, Leofric.'

'Why should I? I am held prisoner while my wife may lie dead somewhere in your forest!' stormed Leofric. 'And how is it that you know my name and speak it as though we are friends?'

'The answer to that is complex, Leofric, I know a great deal about you. More than you do yourself.'

'Spare me your riddles, elf. Answer the question.'

'As you say, I am a witch and thus I know many things. Some I would wish not to know, but that is not for me to choose.'

Leofric surged to his feet, the grey-cloaked elves raising their weapons before them as he did.

'Damn you, woman, tell me where my wife is!' raged Leofric before sitting back down on the stump of wood. 'Please...'

'You will show respect, human,' said Cairbre, raising his spear towards him.

'Leofric, your wife is with the forest now,' said Naieth softly. 'I am sorry. We tried to come to your aid, but we were too late.'

'With the forest? What does that mean?' demanded Leofric, sudden hope in his heart. 'Can we get her back?'

'It means that the spirits of the forest took her,' said Naieth, drawing up her robes to sit on a delicately curved swathe of branches that curled outwards from the walls as she lowered herself to sit upon them. 'Dryads, branchwraiths and tree spirits. As winter draws in they become malicious and spiteful, taking all who cross into the forest as their victims.'

'Victims...' whispered Leofric. 'Then she is dead?'

Naieth reached out to lay a hand on his shoulder, but he pulled back, his face a mask of resentment and pain.

'I am truly sorry, Leofric, but the forest exacts its own vengeance on those who pass its borders.'

'She harmed no one!' shouted Leofric. 'She was an innocent.'

'I know, but she is at peace now,' said Naieth. 'This world is a dangerous place. Orcs and the beasts of the dark places of the world pillage and destroy, the warriors of the Dark Gods lay waste to the lands of your kind and the dead rise from their tombs to slay the living. She is spared that horror now and will live forever as part of Athel Loren. She will live on in your heart, your memories and through your bloodline.'

'But I want her back, I need her!' cried Leofric.

'I'm sorry, but it is not in my power to grant that wish.'

Leofric took a deep breath, attempting to compose himself in the face of the elves. He was a knight of Bretonnia and it did not behoove a knight of the realm to comport himself in this manner.

'She gave me her favour at the Couronne tournament,' he said slowly, 'a silken scarf of blue, edged in white lace.'

Cairbre leaned close to Naieth and she nodded as he whispered something to her.

'I am told it was wrapped around the hilt of your sword,' she said.

'It was,' agreed Leofric, 'and it is precious to me.'

'Then I will see that it is returned to you,' promised Naieth.

He straightened his back and nodded his thanks through red-rimmed eyes at the elf-witch and her guardians as another thought occurred to him.

'The knight who was with you, the one with the heraldry of a dragon, a green one I think. Who is he?' asked Leofric. 'Is he here?'

Naieth shook her head. 'No, he is not. He has travelled beyond this place.'

'Do you know his name? He is one of the holy few is
he not? A knight of the grail…'

'Yes,' agreed Naieth, 'he is that. He is a friend to the
Asrai and that is all that need concern you of him. He is
gone from Athel Loren and will not return for… some
time.'

'The Asrai? Who are they?'

Naieth smiled. 'It is an ancient elven word from
across the seas that means "the blessed ones". It is the
word we use for our race, the kin of the forest.'

'And how is it that a noble knight of the Lady rides
with your people atop an elven steed and wielding an
elven blade? Surely such a thing is unthinkable.'

'He has done great service for my people and I would
speak no more about him, for he is a warrior of great
sorrow and he would not thank me for speaking of
him.'

Seeing he would get no more from Naieth about the
mysterious grail knight, Leofric said, 'So be it, but if I
am to be held here, then surely I deserve at least to
know where I am.'

'Indeed you do,' agreed Naieth, waving her hand at
the branch walls, which parted to reveal a glorious
woodland landscape of golden browns and brilliant
greens. Majestic trees soared upwards, their trunks
thicker than a castle tower and older than the most
ancient ruins Leofric had ever seen. Brilliant lights
wreathed each canopy, haunting melodies and laughter
weaving through the greenery like a gentle breeze.

Elves on foot and elves on horseback moved gracefully
through the trees, and animals – white-furred wolves,
sinuous cats and golden-feathered birds – meandered

through the undergrowth or flitted between the trees without fear.

'You are within the woodland realm of Athel Loren,' said Naieth, 'a guest of Lord Aldaeld Éadaoin of the Asrai in the halls of Coeth-Mara. Lord Aldaeld rules this region of the forest in the name of Isha and Kurnous, and by your way of thinking, we are in the south-eastern part of the forest, near the foot of the mountains you call the Vaults.'

'You say I am a guest,' commented Leofric. 'Does that imply I am free to leave?'

'No, I am afraid that it does not,' said Naieth reluctantly. 'Normally intruders within Athel Loren are killed without mercy. You have lived in the shadow of our forest for enough years to know this.'

'Aye,' agreed Leofric. 'So the question then becomes why am I not dead?'

'Indeed. You are alive only because I decreed it and Lord Aldaeld has consented not to slay you for the time being.'

'So my position is what might be described as "precarious",' stated Leofric.

Naieth made a sound like the opening of a song and it was several seconds before Leofric realised that she was laughing.

'Yes, Leofric, your situation is precarious… as is mine if it turns out I was wrong to save you. Your life depends now on the good graces of Lord Aldaeld, so walk warily in his realm, Leofric Carrard.'

'So why did you save my life then?'

'Not on a whim, I can assure you of that, there was method to my actions.'

'Then I ask again, why did you save my life?'

Naieth hesitated for the briefest of seconds and Leofric knew with sudden clarity that she would not tell him the truth.

At last Naieth said, 'I see many things, Leofric, and the future is not the impenetrable veil to me that it is to others. Nor is it fixed, there are many fates that await us, and not even the mightiest seers can know them all. There is a time of great moment approaching for the Asrai and in many of my waking nightmares of the future, I see you. What part you have to play in the coming days of blood and war I do not yet see, but that you are there is enough for me.'

Leofric sensed that the elf-witch was holding something back, but knew better than to press her too much.

'So what happens now?' he asked. 'You keep me prisoner until this time draws near?'

'No, of course not,' smiled Naieth. 'Lord Aldaeld desires to speak with you before deciding your fate. Once he has made his decision we will resolve what is to be done with you.'

Leofric looked down at his sweat and tear streaked robes, the stain on his hip where his stitches had torn now grown into a large patch of dried blood.

'I am in no fit state to meet a lord,' he said.

'I know,' agreed Naieth. 'That is why I have arranged for someone to take you to the Crystal Mere where you will be cleansed and made presentable to Lord Aldaeld.'

'Who?'

'Don't worry,' said Naieth with a smile, though Leofric saw that it did not quite reach her eyes. 'I'm sure you and Kyarno will get along famously.'

THIS CLOSE TO the forest of the elves, the Beastlord was cautious, having moved the herd slowly through the low, scrubby hills at the foot of the mountains. It knew full well the dangers inherent in being so near the woodland realm. Its senses were alive with the sensation of magic emanating from the trees and ground. It felt it as a sour taste in the back of its throat, a rank, bitter flavour that fuelled its urge to despoil.

A dark rain fell as the forest's edge came into sight over a cold, windswept heath of tall, yellow grasses and stagnant pools of brackish water. The Beastlord waved its thick arms and the beasts of the herd dropped to the ground, crawling and stalking their way towards the edge of the heath. Claws of mist gathered about the dark and twisted oaks of the forest, their trunks and upper branches wreathed with skulls and hides of beasts, orcs and ratkin. Waving, leafy sprouts drooped from eye sockets and a low groaning issued from the depths of the forest.

Drifting lights, sluggish and lazy, wafted between the shadowed trunks deeper in the woods, but the Beastlord paid them no heed, intent on the massive waystone that reared up from the ground at the treeline. Its surface was worn smooth by the elements, though the looping carvings and elven script that spiralled across its surface remained crisp and deep. The Beastlord felt the ancient power that saturated the waystone, reaching deep into the earth to the foundations of the world, and grunted in pleasure as it pictured the stone torn down then corrupted to become its herdstone.

It raised its axe, waving forward a group of around twenty smaller creatures with thin, reddish brown fur and elongated, bestial skulls with small, budding horns. Each beast carried a short, iron-bladed axe and cast fearful glances towards the forest, unwilling to approach it too closely.

The Beastlord sensed their fear and let loose a terrifying bellow, cowing the smaller creatures with its power.

It swung its axe towards the forest once more and the beastmen loped towards the treeline, their instinctive fear of the woodland realm outweighed by the more immediate fear of the Beastlord.

Their braying cries were strangely deadened as they charged, the Beastlord watching as they reached the edge of the forest and waved their axes in the air. Some chopped at low branches with their weapons, some defecated on the trees and others skulked deeper into the forest with low growls.

The altered eyes of the Beastlord could see spiralling lines of magical energy seeping up from the ground and watched as the forest reacted to the intruders.

A beast squatting over the roots of a tree was the first to die, its head torn from its shoulders in a fountain of blood by a looping noose of razor-sharp thorns that whipped down from the tree above. Another died as the earth opened beneath it and swallowed it whole. The ground erupted in rampant growth, slashing, tearing and ripping the beasts to bloody ruin. Soon the forest's edge was a thrashing mass of screaming beasts, lashing branches and jagged bushes that tore at flesh and crushing boles that split skulls.

Snaking branches and curling thorns spiralled from the ground at the edge of the forest and the trunks of the trees, an impenetrable barrier of lethally sharp barbs. A dark hiss and rustle of angered forest life crept across the heath, the sound of screaming beasts sending a ripple of fear through the warherd.

The Beastlord nodded to itself. It had expected no less and the sacrifice of the smaller beasts had simply confirmed its suspicions. Turning from the carnage unleashed by the forest and the pitiful cries of the dying creatures, the Beastlord waved another of its herd forward, a withered, hunched figure swathed in rotted robes of patched leather and hides.

Long, curling horns sprouted from its shaggy, bear-like skull and its hooded eyes held the spark of a dark, malicious intelligence. It carried a long staff of gnarled black wood, its substance slick and somehow alive. The breath of the gods surrounded the creature, a shaman whose powers not even the Beastlord could match.

The shaman looked upon the tall stone that marked the boundary of the forest and nodded, stabbing its staff towards it, grunting and chanting in a language the Beastlord did not understand, although he felt its dark power in the depths of his bones. Powerful winds of magic were stirred and the Beastlord could feel the gathering energy being channelled into the shaman with each passing second.

Another group of creatures stamped forward as the Beastlord again waved its massive axe: thickset centaurs with iron-clawed hooves, hard skins of vermillion and elongated shaggy rumps like powerful dray horses. The reek of powerful spirits was upon them and their snarling faces were flushed with its consumption. Each carried a long, stabbing spear and thick, goring horns curled from their fearsome skulls.

The shaman nodded and the Beastlord ordered them forwards, the bellowing centaurs rearing in wild abandon before thundering towards the trees. As the centaurs charged, the shaman hauled its twisted bulk to its feet and pointed its writhing staff at the barrier of thorns and branches.

Glittering blue flames leapt from the staff and the shaman braced its malformed legs to control the spurting fires. Smoke billowed from the edge of the forest as the magical flames consumed the woodland. White light flared as the magic of the waystone fought the raw power of the god's breath. The barrier swiftly disintegrated under the relentless assault and the roaring centaurs leapt through the gap the shaman's magic had created.

Six of the powerful beasts made it through the barrier of thorns before the shaman's spell was exhausted and it reared up once more. The other beasts turned back as the tearing wall of branches and thorns snatched at them. The forest dragged one down before it could halt its charge, ripping its belly open, breaking its legs and wrenching its limbs off before grinding its ravaged carcass to powder beneath the grasping roots of the trees.

The shaman shook its thick, horned skull and pointed at the base of the waystone, snarling and grunting in pleasure. The Beastlord saw that the grasses surrounding the waystone were blackened and withered, twisting into new and unnatural forms – the influence of the Shadow-Gave reaching from its lair in the mountains…

Once again the Beastlord pictured the waystone as it would soon be – toppled and dragged into the mountains to become the greatest herdstone of all the beasts of Chaos.

CHAPTER FIVE

CAIRBRE WAS WAITING for Kyarno when he rode up to the hall where the prophetess had sequestered the human. The aged warrior wore an expression of faint disapproval, and his stance was guarded. As ever, he was ready to fight in an instant. Kyarno saw that he carried the Blades of Midnight unsheathed, and held the reins of a heavily muscled, human-bred horse with a wide chest and thick limbs.

'Expecting trouble?' asked Kyarno, nodding towards the white-bladed spear as he vaulted from Eiderath's back.

'Where have you been?' said Cairbre, ignoring Kyarno's question. 'You were to be here at dawn.'

'Good morning to you too, uncle,' replied Kyarno, giving the huge, snorting horse a wide berth. There was a crudity to the animal that no amount of grooming could erase; its bulk was powerful, but vulgar. Trust a human to ride something like this, he thought. Curious spites flickered around the beast. The horse's eyes were wide and its ears were pressed flat against its skull.

'That beast is very you,' he said.

'I said you were to be–'

'I heard what you said, Cairbre. I came as soon as Tarean Stormcrow came for me. What more do you want?'

Cairbre nodded stiffly, biting back a response, and said, 'The human is inside. The prophetess asks for him to be taken to the Crystal Mere and for him to be allowed to bathe. Once he is clean enough to be presented to Lord Aldaeld, bring him back.'

'Yes, Tarean told me this,' said Kyarno. 'Is that all?'

'Yes, that's all,' said Cairbre. 'Do you think you can manage that without any trouble?'

'I think so, yes,' snapped Kyarno, tilting his head back to look up into the crisp sunlight as it speared through the autumnal canopy high above. 'It is a fine morning to take a filthy human to the healing waters of the Crystal Mere. I wonder if he will appreciate how privileged he is to see such a sight?'

'I would doubt it.'

'Then why show him, uncle?' asked Kyarno. 'He will only speak of it if he is returned to his lands. And what he speaks of will draw others of his kind here like blights to the dying.'

Cairbre nodded. 'I know, but it is Naieth's wish that he be taken there.'

'Has she seen something?'

Cairbre shrugged, obviously reluctant to speak. 'I do not know. Perhaps.'

'She has been wrong before,' hissed Kyarno. 'Have you forgotten?'

'No, damn you, I have not,' said Cairbre, his pale features ashen. 'And I do not need you to remind me! I see it every day I look at you.'

Kyarno swallowed hard. 'And I see it every time I close my eyes, uncle. Tell me again whose burden is the greater.'

Cairbre was silent for long seconds before he said, 'If I could change things I would, lad. I loved your mother and father, you know that.'

'But you can't change things, can you?' said Kyarno. 'For all your skill at arms, you couldn't save them, could you?'

'I lost a brother that day,' whispered Cairbre.

'No,' said Kyarno. 'You lost a lot more than that.'

NAIETH LISTENED WITH growing sadness to the harsh words spoken between the Hound of Winter and Kyarno. The youngster would never understand the choices she had had to make, the awful truths that woke her weeping in the night with visions of death and ruin. He would never understand that she had needed him to suffer in order to mould him into the weapon she required.

He would never understand and he would never forgive her if he knew.

She closed her eyes, seeing again the wooded glade, the stream that ran red with elven blood, the flames that burned, the guttural brays of the twisted beastkin and the agonised screams that haunted her every nightmare.

What she had told Leofric was the truth: this world *was* a dangerous place and the Asrai had enemies all around. Every rhyme sung to elven youngsters taught them this cold, hard fact.

The forest realm of Athel Loren was one of the last bastions of pure magic in the world, and she would do whatever was necessary to protect it.

Even though the price was sometimes almost too high to bear.

DRESSED IN FRESH clothes – a fine silken shirt of pale cream, downy britches of auburn leather and soft boots that fitted as though they had been made specially for him – Leofric felt almost human again. The air here had a crisp, invigorating quality and, as much as he kept reminding himself that he was in the lair of the enemy, he found himself strangely energised. The ache of loss was still lodged in his heart like a splinter of ice, but he forced himself to maintain a composed exterior in the face of the elves.

It chafed him not to have his armour and sword, but he supposed that if one of the elves had been held prisoner in the oubliettes of Castle Carrard, he would not have allowed it a weapon either.

Though he knew it was autumn, with the season on the cusp of changing to winter, the climate here was mild, far milder than it had any right to be, as though a moment in time of summer had been somehow slowed.

The elf-witch had left an hour ago, though it was difficult to judge time in this place, and the two elf-maids who had earlier brought him food returned with the clothes he now wore. Atop the neatly folded clothes was Helene's silken blue scarf, and Leofric wept once more as he picked up her favour. He had tucked the folded scarf into a pocket of the overshirt while one expressionless maid delicately sewed the wound on his hip. He had thanked them, but they had once again proven to be uncommunicative. Upon leaving, they stared at him blankly as Leofric had bowed graciously, his chivalric code demanding no less a courtesy to ladies, even though these ladies were elves.

The pain in his hip was lessened and the injuries to his chest and head had diminished to a dull throbbing ache. He paced the room, catching fleeting glimpses of the world beyond his confinement – laughter, music and arching voices that spoke of great meaning just beyond his comprehension. His earlier companions, the flitting, winged creatures of light had returned, buzzing around him like irritating insects. He had long since given up trying to dissuade them from annoying him, such attempts only spurring them to greater heights of nuisance.

As far as confinement went, this place was far more salubrious than anything Castle Carrard had to offer, its arched timber walls curved and sweet smelling. Gently waving branches formed the ceiling, the bright sunlight diffusing softly through the canopy of wide green leaves. Nowhere was there anything that appeared to have had the hand of a craftsman upon it, no carved furniture, no hand-blown glass, no skilfully moulded ceramic – everything had a natural, almost… grown quality to it.

But as natural and harmonious as everything was, to his human eyes there was a subtle wrongness to the surroundings. He felt no kinship with his environment, though there a familiarity to it: walls, floor, ceiling, clothes. Everything was familiar, yet at the same time disturbingly different, giving him a caged, impatient feeling.

Just as he was thinking of making his own way from this place once more, an elf clad in simple, practical garb entered. His manner was immediately hostile and his youthful features were fixed in an expression that told Leofric that he would much rather be anywhere else than here.

The elf wore the natural colours of the forest, brown leggings and a pale grey overshirt with embroidered gold stitching along its collar. A feathered cloak of deep blue covered one arm and hung to his calves from his shoulders. A worn, shagreen scabbard housed an elegant, plain-handled sword and across his back hung a long, gracefully curved bow.

Despite its craftsmanship, the bow was still a lowborn peasant's weapon to Leofric's way of thinking and he wondered whether this was some subtle insult. Had the elves sent a peasant to be his gaoler?

'Who are you?' asked Leofric.

The elf did not reply immediately, sizing him up with his wide, green eyes and pursing his lips together. By any human standards, the elf was darkly handsome, with narrow, sardonic features and long, straw-coloured hair that spilled around his shoulders in a fringe of tightly braided locks. Feathers and beads were woven into his hair and Leofric sensed a recklessness in this elf like that of many a knight errant.

'Are you Kyarno?' asked Leofric, raising his voice and speaking more slowly. 'I am Leofric Carrard of Quenelles, knight of the realm of Bretonnia and loyal subject of King Louen Leoncoeur.'

The elf's face twisted in a grimace as he spoke and Leofric wondered if he had somehow insulted him.

'By Kurnous, your voice is ugly and you mangle my name such that I do not recognise it,' said the elf at last, his tone betraying his impatience to be done with this business. 'I know who you are, and yes, I am Kyarno Daelanu. I am to take you to the Crystal Mere.'

'So I am told. What is it?'

'Somewhere you would not be seeing if I had my way,' answered Kyarno.

Leofric nodded in resignation and said, 'Very well, I see we are going to get along like brothers in arms.'

Kyarno ignored the comment and smoothly turned on his heels, heading for the arched exit to the chamber. 'Come. If we do not leave now it will be nightfall before we return and night is no time for one like you to be abroad in Athel Loren.'

Leofric sighed and set off after the truculent Kyarno, following him through the archway and into a passage-way of gently curving branches that swayed in an unfelt breeze. Though Kyarno spoke human language flaw-lessly, there was a stiltedness to his speech that Leofric had noticed in all the elves. Their own language was spoken with a lyrical fluidity, but they voiced the human tongue as though it were unfamiliar and dis-tasteful to them.

The scent of outdoors came to him and he felt a warm gust as his sprightly companions flitted past his head.

Kyarno turned a corner and Leofric, without seeming to pass any boundary that marked the structure he had been in, suddenly found himself outside in a leafy glade, the scent of wood and sap strong in his nostrils and the sounds of life coming from all around him.

He spun, confused and dismayed to find that he could see no sign of any doorway they might have emerged from. Saplings and the towering trunks of mighty trees were all that he could see of the shimmer-ing clearing, and he was seized anew with a fear of this faerie magic.

What manner of race could beguile the senses so?

A familiar and heartily welcome whinny shook him from his discomfort and he smiled as he saw the reassuring form of his horse, Taschen. The horse looked frightened and was without his yellow caparison, his reins held by Cairbre, the warrior elf with the two-bladed spear. Leofric saw that the elven warrior had the reins unwisely wrapped around his wrist like a novice groom. If the horse bolted suddenly, it would wrench Cairbre's shoulder from its socket.

Kyarno stood nearby, beckoning a pale, saffron-maned steed of elvish stock towards him. The beast's neck was clad in a shimmering fabric, its tail and mane braided and woven with colourful garlands, and Leofric was struck by the wonderful impracticality of such a mount. Too narrow chested and slender limbed to carry an armoured warrior into battle, the beast was nevertheless a magnificent specimen of equine beauty and poise.

Cairbre led Taschen towards him, his face a mask of open hostility, and Leofric wondered what he had done to offend these elves so deeply. Was his very presence here an affront to them?

'Thank you,' he said as Cairbre gingerly handed Leofric the reins and Kyarno swung onto the back of his own steed.

'Where is the caparison?' asked Leofric, stroking his horse's mane.

'I removed it,' said Cairbre. 'It was too conspicuous and it is unwise to attract too much attention to yourself, human.'

'Too conspicuous?' replied Leofric, indicating Kyarno's steed. 'That beast is hardly the most subtle of creatures! It could be seen for miles in open country.'

'But it is ridden by one of the Asrai, and you are in Athel Loren,' said Cairbre before turning and marching away. Leofric put the missing caparison from his mind and set his boot in the stirrup, hauling himself onto Taschen's back, relishing the power and security of being back in the saddle.

As he settled himself on his mount's back, Leofric saw that Kyarno's steed had no tack whatsoever, no bridle, no saddle or any other piece of riding equipment. Now he understood Cairbre's careless handling of Taschen's reins.

It felt strange – and, Leofric had to admit, strangely liberating – being on horseback without a suit of heavy plate armour and the sense of weight that it brought. He looked over at Kyarno, who, despite having no saddle or reins, rode his steed as though it were a natural extension of his body.

'That is a magnificent steed,' said Leofric.

'He is indeed,' agreed Kyarno. 'Yours is… strong.'

Leofric patted Taschen's neck. 'He is indeed, he comes from the king's own stables and is said to be have been sired from the line of Tamasin.'

'Who is that?'

'Tamasin was the noble destrier that carried King Charlen into battle against the orcs at the Battle of Blood River in the land of the Border Princes,' said Leofric proudly. 'Thrice was the great steed wounded by foul orcish archery, but ne'er once did he falter in service of his master, bearing him through blood and battle to carry the day. After the battle, King Charlen decreed that his faithful steed had served his master enough and put him out to stud in the royal stables until the day came when his mighty heart beat no more.'

'At least he ended his days well,' said Kyarno. 'Given the chance to fornicate day and night with all the younger, feisty mares in the comfort of a warm stable. Better than being shot at by greenskins.'

'I suppose so,' agreed Leofric, annoyed that such a fine example of Bretonnian horse had been dismissed so flippantly.

Without seeming to guide his horse in any way, Kyarno rode away from him, beckoning lazily for Leofric to follow.

His irritation at this surly elf growing by the second, Leofric dug his heels into Taschen's sides and followed Kyarno into the depths of Coeth-Mara.

And Athel Loren opened up before him.

AWE. WONDERMENT. ENCHANTMENT. Fear.

Emotions whirled in Leofric's head as Kyarno led him through the realm of wonders and rapture that was Athel Loren. The land of the wood elves had been described in dark faerie tales throughout Bretonnia for centuries, telling of magic and spells that wove their domain from dreams. Minstrels and tellers of tales spoke of places where the elves gathered that were not of this world, where the seasons never changed and the inhabitants of the forest could live forever.

As he rode through the place Kyarno had called Coeth-Mara, followed by his darting companions of light, Leofric now knew that those taletellers understood but a fraction of the truth.

Athel Loren was a realm of magic and light, soaring trees as tall as the tallest tower of Castle Carrard with great gnarled trunks of incredible girth. Laughing elves on horseback rode through the trees, followed by more of the darting balls of light. The very air seemed alive with possibility, as though rich with restless motion. This was a place of life, vitality and fecundity – everything he saw, from forest animals to gliding hawks and the elves themselves, had a fierce vigour, the like of which he had never seen.

The peasantry of Bretonnia certainly never displayed such vigour in their daily tasks, never went about their business as though the pleasure in completing a duty was its own reward. They were wretched, hunched specimens and Leofric found himself wondering what manner of beings these elves were to live in such joy.

The heady aroma of sweet sap and pungent blossoms made Leofric feel giddy and light-headed and he had to force himself not to take such deep breaths. As they rode onwards, he saw he was attracting suspicious looks from every elf they passed – first there would be surprise and then either outright hostility or faint curiosity. Nor, he saw, was he the only one attracting suspicious glances. Kyarno drew his own fair share of scornful stares, but if the elf was aware of it he gave no sign.

'Why is everyone staring at me?' asked Leofric.

'Most of them have never seen a human before,' answered Kyarno without turning.

'Really?'

'Why would they have? We have no interest in contact with your kind.'

Leofric bit back an angry retort and said, 'What are they all doing out here in the middle of the forest?'

'What do you mean? This is Coeth-Mara, this is where they live.'

Leofric looked around for dwellings of any sort, but all he could see were the towering trees, verdant greenery and the abundance of forest creatures. A more picturesque scene he could scarce imagine, but he saw nowhere that might be considered a dwelling.

'If this is Coeth-Mara, then where do your people live? I see no homes or dwellings.'

'No,' agreed Kyarno. 'You won't, not unless the forest consents to let you. You ride through one of the greatest halls in Athel Loren, yet you see it not.'

Leofric wasn't sure whether or not Kyarno was making fun of him, and looked harder for any signs of habitation, but try as he might he could see nothing to indicate that anyone or anything lived here. Eventually he gave up, content just to watch the magical beauty unfold around him.

Trees shaped into gently rounded archways formed roofless processionals, like the nave of the great cathedral of Quenelles, and the golds and reds of autumn mingled with the greens of summer in their high branches.

Springs bubbled up through rocky cracks in the ground, gurgling along shaped channels of curved wood and into crystal pools lined with wondrous wooden sculptures that looked as though they had grown there rather than having been crafted. Leofric watched amazed as each of the sculptures began moving as though with an inner life of its own, the wood reshaping itself in newer and more graceful forms.

A soft glow appeared in the centre of one and a dazzling light emerged from the living wood, trilling, musical laughter emanating from it as it zipped towards another of the sculptures. It vanished into the depths of the wood and almost immediately the sculpture writhed with life as the joyous spirits shaped it in new and pleasing ways.

More of the dancing lights capered in the canopy above and Leofric turned in his saddle to see if his will-o'-the-wisp companions were still with him. They bobbed behind him, three impish lights with wings and tiny bodies that Leofric swore were shaped like miniature knights.

'What are these things?' asked Leofric, pointing behind him and then up at the shoal of lights above them.

'Spites,' said Kyarno. 'Magical spirits of the forest that are as much a part of Athel Loren as the trees themselves.'

'Can you make them go away?'

'Not if they've taken a liking to you, no. They are mischievous creatures, but mostly harmless.'

'*Mostly* harmless?'

'Yes, mostly. Like the birds of the air and the beasts of the earth, there are many kinds of spite. Some are harmless, some are not.'

'What about these ones?' asked Leofric, pointing at the spites bobbing after him.

'Mostly harmless,' repeated Kyarno. Leofric glanced warily behind him as they rode through a woven arch of leaves and branches, hung with gem-encrusted belts of gold and silver. Beyond the archway, Leofric immediately sensed a shift in the temperature.

The air here was as invigorating as that he had breathed earlier, but there was a raw, threatening quality to it, as though it possessed a wilder, more energetic essence.

Kyarno had ridden ahead and Leofric quickly dug his heels into Taschen's flanks to catch up with his guide, not wanting to become separated in this darker part of the forest.

The forest itself seemed more alive here, and Leofric shivered, sensing a darker presence lurking in the depths of the wood, a brooding sentience that looked upon him with eyes that were far from friendly.

KYARNO RODE ALONG a wide but overgrown path that Leofric would never have noticed had he not been following the elf, its subtle outline blending perfectly with the forest. Leofric began to see how skilfully the forest's shifting patterns could mislead a person and remembered tales of those who claimed to have become hopelessly lost within the forest despite many a distinctive landmark. Nothing in this place was as it seemed and Leofric knew he would need to be on his guard lest the glamours of the forest beguile him once more with their confusions.

'You still haven't told me where we are going,' said Leofric as he rode up alongside Kyarno. 'What is the Crystal Mere?'

Kyarno brushed a strand of hair from his face and said, 'It is a pool of the clearest water at the foot of a waterfall on the river you know as the Brienne. The water there is so clear and refreshing it is as though it is wept from the eyes of Isha herself.'

'And who is Isha?'

'You humans are ignorant creatures,' said Kyarno, shaking his head. 'No wonder all you can do is take axes to the trees and clear your lands of all that is green and living, grubbing in muddy fields with your bare hands.'

'Why must you always attempt to antagonise me so?' asked Leofric. 'If you wish to fight then give me a weapon and I will fight you in an honourable duel.'

'Fight you?' said Kyarno. 'No, human, I cannot fight you. Lord Aldaeld has placed you in my care and I will see to your protection, but understand this – you are my enemy.'

'Very well,' said Leofric angrily, 'though tell me why I should be your enemy. I have done you no wrong.'

Kyarno rounded on Leofric and said, 'We are enemies because your kind would take what I hold dear and tear it down if you could. Throughout the centuries we have fought to protect our realm from humans, dwarfs, orcs and beastmen who come with axes and fires to slaughter my kin!'

'No…' said Leofric. 'We do not–'

'Yes,' interrupted Kyarno, visibly struggling with his anger. 'You do. You fear us, yet secretly you envy us, and because you fear us you would destroy us.'

Leofric fought for calm and hissed, 'Perhaps there is truth in what you say, Kyarno, but it was your forest that took my wife. It was your forest that snatched away my ancestor all those years ago. I have as much reason to hate your kind as anyone!'

'The forest took your wife?' asked Kyarno, halting his steed with a whispered word.

'Aye,' said Leofric, masking his sorrow with anger. 'Creatures of branch and thorn, with faces of wicked crones, attacked us and took her from me.'

Kyarno turned his steed until he was facing Leofric directly, a measure of understanding now in his eyes. He bowed his head briefly and said, 'The dryads of winter. They are capricious beings and often take great offence where none is intended. Spiteful things they are, and best avoided. I am sorry for your loss, but it changes nothing.'

'Then let us not speak of it,' said Leofric sadly, changing the subject. 'Tell me of this Isha.'

At first, Leofric thought that Kyarno wasn't going to answer as he turned his steed and carried on riding, but eventually the elf said, 'Why should I speak of her? You humans could never understand what she is to my people.'

'Because I want to know,' said Leofric. 'Perhaps if we understand one another better we might not be enemies.'

'I do not think so, human, but I will indulge you for now,' said Kyarno, adopting a tone Leofric recognised as that of a taleteller. 'Isha is the ancestral goddess of the Asrai, the mother of the earth and source of all things. The spirit of Isha pervades the soil of the earth and brings forth the water welling up from the ground. She provides the bounty and life upon which we all depend. She is the breath of warmth on the last of the winter winds and the sigh of life in the first shoots of spring.'

'And she is the god of the elves?'

'One of them,' nodded Kyarno. 'Together with Kurnous and Loec, we honour the gods of earth and life above all others. This forest is sacred to Isha and is potent with her magic.'

Leofric stared with rapt fascination at the forest around him, its fierce beauty beyond anything he had ever seen before, easily able to imagine that the power of an ancient elven goddess gave it such splendour.

'Does Isha have a temple?' asked Leofric. 'It must be a place of some magnificence.'

Kyarno laughed and said, 'How like a human.'

'What is?' sighed Leofric, awaiting Kyarno's next barb.

'Imagining that you would build a temple of walls to enclose a goddess whose very soul is in the wilderness and yearns for the passions of nature,' said Kyarno, raising his hands and spreading them to the heavens. 'Human, you are within her temple even now. The trees and grasses are her places of worship, the ground we ride upon sacred to her.'

'Oh,' said Leofric, looking down at the ground with new eyes.

In truth, the notion of sacred earth was not alien to Leofric, who had seen several groves and pools where the Lady of the Lake had appeared to courageous knights and which those knights who had supped from the grail were pledged to defend with their lives. Such places were holy indeed and Leofric had felt a sensation akin to what he felt in this forest of unearthly beauty.

They rode in silence for what seemed like an hour or so. The wild wood around Leofric was alive with whispers and sounds of faraway voices. The temperature remained chill and knight shivered, wishing he had a cloak of some kind to warm him. Kyarno appeared unwilling to talk and Leofric had no real desire to break the silence, weary of the elf's antagonism.

Though the forest around him had become a darker, gloomier place, there was still the touch of magic on the breeze and Leofric could feel it in every breath he took. What might the magic of the forest do to him were he to spend much more time here? What changes might be wrought upon him by this place, which was plainly steeped in the fey power of enchantment?

As he considered this, he became aware of a prickling sensation on the back of his neck, an instinctive warning of danger. He shook himself from his reverie and looked around, alert for possible danger.

He saw that Kyarno was similarly alert and asked, 'What is it?'

Kyarno silenced him with a gesture, placing his finger against his lips and shaking his head. Leofric's warrior instinct spoke to him of approaching danger and his hand unconsciously strayed to his side before he realised he was unarmed.

He scanned the undergrowth, gripping Taschen's reins tightly and letting his eyes drift over the forest. Dimly he could hear a rustling, thumping sound that he recognised as hoof beats and he looked to Kyarno, who circled his horse and gripped the hilt of his own sword.

A nameless dread settled upon Leofric, though he could still see nothing of the approaching horsemen. Hot fear settled in his gut and he fought the urge to rake back his heels and ride from this place. He remembered the last time he had felt such fear, watching the thunderous charge of the Swords of Chaos coming towards him with the Lord of the End Times at their head.

The sound of approaching riders grew louder and Leofric rubbed Taschen's neck, whispering soothing words as the beast pranced nervously, also sensing the palpable tension in the air.

Leofric saw shapes moving in the periphery of his vision, catching fleeting glimpses of dark riders atop great elven steeds. A single, rising note of a hunting horn sounded, wild and exultant, and Taschen whinnied in fear.

Leofric shared that fear, feeling as helpless as a cornered stag awaiting the hunter's lance.

'Do nothing,' warned Kyarno. 'Say nothing.'

'Who are they?'

'The Wild Riders of Kurnous…' said Kyarno as the riders emerged from the trees like ghosts, a pall of fear travelling before them like a shadow.

Tall they were, and strong: six elves mounted on powerful steeds cloaked with hoar frost, with eyes that shone with an inner fire. Each rider wore a shaggy bearskin cloak the colour of the blood-red sun, and their bare flesh was tattooed and scarred with spirals and blood. Bleached skulls hung from their belts and torques of dark metal banded their arms. Tall helms of bronze with engraved cheek plates and long, curling horns like a stag's covered most of their faces, but Leofric could see pale eyes, as cold as chips of ice, but afire with something magical and terrible. They carried tall spears of silver, looped with coils of thorns and feathers, and tipped with lethally sharp iron blades.

Barbaric and feral, these elves looked more akin to the savage Norse than any of the elves Leofric had thus far seen. A savage death-lust radiated from every one.

'You bring a human into Athel Loren?' said one of the riders, his voice cold, threatening and unnatural.

'We could smell him for miles around,' added another.

'We will kill him,' said a third, drawing a long dagger from a leather sheath at his hip. Leofric looked at Kyarno and was surprised by the tension he saw in the youthful elf's face. He returned his gaze to the wild riders, the power and presence of these elves sending a thrill of fear coursing through his veins.

Another of the wild riders walked his horse forwards, lowering his spear as he spoke. 'It is not permitted for you to be here, human. You travel near the King's Glade.'

As one, the remaining wild riders lowered their spears and closed in on Leofric.

'No,' said Kyarno, sidestepping his horse to put himself between Leofric and the wild riders.

'No?' hissed one of the wild riders. 'You defy us?'

'To defy the wishes of those who serve the King of the Wood is to die,' said the wild rider who had first spoken.

Looking at him, Leofric sensed a fearsome, ancient power. The rider's features were cold and emotionless, and he knew that these elves would kill him without a second thought.

'This human is under my protection,' shouted Kyarno, whipping his bow from his back and nocking an arrow in one swift motion.

The wild rider looked quizzically at the arrow in Kyarno's bow and said, 'You cannot fight the wild riders of Kurnous. My warriors would kill you in a heartbeat.'

'Maybe,' agreed Kyarno, 'but I'd put this arrow through your eye before that happened.'

'Why would you raise arms against the servants of Orion for a human?'

Kyarno did not answer immediately, and Leofric wondered if the elf was now going to give him up to these savage elves, whose spear tips were getting uncomfortably close to his unarmoured body.

'I am Kyarno Daelanu and I have been entrusted with his care. I have sworn an oath that this human will come to no harm.'

'An oath to whom?' demanded the wild rider. 'What kinband do you serve?'

'That of Aldaeld Éadaoin, Lord of a Hundred Battles and steward of this domain.'

'And he wishes this human to live?'

'For now,' nodded Kyarno in a tone that reassured Leofric not at all.

'Where do you take him?'

'To the Crystal Mere,' explained Kyarno. 'To wash as much of the filth from his body as the waters are able.'

The wild rider nodded, putting up his spear. 'The forest warns us of danger, the touch of evil is upon it.'

'Mayhap this human is not the cause of it after all,' said another.

The leader of the wild riders nodded, though his eyes of cold fire never left Leofric.

'A taint is on the land, darkness comes and the king is gone from us until the vernal equinox. There is evil abroad in the forest this day, Kyarno Daelanu of the Éadaoin kinband. Keep your bow and sword ready, Athel Loren may have need of it 'ere the sun sets.'

'I will,' promised Kyarno, lowering his bow and easing the string.

The wild rider turned his horse and without a word being spoken, the rest of the riders set off after him, disappearing into the forest in eerie silence.

Leofric let out a huge shuddering breath, as the dread presence of the wild riders faded into memory. Kyarno slung his bow, leaning over his horse's neck and patting it softly as he too let out a breath of pent-up fear.

When he was sure the riders had passed beyond earshot, Leofric asked, 'What were they? I have never seen the like.'

'They are the king's guard,' said Kyarno. 'The wild huntsmen who ride alongside Kurnous when he awakens in spring and who guard his sacred places while he slumbers.'

'The wild hunt…' breathed Leofric, remembering nights when the horn of the hunter echoed through his lands and the exultant howls and cries of the terrifying charge of the wild hunt tore through the countryside.

Nights when only the foolhardy or desperate dared venture out and both peasant and nobleman offered prayers to the Lady that the wild hunt would pass them by.

These were fearful times of dread, when the long watches of the night echoed to the howls of hunting beasts and the timbers and roofs of the towns shook to the thunder of flaming hooves that beat on the storm-wracked skies. Come the morn, a trail of devastation marked its passage, bodies gathered into the storm of the hunt, torn to shreds and let fly to drop many miles from where they had been taken.

'Yes,' agreed Kyarno, and Leofric was surprised to hear a tremor of fear in his voice. He had not considered the possibility that the elves of the forest might fear the awakening of their king as much as the human inhabitants of the lands nearby.

'Come,' said Kyarno, 'we should be on our way before they change their mind and return for you.'

'Might they do that?'

'Indeed they might. You heard what their leader said. There is something evil abroad in the forest this day and if they do not find it soon, their lust for battle may bring them back to you.'

Leofric nodded, casting nervous glances around him for fear that the wild riders might already be surrounding them. He had no wish to lay eyes on these savage warriors again and knew that, but for Kyarno's words, he would now be spitted on a spear point, his blood soaking the grass at his feet.

'Thank you for speaking for me,' said Leofric. 'I think I would be dead now but for your words.'

'I did not speak for you, human,' said Kyarno. 'I spoke for me. Lord Aldaeld would have my head on a lance if I had let the wild riders slay you.'

'Well, I thank you anyway,' said Leofric. 'You saved my life and I will not forget that.'

Kyarno nodded curtly and urged his mount onwards, Leofric following swiftly behind him, and they rode at a swifter pace through the unseen paths of the forest towards their destination.

Eventually, Leofric could hear the sound of rushing water from ahead and felt a curious lightness touch him, as though even drawing near the Crystal Mere placed a soothing balm upon his soul. The roar of the falling water had a musical quality to it, like the chime of an exquisite crystal goblet.

The trees thinned ahead and he could make out a fine white spray, the rippling reflections of light fracturing on a large body of water.

'The Crystal Mere,' said Kyarno proudly.

Leofric rode into the glade and his breath was snatched away by the ethereal beauty laid out before him.

CHAPTER SIX

KYARNO HAD DESCRIBED the Crystal Mere as something natural, in terms Leofric would understand, but he saw now that the description did not do this incredible place justice. A rock-sided pool filled the wide glade, with a gracefully curved beach of pure white sand opposite a tumbling waterfall of water so pure its sheen was like that of a mirror.

The elf had compared the falls to the tears of Isha and though Leofric had only the vaguest understanding of this elven god, he knew that her sorrow must be sublime indeed to weep such wondrous tears. White water foamed at the base of the waterfall, tumbling a hundred feet or more from the rocky, moss-covered slabs above. Water plummeted in billowing clouds to strike a knife-edged wedge of rock that hurled it back into the air, diffusing multiple rainbows of dazzling colour throughout the glade.

The sun was almost directly overhead, dappling the soft, sweet-scented grass in velvet light and the chill Leofric had felt in the dark of the forest vanished, the fine mist of water imbuing the air with a pleasant coolness.

Wild and vivid flowers of red and yellow blossomed at the edge of the glade, filling it with an incredible perfume that soothed Leofric's troubled heart and gave him a sense of tranquillity that was beyond words. Brightly plumed birds nested in the trees and the ever-present spites darted swiftly between the trunks, chasing each other in the shallows of the pool or cavorting in the waterfall's spume.

'It's incredible...' breathed Leofric, drinking in the unearthly beauty of the scene.

'It's pretty, yes,' agreed Kyarno, gracefully dismounting, while Leofric clambered from his saddle.

'Pretty? This place is beyond such a poor word,' said Leofric, dropping to his knees and clasping his hands to his face in prayer. 'Its beauty makes my heart ache.'

Kyarno released his horse, slapping its rump and setting it loose in the wondrous glade. The elf bounded atop a low collection of rocks at the water's edge and said, 'It's just a glade. A pretty one to be sure, but just a glade.'

Leofric shook his head, unable to comprehend how Kyarno could so blithely dismiss such incredible beauty and wonder. The clearing seethed with life and richness of colour, so much that Leofric felt tears of joy coursing down his cheeks as he wandered like a blind man who had suddenly regained his sight.

Fruits of incredible colours hung from the branches of the nearest trees and Leofric suddenly realised how hungry he was as he caught their intoxicating scent – bitter and rich, but with a strangely sweet aroma.

'What are these?' asked Leofric.

'They are called aoilym fruit,' replied Kyarno with a smile, reclining back onto the rocks and rolling onto his side. 'Try one, they are deliciously sweet.'

Leofric reached out to pluck a scarlet, pear-like fruit, but pulled his hand back at the last second, remembering tales of faerie food and its effects on humans. From the earliest age, children of Quenelles and Carcassonne were taught never to accept food or wine from fey strangers. Bretonnian lore was replete with ballads of those unfortunates who had drunk faerie wines or eaten faerie food and been driven mad with all manner of bizarre and hallucinogenic experiences.

Leofric withdrew his hand from the pungent fruit and said, 'No, I don't think I will after all.'

'Your loss,' said Kyarno, lying back on the rock and pillowing his head on his arms. 'It is a feast beyond anything you will have tasted before, human.'

'Perhaps,' said Leofric, returning to the edge of the water. 'But that is a chance I am willing to take.'

'Well, go on then,' said Kyarno as Leofric continued to stare in wonderment around the glade.

'What?' asked Leofric, startled from his reverie.

'You were brought here to get cleaned up,' said Kyarno, pointing to the sparkling waters of the Crystal Mere, 'so get cleaned up.'

Leofric nodded, eager to bathe in the water. An ache flared in his heart as he thought of how much Helene would have been enchanted by this place, though, shamefully, the ache was more bearable than it had previously been.

As Kyarno lounged on the rocks with a bored expression on his face, Leofric stripped off his shirt, britches and boots, leaving them folded on the soft grass at the edge of the pale beach. Normally, Leofric would have felt incredibly self-conscious stripping naked before a stranger, but such notions of modesty seemed ridiculous in this place.

He descended to the beach, letting out a sigh of pleasure as the soft sand eased between his toes, like the deepest, most luxuriant rug. He wiggled his toes in the sand, smiling as a warm, relaxing sensation eased its way up his legs.

Leofric stared at the pool before him, able to see its sandy bottom, and already wet from the foaming water misting the air from the waterfall. The crystalline waters rippled with life and light, looping sprays of sparkling water spites playing in the shallows.

'Is it safe to bathe with those spites in there?' asked Leofric.

'They won't bite. Nip, maybe, but this is a place of healing and rest,' sighed Kyarno. 'You are safe here.'

THOUGH THE FOREST tore at them and flocks of black-winged birds swooped and dived above them, the roaring centaur creatures did not slow their charge. Powerful muscles, swollen by the breath of the gods, drove them onwards and kept them strong, the intoxicating brew in their wineskins keeping their courage high in the face of the creatures that assailed them.

Branches whipped them, fanged, darting lights befuddled their senses, but ever onwards they charged, guided by an image that burned with an all-consuming clarity in their minds.

One beast was brought low, slashing roots scything its legs out from under it in a flurry of leaves and mud. It crashed down with a mighty roar, its legs flailing as it skidded to a halt. The beast bellowed in pain, the gleam of bone jutting from torn flesh where its back legs had been broken. Ravening spites swarmed from the undergrowth, ripping and tearing and biting and the monster's blood ran in thick rivulets into the ground.

Its companions did not stop to come to its aid or even acknowledge that it had had been caught by the vengeful spirits of the forest. Thrashing bursts of light obscured its form and its roars of pain were muffled and gurgling as it died.

The remaining beasts continued onwards, leaping grasping roots and lashing branches as the forest fought to halt the progress of these bestial intruders, carrying words of warning through the root networks of the trees, the leaves that waved in the air and in the cries of the beasts and spirits of Athel Loren.

The forest closed in around them, pathways shifting and reshaping themselves, but such was the speed of the charge that the monsters outpaced the forest's enchantments and hurtled onwards.

Their nostrils burned with the scent of the choicest meat.

Human flesh.

THE WATER WAS chill, having its origin high in the Grey Mountains, and as he waded deeper into the Crystal Mere its touch felt like cold silk wrapping around his limbs . As the water rose, Leofric felt a pleasant lethargy suffuse his limbs and took a deep, cleansing breath as he lowered himself.

'This water is incredible,' he whispered as it slipped and slid around his flesh, flowing like a living thing, the glittering spites that flitted like underwater fireflies spinning around him with ticklish bursts of speed.

Immediately the pain in his hip lessened and the ache in his head vanished like morning mist as the water rose to his neck. He spread his arms, enjoying the bracing cold of the water and the susurration of spites around his flesh, strangely untroubled by the darting creatures below the surface. Holding his breath, Leofric ducked his head under the water, and swam towards the churning mass of foaming water that marked the base of the waterfall.

The floor of the pool was of the same pale sand that marked the beach, shaped like a gentle bowl and dotted with gently waving fronds. Glittering crystals drifted across the base of the pool and sparkled in the streaks of sunbeams. Sand and water foamed ahead and Leofric swam with powerful strokes towards the mass of bubbles, feeling fresh vigour course through his body with every second.

He surfaced within the deafening torrent of falling water, closing his eyes against the thunderous spray. Water hammered his shoulders, massaging the tension from his body and easing his muscles with its power.

Leofric lowered his head, taking a fleeting breath as the sound of musical laughter drifted through the air, hazy and indistinct over the roaring water. Within the crystal waterfall, Leofric could hear little but the impact of the falling water and had only the vaguest impression of shifting white shapes as they slid gracefully through his field of vision.

He leaned his head back, relishing the incredibly invigorating sensation as he felt years fall from him and the waters cleansed away the dirt and pain of the last few days. Leofric felt a detached quality descend upon him, the rhythmic sound of the waterfall lulling him into a fugue-like state.

He pictured Helene's face, the image of her blonde hair and soft eyes leaping unbidden to his mind, and he smiled as he remembered her sweet laughter, feeling her loss as something less harsh. Instead of the ache that filled his soul with despair, a sense of warmth and gratitude swept through him as he knew he was incredibly lucky to have had any time with Helene at all. This world stood on the brink of falling to Chaos and to have snatched any such happiness was a victory.

He smiled as he heard her laughter in the sound of the waterfall, seeing her pale face in the patterns formed in the spray, a nimbus of soft light playing about her almond eyes and blonde tresses. A dreamlike smile touched him as he realised she had come back to him, her love for him reaching beyond the veil of death.

Nor had she come alone, he saw, as a host of similarly beautiful women ghosted through the misting water, naked and with expressions of faint amusement. He wanted to feel the touch of Helene's ivory skin and reached out to her, trailing his eyes along the soft curves of her shoulders and the fullness of her breasts.

'Helene…' he whispered, but the woman before him shook her head, and Leofric saw that Helene's companions had spread out to surround him. Their slender arms reached out and touched his broad shoulders and muscled arms, stroking them with an unfamiliar hesitancy.

Their touch was light, but intense, as though his every nerve ending were suddenly drawn to the surface of his skin. Hands stroked his chest, running along the nape of his neck and through his dark, soaking hair. Laughter filled the air and he laughed along with it, the magical sensation of her nearness filling him with light and joy.

The woman before him drew nearer, gliding through the foaming spray of the waterfall without a single lock of her hair displaced by the torrent. She smiled and Leofric's heart broke as he finally saw that this was not Helene at all, but some sylvan nymph with eyes of gold and ringlets of hair the colour of ripened corn. Her features were beautiful, ethereal and haunting beyond anything Leofric had ever imagined. The water played over her alabaster skin, the rivulets speckled with light as they trickled down her naked body.

The others were as varied as any other group of elves he had seen, with hair colours varying from flame-red to midnight-black and features with a subtlety of difference that was beguiling and unearthly at the same time.

'Who are you?' he managed at last.

They laughed at him and though he sensed an edge of condescension to it, a wave of desire washed through him.

As they circled him they sang in the silken tones of their native tongue, musical language spinning through his head and enchanting him with its beauty.

He felt their hands upon him, touching, stroking and though he knew it was wrong, he did not want it to stop, the idea of betrayal pushed from his mind by the exquisiteness of sensation coursing through him at the touch of these beautiful women.

All was peace and beauty in Leofric's mind when a discordant, jagged sound intruded on his bliss – a shouting voice and splashes of noise. The women scattered with squeals of false terror and Leofric's eyes suddenly snapped back into focus as an armoured gauntlet reached through the falling water and grabbed him by the scruff of the neck.

'What–' was all he could manage before he was hauled unceremoniously from beneath the waterfall. A powerful grip had him fast, and as he shook off the last of the dreamlike fatigue that had enveloped him, Leofric looked up to see the furious face of Cairbre as he was frogmarched from the water.

The women swam in gracefully lazy circles around them, their hair like great coloured slicks on the surface of the clear water as they pointed and laughed at him.

'Wait!' shouted Leofric, between mouthfuls of water.

Cairbre unleashed a torrent of elvish at him, which, though he knew not what was being said, left him in no doubt as to the mood of the cold-eyed warrior. He splashed and stumbled into the shallows of the pool, suddenly very conscious of his nakedness as the elven women continued to laugh and gawp at him like buyers at a horse fair.

Shame and anger burned hot in Leofric's breast as he saw that these women looked upon him as nothing more than a plaything for their amusement or some sort of savage curio. Cairbre shoved him forward to land in an ungainly heap on the pale sand of the beach.

He heard the whinny of horses and turned to see six grey-cloaked elven riders, their armour and twin-bladed spears brilliant in the sunshine. Thankfully, these were not the wild riders he and Kyarno had encountered earlier that day, but appeared to be the same as those he had seen in Coeth-Mara when he had first awoken. One rider carried a silver banner set with gemstones and fluttering azure blossoms. Kyarno's steed nuzzled one of the newcomers' horses, while Leofric's horse grazed on the rich grass at the edge of the glade.

'Get up!' stormed Cairbre. 'You dare to molest the handmaidens of Lady Morvhen Éadaoin! You are nothing but a base animal, human.'

'Molest? What? No!' coughed Leofric, rolling onto his back and spitting water.

'Then what was it you were doing in there?' shouted Cairbre. 'And get some clothes on! Your hairy body is unsightly to me.'

Leofric pushed himself to his knees and said, 'I was doing what was asked of me. Kyarno brought me here to bathe and clean myself. That's what I was doing when these women came to me. Then you dragged me out here.'

'Morvhen...' said Cairbre angrily, his eyes scanning the glade for something or someone he could not see. 'He must have sent word to her somehow. I knew it.'

'Knew what?' asked Leofric as he reached over to lift his clothes, feeling the warm sunlight swiftly drying his skin. Cairbre marched onto the grassy bank surrounding the waters of the Crystal Mere, his anger a terrible thing to behold.

'Loec's spite! A curse upon that boy!' snapped Cairbre, rounding on Leofric, and unsheathing his twin-bladed spear. 'Where is my nephew?'

'Who?' asked Leofric, nonplussed.

'Kyarno!' roared Cairbre. 'Where is Kyarno?'

Leofric looked around the glade for his surly travelling companion.

But Kyarno was nowhere to be seen.

'Eternal Guard!' shouted Cairbre. 'With me!'

KYARNO LAUGHED AS he and Morvhen ran hand in hand through the twilight beneath the trees, overjoyed that she had received his message to meet him here. Her dress billowed like a great crimson sail, though Kyarno had only ever imagined what an ocean-going vessel might look like.

Her face was alive with the illicit thrill of this tryst and Kyarno felt fierce joy as she let out an exultant, whooping yell like a battle cry.

He was sure to be disciplined by Lord Aldaeld for this, but did not much care any more. He had suffered too many punishments at the hands of Morvhen's father for one more to matter.

And looking at Morvhen's finely sculpted features, the sweeping cheekbones, the chestnut hair, the sparkling eyes and the seductive mouth, Kyarno knew she was worth all the torments that Lord Aldaeld might heap upon him.

Eventually they stopped running, chests heaving and breath hot in their lungs as they circled one another with lustful eyes.

'You got my message then?' chuckled Kyarno.

'Indeed I did,' smiled Morvhen, glancing over her shoulder for any signs of pursuit from the Eternal Guard. 'You are a bad influence on me, Kyarno Daelanu.'

'I know,' nodded Kyarno. 'But that is why you like me.'

'True, but I cannot tarry long. Cairbre will notice I am gone soon and he was suspicious enough on the way here.'

'How did you get away from him?'

Morvhen giggled with wicked glee and said, 'I sent my handmaids into the water to cavort with the human. Cairbre and the others were so mortified that they did not notice me slip into the woods. I can be quite stealthy when the mood suits me, you know.'

'You let your handmaids get into the water with a human?' said Kyarno, aghast.

'Of course! I think they quite enjoyed the opportunity to have a look at one up close,' replied Morvhen. 'For all their graceless thickness of limb, there is a certain savage vitality to humans.'

'They are brutish oafs with all the poise of a wounded bear.'

'A particularly clumsy bear,' added Morvhen, leaning back on the tilted bole of a weeping willow and beckoning Kyarno to come closer with an impish smile.

'A wounded, clumsy and blind bear,' finished Kyarno, leaning in and kissing her as her arms slid around his neck and pulled him into her.

LEOFRIC PULLED UP his britches, averting his gaze from the beautiful elf maids swimming leisurely in the Crystal Mere and trying to shut out their beautiful, but mocking laughter. The warriors on horseback showed no such compunction, openly watching the naked women as though it were the most natural thing in the world. Perhaps for them it was, mused Leofric, wondering again at the alien ways of these woodland folk.

Though he knew he had been little more than a plaything to the women, he felt soothed, as though their touch had imparted some serene acceptance to him.

He saw again Helene's face, but this time the sense of love and wonder she had given him far outweighed the pain of her loss. More than ever he was resolved to leave this place, though how that might be achieved was sure to be problematic. Those held in the realm of the elves did not return unchanged, if they were able to return at all.

Leofric remembered the tale of Duke Melmon, a knight who ruled the Dukedom of Quenelles in the year three hundred and fifty-eight, who was said to have vanished on a night when the wild hunt stormed the skies. The mystery of his disappearance was never solved, though Leofric remembered when he was but a child, the stooped elders of Quenelles once speaking of a knight who was said to have emerged from Athel Loren in the time of their great grandfathers, who presented himself at the doors of the duke's castle. This knight had been brought before the court of the current duke where he had claimed to be none other than Duke Melmon himself, lost these last thousand years.

Of course, the court had scoffed at such a claim, but upon finishing his tale the knight had supposedly crumbled to naught but dust and ashes before their very eyes. Leofric had never really believed the tale of Duke Melmon, thinking it to be no more than the fanciful tale spun by old men who wanted to scare a little boy.

Now, he wasn't so sure, but he had a son to raise, lands to defend and a king to serve – and a knight of Bretonnia did not shirk such duties while he still drew breath and his sword arm was strong.

He ran his hands through his dark hair, feeling more refreshed than he had done for as long as he could remember. The rigours of war and a life of dedication to land and king was a demanding one and took its toll, but here, Leofric felt as though he could defeat almost any foe.

Almost any foe, he reminded himself, again seeing the horror of the battle against the Swords of Chaos and the daemons of the northern tribes. Could anything stand against such warriors, he wondered? When the power of the Dark Gods waxed strong the lands of men were ravaged by war and blood, and each time brought the final victory of Chaos closer.

Trying to banish such melancholy thoughts, he took another breath of the honeysuckle-scented air and awaited the return of Cairbre.

The warrior had ridden off into the forest to search for Kyarno with two of his warriors – the Eternal Guard, presumed Leofric – leaving the remaining four to watch over the elven maids. Elven curses that were no less vile for the beauty of the language had spat from his mouth as he damned his nephew.

Leofric had not noticed the familial resemblance before, but once revealed, it was patently obvious: both elves shared the same confident poise and had the same cruel, warrior features.

Leofric pulled on his overshirt and removed the silk scarf from the pocket, twining the smooth material around his fingers as he knelt on the moist grass.

He closed his eyes and offered a short prayer to the Lady of the Lake, entreating her to guide the spirit of his wife to its final rest. Tears coursed down his cheeks, but they were not shed in bitterness, but fond remembrance.

'Why do you weep?' asked a lilting female voice as he finished his prayers.

Leofric started in surprise, not having heard the elven woman approach. He tucked Helene's scarf back into his pocket and turned to address her, blushing as he saw she was completely naked, water running from her willowy body in glistening droplets.

'I… uh… that is,' stammered Leofric, turning away as the elf circled around to stand before him once again, her head tilted coquettishly to one side and a curious, confused look in her eye.

'Why do you not look at me?' asked the elf. 'Am I not beautiful?'

'Yes, yes you are,' confirmed Leofric, keeping his eyes cast down. 'You are indeed beautiful, but it would be wrong of me to see you like this.'

'Like what?' said the elf, reaching out and lifting his head.

'Without clothes,' finished Leofric, drinking in the vision of grace and beauty before him.

The elven woman tilted her head, puzzled by his answer and spun gracefully before him, 'What is wrong with that? Beauty is a precious thing and should be savoured at all times. You should not deny yourself that pleasure.'

Her body was slender and artfully shaped, though her waist was waspish and too narrow for his tastes. Thick hair the colour of flame hung wetly around her long neck and arched shoulders and her skin was smooth and pale like virgin snow. As she completed her pirouette, oval eyes of a red-gold colour examined him with curious amusement, but no malice, and he kept his gaze firmly locked with hers, lest his eyes stray lower and catch a glimpse of something more libidinous.

'Be that as it may,' said Leofric with embarrassment. 'But it is against my chivalric code to see you thus.'

'You humans are a strange race,' said the elf, shaking her head and sweeping up a diaphanous white gown of a strange, shimmering fabric that slid over her body with the barest shrug of effort. 'Bloodshed and death are second nature to your people, yet the sight of naked flesh leaves you tongue-tied. Baffling.'

Leofric shrugged. 'Yes, it is odd I suppose.'

'Do you have a name, human?'

'Of course I do,' replied Leofric with a deep bow. 'I am Leofric Carrard of Quenelles.'

The elf bowed back to him. 'I am Tiphaine of the Éadaoin kinband, handmaid to Lady Morvhen Éadaoin.'

'It is an honour and a privilege to make your acquaintance,' said Leofric, bowing once more. 'Tell me, is Lady Éadaoin the wife of Lord Aldaeld?'

Tiphaine shook her head. 'No, she is his daughter. A wonderful child, but wilful and drawn to troublemakers.'

'Like Kyarno?' ventured Leofric, nodding towards the reduced numbers of the Eternal Guard.

'Indeed,' agreed Tiphaine. 'Cairbre will not be happy when he finds the lovers.'

Leofric blushed at such frankness, though it explained Cairbre's anger at finding that Kyarno and Morvhen were missing from the glade of the Crystal Mere.

'Is she betrothed to another?' asked Leofric.

'Morvhen? No, she is not, but a wild one like Kyarno does not please her father, who fears he will lead her to ruin.'

'I can see why,' agreed Leofric.

'Truly it is a shame that love choses you rather than the other way round. I knew she was planning to meet with Kyarno and had thought I had dissuaded her, but love is deaf as well as blind it seems.'

'She does not obey the wishes of her father?'

'Sometimes, but she can be capricious and I am only surprised she has not yet sought you out to speak to at length.'

'Me?'

Tiphaine nodded, moving to sit on the rocks at the edge of the pool and stirring it with a languidly circling finger as her fellow handmaids continued to swim and bathe in the spite-rippled water.

'Oh yes, I should imagine she will have many questions for you. Morvhen has an unhealthy thirst for knowledge of that which lies beyond our borders, foolish child.'

'Is it customary for the servants of your lords and ladies to be so forthright about their faults and foibles?' asked Leofric, knowing that he would have had his servants whipped for speaking in such a fashion.

'I say nothing to you that I have not said to her many times before.'

'Oh…' said Leofric, sitting a discreet distance from the beautiful elf woman, watching the warriors of the Eternal Guard glare disapprovingly at him. The sun shone on Tiphaine's hair, making it glow as though afire and the shimmering fabric of her dress did little to conceal her pale flesh.

He looked away as Tiphaine said, 'You still have not told me why you weep in this place of beauty.'

Leofric was silent for long moments, wondering whether to answer or not, but Tiphaine had shown him a kindness he had not experienced thus far in Athel Loren and he was strangely compelled to speak truly.

'My wife is lost to me,' he said at last. 'The spirits of the forest took her. Winter dryads I think they were called, I'm not sure.'

'Ah… now I understand your tears,' said Tiphaine with a wistful smile. 'Well, this is a good place to bring such sorrows, the waters are said to ease the pain of loss and remind us of the wonder of what was once ours. I came here when my brother was killed.'

'I am truly sorry for your loss, my lady.'

Tiphaine nodded in polite acceptance of Leofric's sentiment. 'I thank you, but it was many decades ago and the pain is lessened now by time and the waters of the Crystal Mere.'

'The waters take away the pain?' asked Leofric.

Tiphaine shook her head. 'No, never that, for the pain reminds us of what we have lost and without that, the blessings of the life that has passed are forgotten. And that is the saddest thing of all, Leofric, to forget the joy of life.'

'I feel that more now, though the pain is still there,' said Leofric.

Tiphaine nodded. 'Then your time in Athel Loren has not been misspent.'

Leofric was about to reply when the smile fell from Tiphaine's face and a rustle of thickly-leaved branches shook the treetops, making the brightly patterned birds take to the air with a shrill caw of warning.

Though the sun still filled the glade with its golden light, a shadow passed through it, an elemental cry of warning as the spites in the water flickered into the air with primal hisses of rage.

'What is it?' said Leofric, rising to his feet as the hand-maids began swimming to the edge of the pool and the riders of the Eternal Guard readied their spears with angry yells. Tiphaine sprang nimbly to her feet and called to her fellow handmaids as spites spun angrily through the air, flitting into the trees to the south and changing from shapeless glows to jagged, clawed imps with wings of light.

The Eternal Guard rode to the edge of the pool and began shouting in frantic elvish to the women in the water. Leofric's warrior instincts now spoke to him of imminent danger and he shouted over to the Eternal Guard. 'Give me a weapon! I can fight.'

If they understood him, they gave no sign, but continued to hurry the elven women from the water. Leofric felt utterly helpless and ran over to where Tiphaine helped her fellow handmaids from the waters.

He heard a sudden thunder of hoof beats and looked up in time to see one of the Eternal Guard punched from his saddle by a long, crudely-crafted spear hurled from the edge of the glade.

The elf cried out in pain and landed with a splash in the shallows of the pool.

Leofric spun to face the direction from which the spear had come.

Emerging from the trees were five hideous monsters, their brazen roars and twisted, mutated bodies marking them out as creatures of Chaos. Centaur creatures, they were red-furred and horned, their hideous bodies massively muscled and terrible.

With a terrifying, bestial roar, the monsters charged.

CHAPTER SEVEN

THE TRACKS OF their passing were easy to follow, the lovers not even bothering to conceal their flight into the forest. Cairbre's anger and frustration grew as he rode deeper into the forest, as did his fear that something terrible was going to happen. The forest had an ill-favoured sense to it this day and his warrior soul responded to its unease.

'Spread out,' he ordered, 'and watch for them circling behind us. I don't want to be away from the Crystal Mere any longer than need be.'

The two mounted warriors that accompanied him nodded and peeled away, eyes scanning the forest for sign of Kyarno and Morvhen, their spears held lightly at their sides.

Cairbre followed tracks that led him a merry dance through the thickly gathered trunks of the trees, his route taking him further and further from the Crystal

Mere. Branches and fronds brushed him as he rode, their touch speaking to him of their unease and fear. Something was amiss, and to be abroad in the depths of the forest at such a time was both foolish and dangerous.

He still found it difficult to believe that Kyarno and Morvhen had defied the will of their lord and master once more. Such things were simply unthinkable – to defy the leader of a kinband was to break faith with those appointed guardianship of the forest and such a thought gave Cairbre cold shivers.

But beyond even that, he was angry with himself for allowing this to happen. He was Lord Aldaeld's champion, the Hound of Winter, and to allow his charges to come to harm would be the gravest failure imaginable. The long centuries hung heavily on Cairbre and the twilight of his life was upon him more than ever.

This would not have happened even a century ago, when the summer sun cast its last rays upon his youth and vigour. He was slowing and knew it. His skill with a blade was unmatched by any save the deadly wardancers, but his strength and stamina were a shadow of what they had once been.

The Hound of Winter would soon no longer be the hunting beast of his master, but the aged companion that lives out its days in comfort by the fire. That time was not yet come, and until it did, Cairbre would serve Lord Aldaeld with all his devotion and love.

And if that meant that he had to throw Kyarno from Coeth-Mara?

The youth had had his fair share of chances and though none could doubt the tragedy that had befallen him as a youngster, there was no excuse for his continued reckless disobedience and disrespect.

The trees thinned and Cairbre halted his horse as he came to a leafy glade with white blossoms and shifting branches. Cackling faces creaked in the depths of the gnarled wood and the desperately alluring scent of honey drifted on the light breeze. He turned his horse away as the thorn bushes crackled and moved, dark shapes within them shaking the branches in frustration as he rode away.

Cairbre knew the lovers would not have come this way, the malicious spites of this part of the forest serving to divert them from such a course. Leaving the treacherously scented glade, he rode back along the overgrown path, now seeing the carefully disguised tracks that looped back on the ones he had been following.

So their flight had not been as frantic and reckless as they would have him believe...

Kyarno might be wild, but he had a fine grasp of the hunter's skills.

But the Hound of Winter had hunted the enemies of the Asrai long before Kyarno had been born and, though he may be getting long in the tooth, he had lost none of the fearsome skills that had seen him honoured as Lord Aldaeld's champion.

And his title of the Hound of Winter was well earned.

He rode swiftly but silently through the woods, weaving between the trees and closing on a gathering of gently bobbing spites that circled in the high branches of the trees in the distance. Spites were curious, flighty spirits and were easily attracted to new things, and Cairbre hoped that they might yet lead him to Kyarno and Morvhen.

Laughter drifted to him and his jaw clenched as he recognised his nephew's voice. Morvhen's voice joined

Kyarno's, and there was no mistaking the tone as that reserved for lovers and those who had shared their bodies with one another.

Cairbre slid from the back of his steed and spun the Blades of Midnight in a tight circle, loosening the muscles of his shoulders and forearms as he closed on the sounds of the voices.

He reached the edge of another glade, moving as silently and stealthily as he was able, glancing up at the voyeuristic spites to make sure they would not give his approach away. Through the grass and obscuring branches he could see Kyarno and Morvhen lying naked on a bed of leaves and grass, enfolded in one another's arms. He looked away, relieved that they were safe, but angry at the wilful defiance they had both shown.

Parting the branches with the Blades of Midnight, Cairbre strode into the clearing and said, 'Get dressed, both of you. We are going back to the Crystal Mere.'

Kyarno leapt to his feet, reaching for his bow, but relaxed as he saw who had discovered them.

'Uncle,' said Kyarno. 'You appear with monotonous regularity when I least wish you to.'

Cairbre said nothing, simply stepping forward and backhanding his nephew hard enough across the jaw to draw blood.

'You are a disgrace to your kin, Kyarno,' hissed Cairbre. 'You insult your lord, you dishonour me and you dishonour yourself.'

Kyarno wiped the trickle of red from his chin and spat a mouthful of blood, his eyes full of controlled anger. Without a word, he set aside his bow and turned to pull on his clothes. Cairbre turned to Morvhen, his eyes averted as she too slipped into her clothing.

'My lady, I am disappointed with you,' he said. 'I suspected you might try and see my nephew, but I had hoped you held me in enough regard not to.'

'I hold you in the highest regard, Hound of Winter, you know that,' said Morvhen.

'Then why do you try me so?' shouted Cairbre, taking hold of her arm and marching her towards his horse. 'I am sworn to protect you, yet you behave like a spoilt child. You dishonour your father with such behaviour.'

'Take your hand from her,' said Kyarno.

Cairbre heard the note of warning in his nephew's tone a fraction too late and turned in time to have Kyarno's fist thunder against his cheek. He stumbled, but quickly righted himself, swinging the haft of the Blades of Midnight around and slamming it into Kyarno's midriff.

His nephew doubled over, winded, and Cairbre brought the haft up sharply, cracking it against his jaw and sending him spinning backwards.

'Know your place, Kyarno,' said Cairbre, turning away.

Morvhen looked fearfully at him and he pulled her towards his horse, anxious to return to his warriors. He heard a cry of anger behind him and spun in time to block a hooking right cross with the haft of his weapon as Kyarno came at him again. He spun the Blades of Midnight, twisting Kyarno's arm away and stabbed the blade into the ground between his feet.

Cairbre leapt into the air, twisting around the haft to hammer his boots into Kyarno's chest and fling him across the clearing. He landed lightly as Kyarno rolled to his feet and shouted in frustration, drawing his sword and preparing to charge. Cairbre spread his stance, bringing the Blades of Midnight around to aim at his nephew's heart.

He took a step towards Kyarno then jumped in shock as a long, blue-fletched arrow slashed through the air and hammered into the trunk of a tree, an inch from his head. Another shaft buried itself in the wood beside Kyarno's head and the two combatants were suddenly brought up short.

Morvhen stood beside her lover's steed with Kyarno's recurved bow held horizontally before her, a fresh pair of arrows nocked to the bowstring.

'Both of you put up your weapons!' she yelled. 'Or do I have to put arrows in you to get you to stop this madness?'

'Morvhen, put that bow down,' said Cairbre slowly, seeing the hurt in her eyes.

'Put up your weapons, both of you,' repeated Morvhen and Cairbre could see she meant every word. Slowly he extended a hand towards her, palm-up, and raised the Blades of Midnight until the weapon was upright beside him. Kyarno did the same, taking deep, calming breaths and sheathing his sword once more.

'Morvhen, be careful with that bow,' said Kyarno.

'Yes,' agreed Cairbre. 'Please.'

'Be quiet, both of you!' snapped Morvhen. 'By all the gods of the Asrai, I am heartsick of this constant battle between you. Why must you fight? You are kin!'

'He struck me!' shouted Kyarno.

'You struck me first,' pointed out Cairbre.

'Shut up! Isha's mercy, can't you hear yourselves? You are like children squabbling over a bowstave.'

Both Kyarno and Cairbre opened their mouths to argue, but the creak of the tautening bowstring silenced them both.

Morvhen wept bitter tears as she spoke again, 'I hate this constant bickering between you. You pretend to all the world that you are enemies when everyone can see the love and kinship between you. You are bonded by blood and nothing can break that. As much as you might try to.'

Cairbre plucked the arrow from the tree next to his head and said, 'You are right, Morvhen, but that does not alter anything. I have a duty to my lord and must fulfil it. You need to put down that bow and come with me back to the Crystal Mere. You understand that, yes?'

'I want to hear you say that you will stop this incessant feuding,' said Morvhen, aiming her words as well as her arrows at both Cairbre and Kyarno.

Kyarno nodded and Cairbre could see that, with the surge of anger drained from him, his nephew was deathly worried at what had just happened. True, there was a bond of blood between them, but Kyarno had struck the champion of Lord Aldaeld, and there could be only one punishment for such a blatant attack on the honour of an elven lord.

Cairbre sighed, his duty and honour warring with the call of kith and kin, and he turned from Morvhen to say, 'Kyarno, you are my nephew and I love you dearly, however much you may not want to believe that. You have struck the champion of Lord Aldaeld and you know the penalty for such an attack.'

'Cairbre, no!' cried Morvhen.

'You would take my head with the Blades of Midnight, uncle?' asked Kyarno, trying to sound defiant, but Cairbre could sense the fear of his realisation.

'You know what you have done, Kyarno and were you anyone else, then yes, you would already be dead,' nodded Cairbre, looking beyond Morvhen to see his two Eternal Guard warriors approaching through the forest.

'It is time to leave, Morvhen. Lower the bow.'

Morvhen glanced over her shoulder at the approaching horsemen and nodded, easing the string on the bow and dropping to one knee to slip the arrows back into Kyarno's quiver.

Cairbre turned his back on the Eternal Guard and said, 'Only we three know of this and I see no reason to change that. Clean the blood from your face, Kyarno, and we will say nothing more about this for now.'

'You would do that?' asked Kyarno, obviously surprised.

'I would, but we have much yet to resolve, you and I, so let this be a lesson to you, eh?'

Kyarno nodded warily and retrieved his bow from Morvhen, swiftly cleaning the blood from his face as the two Eternal Guard rode into the clearing.

'I found them,' Cairbre told them needlessly. 'Let's get back to–'

Cairbre's words trailed off as he felt the forest around him cry out in warning, the impending sense of doom he had felt earlier now filling him with dread.

Branch and leaf, earth and water cried out in loathing and Cairbre felt the soul of the land shudder at the touch of something terrible.

Now the growing unease he had felt earlier in the day became clear as the magic of the forest spoke to him of the intruders in its midst.

The creatures of Chaos were upon Athel Loren.

And Cairbre knew exactly where they were going.

ROARS AND WAR-CRIES filled the glade of the Crystal Mere as the beasts charged. Their brazen hooves threw up great clods of earth and grass and the forest itself trembled in rage at such gross trespassers. Leofric felt his limbs as lead weights, unable to move at the sight of such vile, terrible creatures of Chaos.

Memories of the fateful charge into the diabolical ranks of the daemon lord and the horrifying moments of blood and death against the Lord of the End Times flooded him, momentarily rooting him to the spot.

He heard a cry of warning, recognising it as that of Tiphaine, and shook off the torpor that seized him, running to the fallen elf with the beast's spear wedged through his chest. Lady Morvhen's handmaids ran from the water as one of the Eternal Guard began shepherding them towards the edge of the glade and away from the creatures of Chaos. Leofric saw Taschen at the edge of the glade, the beast's eyes wide at the sight and scent of the beasts, but its spirit held it fast and prevented it from fleeing.

With feral, whooping battle cries, the remaining two warriors of the Eternal Guard leaned forward over their horses' necks and charged the thundering, red-skinned monsters. Leofric had seen such beasts before and knew that they would tear the elves from their steeds and feast on their flesh unless the odds were evened.

Leofric splashed into the shallows of the Crystal Mere, through the thickening cloud of blood that fanned from the floating corpse, and reached for the elf's weapon, a long, twin-bladed spear. The weapon was light in his hands and unfamiliar, the fighting style required to wield it effectively unknown to him. He dropped the spear and dragged out the elf's sword, a fine and beautifully forged blade, confident he could spill some enemy blood with this weapon.

'Leofric!' shouted Tiphaine and he turned to see what she was shouting at.

The Eternal Guard and the beastmen smashed into one another, elf-forged iron and jagged-edged obsidian clashing in a flurry of sparks. A flock of ravening spites flew from the forest, transformed from harmless specks of light to snapping, biting imps. One centaur creature fell to the blades of the Eternal Guard, its chest cloven by a blindingly quick slash, its bellow of pain deafening in the once-peaceful glade.

An elven steed reared and lashed out at one of the beastmen, its hooves slashing for its horned head, but instead of quailing before such an attack, the monster lowered its head and lunged forward, hammering its long, curling horns into the steed's belly.

'No!' cried Leofric, loath to see such a fine equine specimen defiled by these monsters. But his denial was in vain as the white steed fell, its innards flooding from its torn flesh. Its rider leapt clear, only to be impaled in mid air by another beast's horns and tossed into the air like a limp and bloody rag.

Leofric staggered from the water and ran towards the handmaids as two of the bellowing creatures broke from the battle with the surviving Eternal Guard. They thundered towards the handmaids and Leofric ran to intercept their course. He could not allow these women to come to any harm; his chivalric code would not permit such an affront. Taschen stamped the ground beside them, the scent of blood provoking his desire to fight, yet needing his rider to enter the fray.

Leofric pushed himself harder as he heard galloping hoof beats behind him. The warrior who guarded the women spun his long spear as his horse reared in defiant challenge to the creatures of Chaos. Leofric continued towards the women, watching in surprise as they retrieved bows from the edge of the clearing. With barely a breath of pause, they pulled on the bowstrings and loosed a hail of arrows towards him.

He cried out as the arrows slashed past him, hearing the hiss of air as some came within a fingerbreadth of him. Grunts and bellows of pain told him that some of the arrows had found homes in the flesh of the beast-men and he spun as he heard the thud of something hitting the earth.

One of the bestial creatures was on its knees, a trio of grey-fletched arrows protruding from its body. Its hideous face, so like a man's, yet so different, was twisted in animal rage as it plucked the feathered shafts from its body. He heard the clash of weapons to one side and knew that battle was joined between the Eternal Guard with the women and the other beastman. The wounded creature began to pick itself up. He could see the two beastmen behind it trample the body of another elven warrior to death. Spites flickered around the monsters, biting them with spirit fangs and blinding them with glittering magicks. The beasts roared and swatted at their tiny attackers, distracted for the moment, and Leofric knew he had seconds at best.

Trusting the defence of the women to the Eternal Guard, Leofric yelled, 'For Quenelles, the king and the Lady!' and charged the wounded monster with his borrowed sword raised high. It saw him coming and its terrible face twisted in a savage grin, holding its spear before it.

'You die, manskin!' it shouted and Leofric's surprise almost cost him his life. The beast's spear stabbed towards his belly, but Leofric frantically threw himself out of the way, rolling to his feet and slashing for the beast's neck with his blade.

The monster lowered its head and his sword impacted against one of its horns, hacking clean through the thick, brass-tipped bone. The roaring beastman rocked backwards under the force of the blow and Leofric didn't give it a chance to recover, spinning on his heel and ramming the sword deep into its chest.

He twisted the blade as he drove it hilt-deep into its body, dark blood pumping from the wound as the creature died.

His breath came in hard gulps, the thick reek of strong liquor from the beast making him gag as he wrenched his blade free. He heard more screams and the hiss of arrows, spinning to see the last warrior of the Eternal Guard dragged from his steed and gored repeatedly by the beastman's wickedly sharp horns. Arrows jutted from its shaggy-furred back, but it seemed not to care, hurling the corpse of the warrior it had just killed to the ground and roaring in triumph as the two surviving creatures turned to join it for the kill.

Leofric ran from the dead beastman towards his horse, knowing that he needed to be mounted to fight most effectively. His steed ran towards him and Leofric gripped the saddle and vaulted onto Taschen's back with a wild yell.

Another flurry of arrows slashed towards the nearest beastman, but its thick hide was proof against the elven archery. It roared and Leofric saw the muscles of its back legs bunch as it prepared to wreak bloody havoc amongst the handmaids.

Leofric dug his heels into Taschen's sides and the horse surged forward.

'For the Lady!' shouted Leofric as he surged towards the beast. Its charge altered direction and man and beast thundered towards each other. The centaur creature raised its spear to plunge down into his chest, but Leofric was a veteran of many a joust on the tilting field and swayed aside from its thrust, slashing his sword across its shoulder.

Vile blood sprayed from the wound and the beast roared in anger as the spear dropped from its useless arm and the two combatants rode past one another. Leofric wheeled his horse quickly and struck again at the monster, opening a deep gash across its thickly furred back.

The remaining two beasts charged towards him through a hail of arrows loosed by the handmaids, though they appeared to be largely untroubled by such hurts. Leofric yelled in challenge as the bloodied beast turned to face him once more, lowering its thick horns to gore him.

Leofric raised his sword above him and shouted, 'Come on then, you bastard! Come on and die!'

But before the bestial creature could move, a pair of blue-fletched arrows slashed from the trees and skewered its skull, the barbed arrowheads bursting from its eyes with a wet thud. With little more than a brutish exhalation, the creature toppled, dead before it hit the ground.

Amazed, Leofric saw Cairbre and two more of the Eternal Guard ride from the trees, the Hound of Winter's twin-bladed spear tucked under one arm as he galloped from the forest. At his heels came Kyarno and a young elven woman with chestnut hair wearing a tight-fitting dress of crimson. His heart lurched at the sight, remembering his last sight of Helene in such a dress. She carried a bow that Leofric recognised as belonging to Kyarno and sent another, wickedly-aimed shaft towards the charging beastmen.

The Eternal Guard rode after their leader as Cairbre charged past Leofric, the Hound of Winter letting loose a feral, ululating yell as his spear came up to spin around his head. The elf rose to stand on the back of his horse, holding his spear two-handed above his head and Leofric yanked on Taschen's reins as he charged after the howling elf.

He shouted wildly, caught up in the thrill of the charge. Cairbre twisted the grip of his spear and Leofric saw the shaft of the weapon split apart to become two long-handled swords.

The venerable elf rode between the two charging centaur beasts, a flurry of screeching spites flying from the folds of his cloak and swarming over his enemies. Cairbre crouched low atop the back of his horse and his flashing blades were streaking blurs of white steel. One centaur crashed to the ground in a pile of thrashing limbs, its head spinning through the air, while the other halted its charge in a spray of earth and grass as it sought to turn to face this new foe and fight off the firefly creatures that clawed its flesh.

Its flanks were exposed and Leofric held his sword out before him, riding hard and slashing its edge through the beast's flesh. It roared and twisted free of the weapon in a froth of blood, its spear stabbing towards him. Leofric brought his sword up to block its powerful thrust, rolling his wrists and stabbing for the beast's throat.

Leofric's blade missed its target as Cairbre leapt from his horse onto the beast's back and it reared wildly in an attempt to throw him.

But incredibly, the Hound of Winter easily kept his balance, ramming his twin swords into the beastman's back. White blades flashed once more and an arcing spray of blood filled the air as Cairbre's swords slashed the monster's throat open. Clawed hands frantically tried to stem the spray of blood, but nothing could halt its demise and the beast collapsed with gurgling grunts of pain.

Cairbre vaulted lightly from the dying beast's body and landed on the back of his own steed, which circled the fallen creature warily. Leofric reined in Taschen and turned to make sure the other monsters were dead.

Relief flooded him as he saw that the handmaids were all safe, their expressions defiant. Tiphaine smiled in gratitude at him and he lowered his sword. The elven woman with the bow ran towards them and Leofric could only assume that this was the Lady Morvhen, seeing the regal cast to her features.

A fierce shout of anger tore the air and Leofric readied his sword once more. He wheeled his horse to face the sound, lowering the weapon as he saw Kyarno hacking at the fallen corpse of the beast Leofric had killed. Kyarno's sword rose and fell, sending blood arcing high into the air as he chopped the foul monster into gory chunks.

The young elf wept as he hacked at the beast's corpse, tears and blood streaking his face as he dropped to his knees. Morvhen ran towards him and he collapsed in her arms, weeping like a newborn babe.

Leofric made to walk his horse towards Kyarno, but a hand gripped the reins and he turned to face Cairbre, who shook his head slowly.

'No,' said the Hound of Winter. 'Leave him be.'

'What is wrong with him?' asked Leofric.

'Nothing that need concern you, human,' replied Cairbre, turning his steed away and riding towards the elven steeds that sadly nuzzled their fallen riders.

'Cairbre!' called Leofric after the Hound of Winter's retreating back.

The champion of the Eternal Guard halted his horse and looked back over his shoulder. 'What?'

'You fight… like no one I have ever seen before.'

Cairbre's expression softened for a moment and he nodded, accepting the compliment, saying, 'You also fought well, human. I will ensure that Lord Aldaeld hears of your bravery defending his daughter's hand-maids.'

Leofric said, 'Thank you,' watching as Morvhen helped Kyarno to his feet and led him towards his horse. Singing lilting songs of lament, her handmaids moved slowly through the glade, gathering up the weapons and bodies of the fallen Eternal Guard, lifting them and gently laying them across the backs of their steeds.

Cairbre himself took up the body of the warrior whose steed had been killed and, with eyes cast down, the sad procession left the glade of the Crystal Mere and began the journey back to Coeth-Mara.

BOOK TWO
Winter's Grey Despair

'Four came over,
Without boat or ship,
One yellow and white,
One brown abounding with twigs,
One to handle the flail,
And one to strip the trees.'

CHAPTER EIGHT

COMING BACK TO her body was always the hardest part. The reunion of flesh and spirit after travelling the secret paths that linked the realms beyond the senses and the beating heart of the forest was becoming more difficult and dangerous for her each time. Naieth felt a momentary claustrophobia as her spirit fought the confinement of her body, eager to be flying on the currents of magic that saturated Athel Loren.

She recited the names of the elven gods one by one, the ancient primal ones of the land and the newer idols of civilisation and culture embraced by the distant kin of the Asrai across the water, forcing her spirit to settle.

As always after journeying through the lines of power that threaded the forest she knew she would be weak, and so lay still, keeping her eyes open to reassure herself that she was indeed back in her body. A hooting caw nearby made her smile and she rolled her head on the soft pillow of leaves.

'I know, Othu,' she said, addressing a grey-feathered owl that perched on a low branch beside her. 'I am getting too old to travel the forest's secret paths.'

The owl hooted again, rolling its eyes and turning its head from her.

'Easy for you to say,' said Naieth, sitting upright with a low moan. 'But I had to see. I had to know for sure.'

Afternoon sunlight dappled this place of branches, gathering in golden pools in the low hollows of the chambers Lord Aldaeld had appointed to her and she smiled at this simple beauty. She enjoyed the sense of peace she felt in Coeth-Mara and felt closer to being at home here than she did anywhere else in Athel Loren. The smile fell from her face as she remembered that she was something of an unwelcome guest; that her skill of divination and her power to pierce the veil of time was both sought after and dreaded.

Naieth sat up, reached over to an artfully shaped wooden bowl and cupped her hands to lift out some water, rubbing the refreshingly cool liquid into her face. As she leaned over the bowl, she saw her reflection staring back at her, the long chin, melancholy mouth and the sad, accusing eyes. Droplets rippled the water in the bowl and she looked deep into her wavering reflection for a moment longer before averting her eyes, unwilling to meet her own gaze.

She had seen much too blood shed in her long life and as she looked at her hands, long, thin and worn, she knew that much of that blood was down to her. For too many centuries she had guided the Asrai along their path, and none of those years had been easy. She thought of Kyarno and told herself once again that it had been for the best, that it would…

That it would what?

Naieth scooped a handful of water from the bowl, shattering her reflection, and drank the gloriously fresh liquid, feeling strength return to her body and a reassuring solidity come upon her limbs. Travelling in the realm of the spirit was incredibly liberating, but returning to flesh grew harder and harder each time.

Her companion, Othu the owl, hooted once more and she said, 'I know I look tired. I *feel* tired and don't need you to remind me!'

The bird hopped from its perch, flying into the higher branches of the tree and Naieth closed her eyes. She took a deep, calming breath, already angry at snapping at Othu; after all, he was right. She *did* look tired.

The owl hooted again and she looked up to see his beak bobbing in the direction of the main hall of Coeth-Mara, now hearing soft footfalls approaching. She closed her eyes and took another deep breath, opening her mind to the souls of those who came to her.

Two of them – one proud and regal and with a will of oak, the other young and courageous, but with the heart of a poet.

She smiled as she recognised them as Lord Aldaeld Éadaoin and Tarean Stormcrow, feeling their suspicion of her like a red ripple in the magical air of Athel Loren.

When she had arrived at Coeth-Mara a week ago and asked for permission to enter, Lord Aldaeld had offered her the hospitality of his halls, but she had seen the wary look in his eyes as he had done so.

Plainly he did not wish her here, but knew better than to offend a spellweaver by refusing her entry. All the

Asrai knew that the mages of Athel Loren travelled nowhere without good reason and were wary of them, even amongst their own kind

Though many kinbands called Athel Loren home, there was often little contact between them and any dealings between them were fraught with suspicion. She turned and lifted her arm, apologising to Othu with a nod of her head as he dropped from above to land on her wrist.

She bowed as Lord Aldaeld and his herald entered, both elves moving with the supple grace of warriors. The Lord of Coeth-Mara wore a long cape of restless leaves and feathers, glowing spites rippling the fabric as they slipped around him. Naieth felt a thickening of the air and smiled inwardly as she realised Aldaeld had somehow persuaded a cluster of radiants to gather about him, tiny imps, little more than colourful lights that sapped the winds of magical energy.

Clearly Aldaeld was taking no chances that she might attempt to cloud his mind with her spells. His tattooed chest was crossed with two thin-bladed daggers and his hand gripped the glowing green pommel of his longsword.

Tarean Stormcrow was clad as he had been when her spirit had watched him speak to Kyarno this morning, his easy smile and confident manner radiating calm.

'Something has happened,' stated Aldaeld, without wasting any words on a welcome. 'The forest is angry and speaks of blood spilled.'

'Yes,' agreed Naieth. 'Blood has been spilled. At the Crystal Mere.'

'You have seen it?' asked Tarean Stormcrow.

'I saw it, yes,' said Naieth.

'Well?' snapped Aldaeld, taking a step towards her when she did not continue. Naieth flinched, the radiants making her skin crawl, and feeling her connection to the consciousness of Athel Loren fade at their nearness.

'Your daughter is safe, Lord Aldaeld. No harm has come to her.'

The elven lord's shoulders sagged a fraction in relief, then straightened as his eyes narrowed and he asked, 'Then whose blood was shed?'

'Four of the Hound of Winter's warriors are dead.'

'Four! Blood of Kurnous! What happened?'

Naieth backed away from Lord Aldaeld, saying, 'Beasts of Chaos penetrated the forest and attacked them.'

'Chaos,' spat Aldaeld. 'How in Isha's name did they reach so far into Athel Loren?'

'And how is it you did not know of them?' added Tarean Stormcrow.

'You know well that beyond the Crystal Mere, Athel Loren is dangerous,' said Naieth. 'The dark fey of the wood dwell in that region of the forest and there is often a sense of danger lurking there, mayhap the beasts knew to approach within its cloaking shadow.'

Neither of her visitors looked convinced and Aldaeld said, 'They are base creatures, mere beasts. How could they possibly know such a thing?'

Naieth shrugged as Othu flapped his wings and flew to land upon the shoulder of Tarean Stormcrow.

'He likes you,' smiled Naieth. 'It is a sign of good favour that he does so.'

Lord Aldaeld frowned at this change of subject and said, 'I do not like this, prophetess. Beasts of darkness reach deep into Athel Loren, the forest grows restless as winter comes and you bring a human into my halls. I tell you, I do not like it. A barbarian human! You know he should be dead already.'

'Leofric is just one human, you should not trouble yourself with him.'

'I do not have that luxury, prophetess,' spat Lord Aldaeld, waving his arm towards the south and dislodging several of the jostling radiants that gathered in the folds of his cloak. 'We dwell within reach of unnumbered enemies who bend their every effort to destroying everything I hold dear and have sworn to protect.'

'I know that, Lord Aldaeld, and–'

'I am not sure that you do, prophetess,' cut in Tarean Stormcrow. 'Winter is upon the forest and the King of the Wood prepares to go to his pyre. If we be not vigilant against such threats, then who?'

'There are many threats to this realm, Tarean Stormcrow, and know that I have seen them all. I have fought the secret war since before the seasons of your father, and I have seen a time beyond this where the restless dead rise from their tombs once more and red-skinned daemons of the Dark Gods stalk the lands where men once dwelt.'

'And what has that to do with this human?'

Naieth hesitated briefly before saying, 'In this time of blood and war we will have need of this human.'

'Humans live short, brutal lives, prophetess, surely he will be long dead by then?' said Aldaeld. 'And in any case, since when do the Asrai need the help of a human?'

'Without this human, the handmaids of your daughter would now be dead,' pointed out Naieth. 'He fought alongside the Hound of Winter and slew one of the creatures of Chaos in single combat.'

Tarean Stormcrow moved to stand at the edge of her chambers, looking beyond the woven branches and said, 'I still find it strange that you were not aware of these creatures. You speak of things far distant from us, but see not what is to pass within days. How can that be?'

Othu flapped and flew from the chamber, hooting loudly as Tarean Stormcrow spoke. Aldaeld's herald watched the bird go, turning his eyes back to Naieth as the owl vanished from sight.

'The future is not a straight path, Tarean Stormcrow, it weaves and misleads like a befuddlement of mischiefs, twisting and teasing with half-truths and shadows. There are none who can see where it leads with certainty.'

'And yet you would have us hold this human here as though you see it with the surest certainty?' asked Aldaeld.

'Yes, I would,' agreed Naieth, lifting her wrist as Othu flew back into the chamber to land on her arm. 'In all the futures I see Leofric standing beside the Asrai in defence of Athel Loren. Trust me Aldaeld, put your hatred of them aside, for more is at stake than the fate of one human.'

'Tell me of it,' demanded Aldaeld.

'I cannot,' said Naieth, shaking her head. 'To speak of the future is to change it.'

Othu hooted at her ear, a trilling series of clicks and whistles, and Naieth smiled.

'What does he say?' asked Lord Aldaeld.

'He brings word of another visitor to your halls,' said Naieth. 'One I bade come.'

Before Aldaeld could ask more, a grey-cloaked warrior of the Eternal Guard appeared at the entrance to the chamber with an anxious expression. Tarean Stormcrow nodded towards the warrior and Lord Aldaeld turned to face him.

'What news?' he asked, wary of the answer.

'The Red Wolf is come to Coeth-Mara,' said the warrior.

'Cu-Sith?' hissed Aldaeld, turning to Naieth, his face a mask of anger and not a little fear. 'Why would you bring the Red Wolf here?'

Naieth lifted her staff and said, 'He and his wardancers will perform the Dance of the Seasons at the Winter Feast. It is a great honour he does you by consenting to come here.'

'Indeed,' snapped Lord Aldaeld, turning to march from her chambers. 'Be careful that you do not heap too many honours upon me, prophetess. I do not think I would be thankful for any more.'

LEAVING THE CRYSTAL Mere, Leofric was both saddened and relieved to bid farewell to such a vista of incredible beauty. Its wonder was something he knew he would never forget, but it had been sullied for him by Chaos. Much as everything in this world, he mused.

All that was good in the world would eventually be tainted by Chaos, no matter how remote or seemingly untouchable. Even this place of beauty and magic, hundreds of miles from the northern steppes and protected by faerie magic, could not protect itself from the predations of the Dark Gods. Every victory won, every invasion defeated was but a respite – a pause in the inevitable doom of this world.

Any fool could see that…

He had helped drag the bodies of the beastmen into the forest where Leofric had assumed they would be burned, but Cairbre had shaken his head, saying, 'Leave them. The forest will claim them and they will return to the earth.'

The Hound of Winter had then extended his hand and said, 'That weapon you carry is an elven blade and does not belong to you.'

Briefly Leofric considered refusing to return the weapon, but knew that Cairbre could take it from him without even trying. Though he was loath to render himself unarmed once more, he reversed the blade and handed the sword, hilt first, to the Hound of Winter.

Cairbre had nodded and said no more, riding off at the head of their column back to Coeth-Mara. Once they had set off, Leofric had offered his mount to Tiphaine, uncomfortable with the idea of riding while a woman walked, but she had politely refused, walking hand in hand with one of her fellow handmaids.

Kyarno rode in silence, his head hung low over his chest and his braided hair cloaking his face in shadow. The chestnut-haired elven woman in the red dress who had loosed the deadly accurate shafts rode alongside him, speaking soft words of comfort.

As their journey back to the elven halls continued, Leofric found himself glancing warily into the darkness of the forest, wondering what fey creatures might dwell in the depths of Athel Loren, as a soft chorus of plaintive voices drifted from the trees.

Were the wild riders of Kurnous still out there? Might they come for him again?

His pack of spites still followed him, all now changed to resemble bobbing unicorns of light, the sight of them now mildly alarming after he had seen the fury with which they had attacked the beastmen.

It seemed as though there were low whispers coming from beyond the trees, hissing, sibilant tones like branches and leaves rustling in a chorus of wondrous ancient voices. As he listened, the sound filled his head with magic, lilting words like songs and beguiling tones like symphonies of joyful nuance. Leofric had thought that the language of the elves was like sweet music, but this was greater still, like the language of the soul made real. Leofric tugged on Taschen's reins, eager to hear more of this incredible sound, but a light hand reached out and gripped his wrist.

'Don't,' said the Lady Morvhen. 'You are human and the forest is not kind to humans.'

'What is it?' asked Leofric. 'It sounds like the forest is speaking.'

'It is.'

'What is it saying?' asked Leofric.

'It is the ancient language of the world, spoken only by the tree-kin and ancients of the wood,' said Morvhen. 'None but the spirits of the forest may speak it.'

'It's beautiful,' said Leofric.

Morvhen nodded and said, 'Yes, it is. There are only two places left in the world where it can be heard. Here and the Forest of Avelorn.'

'Avelorn? I have not heard of such a place.'

'It is far away on the island of Ulthuan, the birthplace of the Asrai.'

'What is it like there?'

Morvhen shook her head. 'I do not know, I have never seen it. Our people left this land many thousands of years ago to return to Ulthuan, but my kin remained behind in Athel Loren.'

'Why?'

She smiled, looking around at the wild beauty of the forest around her. 'Could you leave this place? No, our forebears had made their home here and, though it broke their hearts never to see the land of their birth again, they could not bear to leave the forest to the beasts and...'

Morvhen's voice trailed off and Leofric said, 'Humans.'

'Yes,' she said, 'humans. By the time the Phoenix King called his subjects home our kin had become part of the forest, their souls and fates entwined forever. We could not abandon the forest to the axes of the lesser races.'

'I understand,' nodded Leofric, wanting to rise to the defence of his race, but knowing that Morvhen was right.

'I am the Lady Morvhen Éadaoin, daughter of Lord Aldaeld Éadaoin,' said Morvhen. 'I think you know that already, but it is only proper that I introduce myself.'

'Yes, I know who you are, my lady,' replied Leofric, seeing Cairbre keeping a close eye on him as they spoke. 'Is Éadaoin your family name?'

'It is,' said Morvhen. 'In your language it means Fleet-mane.'

'I am Leofric Carrard, but then I am sure *you* know that already.'

Morvhen laughed, a wonderful, enchanting sound, and said, 'There are few in the forest who do not. The trees have carried word of your presence to all the corners of Athel Loren. Hence it might be wise for you not to go into the woods on your own. As I said, the forest is a dangerous place for humans.'

'I know,' said Leofric bitterly. 'It took my wife.'

'Yes,' said Morvhen. 'I know and I am truly sorry for your loss, but the waters of the Crystal Mere helped, yes?'

Leofric nodded, 'Aye, they did, and, Lady forgive me, I feel Helene's loss less keenly now.'

Morvhen frowned at his tone and said, 'But that is a good thing, surely?'

'Is it?' snapped Leofric, waving an arm at the forest around him. 'This place is eroding what I have of her, taking away the pain of my grief.'

'Why should you wish to hold onto grief?'

'Because it is *my* grief,' said Leofric. 'I desire to carry the pain of her loss; I do not want it taken away by faerie magic. I will grieve for my lost love in my own way, not yours!'

'Yours is a strange race, Leofric,' said Morvhen, echoing Tiphaine's earlier sentiment. 'You suffer when you do not need to.'

'Perhaps,' agreed Leofric, already ashamed at giving vent to such passion in front of a lady, 'but it is what I wish for. Leave me my grief. I will remember Helene in my own way.'

'As you wish, Leofric,' shrugged Morvhen, as Cairbre turned his horse and dropped back along the column of riders towards them, lowering her voice to a conspiratorial whisper. 'But when we return to Coeth-Mara may I speak with you some more? I would know of your adventures, the strange things you have seen and the far-off lands you have visited.'

Leofric shook his head. 'Regretfully, I must decline, my lady, for I shall be leaving Athel Loren upon returning you safely to your father. I have lands to rule in the name of my king and a son to raise without his mother. I cannot stay here.'

The crestfallen look on Morvhen's face cut Leofric deeply. He was unused to declining a lady's request, but there was little she could do to persuade him to stay in Athel Loren when he had responsibilities back in Bretonnia.

'Surely you can stay a little longer?' said Morvhen, and Leofric detected a note of petulance in her tone.

'No, my lady, I cannot, and please do not ask me again, for it ill becomes a knight to refuse a lady twice.'

'Very well,' said Morvhen sharply as Cairbre rode alongside them.

'My lady,' he said, 'you should not be talking to the human. You know what your father would say.'

'No matter, Hound of Winter,' said Morvhen, turning her horse to ride back to Kyarno. 'He does not wish to speak anyway.'

As she rode away, Cairbre said, 'If I were you, I would stay away from the Lady Morvhen.'

'Is that a threat?' asked Leofric, unable to take his eyes from the dead warrior laid across the rump of Cairbre's steed.

'No,' said the Hound of Winter. 'A warning between warriors.'

'How so?'

'She is the daughter of Lord Aldaeld and he holds your life in his hands. It would not please him to know that she was associating with a human.'

'I understand,' nodded Leofric. 'Then I thank you for your words. Tell me, why do they call you the Hound of Winter?'

At first, Leofric thought Cairbre wasn't going to answer, but the venerable elf smiled and said, 'I am Lord Aldaeld's champion, a warrior of the Eternal Guard and I hunt down the enemies of my kinband. None who have earned the wrath of Lord Éadaoin have escaped my hunt and none ever shall.'

Leofric nodded. In any other warrior, such a boast would have been arrogant, but having seen the Hound of Winter's deadly skills in battle, Leofric had no trouble believing Cairbre's words.

'The Eternal Guard, is that the name given to the army of Athel Loren?' he asked, pointing at the body behind Cairbre.

'Army?' said Cairbre, 'We have no need of such a thing, human. Every member of a kinband has a duty to guard the domain entrusted to their lord, and every elf of the forest has great skill with a bow. No, the Eternal Guard is no army of Athel Loren; we are its guardians through the long dark of winter, when branch and tree slumber. It is our duty and privilege to defend the sacred places of the forest and the lords and ladies that dwell within.'

'A heavy duty indeed,' said Leofric. 'But a welcome one, I should think.'

'It is a great honour to be chosen by the Eternal Guard, an honour earned through skill at arms. To meet death in the service of something so noble as Athel Loren is more than any warrior can ask for,' said Cairbre. 'But I see that you are a human who understands such things.'

'I do indeed,' agreed Leofric. 'Only by such feats of arms may a knight rise to become a knight of the realm. The king desires only warriors of courage and honour to defend his realm and there are none greater in all the lands of men than the knights of Bretonnia.'

'You are a great warrior in your lands?'

'A warrior, yes,' nodded Leofric. 'I have some skill with lance and blade, but modesty forbids me from vulgar boasts of prowess.'

'Spoken like a true warrior,' said Cairbre with a wry grin. 'One who lets his deeds attest to his mettle.'

Despite himself, Leofric found himself warming to Cairbre; the elf had the easy confidence of a warrior born, coupled with a manner that spoke of a life of great experience and wisdom. As he looked at the regal profile of the Hound of Winter, he found it increasingly difficult to reconcile this softly spoken, yet powerful warrior as being kin to the brash, argumentative Kyarno.

'Perhaps we are not so different after all,' said Leofric.

Cairbre shook his head. 'Do not mistake a warrior's respect for anything other than that. You are human and I am elf, and we will always be different. Though we can speak in the same language and live mortal lives, your kind will never understand mine.'

'That is a shame,' said Leofric. 'We could learn much from each other.'

'I do not believe so,' replied Cairbre, his cold-eyed expression settling upon his features once more. 'You humans have nothing we wish to know, and we do not wish to be part of your world. Let us leave it at that.'

'As you wish,' said Leofric as Cairbre rode off to the head of the column.

Alone once more, he glanced over to where Kyarno rode with Morvhen, catching the eye of Tiphaine and smiling at the scarlet-haired handmaid. Leofric saw that Kyarno had roused himself from his melancholic reverie, talking in a low voice with Morvhen and casting wary glances his way.

He did not know what had driven the young elf into such a bloody frenzy back in the glade of the Crystal Mere, nor did he have any reason to believe that Cairbre would be more forthcoming than he had been earlier.

Such matters were none of his business and since he had resolved to leave Athel Loren tonight – Naieth's wishes be damned – there was no need for him to pry further.

Whatever inner torments plagued Kyarno would remain his own to face.

He returned his attention to the path before him, allowing the gentle rhythm of the forest's song to carry him onwards.

To Coeth-Mara and then home.

CHAPTER NINE

RIDING BACK INTO Coeth-Mara through the same woven arch of leaves and branches, Leofric felt a familiar warmth enfold him, like the homely sensation he had every time he rode through the arched gateway of Castle Carrard upon his return from campaign. It felt like coming home, as though he was somehow welcome now...

The hanging belts of jewels and gold tinkled musically as they passed beneath them, sad and mournful at the dead they brought with them. The sense of things moving in the dark of the forest receded and Leofric again felt the strange sensation of feeling like he had moved from one season to another.

Cairbre's normally stony exterior softened as they entered the realm of his kinband and even Kyarno's face lit up with relief and pleasure at his return home. He saw the same expressions on every face – Morvhen's,

Tiphaine's and all the handmaids. He could not deny that the uplifting feeling was palpable and fought against its lulling qualities.

He was not long for this woodland realm and could not fall prey to its faerie magicks now. Leofric rode through the golden splendour of Coeth-Mara, remembering the words that had passed between him and Kyarno only this morning as he saw subtle hints of archways and pillars, suggestions of roof and beam and the barest outlines of passages and doorways. Where once he had seen nothing but tree and branch, forest and bush, he now saw signs of habitation, of life and living.

Here he saw a mother and child shaping a bowstave, there an elf skinning a brace of coneys. Leofric smiled as he passed many such domestic vignettes, amazed that he had not seen them before. Had he simply been ignorant of what to look for or was the forest now allowing him to see its gracefully shaped structures? Or was there something more sinister at work? Was the magic of the forest even now altering him in ways he could not fathom, reshaping what his human senses could perceive?

Such a worrying notion only heightened his desire to leave Athel Loren and, once night fell, he decided would make his way from this place before he was lost to its fey power forever. He had no wish to suffer the same fate as the vanished Duke Melmon and knew that the longer he stayed here, the more likely such an end became.

The handmaids of Morvhen seemed to glide past him, each one offering him a shy smile and a bow of gratitude as they did so and Leofric felt a great humility at their recognition. As she passed him, Tiphaine whispered, 'They want me to tell you that they are sorry for teasing you at the Crystal Mere and to thank you for rising to their defence against the monsters.'

Leofric shivered as he remembered how close the arrows loosed by the handmaids had come to his head and said, 'I am not sure they really needed my help, but I am glad to have been of service.'

Tiphaine smiled, reaching up to touch his arm and Leofric felt a soothing warmth to her touch. 'Take care, Leofric Carrard. I wish you well.'

'Thank you, my lady,' said Leofric as she moved away. 'I hope I may one day be of service to you again.'

Looking over her shoulder as she joined Morvhen and the rest of her handmaids, Tiphaine smiled and said, 'As do I.'

Leofric watched as Morvhen and her handmaids gently relieved Cairbre of the body carried on the back of his horse and led the elven steeds bearing the other dead warriors of the Eternal Guard into the winding paths of Coeth-Mara. Soft laments sighed from their lips as they vanished and Leofric found himself sad to see Tiphaine go, but shook such thoughts from his mind as Kyarno rode alongside him.

'Where are they taking the fallen?' asked Leofric.

Kyarno looked up and Leofric saw that the young elf's earlier manner had reasserted itself in his suspicious stare.

'They are being taken to be cleansed before being laid to rest in the forest,' said Kyarno, 'but it is not fitting for a human to speak of elven dead.'

'I am sorry,' said Leofric. 'I meant no offence.'

'No,' replied Kyarno slowly, 'it is I who am sorry.'

Leofric could see the difficulty Kyarno had in making such an admission as he spoke again. 'You fought to defend my kin when all I have offered you is anger and hostility. For that I thank you.'

'No thanks are necessary. They were creatures of Chaos and though, in the end it is fruitless, evil must be fought at all times.'

'Fighting Chaos is never fruitless… Leofric. May I call you that?'

Leofric bowed his head and said, 'Yes, you may. But I have seen the face of evil, Kyarno. I rode with my king down the east causeway of Middenheim to face the lord of daemons and though we fought like Gilles and the Companions, we could not defeat it. The best and the bravest of Bretonnia, and still we could not defeat it.'

'Perhaps you were not strong enough?' said Kyarno without malice.

'On the charge, there are no mightier warriors than the knights of Bretonnia,' said Leofric proudly. 'Or at least… at least I thought so… until…'

Leofric's eyes misted over and the gold and greens of Athel Loren faded from sight as he saw again the mud- and corpse-choked wasteland around the great northern city of Middenheim. The Ulricsberg towered over the group of knights, its tall spires wreathed in smoke and flames as the shamans of the Dark Gods hurled their vile magicks at its walls and terrifying dragons and other nameless, winged horrors breathed gouts of fire.

Smoke and a thick, cloying mist hung over the battle-field, the twisted corpses of slaughtered beastmen lying strewn about amid the hacked apart bodies of men in various liveries of the Empire's provinces. The red and white of Talabheim mingled with the gold and yellow of Nuln and the blue and red of Altdorf. Shattered breastplates, discarded halberds and dented sallet hel-mets rusted in the open air. Leofric remembered the stench of death, the rotten aroma of opened bowels and decomposing flesh.

The knights had walked their horses through the battlefield, scattering carrion birds as they feasted on eyes and tongues, as well as foxes and dogs fighting over the contents of ruptured bellies. Here and there, looters of the dead scurried from corpse to corpse, slitting open purses for coin and pilfering gold teeth or trinkets.

Where they came upon such animals they killed those they could and drove away others, though Leofric knew it was a hopeless task, for as soon as they moved on, the scavengers, both human and animal, would return.

It had begun slowly, as a soft drumming noise like far away thunder.

Then it had grown to a rumbling storm of slow hoof beats and the knights had circled their horses and twisted in the saddle to pinpoint its direction, for none now could doubt that the sound was approaching cavalry. And in the forests around Middenheim, it could only be that of the enemy.

The hateful mist had conspired to confound their efforts to locate the approaching foe and Leofric had felt the tension rise as the noise grew louder and louder. Some of the younger knights cried that the mist was unnatural, that it was the result of an enemy spell. Older, wiser heads scoffed at such protestations, but Leofric had heard the unease in their denials as the mist closed in.

The maddeningly slow drumbeat of hooves grew louder with every passing second and though it seemed their foe must surely be upon them, there was still no sign of them.

None could now doubt the sorcerous nature of the mist as it thickened and coiled about them, acrid and unpleasant, and dulling the sound of the approaching riders. A carnyx horn sounded in the mist and Leofric could hear the galloping jingle of trace and the metallic scrape of swords being drawn.

The knights lowered their lances, but by now it was already too late as the mist suddenly rose and the thunderous charge of the riders of Chaos struck them. A single dread rune blazed with power on a banner carried by one of the knights and Leofric's heart trembled as he recognised to which warlord the rune belonged.

Riding at the head of the terrifying knights of Chaos was Archaon himself, seated astride his monstrous steed of the apocalypse, swollen by dark magicks to many times the size of even the mightiest Bretonnian steed. Its eyes were burning coals, its breath that of a furnace.

The Lord of the End Times was vast and awesome in his evil, clad in armour forged of brazen iron and a horned helmet blazing with fell energies. A great bearskin cloak flared out behind him and he carried a terrible, flaming sword, its blade screaming with a soul-destroying roar.

Knights fell, both they and their mounts hewn in twain by each swing of Archaon's colossal blade. Bloody arcs clove the air as Chaos-forged blades shattered armour and weapons alike, killing men and beasts without pity or remorse. Leofric's shield was smashed from his arm, his body numbed by the force of the blow. The knights fought bravely, but against such brute ferocity there could be no victory.

Though it shamed every knight among them, they had turned their horses and fled from the battle, the raucous cries of the chosen warriors of Chaos ringing in their ears as they rode on to find more prey.

The shame of that rout had not lessened, and though the king had honoured each and every one of them after the final victory, they had all left the Empire with the guilt of fleeing before the enemy festering in their hearts. Men who Leofric had fought alongside for years would no longer meet his eye, the shared guilt making each man loath to seek out the company of his fellows.

It had been a black day for honour and the memory of it had all but unmanned him. Leofric had seen the raw power of Chaos that day and it had settled like a shroud upon him, filling him with dread for the day when the Dark Gods finally took the world for their own.

Filled with such gloomy thoughts, all he could picture was Helene's face, wishing he could have spent the last days of this world's life by her side. Such selfish thoughts did not become a knight of Bretonnia, but faced with the inevitability of the fall of nations, he knew he was but a man, with a man's desires.

And yet, amid such darkness was life. The image of his son's face, smiling and full of innocence leapt unbidden to his mind. Beren's green eyes were the image of his own, his laugh like an angel's. There was no malice or guile to his son, only a child's unquestioning love and purity. While such things existed in the world, there was something worth fighting for, even if only to preserve it for a little longer.

Leofric smiled ruefully, the darkness of his thoughts retreating in the face of the love he felt for his son. The battlefields and horrors of the Storm of Chaos faded and he saw that he was once again in Athel Loren, its enchanted boughs of red and brown leaves like a fire above him, its beauty almost painful against such horrors as he had just relived.

The sweet scent of wood sap and leavening bread caught in his nostrils and Leofric felt a strange peace settle upon him, as though such homely, domestic scents had somehow brought his soul back to him.

He saw Kyarno looking strangely at him and said, 'Athel Loren is a place of wonders and miracles, but I can never forget that, for my kind, it is also a place of fear and death. I think that if I were to remain here I would soon have a surcease of sorrow, but that is not for me and I must go before I forget my duties.'

'Leave?' said Kyarno. 'You still do not understand, human. You cannot leave.'

'No?' replied Leofric coldly.

'No, you are deep in Athel Loren and without the leave of Lord Aldaeld and the forest you would be dead before you were out of sight of Coeth-Mara.'

'Be that as it may, I have to try.'

'I wouldn't if I were you,' shrugged Kyarno, 'but then who am I to give advice on what to do?'

'Then tell me where I may find this Lord Aldaeld,' said Leofric. 'If I must secure his leave to travel through his lands, then so be it.'

'It looks like he has come to find you,' said Kyarno, pointing towards a group of horsemen that approached along the main thoroughfare of Coeth-Mara.

Leofric followed Kyarno's gaze and saw Cairbre riding out to meet a group of elves led by a powerful-looking elven warrior atop a golden-coloured horse with a pale mane and tail. The elf's bare chest was adorned with numerous tattoos of twisting, knotted torques, thorns and wild beasts, his long cloak of leaves and feathers rippling with motion.

The warrior carried a long, green-hilted sword across his back and wore a crown of woven branches and leaves atop his patrician features. His oval eyes were utterly dark, seemingly without pupils, and Leofric sensed a power to this elf beyond anything he had felt from any other – even Cairbre or Naieth.

This elf was empowered with the magic of the forest and Leofric knew that this must be none other than Lord Aldaeld Fleetmane, lord of Coeth-Mara and protector of this domain of the forest.

He saw an unmistakable hostility and disdain in Lord Aldaeld's eyes, and knew that if his fate truly lay in this elf's hands, then it was doubtful that it would be a happy one. Accompanying Lord Aldaeld was Naieth, clad in a long dress of green velvet with a grey-feathered owl sitting on her shoulder, and a golden haired elf in clothing similar to Kyarno's but of exquisitely tailored reds and blues. A trio of the Eternal Guard followed behind their lord on foot, their twin-bladed spears held at their sides.

Cairbre dismounted and stood before the elven lord, the Blades of Midnight held across his body in a defensive posture. Turning back to Leofric, he said, 'You are required to dismount.'

Leofric nodded and climbed down from Taschen's saddle, holding himself tall and proud before this elf. Aldaeld may be lord of this place, but Leofric was a knight of Bretonnia and bowed to no king but his own.

The elven lord spoke to the richly dressed elf riding alongside him who bore a longsword and carried a short, recurved bow slung over one shoulder. His hair was long and golden, held in place by a silver circlet, and Leofric saw a softness to his features that he had not seen in other elven warriors.

The elf nodded and said, 'I am Tarean Stormcrow, and I am herald to Aldaeld Éadaoin, guardian of the forest realm of Athel Loren and Lord of Coeth-Mara. Lord Aldaeld welcomes you to his hall.'

Leofric switched his gaze from the herald to Aldaeld himself, seeing no hint of that welcome in his patrician features. Behind the elven lord, Leofric saw Naieth's owl hoot nervously and had the distinct impression it was talking to her. The faerie legends spoke of elf sorcerers who could speak to the beasts of the forest, and it appeared that Naieth was one of them.

Leofric ignored Aldaeld's herald and addressed the elven lord directly. 'Do you not speak for yourself? Must you hide behind another?'

'Lord Aldaeld does not lower himself to speak the tongues of men,' explained the elf named Stormcrow. 'You will address me and, through me, Lord Aldaeld may consent to speak to you.'

Leofric folded his arms across his chest as Aldaeld spoke again to Stormcrow, who shook his head and said, 'Lord Aldaeld asks why you insult him by speaking to him directly. Do you not accord honour to other kings besides your own?'

'I do,' acknowledged Leofric, 'when I am their guest or supplicant. But not when I am their prisoner.'

'Ah…' said Stormcrow, spreading his arms wide and smiling broadly. The elf's smile was contagious and Leofric found himself smiling as well. 'You think you are a prisoner here?'

'Am I not?'

'No,' replied Stormcrow, shaking his head. 'You are a guest in Athel Loren, though, for your own safety, it would be wise not to enter the forest without the consent of Lord Aldaeld or the trees themselves.'

'A prison may be called many things, but if one is not free to leave, then it amounts to the same thing does it not?'

'There is truth in what you say,' nodded Tarean Storm-crow, looking over Leofric's shoulder at Kyarno, 'but Coeth-Mara truly is not a prison, save for those who choose it to be so.'

Lord Aldaeld spoke a swift burst of elvish and his her-ald took a step towards Leofric, saying, 'The lord of Coeth-Mara wishes it known that he is grateful for the aid you gave to his daughter's handmaids. To have fought the beasts of Chaos took great courage for a human and he is pleased that you survived.'

'The Lady Tiphaine has thanked me on their behalf, and the gratitude of a lady is its own reward.'

Tarean Stormcrow bowed slightly to Leofric and said, 'You are a human who knows the value of honour. Nev-ertheless, Lord Aldaeld is indebted to you and extends to you the hospitality of his halls for so long as you remain within them.'

Leofric glanced at Naieth, wondering how much of Lord Aldaeld's hospitality was as a result of her and how much of it was resented. Even he could sense the frostiness between Aldaeld and Naieth.

'In addition to this great honour, he bids you to attend upon his kin at the Winter Feast, when the War-dancers of the Red Wolf will perform the Dance of the Seasons.'

Though nothing was said, Leofric could sense a sud-den shift in mood and felt a shiver of fear work its way up his spine at the mention of this Red Wolf.

He shook off his momentary unease and said, 'Con-vey my thanks to Lord Aldaeld and inform him that I accept his gracious offer of hospitality for as long as I shall remain here.'

Tarean Stormcrow smiled broadly, nodding slightly to Lord Aldaeld, who wheeled his horse and rode away without another word. The herald swung onto the back of his own horse and he, Cairbre and the Eternal Guard, followed their master as he departed.

As they left, Naieth rode forwards, the owl flying off towards the treetops above, a strange, sad expression on her face as she spoke to Kyarno in the gentle cadences of her native tongue.

Kyarno shook his head at whatever she said and spat some harsh elven words back to her before riding off, leaving Naieth and Leofric alone together in the forest.

'What did you say to him?' asked Leofric.

'Nothing,' said Naieth. 'It is not important.'

Leofric turned from the elf witch and climbed back into his saddle, running a hand through his unruly hair and brushing grass and dirt from his clothes.

'Well, it seems as though your idea of sending me to the Crystal Mere was not entirely successful,' said Leofric.

'I wouldn't be so sure, Leofric,' said Naieth, her voice taking on a distant, ethereal quality... as though she looked straight *through* him. 'I think perhaps it achieved exactly what was intended.'

'What does that mean?'

'It means that there are often many things that need to happen for the present to choose the right path into the future,' said Naieth, and Leofric was unsure as to whether she was talking to him or herself.

THE CHAMBER OF branches was clearer to him now than when he had first awoken here, the distinct outlines of shaped wood and curved bough now obvious. Where first he had seen nothing but the riotousness of nature, he now saw the guiding hand of artifice, though nowhere did he see anything as crude as a straight line.

Late evening sunlight streaked the branches of the trees, the distant sounds of melodic voices and the warm smells of summer mingling with the crispness of autumn and the bite of winter, and Leofric had a sense of time slipping away from him.

'Time to be away from this place,' he whispered to himself as he dismounted and unbuckled the girth. He looked for somewhere to hitch his steed's reins, but saw nothing that would serve. He turned back to the horse and watched with amazement as the glowing spites – that seemed now to be his constant companions – flitted past his head and vanished into the low, twisting branches of the tree. The wood writhed and swelled, growing and reshaping itself into a knotted branch at just the right height to form a hitching rail.

Leofric chuckled, already becoming more used to the strange creatures of the forest, and said, 'Thank you, little ones,' as he hitched Taschen's reins to the newly formed branch. The glowing spites emerged from the wood and resumed their bobbing pattern above his head as he began stripping the tack from his horse.

With a grunt, he hauled off the saddle and dropped it onto the hitching rail then began rubbing down the flanks of his weary horse. In this place of magic and mystery, there was a reassuring sense of reality in this simple task that, ordinarily, he would have ordered his squire attend to.

Having seen to the needs of his mount, who now began feeding on the long grass, he entered the chambers Naieth had escorted him to. She had left him to his own devices, saying, 'Rest well, Leofric, we will talk again soon.'

He had merely nodded, seeing no reason to speak to her of his plans to depart Athel Loren this very night. As he had watched her depart he felt no guilt at this deception, merely a desire to be away and to be reunited with his son.

Inside, the trees and branches of his chambers smelled of warm jasmine and were filled with light, softly glowing traceries as though the sap within ran like liquid amber. He saw the same bed of leaves where he had awoken and, beside it, a deep wooden bowl of water and another set of fresh clothes, identical to the ones he wore.

But beside them – and a much more welcome sight – was a tall, intertwined arrangement of branches upon which was hung his armour, polished to a mirror sheen, and his scabbard. The hilt of the Carrard sword glittered in the fading light and he marched across the chamber to grasp its soft, leather-wound hilt.

Drawing the sword, he cut the air with its silvered blade, running through a series of martial exercises designed to loosen the muscles of his shoulder. He frowned as he swung the blade, twisting its length through the air in a series of dazzling thrusts, ripostes and cuts. Though he performed each move flawlessly, the sword's weight felt strangely different, and it took Leofric several moments to realise why.

Next to the elven blade he had wielded in battle earlier, this sword felt clumsy and inelegant, heavy and ponderous, though he knew the blessing of the Lady was upon it and it was many times lighter than any similar blade.

Disturbed, he sheathed the sword and placed his palm against the breastplate of his armour. The surface was smooth to the touch and the gold chasing along its edges and the unicorn in its centre shone like fire with the touch of the setting sun.

Leofric turned from his armour and stripped off the bloodstained clothes he wore, washing himself with water from the bowl and using the bunched garments as a cloth. When he was as clean as he could make himself, he dressed quickly in the fresh attire, noting that the scar on his hip from the forest spirit's attack had completely vanished. Leofric was a fast healer, but he knew that such speed was unnatural – there was not even a blemish to mark its passing.

Perhaps the waters of the Crystal Mere had healing properties beyond those of easing the torments of the bereaved?

Putting the vanished wound from his mind, Leofric lifted his greaves from the frame of branches, buckling them onto his shins. Normally he would be wearing quilted hose beneath his armour, but there was no sign of the ones he had been wearing upon entering Athel Loren, so he had to content himself with buckling the armour on tighter than normal.

Piece by piece, Leofric donned his armour, shrugging into his heavy mail shirt and coif and wincing as the links bit into his skin through the thin shirt he wore. Silver moonlight streamed into the chamber as he lifted the breastplate and fitted it across his chest, smiling at the familiar feel of armour again.

Only then did he realise how difficult putting it on was going to be without his squire to help him.

With some difficulty, and not a little distraction from the curious spites that circled him, he was able to get one strap buckled and reached around in vain for the next.

'Instead of just watching me, it would be useful if you could help,' snapped Leofric as a spite shaped like a tiny dragon circled his flailing hands as he tried to grasp the next buckle.

No sooner had he spoken than he felt the buckle pressed into his palm and looked down to see a tiny glowing figure, no larger than his hand floating beside him. Like a miniature elf, the small, red-capped figure smiled with a wicked grin and nodded towards the next buckle.

'Now then, what are you, my little friend?' asked Leofric, but the diminutive creature didn't answer, content merely to hover in the air beside him. Despite himself, Leofric couldn't help but smile at this absurd little creature. Here, in this place, he supposed he should not be surprised at anything any more.

'Thank you,' he said, pleased that the little spites appeared to have taken a liking to him. 'Your help is most welcome.'

The glowing spite giggled, the sound like the chiming of glass, and Leofric buckled the strap of his armour and moved onto the next, not surprised when it was also pressed into his hand.

'I may make you my squire…' said Leofric, the smile falling from his face as he suddenly pictured Baudel, his guts spilling over the forest floor as he was disembowelled by one of the deadly forest spirits. Without speaking again, he finished donning his armour and turned to put on his sword belt.

He felt better now that he was armed and armoured once again, as though the mere act of putting on the apparel of a knight of Bretonnia had reminded him of his duty, a duty the magic of this forest seemed keen to erode the memory of.

He drew his sword once more and dropped to his knees, holding the sword by the hilt with its point resting on the soft floor of the chamber. Taking Helene's favour, he wrapped the scarf around the hilt and quillons of the weapon, entwining it with his fingers as he knelt in prayer.

Closing his eyes and resting his forehead on the pommel of his sword, Leofric softly recited the vow of the knight: 'Lady, I am your servant and in this time of trial I once again offer you my blade and service. When the clarion call is sounded, I will ride out and fight in the name of liege and Lady. Whilst I draw breath the lands bequeathed unto me shall remain untainted by evil. Honour is all, chivalry is all. Such is my vow.'

With each word spoken came a feeling of peace and tranquillity and Leofric knew that his prayer had been answered.

He stood and sheathed his sword in one smooth motion, lifting the last of his armour from the frame. He slid his helm over his head and snapped shut the angled visor, before turning and marching from the chamber.

The Lady herself had come to him, easing his troubled mind, and he knew that the time was now right for him to leave Athel Loren.

CHAPTER TEN

EVEN AT NIGHT, Coeth-Mara was a place of light and magic, the boughs and branches of the forest garlanded with moonlight and starfire. Snow was falling, carpeting the ground in white and the sense of hostility Leofric had felt before was much lessened now, though he knew that the forest would never be a safe place for a human.

His armour chafed against his skin and clanked loudly with every step, but Leofric knew there was no sense in trying to be stealthy – such a thing was next to impossible in a suit of heavy plate armour anyway. He left the chamber of branches and passed through the blurred boundary between his dwelling and the forest itself, seeing Taschen still feeding on the grasses of Athel Loren. The horse had eaten its way through a wide swathe of grass and Leofric rubbed his mount's neck, saying, 'Elven grass obviously agrees with you, my friend. I wonder, would you prefer it to grain?'

Taschen ignored him as he threw his saddle blanket over the horse's back then lifted his saddle from the spite-formed hitching rail. It had been many years since Leofric had saddled a horse himself and the process took longer than he remembered it taking Baudel. Nevertheless, it was a skill that, once learned, was never forgotten, and soon he had his steed saddled and ready to ride.

Leofric climbed into the saddle, settling himself and adjusting his scabbard before grasping the reins and spurring his horse onwards into the night.

In the veiled twilight of darkness, the forest was perhaps even more spectacular than during the day, though there was a chill to the air that felt to Leofric like the depths of winter rather than its onset. The sense of time slipping away from him felt more acute at night, as though the moons above him were circling the world differently.

He angled his horse along a trunk-lined processional, the leafy arches shining with reflected light from the glittering snowflakes on the wide leaves and drooping foliage. As spectacular as it was, there was also something infinitely sad and fearful to the forest, a sense of things dying and never to be seen again. Leofric felt a sense of ancient melancholy as he rode through the leaf-strewn paths of Coeth-Mara, the sounds of faraway voices and tree-song filling him with an unexpected wistfulness.

'I will remember this,' whispered Leofric. 'For good and ill, I will remember this.'

Whether it was the moonlight shadows or his apparent acceptance by the forest, he did not know, but he could now clearly see the softly lit outlines of tall columns of trees and gently curving roofs of branches and leaves. He had noticed the same thing upon his return to Coeth-Mara, but only now in the moonlight were the song-woven structures of the elven halls truly visible. Only a day before he would have ridden through here and seen nothing of Lord Aldaeld's domain and Leofric's would have been the loss.

But for all its beauty, it was still a place of shadows and fear. It was still the forest that had taken his wife and though the pain of her death was still fresh, it felt like a lifetime had passed since the spirits of the wood had taken her. He could feel the pain of her loss diminishing, as though the forest itself sought to heal his hurt, and knew he had to leave before he forgot her completely.

He could feel many eyes upon him, though he saw not a single soul. The eyes of Athel Loren were ever watchful and he knew that his departure from Coeth-Mara would already be known. He gripped the hilt of his sword, hoping that he would not need to draw it, but knowing that such a hope was ultimately doomed.

A red-furred wolf padded softly from the trees, its coat gleaming like copper in the moonlight and its eyes a glistening red. A golden hawk with a curious expression sat on its back and examined him carefully. Leofric tensed, wondering if the wolf would attack as it turned to face him and bared its fangs.

But before the wolf could advance, a hunting hound with fur the colour of snow ghosted from the shadows, a low, threatening growl building in its throat.

Leofric slowly drew his sword, holding it close to his side as the hound leaned forwards and barked in the wolf's ear. The wolf ignored the hound and took slow, stalking steps through the snow towards him, never once taking its eyes from his. Leofric rubbed Taschen's neck as the animal approached.

He raised his sword and pulled on his horse's reins to better angle himself to meet the wolf's attack.

As he drew back his sword arm, a gentle voice whispered, 'I wouldn't if I were you...'

Leofric risked a glance over his shoulder, seeing Morvhen Éadaoin atop a glorious roan mare with a mane the colour of snow on the mountains. She had changed from her red dress into more practical attire of buckskin trews and a feather-laced jerkin with strips of gold woven into the fabric. Her long, chestnut hair was teased up into a high, feather-woven cascade of silver pins, leaves and braids. Her long, delicate features were curious and unafraid, her wide eyes dark in the shadowy night.

'What are they?' asked Leofric.

'Spirits of the wild,' said Morvhen. 'The spirits and beasts of the forest have a strange relationship and not even we really understand it.'

'Are they dangerous?'

'That depends on whether you mean them harm,' said Morvhen. 'Do you?'

Leofric shook his head and sheathed his sword as the hound again barked at the wolf. The wolf stopped in its tracks and held his gaze for a second more before bobbing its head towards Morvhen and turning to pad back the way it had come, crossing the path and disappearing into the forest across from them. Satisfied that the wolf had gone, the hound also bowed its head to Morvhen and ran off into the forest after its red-furred companion.

Leofric let out a deep breath, shaking his head at such strangeness.

'Where are you going?' asked Morvhen. 'Are you leaving my father's halls?'

'I have to,' said Leofric, raking his spurs back and riding onwards. 'I have to return to my son and my lands.'

'Yes, you said that before,' said Morvhen, riding to catch up. 'I didn't think you really meant it.'

'Why would you think that?'

'I don't know,' shrugged Morvhen, pointing at the glowing spites that followed Leofric. 'It doesn't look like they want you to leave and my father says that you humans change your minds all the time. I just thought that once Coeth-Mara welcomed you, you might want to stay for a time.'

'What do you mean by that?'

'That once you'd seen how beautiful Athel Loren was, you'd want to see more of it and speak more with me. I told you, I want to hear all about your adventures.'

'No,' said Leofric, halting his horse. 'I meant what you said about humans changing their minds. What do you mean?'

Morvhen pulled ahead of him, riding her horse in a tight circle and Leofric could see that she was armed. An elven bow was slung from the flank of her steed and she wore a narrow, short-bladed sword across her back. Had she come here to stop him leaving?

Cunning of them to send a woman, knowing he would not harm her.

'Well, he says that you make war on each other all the time and that a human's word is like summer mist. My father fought in a land called the Empire before I was born in the time when they had three emperors. He said that the leaders of the humans couldn't decide on who was to rule them and that they fought bitter wars with one another with alliances like shifting sands.'

Leofric cast his mind back to Maixent's history lessons in the draughty garrets of Castle Carrard, trying to recall his teachings of the land of Sigmar to the north of Bretonnia. Since the time of Magnus the Pious, a single Emperor had led the Empire, though there had been a time...

'But that was over five hundred years ago,' said Leofric. 'How could your father have fought in the Empire then?'

'He was young then,' admitted Morvhen. 'But we elves have a greater span of years than you humans. Didn't you know that?'

'There are stories that say you are immortal, but I had taken them for flights of fancy. I never believed you were so long-lived.'

Morvhen laughed. 'We are not immortal, Leofric. Nor is it that we are long-lived. It is just that your kind exists so fleetingly that all others appear to be immortal. It is no wonder your people live such rushing, desperate lives. To have such a limited time to experience the joys that life has to offer must be terrible indeed. How do you cope with it?'

Leofric tugged on Taschen's reins and rode around Morvhen, saying, 'You have never ventured beyond the borders of Athel Loren, have you?'

'No. What has that to do with anything?' replied Morvhen, riding to catch up with him once more.

'It means that you have no idea what you are talking about,' snapped Leofric. 'Try living in the world beyond your cosy forest paradise and then ask me about the joy of living, little girl! I have been a warrior for most of my adult life. I have killed men and I have killed monsters. I have seen good men slaughtered by warriors of the Dark Gods and seen my wife murdered by the creatures of this damned forest. So don't you dare talk to me about living! I have done my share of living in the brief span allowed to me by the gods and I am going home to spend the rest of it with my son.'

Morvhen's jaw dropped open and Leofric could see that she had clearly never been spoken to in such a manner. No sooner had her shock faded than her regal blood flushed her face and she said, 'I forbid you to go. I want you to stay and tell me of faraway lands, of monsters you have slain and wars you have fought.'

'You want to know about the wars I have fought?' demanded Leofric.

'Yes,' said Morvhen. 'I do.'

'Very well, Lady Éadaoin. Shall I tell you of men screaming for their mothers as their guts spill from their bellies, of boys carried from the field of battle with their legs no more than a bloody pulp because they tried to stop a rolling cannonball? Is that what you want to hear? Or maybe I should tell you of the women beaten and raped by passing soldiers and left to die by the roadside, of the children dragged off to a life of slavery by the northmen, or the field hospitals that stink of gangrene from wounds that have become infected because injured men lay in a bloody field for days before being found by their fellows?'

Morvhen's face twisted in disgust at such things and though Leofric regretted such a breach of his chivalric code, he was in no mood to humour this spoilt little girl. He took a deep breath to try and calm himself, softly reciting the vow of the knight under his breath.

'You speak as though I am innocent of war,' spat Morvhen. 'I am not. Athel Loren is forever threatened. We have enemies all around and I have lived a hundred years and shed my share of blood in its defence. I too have known the loss of friends and loved ones.'

Morvhen wheeled her horse and Leofric could see a cold hardness to her eyes and a defiant strength he had not noticed before.

'Those who died at the Crystal Mere?' she said. 'They were not strangers to me.'

He opened his mouth to speak, but Morvhen dug her heels into the mare's flanks and rode off in the direction of Coeth-Mara.

Leofric cursed and watched her ride away, sorry for hurting her, but unwilling to be diverted from his course. The spites following behind him hung motionless in the air and he could sense their disapproval of him.

'Don't say a word,' he cautioned them, before realising he was talking to glowing balls of light. Surprised at his own foolishness, he turned from them and rode onwards.

THE FOREST FLASHED past her in a blur, emotions raging within her head at the human's words. Though part of her knew there was some truth to what he had said, her pride would not yet allow her anger to diminish. Morvhen pushed the mare hard, releasing that anger through the speed of her horse. She was not worried about Ithoraine stumbling or plunging her leg into a rabbit hole or root; the horse knew the forest well enough to gallop headlong in the darkness without fear of such things.

She rode hard through the overgrown paths of the forest, feeling branches and leaves pull themselves from her path as her mad gallop continued. The human thought her ignorant of the harsh realities of life, that she knew nothing of loss and pain.

Well, he would soon know of loss and pain if he rode further into the forest without her father's blessing. The dryads of winter were far from welcoming to outsiders and though he rode *from* Coeth-Mara, they would offer no mercy to a human in their forest.

The thought gave her pause and she leaned over Itho-raine's neck and whispered to her, entwining her fingers in the horse's mane. Her steed circled, coming to a halt with a neigh of disappointment that their wild ride was over.

As she rode back into Coeth-Mara, the reality of the human's fate sank in and her anger vanished as she knew who would bear the full wrath of her father should he be killed by the forest spirits.

Kyarno.

With a whooping yell, she rode to warn her lover.

WITH MORVHEN GONE, the forest took on a darker aspect, the moonlight now imparting a sinister, spectral glow instead of the silver sheen it had once provided. Where before there had been a strange warmth to the inky blackness between the trees, there was now only the chill of the grave.

'Foolish,' Leofric muttered, 'very foolish.'

Had the forest sensed the anger of the words that had passed between him and the elven princess? Was it even now withdrawing the welcome it had offered him at Coeth-Mara? If so, he would need to hurry.

Clouds covered the moon and as he rode deeper into the woods, the snow fell more heavily, and it became increasingly difficult to see the path before him. Rustling in the undergrowth and a high pitched whis-pering that sounded as though it came from all around him set his nerves on edge.

Leofric kept one hand loose on Taschen's reins, the other tight upon the hilt of his sword. An owl hooted nearby and he saw the grey-feathered bird perched on a snow-laden branch, watching him intently with its saucer eyes. He ignored the bird and kept his eyes flitting from shadow to shadow as they danced before him.

The sounds of the forest were magnified by his isolation – every creak of a wind blown branch or rustle of leaves made him jump, ever fearful of the creatures that had killed his men-at-arms. A clammy, creeping mist snaked through the trees and coiled around their tall trunks.

'I am a knight of Bretonnia and servant of the Lady, no harm can come to me.'

Taschen whinnied in fear and Leofric could feel a shadow steal across his soul, a dark pall of fear that he could not name or pinpoint. Unseen things rustled in the depths of the wood and a hundred whispering voices seemed to hiss from the depths of the unnatural mist.

A branch caught his armour and his sword flashed from its scabbard before he realised that he was not under attack. He rode on, not sheathing his weapon, but keeping the blade bared.

'I am a knight of Bretonnia and servant of the Lady, no harm can come to me,' he repeated, willing the simple prayer to work in the face of this darkness.

Taschen's progress through the undergrowth became slower and slower, branches, roots and bushes growing thicker with every yard gained. Leofric pushed aside low branches and twisted in the saddle as grasping thorns and briars snagged on his armour. Though he kept his sword at the ready he was unwilling yet to use its edge to clear a path, his instincts warning him of the danger of such action.

The hoot of an owl sounded again and Leofric turned to see the bird close by once more.

'You are said to be wise, friend. Do you know an easier way out of this damned forest?' he called up to it.

The owl did not reply and Leofric found himself surprised that it did not, having seen stranger things than talking animals in Athel Loren. The bird turned its head to the left and then to the right and Leofric had the distinct impression that it was shaking its head at him.

Despite his growing unease, he laughed and said, 'Perhaps you are wise after all.'

The owl bobbed its head up and down and Leofric's laughter died in his throat as it continued to watch him struggle through the gathering forest. He turned from the bird and continued onwards.

The moon emerged from behind the clouds and a deathly chill seized his heart, the light like ice-water pouring from the skies and filling his veins with the touch of death. Shadows gathered at the edge of his vision as he felt the approach of something of terrible power through the silver-streaked mist.

Leaves snatched at his helm, branches caught on his armour and roots twisted around the legs of his steed. Though his determination was still strong, he began to question the sense of his current course. Should he continue or retreat?

The hiss of something dreadful in the depths of the rising mist told him that he had long since passed the point where such a choice could be made. Shapes moved all around him, shadowy and sinuous, like ghosts in the mist, and he heard a cackling laughter. There was no humour or warmth in it though, only malice and a spiteful glee at his predicament.

His breathing came hard and fast, his heart hammering fit to break his chest, and he shouted, 'The Lady of the Lake protects me, so if you come seeking death then come out and face me!'

No sooner had the words left his mouth than the mist retreated and a blinding radiance emerged from the trees.

Leofric cried out and shielded his eyes against the glare as its shining brilliance turned the forest from night into day.

KYARNO PUSHED EIDERATH hard, galloping into the dark, moonlit paths of the forest with terrible urgency. The foolish human was going to get himself killed and Kyarno knew that he would be the one to suffer for Leofric's stupidity. The snow was falling in earnest as he reached the edge of Coeth-Mara and though he barely felt the cold, he shivered in fearful anticipation.

He plunged headlong into the trees, taking the secret ways that only the Asrai knew of, travelling in a manner beyond the purely physical. Eiderath's speed was great, the horse having been raised from a foal for a swiftness and agility that no thick-limbed human beast could ever match, but Kyarno only hoped that he could reach the human in time.

Morvhen had come to him, breathless and afraid, and as he sought to discover the source of her distress, he had felt the ancient soul of Athel Loren rise up somewhere deep within the forest.

She had told him what had passed between her and the human and unless Kyarno reached him soon, the forest would deal with him as it dealt with all intruders.

'Come, my friend,' he yelled to Eiderath as they rode. 'Tonight I need you to fly as never before!'

* * *

LEOFRIC SQUINTED THROUGH the halo of white light, seeing a shimmering figure emerge from the trees, and he raised his sword. The growing nimbus of light that surrounded the approaching figure began to dim and where Leofric expected to see more of the hag creatures of branch and tree, he instead saw something far more astonishing.

Beauteous and divine, a woman of unearthly grace stood revealed in the new sunlight, unseen winds swirling around her and rippling her pale green robes. Artists would weep to see her face, knowing that they could never capture such beauty, and her eyes pierced Leofric with their kindness and wisdom. Her body shone with an inner radiance, like captured moonlight, and her arms reached out to him, trailing streamers of glittering stardust.

Leofric wept to see such splendour and felt his sword tumble from his hand, the very thought of raising arms against this goddess abhorrent to him. Helene's favour trailed from the hilt of the falling sword, blue and stark against the brilliant glow of this wonderful apparition.

'My Lady...' he whispered, his soul crying out with the rapture of this vision before him. She smiled and his heart sang with joy to be blessed so.

Leofric dismounted and dropped to his knees, clasping his hands to his breast and averting his eyes. Magical zephyrs spun her robes around her, billowing around her back like pale, gossamer wings.

Leofric...

He raised his gaze to the Lady of the Lake, for it could surely be none other, and cried out in wonder at her giving voice to his name. Leofric struggled to find words to say, but who could ever express what it was to be in the presence of a goddess?

Every knight of Bretonnia longed and dreamed for this, to be judged virtuous and valorous enough to be granted a vision of the Lady of the Lake. That such a vision should come to him here, in this place of magic and terror, was surely a sign that he had earned her favour.

Whither goest thou?

Though he was loath to defile such a divine moment with his own crude words, Leofric said, 'I return to your lands, my Lady. To your service and to my son and heir.'

You would abandon me so soon?

'No! Never!' cried Leofric.

Then why do you leave this place?

Confused, Leofric stared into the liquid pools of the Lady's eyes, awed by the power and compassion he saw there and feeling all the hurt and sorrow of the last few days rise up inside him in an unstoppable wave.

'My wife is dead!' he cried. 'This place took her from me and now I am lost!'

Leofric fell forwards onto his elbows in the snow, weeping as the full force of his grief poured from him in great, wracking sobs. The light of the Lady surrounded him and he felt her healing warmth enfold him, like a mother's comfort or a lover's embrace.

No, she is not gone from you. She is with me.

Soothing, wordless song came to him and he saw Helene standing beside the Lady, smiling and with her ringleted hair caught in the same impossible winds that stirred the Lady's robes.

'Helene…' he cried, reaching out to her.

She dwells at my side and awaits the day when you will come to her.

Leofric pushed himself to his knees and watched as the vision of Helene faded, his last sight of her a wistful smile on her lips and a playful glint in her eye. Though his heart broke to see her go, he felt a great weight lift from his shoulders at the thought of her at peace with the Lady.

'Tell me what I must do,' said Leofric. 'I am yours to command.'

There was a time when the knights of Bretonnia and the folk of this realm stood together as brothers. That day must come again. You must return.

'Return? To Coeth-Mara?' asked Leofric. 'But what of my son?'

Those around him will love him and he will grow to be a fine man.

'Will I ever see him again?'

You shall, but not now. You and Helene may yet raise him to manhood.

'I don't understand, my lady... Helene and I? How is that possible?'

Time is a winding river beneath the boughs of Athel Loren, Leofric, and many things are possible here that some would think hopeless. Paths once trod may be trod again and their ends woven anew.

Leofric fought to follow the Lady's words as they echoed within his head, their beauty and meaning slipping through his grasp like water.

Times of war and blood are coming and you must be ready, Leofric.

'I will be,' he promised.

THE VERY AIR was alive with magic. Kyarno could feel it in every breath and see it in the luminescence that filled every tree with light. The song of the trees grew stronger, a rousing chorus of wondrous power that leapt from branch to branch as it spread outwards from somewhere ahead. Ghostly mists conspired to mislead and befuddle him, but Kyarno had ridden the wilder parts of the forest for decades – the groves of the dark fey and the chasm glades of Beithir-Seun – and was too clever to be taken in by such petty diversions.

Eiderath was as surefooted as ever, weaving in and out of the close-pressed trees like liquid, with barely a motion from him. Like all riders in Lord Aldaeld's kindred of Glade Riders, Kyarno had a bond with his steed nurtured from birth, and rider and mount were in perfect synchrony.

There was power afoot in the forest this night and Leofric was riding blindly into it. This was no orc-infested wood: this was Athel Loren and a thousand times more dangerous.

Apparitions moved in the mist, the cackling faces of crones and thorn-clawed harridans of winter, but Kyarno ignored them all, riding towards a brilliant glow and potent sense of magic that filled the forest ahead.

'This human will be the death of me,' he whispered as the full force of the magic rushed towards him. His skin prickled and he felt the power of Athel Loren reach deep inside him, its warmth and love coursing through his veins like an elixir.

Kyarno gasped as the power sought out all his hurts and pain, soothing them and filling him with peace. He whispered to Eiderath and the horse pulled up, stamping the ground and wishing to be at the gallop again.

The light from ahead was eclipsed as a rider emerged from the glow and Kyarno cried out as it began to fade, the wonderful light retreating into the depths of the forest. He wanted to follow, to bathe in its radiance again, but a warning voice in his head told him that such would not be permitted.

He looked up at the rider, amazed to see Leofric alive and well.

Better than that in fact. The glow that had bathed the forest in its light seemed to have left some lingering radiance on the human, his flesh and armour rippled with luminescence and elven magic. Leofric's armour shone like new and his face was alight with purpose and life.

'What happened?' managed Kyarno.

'The Lady came to me,' said Leofric, his voice awed and humbled.

'She came to you?' he asked as the knight rode past him, amazed that she would deign to take an interest in the fate of one human.

'Yes.'

'Where are you going?' asked Kyarno, turning his horse and following.

'Back to Coeth-Mara.'

'Why? I thought you wanted to leave?'

'I will leave, Kyarno, but the Lady has charged me with a quest and I am sworn to its completion.'

'A quest?' asked Kyarno. 'What quest?'

Leofric smiled and said, 'To save Athel Loren.'

CHAPTER ELEVEN

WINTER REACHED ITS zenith the following morning, layering the forest in a crisp white blanket and dropping the temperature quicker than Leofric could ever remember. Snow lay thick on the ground, snapping branches from the trees with its weight and robbing the forest of its life and vitality.

But what the forest lost in life, it gained in magical beauty. Long spears of ice drooped from the branched archways, glittering in the cold sun like vast chandeliers, and snowflakes glimmered and shone like shimmering rose petals as they floated through the air. Coeth-Mara still breathed with life, but it was a still, silent life as its inhabitants awaited the first breath of spring.

The elven halls became a new home to Leofric, this dwelling of branch and leaf never cold despite the biting chill of winter beyond its confines. Whether magic or his ever-present spites kept it warm, he didn't know, but each passing day made him feel more comfortable.

Though few of the elven halls' inhabitants spoke to him, he could sense a lessening of the hostility towards him as word spread of his encounter in the woods. How the elves of the forest could understand the rapture of the Lady of the Lake was beyond Leofric's comprehension, but it was further proof that the course he had chosen was the correct one.

Weeks of winter passed, with Leofric and Kyarno often riding out into the silent forest to explore the twisting paths that lay hidden beyond the trees. Such ventures beneath the icy, snow-wreathed boughs of Athel Loren further thawed their dealings with one another, as though the shared experience in the forest that night had allowed human and elf to find some common ground, though the hostility that had characterised their previous meetings had not entirely vanished.

This was brought home to Leofric one afternoon when Kyarno had offered to teach him how to use a bow.

'No, Kyarno,' Leofric said. 'Such a weapon is fit only for peasants and those of low birth. As a warrior who follows the rules of honour I cannot countenance using such a weapon for battle.'

Leofric had seen the anger in Kyarno's face and though he now regretted his harsh words, he could not change his belief. A hurled weapon had slain Gilles le Breton, first king of Bretonnia, and, since that day, no knight had ever loosed an arrow or hurled a spear in battle.

Sometimes Morvhen would join them, chaperoned always by the Hound of Winter, and Leofric found himself looking forward to their arrival, as it invariably meant that Tiphaine and some of her handmaids would be present.

Though they never spoke, Leofric would sometimes catch Tiphaine stealing a glance towards him, and though he often wished to converse with her, he felt it would somehow sully their courtly relationship were he to thank her for the gift he was sure had come from her.

Upon waking one morning, Leofric had found fresh clothes awaiting him as he always did, but atop them was an exquisitely fashioned quilted jerkin of tan leather and silky fabric, together with soft buckskin hose. Twisting patterns of leaves and thorns were embroidered along the jerkin's sleeves and a rearing unicorn was picked out in gold thread above the heart. The garments were extraordinary, comfortable and warm, and fitted him better than anything he had ever worn before.

He had worn the jerkin beneath his armour and it had felt as natural as any armour ever had, the links of his mail shirt soft against his skin instead of biting into his flesh. He had said nothing, but Tiphaine smiled slyly when she had seen him wear it and he resolved to do her honour by wearing her gift in whatever battles were yet to come.

KYARNO RAN A hand through his long hair, the beads and jewels woven there jingling as he walked below the branches that twisted above him and marked the entrance to Lord Aldaeld's halls. The Eternal Guard stood to attention further down the leaf-strewn nave of the glittering hall. The spell-sung walls rippled with inner life and movement and Kyarno could feel the magic of the spites moving beneath the surface.

He ignored them and the sculptures of wood they formed as they played, moving through the curving paths of the inner halls towards his destination. Dressed in his finest attire, a soft green tunic embroidered with silver thread and woven with intricate patterns of leaf and tree, he hoped he looked less like Kyarno the troublemaker and more like Kyarno the peacemaker.

He sensed the stares of the Eternal Guard and those who served Lord Aldaeld upon him, their wary eyes ever vigilant for him causing some mischief. He felt his anger growing with every suspicious glance that came his way and fought to control it, casting his mind back to the divine presence he had witnessed in the forest.

Though he knew what it was he had seen, that knowledge made it no less miraculous and he held to the peace and love he had felt at that moment, calming his simmering emotions with the memory.

He saw Cairbre across the hall, but kept his head down and walked on, not yet ready to face his uncle and the issues they had between them. Until he understood more about himself and the newly unlocked feelings within him, he knew that his anger would only get the better of him, and he didn't want that.

Kyarno found who he was looking for in a snowy glade, open to the skies and utterly silent, no sounds of bird or beast to disturb the peaceful solitude. A lone horseman galloped around the circumference of the glade, bare-chested and with an unsheathed sword.

Tarean Stormcrow swung from the back of his horse and slashed his sword at an imaginary enemy before pulling himself back up and bounding smoothly to stand on the beast's back. He drew another blade and threw himself forward in a twisting pirouette, his swords flashing left and right like silver darts. The golden-haired elf landed lightly on the back of his steed, directing it in a zigzag course through the glade with gentle pressure of his knees.

Kyarno let Tarean finish his basic exercises, watching the consummate ease with which elf and steed worked together. Tarean Stormcrow was a fine rider, though Kyarno knew that in a kindred of Glade Riders, there were others of much greater skill.

'You are leaning too far to your left, Tarean Stormcrow,' called out Kyarno as Lord Aldaeld's herald finished his exercises. 'A right-handed enemy with a longer reach would kill you first.'

Tarean leapt lightly from his horse, a light sheen of sweat coating his lean, tattooed body, and sheathed his twin swords. He nodded in recognition as he saw who observed him, and pulled his hair back to settle his circlet upon his brow as Kyarno walked towards him.

'Thank you for the advice, Kyarno, I will remember it.'

'Your next battle would have reminded you soon enough.'

Tarean nodded, sensing that Kyarno was not here to argue or berate him for some real or imagined slight, and slapped his shoulder, saying, 'To what do I owe the pleasure of this visit, my friend? You didn't just come here to advise me on my swordplay.'

'You do not miss anything, Tarean, do you?'

'You are not hard to read, my friend.'

Kyarno smiled weakly. 'I suppose not. But you're right, I did come here for more than that, though Isha knows you need it,' he said, reaching up to pat the bay gelding Tarean had been riding. The beast was magnificent, easily one of the finest steeds of the Éadaoin kinband, its flaxen coat smooth and shining. 'I came to apologise to you, Tarean.'

'Apologise to me?' said Tarean, wiping the sweat from his face with a fine cloth.

'Yes,' nodded Kyarno. 'You once said that you offered me friendship. I threw it back in your face, and for that I am sorry.'

'No apology is necessary, my friend,' said Tarean, offering his hand to Kyarno.

'Does your offer still stand?'

Tarean nodded. 'Of course it does, Kyarno. I do not make such offers just to retract them later.'

'Good,' replied Kyarno and reached out to grip Tarean's hand. 'I think that you and I could be friends and am willing to see if such a thing is possible.'

Tarean walked to a tree where his overshirt hung and pulled it over his head, settling it over his shoulders and straightening his sword belt.

'I am glad you think so, Kyarno, but tell me, what brought about this change of heart?'

'I'm not sure,' admitted Kyarno, unwilling yet to share what had happened in the forest. 'I think that I carried a great bitterness and it poisoned me to those who loved me. I shut myself off from them and my heart became like one of the humans' hateful fortresses of stone.'

Kyarno paced as he spoke, having to force every word and finding each one both difficult and cathartic to say.

'When my parents were killed... I... I...'

'You blamed Cairbre,' finished Tarean. 'I know. He rescued you from the beastmen attack and carried you to safety. You blamed him for not reaching you in time to save your parents.'

'No,' said Kyarno, shaking his head. 'That's not it.'

'No?'

'No,' repeated Kyarno. 'I blamed him for not let me die with them.'

Tarean said nothing, plainly surprised at his admission, but the well was undammed now and Kyarno's words would not stop.

'But then I learned that it wasn't his fault that he hadn't got to us in time. It was Naieth. She was to blame.'

'Why do you think this?'

'Cairbre told me years later that she had come to Lord Aldaeld with a vision of beastmen raiding the Meadow Glades in the south. Cairbre's Eternal Guard and the Waywatchers had been sent to destroy them.'

'I remember now,' whispered Tarean. 'But she was wrong, wasn't she? They were not in the Meadow Glades at all.'

'No, they were not,' said Kyarno. 'The creatures of Chaos had penetrated deep into Athel Loren and came upon the halls of my father. They came with burning brands and bloody axes and killed everyone they found. My mother, my father and my sisters… all of them died that day.'

Tarean laid his hand on Kyarno's arm, and he could feel the pain of those memories rise up in a suffocating wave. 'I was just a child, but I remember it all, the flames, the fear and the blood… so much blood. I can see it even now, clear as a winter's morning. Cairbre must have heard the forest cry out in anger or felt his brother's fear for his kin, I don't know, but he and the Eternal Guard swiftly travelled the secret paths of the forest and destroyed the monsters. But it was too late, I was the only one left alive.'

The two elves sat in silence for some time, Kyarno lost in the pain of a time long passed and Tarean sitting patiently with a fellow elf and letting him speak in his own time.

'Cairbre saved you,' said Tarean at last. 'You should be thankful for that.'

'I know,' agreed Kyarno, 'but I was young and foolish. I screamed and cursed him for not coming sooner, for deserting his kin and letting them die. Isha alone knows why I said the things I did, for they must have cut him deeply. But I did say them and when I finally accepted that it wasn't even his fault, it was too late, we had erected impenetrable walls between us.'

'No wall is impenetrable, Kyarno,' said Tarean. 'Remember that.'

THE BREATH OF the gods blew strong, the power of the shaman growing with each passing heartbeat. The presence of the Shadow-Gave in the mountains aided its magic, empowering the shaman as one chosen by the Dark Gods. The rain continued to fall around it, black and noxious, and the ground turned to a stinking quagmire beneath its hoofs.

The wind blew cold and hard, flapping the tattered and rotted robes around its twisted and hunched body of shaggy fur. Its horns dripped with black moisture and its magically attuned eyes were filled with the crackling lines of magic that flared from the waystone before it.

The lethal wall of thorn and branch still stood, though the shaman could see the tips of the furthest growths were blackened and twisted, dying as the power of Chaos touched it. Time had ceased to have meaning for the herd, days and nights blurring into one continual span, though the shaman was dimly aware of enemy magic at work, some unknown force sweeping them up in its wake. Snow froze them, rain lashed them and the sun baked the mud on their backs to hard clay, all within the space of a passing of the sun.

But for each faerie trick unleashed by the forest, the shaman had an answer, his greater power causing black veins of necrotic energy to leech their way up the length of the waystone. The enchantments woven into the living rock were strong, forged when the world was young, but the breath of the gods was eternal and unyielding.

The shaman's staff crackled with energy, bruised arcs of light flaring from its gnarled tip and the stink of raw, dangerous magic.

The Beastlord paced like a caged thing, its impatience to be about its bloody work palpable and the shaman knew that if it did not bring the waystone down soon, then its life was forfeit.

Soon the waystone's magic would be all but spent and it would fall, unable to bend the dark forest around it to its will.

And then the Beastlord's herd would hunt.

As THE WINTER locked Coeth-Mara in its enveloping crystalline grip, the days passed with funereal slowness, each short span of daylight gratefully seized by the inhabitants of Lord Aldaeld's halls. Leofric spent his days riding into the forest with Kyarno and learning more of the culture he now found himself immersed in.

Though he and Kyarno often spoke of the Asrai, their history and their society, he never felt any real connection to them, as though there was a barrier between man and elf that no amount of conversation could ever erode. He and Kyarno, and, to a lesser extent, Morvhen, had become friendly enough, but Leofric would not count them as friends. In every word that passed

between them, he always sensed a faint air of condescension, as though the elves were somehow lessening
themselves by talking to him.

Of Naieth he saw almost nothing, save for a chance
encounter at the spite-wrought sculpture pools where
Leofric performed his ablutions each morning. The day
was crisp and clear, though not cold, and Leofric had
taken off the jerkin Tiphaine had fashioned for him and
was in the process of trying to shave when Naieth had
silently come up behind him. The sudden appearance
of her reflection behind him made him jump and his
razor nicked his cheek.

A drop of blood fell into the pool and the water
instantly foamed as though boiling, a trio of water-
formed tendrils leaping up from the water, a dazzling
core of light in each one. Leofric dropped his razor and
stumbled back from the pool as the tendrils angrily
reached for him.

Before they could touch him, his own spites sped forward and interposed themselves between the water
spites, shifting to become angry red balls of light with
fanged mouths and gleaming stag horns of light. Both
groups of spites hissed and spat at one another until
Naieth's lyrical elven tones sang out and the three tendrils of water retreated back into the pool, mollified by
whatever she had said.

'Greetings, Leofric,' said Naieth. 'You are well?'

'Well enough,' nodded Leofric, rubbing his cheek
where his blade had cut his skin. 'What happened there?'

'The water spites don't like human blood,' explained
Naieth, sitting on the edge of the pool and waving to
something high in the snowy treetops. 'They feel it is
impure and should not be mixed with the waters of
Athel Loren.'

'That suits me, I would prefer for my blood not to be shed,' said Leofric as a familiar looking, grey-feathered owl dropped from the trees and landed on Naieth's shoulder. It hooted once and bobbed its head in Leofric's direction.

'Is that your owl?' asked Leofric, recovering his razor and warily rinsing his face in the pool.

'Yes, his name is Othu.'

'I saw him,' said Leofric. 'In the forest.'

The owl hooted again and made a sound that Leofric could only interpret as laughter.

'Indeed you did,' smiled Naieth. 'Othu asks if you have recovered from your journey?'

Leofric nodded as he gathered up the rest of his clothes, pulling his dark hair back and tying it at the base of his neck with a leather cord. He was becoming unkempt here without his servants to keep him presentable and he knew his appearance was becoming closer to the elves than a knight of Bretonnia.

'Tell him I have, thank you very much.'

'Tell him yourself, he is right here.'

Leofric looked at the owl and said, 'I feel foolish talking to an owl.'

'Then imagine how *he* feels,' sniffed Naieth, rising from the pool and walking away. As she departed, the owl turned its head and shifted its feathers in a manner that looked for all the world like a weary shrug.

Gathering up his things, Leofric left the pool and made his way back through the leafy paths and hollows of Coeth-Mara, intending to change into his armour and practise his swordplay. He might be far from home, but that was no excuse to let his skills become rusty.

As he made his way through the silent forest of ice, he felt he might as well be walking alone, such was his sense of peaceful solitude and tranquillity. His heart still ached to see his son again and he missed Helene's soft company, but each day the hurt was lessened and his will to serve the quest entrusted to him by the Lady of the Lake grew stronger.

He smiled as he again pictured the Lady's wondrous, aquiline features, her hair of gold and overwhelming powers of healing and renewal. Such visions were a thing of beauty and rarity and he wanted to remember every detail flawlessly.

So caught up in his reverie was he that he didn't hear the first shrill yell as it echoed through the forest. It took a second, high-pitched shriek to intrude on Leofric's senses before he realised that he was not alone any more.

Fast-moving figures spun from the trees around him, leaping from branch to branch and corkscrewing madly through the air. Elves, that much was obvious, but these were of a kind he had not seen before. How many there were, he couldn't say, their speed was too great to make any kind of guess.

They circled him with whooping yells and bared blades, and as the noose closed tighter about him, Leofric dropped his towel and shaving razor and gripped the hilt of his sword. One of the figures stopped moving long enough for him to take a proper look at his new companions.

The elf was tall and slender-limbed, though the taut, corded muscles of his chest, stomach and arms belied his frailty. Despite the snow and ice that lay over the forest, the elf was nearly naked, a thin loincloth and golden torques on his upper arms the only concession to attire. His body was covered almost entirely in tattoos, weaving thorns and briars, and a snarling blood-red wolf decorated his chest.

His hair was a wild coxcomb of red, raised in jagged points, and his face was as tattooed as his body, with looping spirals of thorns decorating each cheek and sharpened jawbones and teeth adorning the skin around his own jaw. The elf wore a thin necklace of gold and bronze, his wild eyes alight with savage mischief.

Leofric tore his gaze from this barbaric-looking elf as the others closed in, their wild cries and yells disorientating as they leapt and bounded around him.

Each one carried twin blades and their swords snaked around their bodies like liquid trails of silver, their every movement lithe and supple. One leapt from the ground and seemed to run up the side of a mighty oak before bounding to perch, bird-like, atop a thin branch that was surely too slender to bear his weight. Another spun through the air, her swords like striking snakes as they danced and she pirouetted to land before him with her blades aimed at his heart.

Each one performed impossible feats of acrobatics, leaping and twisting through the air in defiance of gravity before landing in aggressive stances around him, not one looking even slightly out of breath.

Leofric looked beyond the warlike elves, but saw no one that might come to his aid anywhere near. The elf who had stopped moving first spat something in elvish and the others took a perfectly choreographed step towards him, their swords cutting the air with a slow, purposeful grace. The leader, if such he was, looked at him with naked hostility, his perfect features curled in contempt and disgust. As he approached, Leofric saw that the tattoo of the wolf on his chest rippled with life, its fangs baring and its eyes narrowing in feral anticipation.

Looking at the tattoo he realised the identity of the elf he stood before.

'The Red Wolf...' said Leofric.

Quicker than he would have believed anyone could move, even an elf, a tattooed hand snatched out and gripped his throat, the tip of a long knife an inch from his eye.

'You dare speak of Cu-Sith?' hissed the elf. 'Cu-Sith should kill you now. Loec? What say you, shall Cu-Sith kill him?'

'No!' gagged Leofric, hoping whichever of these elves was Loec could hear him.

'Let us perform the Dance of a Hundred Wounds,' said another of the elves as they slowly began circling Leofric like stalking cats. A sword slashed out, cutting a lock of hair from Leofric's head.

'No, the Masque of the Red Rain,' said another, leaping into the air and stabbing his swords either side of Leofric's head, a fingerbreadth from his ears.

'The Tarantella of the Wailing Death!' cried a third, her blades flicking out and kissing the underside of his jaw. Leofric's heart pounded in fear of these wild elves, fighting to keep his panic in check as more blades licked out and wove a tapestry of silver steel around him. He knew that if he moved so much as a muscle he was a dead man, though the Red Wolf was clearly untroubled by the storm of blades flashing around them.

'Enough!' said the Red Wolf, cocking his head to one side. 'Loec tells Cu-Sith that we need something special for this one!'

Leofric took a great, gulping breath of air as the iron grip around his throat was released and the Red Wolf took a step back. With the flashing blades no longer weaving around him, Leofric felt his heartbeat begin to slow, and he watched as the elves began circling him again. Each one was practically naked, but for golden torques and thin harnesses of leather. Their skin was daubed with chalk and lime and heavily painted with vivid dyes, and they wore their resin-stiffened hair in wild, elaborate styles. They watched him with predatory eyes, but moved like the most graceful dancers and Leofric realised he looked upon the Red Wolf's troupe of wardancers.

'I am a guest of Lord Aldaeld,' said Leofric, massaging his bruised throat.

The Red Wolf lunged forward, baring his teeth like the wolf on his chest. 'You think Cu-Sith doesn't know that? Cu-Sith knows everything Loec does!'

'Loec...' said Leofric, now remembering Kyarno mentioning the name. 'Wait, isn't he one of your gods?'

'That he is,' nodded the Red Wolf, reaching up to dab his finger in the blood on Leofric's cheek. 'And a close friend of Cu-Sith, human.'

'I see,' nodded Leofric.

'Kill him and garland the trees with his entrails!' shouted one of the wardancers.

'No, present them to Lord Aldaeld!'

'Silence!' shouted the Red Wolf, somersaulting backwards onto the bough above Leofric. 'Cu-Sith likes this one. Didn't flinch during the sword dance. Sensible. Might keep him as a pet.'

'Pet! Pet! Pet!' chanted the circling wardancers.

'Are you Cu-Sith?' asked Leofric, as the Red Wolf swung from the branch to land lightly in a crouch before him. The leader of the wardancers nodded, rolling forwards and twirling a pair of swords as he rose to his feet with a grace no human dancer could ever hope to match.

'Cu-Sith heard that a human was kept in Lord Aldaeld's halls, but did not believe it. Now Cu-Sith sees him and wonders why he is not dead,' said the war-dancer, the eyes of his wolf tattoo following Leofric as Cu-Sith circled him in the opposite direction to his troupe.

'Tell me, human, why are you not dead and why should Cu-Sith not make it so?'

Leofric tried to stay calm as the snarling, hissing elf stopped behind him, sniffing his neck and shoulders like a wild animal.

'I… I was spared from the forest spirits by Naieth,' said Leofric.

'The prophetess?'

'Yes, yes, the prophetess.'

Cu-Sith circled back around, leaning in close and turning Leofric's head with the flat of his blade. 'She wants you alive? Why?'

'I don't know for certain,' said Leofric, the words tumbling from him in a frantic rush. 'She says there are times of war coming and that I am to fight alongside the elves of Athel Loren.'

'You?' spat Cu-Sith, spinning his blades and sheathing them before catching another pair hurled towards him without his asking. 'Cu-Sith does not believe you. What about you, Loec?'

The leader of the wardancers closed his eyes and cocked his head to one side, as though listening to a voice only he could hear. The other wardancers looked on in awe as their leader nodded and laughed to himself at some unheard jest. Suddenly Cu-Sith's eyes snapped open and he brought his new swords up in a cross-wise slash, each blade slicing the skin of Leofric's cheeks.

Leofric flinched from the thin cuts, more in surprise than pain, as Cu-Sith spoke again. 'Loec says for Cu-Sith to let you go, but you are marked now, human. Cu-Sith's pet you are now!'

The wardancers laughed and spun faster and faster around him, peeling off one by one and disappearing into the forest in bounding somersaults and incredible leaps from tree to tree.

The Red Wolf remained before him for a second longer before giving out a manic laugh and flipping up into the high branches above. Leofric tried to follow his progress as he leapt higher and higher into the branches, but was forced to look away as dislodged powdery snow fell into his eyes.

And when he looked again, Cu-Sith was nowhere to be seen.

LEOFRIC MADE HIS way back down into the more populated halls of Coeth-Mara, shaken to the core by his brush with the wardancers. Cu-Sith had terrified him with his fearsome display of lunacy; the leader of the wardancers clearly insane to believe that he spoke directly to a god.

There had been a wild madness to the Red Wolf and its sheer unpredictability scared him more than anything else. Who knew what such an individual might do?

As he descended into Coeth-Mara, he dabbed the cuts on his cheeks, wondering if he actually was Cu-Sith's pet in the eyes of the elves, or whether it was just another indication of his madness.

Now Leofric understood the wariness and unease he had sensed when Tarean Stormcrow had first mentioned the leader of the wardancers.

Leofric shivered, feeling a tremor of unease pass through the boughs and branches around him and a sudden chill pierced him. He looked around him for the source of his unease, but could see nothing specific.

Elves moved through the snow-wreathed paths of Coeth-Mara, but there was an urgency to their movements now, a suspicious fear in their glances as they retreated to their halls.

Ahead, Leofric could see a group of riders coming towards him and stood aside as the Lord of Coeth-Mara and his daughter rode past, accompanied by Tarean Stormcrow, Naieth, the Hound of Winter and a dozen of his warriors. Both Aldaeld and Morvhen were regal and magnificent in pale robes of cream silk and embroidered gold. Lord Aldaeld wore a crown of antlers and carried his green-hilted longsword belted at his side, while Morvhen was unarmed.

Neither gave him a second glance as they passed.

Naieth gave him the briefest of acknowledgements, her robes of gold shining in the morning sun and her staff of woven branches shimmering with dew. Tarean Stormcrow, dressed in an elaborate tunic of sky blue silk and silver, and carrying a long, hardwood spear, peeled away from the procession to stop before Leofric.

'What happened to you?' he asked, noticing the cuts on his face.

Leofric glanced over his shoulder and said, 'I met the Red Wolf.'

'Cu-Sith!' hissed Tarean. 'You encountered his war-dancers?'

'Yes,' nodded Leofric. 'It was… a memorably frightening experience.'

'I should imagine it was,' agreed Tarean. 'I am surprised he let you live. Cu-Sith has no love for those of your race.'

'So I saw,' said Leofric, dabbing at the cuts once more.

'Be that as it may, Leofric, you must return to your chambers and prepare yourself. Clean the blood from your face, put on your finest clothes, polish your armour then await my summons.'

'Why? What is happening?'

Tarean nodded in the direction of the group of Lord Aldaeld's riders as they disappeared into the trees.

'The Laithu kinband has arrived for the Winter Feast,' he said.

CHAPTER TWELVE

Two score of them there were. Each was richly attired, outlandishly so, thought Caelas Shadowfoot as he watched the procession of riders from his vantage point in the heights of a hoary old willow tree. The easily recognisable figure of Valas Laithu rode at the head of the column, his cloak of red a bad omen in these times of trouble, knew Caelas.

A human in Coeth-Mara and the Red Wolf attending the Winter Feast. No good could come of it. Where the Red Wolf danced, trouble followed.

He watched Valas turn to say something to a young, sharp-featured elf beside him, the youth nodding curtly, as though he had heard these words many times before. Caelas recognised the stripling as Sirda, son of Valas, and felt a shiver travel up his spine that had nothing to do with the frost that coated the gnarled bark of the tree he clung to.

Both Valas and his offspring were known to the Éadaoin kinband, as was their reputation for deviousness and cruelty. Where other kinbands might kill intruders to Athel Loren or send them back the way they had come in equal measure, the Laithu kinband would see all such trespassers dead, their bones left at the forest's edge as a grim warning to others.

Even from hundreds of feet up, Caelas could see the cruel lines on Valas Laithu's pale face and did not envy Lord Aldaeld the coming gathering. Sirda was no better, having inherited the worst of his father's traits as well as developing some bad ones of his own.

Caelas edged around the bole of the tree, leaning out onto a snow-covered branch and signalling that the Laithu kinband drew near to one of the Éadaoin kinband's waywatchers nearer to Coeth-Mara. Though, truth be told, none needed warning, as the riders below had made no attempt to disguise their approach. A single scout had travelled before them, Caelas and his waywatchers having tracked him for the past week, oft times passing within a few paces of his position to test his skills – but not once had the Laithu scout observed them.

Caelas was disappointed in the lack of caution shown by the Laithu kinband. Everything he had heard of them had led him to believe they were warriors of skill and cunning, though what he had seen over the last week did not bear such a reputation out. He and his waywatchers could have ambushed the Laithu kinband a dozen times or more, slaughtering them in a hail of arrows before their prey had even known they were there.

But such were not their orders. These visitors to Coeth-Mara were to be allowed to approach unmolested. As he watched them draw away from him in the direction of Lord Aldaeld's halls, Caelas briefly considered following them and returning to the place where he had been born. It had been many years since he had seen his kin, but the thought of being amongst others sat uncomfortably with him.

He loved his kin and kinband, but only here, in the magnificent wilds of the forest, did he feel truly at home. Indeed, it had been months since he had laid eyes on any of his fellow waywatchers, content to read their signs in the wild and communicate through the secret language of the forest known only to them.

Caelas ran along the tall branches of the willow and leapt across the gap between it and a white-leaved chestnut, swinging around its thin trunk and looping his way down the tree. Even before he landed, his bow was drawn and an arrow nocked as he scanned the undergrowth for signs of life. He already knew there was nothing around here for hundreds of yards that he was not already aware of, but a waywatcher did not live to be as old as Caelas by relaxing his guard.

He risked a glance around the chestnut's trunk, watching the last signs of the Laithu kinband vanish from sight. Something sat ill with him and the decades spent alone in the wilderness had taught him to trust his instincts.

Caelas ghosted from tree to tree, invisible in his grey cloak and stealthy movements, examining the trail left by the riders. He shook his head as he silently gauged the depths of their tracks, seeing that they had taken no care to cover their back trail or ride in single file to better disguise their numbers.

No, something sat ill indeed and Caelas was not one to let such things lie.

The waywatcher set off into the forest, determined to find the truth of what was going on.

'BLOOD OF KURNOUS,' whispered Lord Aldaeld as he watched Valas Laithu and his retinue come into view over the snow-covered rise ahead. 'This will be a trial indeed.'

'My lord?' said Tarean Stormcrow, adjusting his cloak and tunic so that it sat perfectly. Tarean altered his grip on the spear he held, brushing a melting snowflake from his shoulder. The rituals of elven greetings were highly formalised and were Tarean to fail in his duty as herald, the dishonour would pass to Aldaeld himself.

Aldaeld and his most trusted kin, his herald, his daughter, his champion and a dozen of his loyal Eternal Guard, had come for this rare meeting of elves from across the forest. The prophetess had insisted on accompanying him too, and while he had only grudgingly offered her the hospitality of his halls, he was glad of her presence here now. Lord Valas was known to be a dabbler in the mystic arts and Naieth's presence was, this time, a welcome one.

The tension in this leaf-strewn archway of ice and snow was palpable, none able to deny the apprehension that Lord Valas's visit had brought.

'I will be glad when this snake is far from my halls,' said Aldaeld.

'I understand, my lord, but custom demands that we make him welcome,' pointed out Tarean Stormcrow.

'I know that,' snapped Aldaeld, gripping the hilt of his sword tightly. 'It does not mean I have to like it.'

'Perhaps you should not hold your sword thusly,' suggested his daughter.

He looked down, startled that he had not even noticed he was gripping the hilt so tightly. Aldaeld smiled at his daughter and said, 'Yes, you are probably right, my dear.'

She was beautiful, thought Aldaeld, regal and every inch the daughter of an elven lord and, were circumstances different, he had hoped Morvhen would have plighted her troth to Tarean Stormcrow by now. Alas, her heart had gone to the ne'er-do-well, Kyarno, and as much as he had tried to keep her from Cairbre's nephew, his every attempt had served only to bring them closer.

Thinking of the miscreant Kyarno brought a scowl to his rugged, ancient features. His every instinct was to throw Kyarno to Valas Laithu, but both Tarean Stormcrow and the Hound of Winter had recently spoken to him of their belief that Kyarno was not yet a hopeless case. Aldaeld was still to see proof of that and this visitation by the Laithu kinband was yet another reason for Aldaeld to wish him gone from his halls.

'Do not worry, father, this will be over with soon,' promised Morvhen.

'I fear it will not be over soon enough, daughter,' said Aldaeld. 'Valas will want his pound of flesh for your lover's mischief before this is out and I only hope his foolishness does not cost us all too dearly.'

'Father–' began Morvhen.

'You should not think to defend him, Morvhen,' interrupted Aldaeld. 'He would not thank you for it and he does not deserve it. Do not think me ignorant of all that passes in my domain, daughter. I know what happened in the forest between Kyarno and the Hound of Winter before the creatures of Chaos attacked.'

Morvhen flushed and looked away and even Cairbre had the good grace to look embarrassed at Aldaeld's words. Seeing the hurt in his daughter's eyes, Aldaeld's expression softened and he reached out to touch her shoulder.

'Neither am I blind to the desires of your heart towards Kyarno, but I must put the welfare of this kinband before anyone's feelings. Even yours. Kyarno has a good soul, I see it, truly I do, but until he *learns* his place in my kinband, there is no place for him in it.'

'My lord,' said Tarean Stormcrow. 'Perhaps this is a conversation best had another time? Lord Valas approaches.'

Aldaeld kept his eyes on his daughter for a few seconds more before turning to face Lord Valas and his warriors, his stern, patrician demeanour reasserting itself once more.

Lord Valas was tall, thin and pale-skinned, even for an elf, his slender frame clad in rich robes of heavy furs and soft tan leather. The hood of his spite-rippled cloak of red leaves was pulled back and his long, dark hair was swept into a tight ponytail with a circlet of gold across his brow. His tapered ears were hung with beads of gold and his eyes were a brilliant shade of blue.

Valas nodded to Aldaeld and bowed his head a fraction. Aldaeld echoed the gesture as Tarean edged his horse forward, a precise bowstave-length away from the newcomers. His herald lifted the long spear he carried; its shaft was etched with spiral grooves and tipped with a patterned copper blade engraved with eyes that were said to seek out and defeat an enemy's blows.

'Lord Valas,' began Tarean, holding the spear by the hardwood haft and offering it to the lord of the Laithu kinband. 'Aldaeld, Lord of a Hundred Battles, bids me welcome you to Coeth-Mara and offers you this gift as a token of our kinbands' fellowship. Fashioned at Vaul's Anvil by Daith, master craftsman of the Ash Groves, it is potent with the magic of Athel Loren and was wielded in battle by the great eagle-rider Thalandor.'

Valas Laithu reached out and plucked the spear from Tarean's hand, examining the magnificent weapon without apparent interest. He nodded briefly and handed the weapon to his son, who gave the spear a much more thorough examination.

Sirda was the image of his father, saw Aldaeld, sharp-featured and without the grace of the Asrai who dwelt in harmony and balance with the forest. Sirda seemed furtive, always looking beyond the Éadaoin Eternal Guard, and Aldaeld could guess who he was looking for. The Laithu were a harsh kinband, merciless to those not their own, even other elves, and unlike his father, Sirda was armed, bearing a pair of elegant swords and a long, ornamented bow across his back.

'Lord Aldaeld's gift is most welcome,' said Valas Laithu. 'I thank him for it and bid him greetings from my kin. Will he permit us to enter his halls freely?'

Tarean Stormcrow turned back to Aldaeld and the elven lord held the moment before saying, 'I will indeed. I offer you the freedom of Coeth-Mara and bid you join my kin for the Winter Feast.'

'You honour me,' said Valas. 'Rightly is it said that even the lowest that arrive at Lord Aldaeld's hall will receive his charity.'

Aldaeld bristled at Valas's words. Obviously Valas knew of the human in Coeth-Mara and was keen to show his disapproval.

He nodded and said, 'All are welcome within my halls, even those who would normally be turned away.'

Valas smiled, though there was no warmth to it, and said, 'Happily we are all in accord here. Is that not so?'

'It is indeed,' said Tarean Stormcrow quickly. 'Lord Aldaeld has spoken of little else but your visit to his halls.'

'I'm sure,' laughed Valas and Aldaeld fought to control his temper as he saw Sirda Laithu cast secretive, lascivious glances towards Morvhen. Catching Aldaeld's eye, Sirda gave a guilty smile and returned to surveying the forest behind them.

'He is not here, Sirda,' said Aldaeld, now sure of the object of the young elf's search.

'Who?' replied Sirda, feigning ignorance.

'You know who I mean, boy. Kyarno.'

'I am not a boy,' snarled Sirda. His face flushed and he reached for his sword. His father's hand snatched out and gripped his son's wrist.

'Ah, yes, the outlaw,' said Valas, easing his son's hand from his sword hilt. 'His theft of our steeds was an act of great skill and cunning. I much desire to meet him. He still resides within your halls, Lord Aldaeld?'

'For now,' nodded Aldaeld.

'Then bid him attend the Winter Feast,' said Valas. 'I wish to meet this elf who can evade my waywatchers and steal away with our most beloved steeds.'

'Kyarno let them loose as soon as he stole them!' snapped Morvhen. 'They must have returned to their stable glades soon after.'

'Daughter!' barked Aldaeld. 'Know your place here! Be silent!'

Aldaeld could see the amusement in the faces of the Laithu kinband and knew he had to end this farce of a welcome.

'Come,' he said, turning his steed. 'The Winter Feast awaits!'

LEOFRIC THOUGHT HE had already seen the full majesty of Coeth-Mara, but as he sat in the inner halls of Lord Aldaeld, he realised that what he had seen thus far had been but a taster for this miraculous sight.

The abiding impression he would take to his grave was that of light.

Though winter had laid its velvet blanket of night upon the forest and the darkness crept back into the world almost as soon as it had left, the feast hall of Coeth-Mara was lit with dazzling brightness and colour.

'Close your mouth,' said Kyarno. 'A spite will fly in and then you'll be sorry.'

Leofric snapped his mouth shut, having not realised it had fallen open again at the awe-inspiring sight of such incredible beauty. He and Kyarno sat at a gracefully curved table that grew from the soft earthen floor of the hall, alongside laughing elves who told lyrical tales and sang heartbreakingly beautiful ballads in their wonderfully musical language.

'Sorry,' he mumbled, taking another drink of water.

The spell-sung walls were tall and majestic, twisting, looping spirals of pale branches weaving in intricate, natural patterns towards an arched ceiling of great, needle-pointed icicles. Each one was home to a spite of some sort, the ice glittering with the golden light of the creatures at play within.

Tresses of branch and flower garlanded every wall and a tall fire of dead wood burned in the centre of the hall, surrounded by tables and benches shaped from the roots of the mighty trees that enclosed Lord Aldaeld's hall.

Warmth and life filled the hall as the elves of Coeth-Mara gathered for feasting and song, perhaps a hundred souls come to make merry with their fellows. Attending to the elves of Coeth-Mara were youngsters who bore platters of meats and fruit and jugs of wine throughout the hall. None looked older than ten summers and the sight of them reminded Leofric of his own son's face once more. The boys each wore a simple tunic of pale green, upon which was embroidered a white stag, and the sight of these youths sent a pang of aching sadness through Leofric.

Through previous discourse with Kyarno, he had learned that winter was a time of sadness within Athel Loren as the forest slept away the long watches of darkness before the joyous coming of the spring.

But even amidst this time of darkness it seemed there was life and joy to be had, the darkness tempered by the sure and certain knowledge of the forest's rebirth.

Such was the purpose of the Winter Feast, a celebration of life amid death.

The scent of new blooming flowers was incongruous, but welcome, and the sense of shared kinship and love amongst Lord Aldaeld's people was contagious, even though Leofric knew he was not truly a part of this celebration.

Leofric wondered if perhaps it was that very detachment that allowed him to better see the tension lurking behind the smiling faces of the revellers, for he could sense an underlying current of wariness among Lord Aldaeld's people. Whether that wariness was due to the surly presence of the newly-arrived warriors of the Laithu kinband or Cu-Sith and his prowling wardancers, who stalked through the hall like predatory cats, Leofric did not know, but he had felt it the moment he had entered.

Leofric wasn't even sure why he was here, Tarean having sent for him as the pale light of afternoon turned to the soft purple of dusk. True to his word, Leofric had cleaned himself up as best he could – though his beard and hair were beginning to get the better of him – put on Tiphaine's jerkin and hose, polished his armour and awaited his summons. More used to the stiff formality of the court feasts at Quenelles, Leofric had been pleasantly surprised by the informality he saw here.

Though even in such apparent informality he saw there was a hierarchy at work. Seated at the far end of the hall, on a raised dais of pale wood, were Lord Aldaeld and his closest kin. Naieth and Morvhen sat beside the lord of Coeth-Mara, together with Tarean Stormcrow, while behind them stood the warriors of the Eternal Guard.

'What manner of weapon does Cairbre wield?' asked Leofric as he watched the Hound of Winter complete another circuit of the hall with his long twin-bladed spear held beside him.

'It is called a *Saearath*, which means "spear-stave" in your tongue,' explained Kyarno, procuring himself a plate of aoilym fruit and another jug of wine, 'though the weapon Cairbre carries is unique. He is the bearer of the Blades of Midnight.'

'Unique? Is it magical?'

'It is said so,' nodded Kyarno, 'but none but the bearer may know its powers.'

'Why is that?'

'I don't know,' shrugged Kyarno, obviously unwilling to be drawn further. Leofric decided to change the subject and looked over to the end of the hall at the guests of Lord Aldaeld, saying, 'Is that the leader of the Laithu kinband with Lord Aldaeld? He looks quite different from the elves I have seen in Coeth-Mara.'

'As well he ought,' nodded Kyarno, taking a bite from the red-skinned fruit, the bittersweet aroma filling the air and making Leofric's mouth water. He longed to taste the strange fruit, but the dire consequences that would result from partaking of magical faerie food and wine had been drummed into him from boyhood.

He shook his head clear of the desire to eat the elven fruit as Kyarno spoke again of the Laithu kinband. 'They hail from the Vaults of Winter, a gloomy place of permanent darkness and cold, where the season never changes and the glow of the moons is the only light to touch their skins.'

'That sounds like a terrible place,' said Leofric. 'Why do they stay there?'

'It is their home,' replied Kyarno, as though the answer should be obvious. 'In your tongue, the name Laithu means Moonblade, and it is said they work their finest enchantments with the light of the stars.'

'And why are they here?'

'Ah...' said Kyarno, wiping the aoilym fruit's juice from his chin and taking a long drink of wine from the jug. 'That might have something to do with me...'

'What do you mean?'

'During the summer I crept into their stable glades and took some of their steeds.'

'You stole from them?'

'Only for a while,' protested Kyarno. 'I let the horses go once I was clear of their domain. The steeds would have returned to the stable glades soon after.'

'If you let them go then why did you steal them in the first place?' asked Leofric.

'It was a bit of harmless fun,' sighed Kyarno. 'Isha's tears, you are starting to sound like Cairbre! I took them to show that I could. Haven't you ever tried something impossible just to prove that it could be done?'

Leofric started to shake his head, then stopped as a memory surfaced. Kyarno saw his realisation and said, 'You have, haven't you? Come on, tell me of it.'

'No, it's not the same.'

'Come on, tell me!' laughed Kyarno, relishing Leofric's discomfort and drinking more wine.

Leofric spread his hands and said, 'All right, all right. You have to understand though, that I was but a knight errant at the time and young and foolish.'

'You're stalling. Come on, tell me what you did,' urged Kyarno.

'Very well,' said Leofric. 'To be worthy of the chance to court Helene, I rashly challenged Duke Chilfroy of Artois to a joust on the tilting fields of Couronne. He was the best and bravest knight in Bretonnia, skilled beyond all others with a lance, and no man had ever unhorsed him. We faced each other down the length of the field and though I was shaking fit to soil my armour, I knew... somehow I just knew that I could best him.'

'How?'

'I don't know, I just knew,' shrugged Leofric. 'It was as though the Lady had whispered it as a certainty in my ear.'

'And did you beat him?' asked Kyarno, finishing the last of the wine.

'Yes,' nodded Leofric proudly. 'My lance took him clean in the centre of his chest and sent him flying from the back of his horse. I do not think I have ever had as sweet a memory as that.'

'You see?' said Kyarno, putting down the empty wine jug and rising unsteadily to his feet. 'Don't pretend you don't understand what I did. It's the urge to achieve what can't be achieved, the drive to succeed in the impossible task that makes us feel really alive! You felt it as you challenged the knight and I felt it when I stole the Laithu kinband's steeds. And I'd do it again!'

'Really? Even after the trouble it's caused you?'

'Are you saying you wouldn't challenge that knight again?'

Leofric shook his head. 'I am older and wiser now, Kyarno. I have become a knight of the realm and I recognise the difference between valour and impetuosity.'

'That's no answer!' cried Kyarno. 'And anyway, I need some more wine.'

Kyarno's voice was getting louder and louder, and Leofric could see he was attracting some unwelcome stares, but before he could say anything, Kyarno set off in the direction of the serving tables in search of fresh wine.

Leofric let him go, watching the smooth grace of the wardancers as they circled the tables and firepit with unhurried dances. The inhabitants of Coeth-Mara were deferential to the painted elves, but Leofric could see that none were entirely comfortable being near them. Cu-Sith himself leapt and tumbled through the high arches of the hall, moving as though free of the constraints of gravity.

Leofric remembered the performance of the companion of the troubadour, Tristran, when he had performed for Duke Tancred in Quenelles, dazzling the assembled court with his wonderful acrobatics and somersaulting. But even the most graceful human acrobats moved like a pregnant sow when compared to the savage grace of Cu-Sith.

He reached for the water jug, only to discover it was empty. He was about to search for more when a small voice beside Leofric asked, 'Would my lord wish more water or fruit?'

Leofric looked down to see one of the green-liveried serving boys standing behind him, a brimming jug of water held in one hand and a platter of fruit in the other. Leofric nodded, holding out his goblet to be filled, noticing that the boy's face had a ruddy, healthy glow, quite unlike the alabaster skin of the elves.

The boy poured some water into Leofric's goblet and asked, 'Does my lord require anything else?'

'No, thank you,' said Leofric. 'That will be–'

His words trailed off as he looked closer and saw that the boy was not what he had first taken him to be.

'You are human…'

Leofric put down his goblet and turned to face the boy, now seeing the more rounded face, the darker skin and the ears of a human being. The boy turned to leave, but Leofric gripped his tunic and held him fast.

'You are human,' repeated Leofric.

'My lord?' said the boy, a puzzled look in his eyes. Leofric kept hold of him and cast his gaze throughout the hall, looking at the rest of the serving boys. Confronted with the truth, it was now obvious that all the children who served the elves of Coeth-Mara were human.

'Can I go now, my lord?' asked the boy.

'No,' said Leofric, still struggling with the humanity of the child. 'Not yet. What is your name, boy?'

'My name?'

'Yes, what do they call you?'

'Aidan, my lord.'

'A good Bretonnian name,' said Leofric. 'Tell me, Aidan, why are you here?'

'I am here to serve at the Winter Feast.'

'No, I mean here in Athel Loren. How did you come to be here?'

'This is where I have always been,' said Aidan with a puzzled expression.

'Always? How long have you been here?' asked Leofric, a terrible suspicion forming in his mind.

'Since… I don't know, my lord. Always.'

'Very well, Aidan. Tell me which king sits upon the throne of Bretonnia?'

'The king?' said Aidan, pulling his face in the grimace of concentration common to all small boys. 'I think his name was Baudoin. I remember they called him the Dragonslayer.'

Leofric sat back, releasing his grip on the boy's tunic, feeling as though he'd been punched in the gut. King Baudoin had indeed been known as the Dragonslayer after he had slain the great wyrm, Mergaste – a great fresco in the cathedral of Bastonne commemorated the heroic deed.

'How could that be?' said Leofric. 'King Baudoin slew the dragon more than a thousand years ago.'

'Really? It seems like only yesterday. I don't remember much about it. My mother told me the tale.'

'And where is your mother? Where do you come from?'

'I don't remember,' shrugged the boy. 'I come from Athel Loren, my lord.'

'But you are not elven, you are human. You must have come from somewhere.'

'I don't know, my lord,' said Aidan. 'I have always been here.'

'Stop calling me "my lord", boy,' snapped Leofric, his exasperation growing with every obtuse answer.

'What should I call you then?'

'Call me Sir Carrard,' snapped Leofric. 'Now tell me–'

'Carrard?' exclaimed the boy. 'There is another here called that. Shall I fetch him for you?'

Leofric felt a sudden chill seize him at these words and the colour drained from his face. If the boy spoke the truth and he had served the elves of Coeth-Mara since ancient times... might then this Carrard boy be his...

Looking closely at the boy, Leofric saw a ghostly luminescence to his skin, an ageless quality that spoke of a moment frozen in time. The boy's eyes were differently coloured – one blue, one green – and Leofric knew that such fey children of Bretonnia often received a visitation from the prophetesses of the Lady before being spirited off to the Otherworld.

Though it was a great honour for a child to be chosen, families mourned their sons and daughters as lost, believing they were going to a better place to serve the Lady of the Lake. Sometimes the girl-children returned to Bretonnia many years later as damsels of the Lady, but of the boy-children's fate, nothing was known.

Was this what befell them? Doomed to live here in Athel Loren, ageless and unchanging, forever...

'My lord?' asked the boy. 'Are you unwell?'

'What?' whispered Leofric. 'No... no, I am well, Aidan, but I wish you to go now.'

The boy nodded and bowed to Leofric, returning to his duties in the hall.

Leofric watched him go, a mix of emotions vying for supremacy in his heart. The life of most children in Bretonnia was one of misery, pain and poverty, but the thought of a child denied the potential of his natural span of years horrified him.

Who was to say that this life was better or worse?

KYARNO THREADED HIS way through the thronged hall, smiling at folk he knew and enjoying the warmth he now felt in Coeth-Mara. Was this how it felt to belong to something? All his life, he had felt like an outsider, but now he felt accepted and welcome. Perhaps he was ready now to take his place within the Éadaoin kinband.

He knew the wine was making him mellow, but didn't care. Not even the hostile stares of the Laithu kinband could dampen his spirits. Yes, he decided, he would do honour to his kin by accepting his place within the kinband and thus secure Lord Aldaeld's blessing to wed his daughter. He chuckled to himself at the thought, knowing that the wine put such spring fantasies into his head, but he could not deny he desired them.

Kyarno paused to join a group of elves watching a female wardancer give a display of incredible martial acrobatics, the near-naked girl leaping and twirling in the air while slashing a long, two-handed sword around her body. The blade swept around her like silver wire, its edge cutting the air no more than an inch from her painted flesh.

Though the presence of wardancers had put everyone on edge, not least because it was the troupe of the Red Wolf, there was much to admire in the incredible skills they had. Though he had seen the Dance of the Seasons before, Kyarno looked forward to witnessing it performed by Cu-Sith and his warriors, for it was certain to be something spectacular.

The wardancer's display ended as she landed in a crouch, the sword angled upwards behind her body, and Kyarno joined her audience's rapturous applause. The wardancer stood, her every movement fluid and graceful, and stalked away without acknowledgement, joining her kindred warriors as they gathered around the fire at some unheard summons of Cu-Sith. The Red Wolf stood with his arms upraised, holding a long spear garlanded with leaves in a spiral pattern in both hands. The taut muscles on his chest rippled with the motion of the great wolf tattoo while his wardancers adorned his flesh with chalk, lime and fresh talismanic paint.

Kyarno looked for one of the human serving boys and made his way towards him, looking for more wine. He saw Morvhen weaving her way through the crowd and forgot about wine, angling his course towards her. She saw him and smiled, and Kyarno felt the sun on his face to be in love with a sylph of such beauty. Attired in a regal gown of cream silk and gold, she looked every inch the daughter of an elven lord, the fabric clinging wonderfully to the curves of her lithe body.

'Morvhen,' he said. 'It is a glorious night is it not?'

She nodded, 'It is, though I'll be happier when Valas and Sirda are gone from here.'

'As will I,' said Kyarno, slipping his hand into hers. 'Has Laneir not come with his father and brother?'

'No,' said Morvhen, 'and for that I am glad. Sirda is bad enough, but his brother carries more ill-will than a blight of terrors.'

'True,' agreed Kyarno. 'His absence here will not be mourned. Least of all by me.'

Kyarno leaned down and gave Morvhen a quick kiss, slipping his arm around her shoulder.

'Walk with me,' he said.

'Where to?'

'Nowhere, just walk,' he said. 'For I am happy to see you.'

'And I you, but we must talk. My father knows what passed between you and your uncle in the forest. He knows you struck him.'

Kyarno nodded in understanding and said, 'That doesn't matter any more.'

'No? Why not?'

'Because I think I am ready to become truly a part of this kinband now. I am ready to pledge myself to Lord Aldaeld and take my place within the halls of Coeth-Mara.'

Morvhen stopped and gave him a piercing look, as though searching for any sign of mockery. 'Truly?'

'Yes,' he smiled. 'I love you, Morvhen, and I know that I am nothing without you. Your father will not countenance our union while I am an outsider, so, yes, I am ready.'

Morvhen put her hand to her mouth and said, 'I have waited so long for you to say these words, Kyarno.'

'Then you will have me?'

'Of course I will, my love,' she cried, throwing herself into his arms. 'I thought I would lose you, that you would never come back to us.'

'For you, Morvhen, always,' said Kyarno, kissing her and holding her tight.

'How very touching,' hissed a voice behind them and the lovers broke apart, turning to see the mocking features of Sirda Laithu. The son of Lord Valas was dressed in thick furs and a black and silver tunic with rich embroidery at the cuffs and seams; a pair of swords was sheathed across his back. Kyarno could see the tension and aggression in Sirda's eyes, the knuckles of his right hand white where he gripped his sword hilt.

Sirda cast an appreciative eye over Morvhen's body and said, 'I had thought the daughter of Lord Aldaeld would have known better than to associate with a common reaver.'

'Sirda,' said Kyarno with a forced smile. 'You are welcome in Coeth-Mara.'

'Such welcome is not yours to give, outlaw,' snarled Sirda.

'Perhaps not, but I offer it anyway,' said Kyarno.

'I should cut you down where you stand,' said Sirda, stepping close to him.

'Why are you so angry, Sirda?' snapped Kyarno. 'Your steeds returned to their stable glades. No harm was done.'

Sirda laughed, a high, almost hysterical quality to it, and said, 'No harm was done, he says. You are a bigger fool than even I took you for!'

Kyarno fought to quell his rising anger, saying, 'Sirda, this is not the place for this. If you must have a reckoning with me, then it can wait until tomorrow, yes?'

'Oh, there will be a reckoning, outlaw, sooner than you think!'

'What in the name of Kurnous does that mean?' asked Kyarno, taking his arm from Morvhen and sliding his hand towards the hilt of his own sword. Sirda altered the grip on his weapon and Kyarno saw that he was itching to plunge the blade into his body.

'Sirda!' said Morvhen, stepping between them. 'You are a guest in my father's halls, remember that. Do not bring shame to your kinband by your behaviour.'

'It is too late for that,' snapped Sirda, taking a deep breath and Kyarno could see bitter tears in his eyes. 'There is blood between us and only in blood will it be settled.'

Kyarno slowed his breathing, knowing that whatever was driving Sirda's aggression would not be calmed by any of Morvhen's words.

But before either he or Sirda could draw their weapons, the fire in the centre of the hall erupted in a great blazing pillar. The wardancers leapt and spun through the flickering flames, whooping and yelling songs of war and death.

Cu-Sith stood before the roaring fire, his face savage and daemonic in the red glow. The wolf on his chest howled in time with the cries of his wardancers, its eyes alight with feral anticipation.

Throughout the hall, elves stood transfixed as the Red Wolf lowered the spear he carried and let loose a piercing cry that echoed through the branches of the trees and touched the primal heart of every elf with a fierce longing.

The Red Wolf turned and bowed to Lord Aldaeld, saying, 'Coeth-Mara is fortunate. Cu-Sith and his wardancers shall perform the Dragon Dance.'

CHAPTER THIRTEEN

THE HALL FELL silent at Cu-Sith's pronouncement. The Dragon Dance was performed but rarely, only the greatest wardancers of Athel Loren were able to perform such a dangerous, intricate dance. The pillar of flames that reared from the centre of the hall dropped in a flurry of sparks, the fire reduced to its natural state, and the elves of Coeth-Mara swiftly returned to their tables as the wardancers took up their positions around the fire.

A hush descended on the hall and without another word spoken, the dance began.

LEOFRIC WATCHED THE wardancers hurl themselves around the fire, not truly understanding what was happening, but content to watch the spectacle unfold before him. The paint on the wardancers' bodies blurred with the speed of their movements, a weaving pattern of colours as they danced with fierce, savage abandon. Cu-Sith stood motionless behind the fire as his troupe danced faster and faster, a singing sensation of loss, pain and joy spreading outwards from the dancers in the centre of the hall.

The dancers became wilder, their passions stronger and their joys more extreme, more menacing. They leapt, cartwheeled and somersaulted through the flames, coming together like a whirlpool and breaking apart as Cu-Sith landed in the centre of the fire.

Leofric gasped as sparks and embers were thrown up by Cu-Sith's landing, but the leader of the wardancers seemed untroubled by the flames licking around him. He bounded from the firepit with a wild yell, his spear trailing fire behind him.

The wardancers leapt towards him with wild howls of exultation, but with a cry, he flew above their heads, tumbling in flight to land facing them. As they tumbled, he leapt again, the weapons of the troupe clawing empty air as he passed between them.

Cu-Sith laughed maniacally as he leaped and spun, evading the darting swords and spears with ease. A soft wind tugged at Leofric's hair as the dance grew wilder and wilder, he could hardly believe that any being could move so swiftly or so gracefully. The beat of a pounding drumbeat filled the hall, thumping in time with his rising heartbeat and Leofric could not tell whether he truly heard the rhythmic music or if it resounded deep in his soul.

Almost too fast to follow, the wardancers broke apart from the centre of the hall, spinning and twisting through the air to land amid the stunned onlookers.

As one, their blades flashed quicker and quicker, spear and sword spinning in silver blurs of steel that whipped the air into frantic motion. The wind built and filled the hall, rising from a soft zephyr to a sighing breeze and finally to a howling gale.

Leaves spun from the ground, fluttering round the hall as the wind carried them upwards and within moments, the air was thick with gold and red. The beauty of the sight took Leofric's breath away as the leaves spun around the hall with ever increasing speed.

The shrieking wardancers closed on the firepit once more, their flashing blades spinning and keeping the tornado of leaves afloat with their movements. Cu-Sith spun like a dervish through the gathering spiral of flying leaves, his blade carving looping spiral patterns through them as he bounded from table to table.

Slowly the tornado of leaves shifted in its movements, its course angling until each one passed through the roaring fire at the heart of the hall. Each leaf burst into flames, blazing like a firefly as it spun through the air.

Leofric watched amazed as the blazing leaves, thousands of them surely, looped upwards as the wardancers spun around the column of fire, their swords and spears spinning and moulding it into some new and magnificent form. The dance spoke to him on some deep, instinctual level and his flesh answered with fierce exultation, his soul soaring at the magic he was seeing.

Slowly at first, but with greater speed as the shape took form, Leofric saw the sinuous form of a great beast emerge from the burning leaves. A great body of light was shaped, then a long tail and massive flaring wings of fire emerged from the wardancers' creation. Finally, a vast, draconic head was fashioned from the blazing leaves, its jaws wide and powerful.

Scarce able to believe his overwhelmed senses, Leofric saw the great dragon of fire twist and spin through the air, the leaping wardancers sustaining it with their deadly dance and flashing blades. It swooped and dived, the roar of the flames giving the dragon a mighty voice.

A lone figure stood before the might and majesty of the fiery dragon. Cu-Sith stood unmoving with his spear held before him, and laughing with wild abandon. The dragon leapt towards him, its blazing jaws spread wide to swallow him whole and Leofric had to fight the urge to draw his sword and fight the monster.

Cu-Sith leapt from the path of the dragon, somersaulting over its long neck and slashing with his weapon. The dragon came at him again and again, directed by the energies of the wardancers, but each time it bit thin air as Cu-Sith expertly evaded its attacks, turning to strike back each time.

The confrontation went on and on, the dragon snapping and biting, and Cu-Sith cartwheeling and leaping around it. Leofric was lost in admiration for the incredible beauty of the sight before him and the unbelievable skill of Cu-Sith. The memory of Cu-Sith's blades at his throat was swept away as the wild exultation that had seized every elf in the hall reached deep inside him and stirred his primal heart.

Unable to stop himself, he beat his palm against the table in time to the drumming beat of the unheard music, swept up in exultation by the phenomenal exhibition.

Instantly, the dragon of fiery leaves dropped from the air, its mighty form extinguished as the wardancers abruptly stopped their dance.

Every eye in the hall turned upon him and Leofric knew he had made a terrible mistake.

A blur of colour and movement exploded beside him and the breath was knocked from his body as he was hurled to the ground. A blur of silver steel flashed before him and he found himself looking into the crazed eyes of Cu-Sith.

'You interrupted Cu-Sith's dance,' said the wardancer, hauling him to his feet and pushing him back towards the table.

The Red Wolf spun in the air, his foot lashing out to strike Leofric square in the chest and hurl him onto his back on the table. Fast as quicksilver, Cu-Sith was upon him and Leofric felt the touch of cold steel at his groin.

'You should keep your animals on a leash, Lord Aldaeld!' yelled the wardancer.

'I'm sorry,' gasped Leofric, fearful of moving lest Cu-sith's blade unman him.

'Sorry?' hissed Cu-Sith. 'The Red Wolf will geld his pet and then you will know your place, human!'

'No!' shouted Leofric as he felt the tip of Cu-Sith's blade pierce his flesh.

THOUGH DARKNESS HAD closed in and the snowfall had grown heavier, Caelas Shadowfoot could follow the trail of the Laithu kinband without difficulty. Their tracks were easily visible through the powdered snow that fell, and the more he saw of them, the more uneasy he became.

Elves did not travel the paths of Athel Loren so recklessly. Something was amiss, and it sat ill with him that he did not yet see what.

Kneeling beside the deep tracks of a horse, he knew there was little point in following the back trail anymore and turned to head back towards Coeth-Mara. The moonlight pooled in the glade, filling it with a silver glow and long, angled shadows.

He slung his bow, pulling his green scarf over his face and setting the hood of his cloak over his head.

And then he saw it.

Sudden fear seized him as he ran lightly across the snow and dropped to his belly beside the tracks. Caelas drew his long knife and reached gently into one of the tracks with the blade, an angled shadow within showing a subtle difference in the shade of snow. He cursed as he realised what he was looking at, the fresh fall of snow having hidden it from his keen eyes.

He had thought the new snow accounted for the deepness of the tracks, but as he looked closer, he saw that the original prints were deeper than would normally be expected of a single rider. He leapt to his feet, caution forgotten in the wash of fear that chilled him worse than the weather.

Swiftly, he checked the tracks of the other riders, finding the same depth of tracks.

These horses had carried more than one rider.

Somewhere between here and the time he had seen the Laithu kinband, these horses had shed a rider. Which meant that somewhere between here and Coeth-Mara were at least forty warriors hidden in the wilds.

Caelas had no idea why Valas Laithu would want to have warriors stealthily approach Coeth-Mara, but such concerns were irrelevant just now.

Warning had to be taken back to Lord Aldaeld of the threat to his domain.

Now he understood the Laithu kinband's apparent lack of caution, and he cursed himself for assuming that they had rode blindly into Coeth-Mara, allowing his disdain for their skills to blind him to their true wiles.

He cleaned the snow from his knife and, as he prepared to sheath it, the briefest reflection ghosted across its mirror sheen. Without thought, Caelas threw himself forward as a trio of arrows slashed through the air above him.

Caelas dropped his knife and rolled, his bow drawn and an arrow nocked as he rose to one knee. He loosed a shaft to where the arrows had come from and was rewarded with a cry of pain and the sound of a falling body.

He dived to one side as two more arrows flew from the undergrowth, one passing within a finger's breadth of his shoulder. But the second archer had anticipated his move and the arrow thudded home in his chest. Caelas grunted and tore it from his body, feeling warm blood wet his cloak. He scrambled painfully into the cover of a stately birch tree as another pair of arrows thunked into its trunk.

His breathing came hard and fast; by now at least one of his unseen foes would be circling him, aiming for a clear shot while the other kept him pinned behind the tree.

There was no way out and his eyes darted from tree to tree as he tried to guess where the next attack would come from. He could see four places where an enemy might loose a killing arrow, but there was no way to tell which one his attackers would head for.

But then Loec smiled upon him as a stray moonbeam glittered from something in the undergrowth over to his right. Caelas nocked a fresh arrow and waited. Once he was sure the second archer would have reached his new position, he stepped out from behind the birch, his arrow aimed to the left.

No sooner had he moved than an archer rose from the undergrowth where the reflection had come from and Caelas spun, dropping to one knee and sending his arrow through the throat of the cloaked figure before he could fire.

He dropped his bow and dived forwards as a second arrow flashed towards him from a cleft in a boulder before him. The arrow sliced across his shoulder, but Caelas continued his roll, scooping up his fallen knife and hurling it towards the shadowy outline of the hidden archer. A strangled scream told him he had struck his target and Caelas fell to his knees as blood bubbled up in his throat.

He knew his lung had been punctured and he was losing blood rapidly, but before he tended to his wound, he slipped silently around the boulder to discover the identity of his attackers.

An elf in furred winter garb in the colours of the forest lay dead with Caelas's knife buried in his throat. He knelt and pulled open the elf's cloak, nodding to himself as he saw the Laithu kinband's rune of moonlight.

A waywatcher of Valas Laithu.

Dizzy from blood loss, Caelas wrenched his knife clear of the body, wiping the blade clean on the corpse's tunic then taking the arrows from its quiver. He cut the dead waywatcher's cloak into strips to fashion an impromptu bandage, plugging the sucking hole in his chest, then pulled himself to his feet.

His senses tingled and his warrior instinct warned him that these three would not be alone. Time was of the essence, knew Caelas, and though it was doubtful that he would survive to make it back to Coeth-Mara and warn Lord Aldaeld, he had to try.

LEOFRIC GASPED AS the razor-edged steel of Cu-Sith's blade touched the skin of his inner thigh and tried in vain to pull free of the wardancer's grip. His efforts were to no avail as he was held fast by the wild elf. The tattoo of the red wolf on Cu-Sith's chest snarled at him, relishing the prospect of spilled blood.

'Cu-Sith does not suffer interruptions to his dance, human,' snarled the wardancer. The tip of the blade broke the skin and Leofric felt a trickle of warm blood run down his thigh.

'I am sorry,' cried Leofric. 'The music! It roused my soul with its magnificence.'

'Cu-Sith needs no human's appreciation. Cu-Sith already knows he is the greatest wardancer of Athel Loren. No enemy has ever laid a blade upon Cu-Sith, nor does he bear scar or bruise.'

Leofric twisted his head from side to side, hoping that someone would come to his aid, but all he could see was a tightening circle of angry wardancers, their weapons drawn and once exultant features now curled in anger.

'Cu-Sith!' shouted a voice, and Leofric recognised it as Naieth's. 'Wait!'

The wardancer looked up as the prophetess moved through the circle of wardancers, their whooping cries angry and hostile as they parted before her. They spat insults at her, leaping close and slashing around her with their blades, but she did not react to their taunts.

'You speak for this human?' asked Cu-Sith. 'Loec is listening.'

'I ask you to release him.'

'Why should Cu-Sith do such a thing? Cu-Sith has already marked him and may do with him as he pleases.'

'It would displease Loec were you to kill him now,' said Naieth.

The wardancer leapt from the table and landed lightly before the gold-robed Naieth, circling her with a wary look in his eyes. Leofric sat up, hyperventilating at the thought of Cu-Sith's promised castration. The Red

Wolf's spear spun in a glittering circle as he leaned close to Naieth and looked straight in her eyes.

'Loec speaks to you as he does Cu-Sith?'

'Yes,' agreed Naieth, 'and this is not his will.'

'No? Cu-Sith will ask him!' yelled the wardancer, leaping in a backwards somersault to land astride Leofric once more, placing his blade at his throat.

'Loec! Does this base human deserve to live?' he yelled into the air.

The wind that had built when the wardancers had performed the Dragon Dance gusted once more, a flurry of blackened leaves taking to the air in a miniature spiralling whirlwind. Cu-Sith laughed and bent down until his face was inches from Leofric's.

'You are lucky, human,' hissed the wardancer, dragging Leofric to his feet. 'Loec says you get to keep your manhood today.'

Leofric was barely able to stand, his legs unsteady beneath him. Cu-Sith hurled him from the table and vaulted away, shouting, 'Loec smiles upon you, human. Don't waste that fortune!'

He felt hands at his shoulders and looked up to see a pale-faced Kyarno above him. The elf hauled him to his feet and dragged him away from the wardancers who followed their leader, bounding and leaping towards the fire.

'Even for a human, that was stupid,' said Kyarno, watching as the wardancers gathered around the fire to drink.

Leofric did not reply, his heart was hammering in his chest and his limbs were shaking in fear. He reached out and grabbed the nearest goblet, desperate for a drink to calm his shredded nerves.

He lifted the goblet to his lips and drank gulping mouthful after gulping mouthful of its contents. The sweet, honeyed scent of the elven wine flooded his senses and the warm nectar of its taste was beyond anything he had ever drunk before.

Leofric put down the empty goblet, only now realising what he had just done.

'Oh no...' he heard Kyarno say before his world exploded in golden light.

Light and colour filled his senses and he gasped as the sky changed hue as though the branches of the trees had caught fire. Brilliant lights and colours filled the air, rising in clouds of vermilion, azure and jade smoke. The fire in the centre blazed a vivid blue and Leofric could see the threads of golden life that saturated every living thing in Coeth-Mara.

His normal sight began to fade until he saw nothing mundane, neither flesh nor fabric of his perception of reality. He laughed as he saw the golden haloes of life everywhere, touching and connecting everything in the hall, the colours of movement and emotion writ large in the auras of those around him.

'I can see...' slurred Leofric as he slid from his chair, his mind overloading with sensation. As he toppled to the ground the colours spiralled and spun, blending together in a blur of vital essence. He could see the answers to everything – they were encapsulated in the hues, if only he could find the words to express them.

'Isha's tears,' hissed Kyarno, pulling him to his feet. Leofric smiled dreamily as the elven wine coursed through his newly refined and elevated senses. He giggled drunkenly, waving his hands before him and laughing at the colours that rippled around them as they moved. He saw no flesh or bone, just the pulsing yellow light of his life as it thundered around his body.

'What is wrong with him?' asked a woman's voice. Naieth's, thought Leofric.

'He drank some wine when I wasn't looking,' replied Kyarno.

'Elven wine is not for humans!' snapped Naieth. 'We'll be lucky if he ever comes back! Take him outside and get him some air. Keep talking to him, give him a connection to this world.'

Leofric wanted to speak, but felt that the words would choke him, clamping his hands across his mouth as Kyarno dragged him through the hall. Sparks and swirls of light followed him and Leofric gagged as a vertiginous nausea seized him. His legs buckled and but for Kyarno's support he would have fallen.

Sudden cold hit him and he gasped, feeling his stomach clench agonisingly. Embers of fire fell around him, spinning in a sickening web of gold.

'Come on, Leofric,' urged Kyarno. 'Remember who you are. You are a knight of Bretonnia. Stay with that!'

Leofric barely heard the voice, feeling as though he was falling into a dark pit without bottom, spinning and tumbling end over end into a swirling maelstrom of vibrant colours.

The voice grew fainter and fainter, echoing within his skull as though coming from along a faraway corridor. Something within his crude flesh came loose and with a start, Leofric's sight spun from his body out into the forest.

He saw trees as columns of fire, their leaves as bright spots against the dark of the night. Sap ran in molten rivers through the trees, flowing into the ground and spreading through the forest in an interconnected web that linked all things.

Everything was connected by life and the realisation was so profound and clear that he was amazed no one had seen it before.

All life was one and everything was a circle.

All he had to do was hold on to that realisation and everything would be all right. He heard a voice again, but ignored it, revelling in his newfound freedom as he soared through Athel Loren, his spirit no longer shackled to his flesh.

Was this what it was like to be divine? Journeying through realms hidden from the sight of mortals, able to see and hear the beating heart of the world as it seethed with all its myriad fecundities. Everywhere was life…

No… not everywhere, he saw.

In the depths of the forest, Leofric saw pain. Hot, searing and deathly. His spirit form flashed through the golden fires of the trees towards it, eager to soothe the pain he felt.

An elf, his life-light weak and flickering, stumbled from tree to tree, desperation flaring from him in bright red waves as he fought a losing battle to outdistance three pursuers. Leofric could see the goodness of his failing heart and the thought of this noble elf dying at the hands of these villains pierced Leofric's heart with sorrow.

CAELAS SHADOWFOOT FELL against a tree trunk, blood pouring from the sucking wound in his chest, and knew that he could not run any further. He had run as fast as he was able to bring them to this place, but now the game was over. He turned to face his hunters as they emerged from the trees, their bowstrings pulled taut and gleaming arrowheads aimed at his head.

'You have great skill, old man,' said one.

'It took you long enough to catch me,' hissed Caelas, drawing his knife.

'You think to fight us?' said another. 'Don't. It will be less painful for you.'

'I'll fight you if I have to,' wheezed Caelas.

'No need,' said the third, sadly. 'You will be dead in minutes anyway.'

Caelas pushed himself painfully from the tree, intending to gut one of these Laithu swine before they finished him. They lowered their bows, but as the first stepped towards him, Caelas felt the fury of the forest rise up around him. Something powerful rippled through the forest and even as he felt it, the hunters realised the trap he had led them into.

Branches and roots ripped from the snow as the dark fey of this haunted glade arose, smashing the nearest of his pursuers to splintered bone and pulverised meat. Thorned barbs slashed from the undergrowth, whipping the second to the ground where heaving, groaning roots crushed his trapped body. The third waywatcher turned and fled into the forest, but cracking branches and screams told Caelas that he didn't get far.

The rippling branches and grasping thorns turned towards him and Caelas knew he had to get out of this glade before they killed him too, but a wave of dizziness swamped him and his vision began to grey at the edges. He dropped to the ground as the last of his strength left him, seeing a shimmering, ghostly image hovering in the air above him.

He felt its compassion and knew that he had been offered one final chance. Caelas tried to form words of warning, but blood burst from his mouth and he toppled to the snow as his life faded.

With his last breath he fought to speak, tears of frustration freezing on his cheeks at his inability to communicate, but the spirit being nodded and he knew that it understood.

Caelas Shadowfoot died knowing he had fulfilled his duty to his kinband.

LEOFRIC'S SPIRIT WATCHED the elf's life-light fade, immense sadness smothering his soul as the brave warrior before him died. The blood of the elves the forest had slain was like molten gold against the snow and Leofric felt the wrench of reality strike him with great hammerblows.

Without warning, the scene before him sped away as he rushed back through the forest, the irresistible pull of flesh wrenching him back to his body. He screamed as his spirit form plunged into his frame of meat and bone, rolling onto his side and vomiting explosively onto the snow.

His stomach heaved as he expelled the last of the elven wine, his senses feeling dull and deadened without the freedom of the spirit. The acrid taste of vomit burned his throat and he heard Kyarno say, 'Maybe that will teach you not to drink our wine.'

He struggled to stand, his body feeling leaden and clumsy after his flight through the forest.

'No...' he gasped. 'No, no, no...'

'No, what?' asked Kyarno. 'Are you sure you're all right?'

'They're coming,' cried Leofric. 'They're coming to kill you all.'

'What? Who are?'

'Warriors of the Laithu kinband,' said Leofric stumbling like a drunk as he fought for balance. 'He found them.'

'Who did? What are you talking about?' asked Kyarno.

'Shadowfoot he was called,' wept Leofric. 'Caelas Shadowfoot. He found them and died to bring warning to Coeth-Mara.'

'Shadowfoot?' demanded Kyarno. 'You saw Caelas Shadowfoot?'

'Yes... They're coming!' pleaded Leofric. 'You have to warn them!'

Kyarno dropped Leofric and ran for Lord Aldaeld's hall.

'THIS IS WHAT happens when you bring humans into Athel Loren,' said Lord Valas, shaking his head and sipping his wine. 'Your halls have become the refuge of outlaws, vagabonds and animals, Aldaeld.'

Lord Aldaeld struggled to keep his temper in the face of this latest insult. Throughout the feast, the tension had been almost unbearable as Valas kept up a steady stream of jibes and veiled threats. Watching Kyarno drag the human from Coeth-Mara was but the latest barb for Valas to prick him with.

But as Valas was his guest, Aldaeld could do little but grit his teeth.

'These are strange times, Valas,' replied Aldaeld. 'There is much that displeases me about the human's presence, but he has a crude form of courage and fought beside the Hound of Winter against the creatures of Chaos.'

'Pah!' sneered Valas. 'Is the Hound of Winter now so old that he needs the aid of a human to triumph? Truly this is a sad day for the Asrai.'

Aldaeld glanced over his shoulder towards Cairbre, but his champion made no indication that he had heard the jibe.

'The Hound of Winter's fangs are as deadly as ever, Valas.'

'We shall see,' muttered Valas. 'But it matters little any more.'

'What do you mean by that?'

'I mean that it is time for you to make good to me the dishonour done to my kinband, Aldaeld,' said Valas.

Aldaeld kept his tone even as he said, 'Valas, there is no need for us to be enemies. Your steeds were taken, that is true, but I have punished Kyarno for his reckless-ness.'

'There is a blood debt between us, Aldaeld, and only in blood will it be settled.'

'I don't understand,' said Aldaeld warily. 'What blood is there between us?'

'The blood of my son, Laneir,' hissed Valas. 'As he gave chase to the reaver who thieved our steeds his course took him through the wild glades of the forest and the dark fey arose and claimed his life.'

Aldaeld felt his blood chill at Valas's words, his instinct for danger screaming that something was very, very wrong.

He struggled to keep his expression neutral as he said, 'I did not know that, Valas. My heart is saddened at your loss and whatever is in my power to grant is yours.'

'Really, Lord Aldaeld? Are your powers now so great as the Lady Ariel's as to be able to bring the dead back to life?'

'No, of course not, but−'

'Can you bring my son back, Aldaeld?' asked Valas with cold fury, reaching inside his furred cloak. 'Can you restore my son to me?'

Aldaeld heard the sound of frantic shouting from the entrance to the hall and tore his gaze from the anguished Lord Valas.

He saw Kyarno fighting his way through the crowds of his people, shouting and yelling at the top of his voice.

Lord Aldaeld turned back to Valas in horror as he heard what Kyarno was shouting and the Hound of Winter gave a cry of warning.

'Only in blood will it be settled!' shouted Valas as he surged from his seat and plunged a curved dagger into Lord Aldaeld's heart.

CHAPTER FOURTEEN

KYARNO SAW VALAS Laithu lunge from his seat and thrust a curved blade between Lord Aldaeld's ribs. He screamed in warning, but could only watch helplessly as bright blood burst from the wound and the lord of the Éadaoin kinband slumped in his throne. The Blades of Midnight stabbed for the throat of Aldaeld's attacker, but a copper-headed spear leapt to Valas Laithu's hand and the blow was intercepted.

Kyarno's sword was in his hand as the hall of Coeth-Mara erupted in yells of outrage and anger at this terrible, treacherous attack. He saw Morvhen run towards her father and followed her, shouting, 'To arms! To arms! We are betrayed!'

Warriors of the Laithu kinband threw off their fur cloaks and drew their weapons, but the Éadaoin kinband was not as helpless as they had expected. Arrows flashed through the air and elves of Valas Laithu fell, their throats pierced by deadly accurate shafts. Swords and spears were readied as elves clashed, leaping across the tables of the hall to do battle with one another.

Kyarno leapt a fallen warrior, sprinting towards the raised dais where Lord Valas expertly parried Cairbre's blows with a long, spiral-patterned spear. The Hound of Winter attacked with all the grim, brutal ferocity he was famed for, but nothing could penetrate Valas's defences.

Morvhen knelt beside her father with Naieth, fighting without success to stem the bleeding from the grievous wound in his chest.

Morvhen looked up through her tears and shouted, 'Kyarno! Look out!'

He risked a glance to his left, throwing himself flat as he saw Sirda Laithu loose an arrow towards him. He hit the ground and rolled, putting the fire between himself and Sirda.

The air was thick with arrows and cries of pain. Kyarno edged around the fire as the clash of steel on steel rang from the walls of Coeth-Mara. Denied complete surprise, the Laithu kinband knew they had a fight on their hands. A shape moved through the flickering flames and he dropped as another arrow flew through the fire, thudding into a root-formed table a handspan from his head, its goose-feathered fletching aflame.

'Nowhere to run, outlaw!' shouted Sirda as he circled the fire, looking to deliver the killing shot. Kyarno circled with him, keeping the fire between them.

'I told you there was blood between us, outlaw! Your death for my brother's!'

'Your brother is dead?' shouted back Kyarno. 'What has that to do with me?'

'Laneir died chasing you from our stable glades!'

'I didn't kill him,' cried Kyarno. 'I swear by all the gods I did not!'

'It doesn't matter, you're going to die anyway,' said Sirda.

He could not go on like this. Unless he could close the gap – or get Sirda to close it – there could only be one outcome between a swordsman and a bowman.

'Your brother was a treacherous cur!' shouted Kyarno. 'Just like you, Sirda.'

He heard Sirda give a strangled cry of rage and hurled himself backwards as another arrow struck the table between his legs. He rolled over the table in a clatter of plates and goblets as Sirda leapt around the fire and drew another arrow.

A spinning platter struck Sirda square in the face and the elf tumbled to the floor, dropping his bow and clutching his head. Kyarno vaulted the table, and sprang towards the fallen Sirda with his sword raised.

His foe rose quickly to his feet, his swords flashing in his hands as he shook his head free of the impact of Kyarno's makeshift missile.

Kyarno's sword struck for Sirda's heart, but the twin swords of the Laithu swordsman swept up and blocked the blow. A streaking riposte tore a gash along Kyarno's left arm and he dodged away from a low cut intended to gut him. Sirda followed up his counterattack with a blistering series of cuts and thrusts, Kyarno just barely managing to block them.

He parried a blisteringly quick lunge and had a moment of sick realisation that Sirda was a far better swordsman than he.

Sirda saw the awful knowledge in his eyes and grinned.

'You are going to die, outlaw,' he promised.

'We'll see,' said Kyarno as the battle raged around them.

CAIRBRE SENT ANOTHER lethal blow arcing towards Valas Laithu's head, the white blade slashing in to behead the traitorous vermin that had attacked his lord and killed three of his warriors. Once again the copper spearhead caught his blow and turned it aside at the last moment. The haft spun and jabbed at his head, and Cairbre barely evaded the blow.

Beside him, Tarean Stormcrow attacked with his golden sword, his blows parried by the magical spear.

'You cannot defeat me,' said Valas Laithu. 'So why try? Your lord is dead, but neither of you need to die. You can serve me.'

'Serve the murderer who betrayed the hospitality offered him? Never,' swore Tarean, nodding towards the furious battle between the elven kinbands that filled the hall with blood and violence. 'You bring dishonour on us all.'

Cairbre slashed the Blades of Midnight towards Valas once more, but again the magical spear thwarted his attempts to gut Aldaeld's killer, turning aside his blow with unnatural ease.

'Aldaeld was weak,' sneered Valas. 'He gave shelter to base humans and welcomed them into his hall! Where will it end, Cairbre? I know you, Hound of Winter – it must have sat ill with you that a human dwelt in Coeth-Mara.'

'It is not for me to question my lord's decisions,' gasped Cairbre as the Spear of Daith laid his bicep open to the bone. His hand spasmed and he lost his grip on his weapon, the Blades of Midnight dropping to the floor of the dais.

Valas Laithu darted in, thrusting the spear at his stomach, but Cairbre dodged aside and gripped the haft with his good hand, spinning inside his foe's guard and hammering his elbow against his temple.

The lord of the Laithu kinband staggered, dropping to one knee and dragging the spear back, slashing Cairbre's palm open. But before either Cairbre or Tarean could take advantage of Valas's stumble, a flurry of black, bat-like malevolents erupted from his cloak, spitting darts and chittering cries as the vicious little spites swarmed them.

They fell back before their onslaught, feeling needle-like claws and teeth tear and cut them. The spites were small, but they were numerous. Cairbre shook them clear, swatting them away with his uninjured arm, seeing Tarean Stormcrow launch another attack at Valas.

Tarean was brave and a swordsman of great skill, but the Spear of Daith had been fashioned with some of the most powerful magic of Athel Loren and his blow was easily intercepted. Cairbre saw Valas aim the weapon at the herald's stomach, the engraved eyes on the leaf-shaped blade glowing with bright magic as they sought out the swiftest route to his vitals. The spear lanced towards Tarean, the herald swiftly bringing his sword down to block, but quicker than Cairbre would have believed possible, the weapon altered direction.

'No!' shouted Cairbre as the spear rammed up into Tarean's chest, the tip erupting from his back in a bloody shower. Lord Aldaeld's herald shuddered and cried out in agony as the spear spitted him like a wild boar. The blade was wrenched clear and Tarean fell to the dais, his eyes glazing over as he died.

* * *

LEOFRIC STUMBLED TOWARDS his horse, his senses only
just recovering their equilibrium after his inebriation
with the elven wine. Before he had run into the hall,
Kyarno had alerted the Glade Guard still on duty of the
threat to Coeth-Mara and within moments, sixty riders
had assembled on snorting steeds, their blades bared
and ready for battle.

He had briefly considered following Kyarno, but
knew that he could fight best from the back of a horse.
Cries of alarm and shouts of anger echoed from the
starlit avenues and processionals beyond Lord Aldaeld's
hall as the riders circled in the moonlight, ready to take
the fight to their enemies.

Leofric found Taschen hitched to the rail in front of
his abode and climbed into the saddle, unsheathing his
sword and galloping back to Lord Aldaeld's riders as a
hail of arrows flashed from the treeline.

Against an unprepared foe, such a volley would have
been deadly, but the Glade Riders of the Éadaoin kinband
had been waiting for this moment and surged forwards to
meet their attackers. A handful of warriors fell to the enemy
arrows, but the skill of the Glade Riders was so great that
the majority were able to evade the deadly shafts.

An arrow ricocheted from the solid plate of Leofric's
armour, but a knight cared not for such things, and he
urged his steed onwards as the faster mounts of the
Glade Guard pulled away.

More arrows slashed out and more riders were punched
from their steeds by the enemy bowfire. An arrow thudded into Leofric's breastplate; the point slowed, but not
stopped by his armour. He felt its point break the skin
and wrenched it clear as he thundered onwards.

Then they were through the treeline and Leofric saw
the archers of the Laithu kinband running for fresh

cover as the Glade Riders rode them down without mercy. Leofric angled his horse towards a fleeing, grey-cloaked archer, raking his spurs viciously into Taschen's flanks.

The elf dodged nimbly, but Leofric was in his element, having ridden down broken enemies in countless battles, riding just ahead of his prey and slashing his sword back into his foe's face.

The elf screamed horribly, his skull split open and Leofric set off in pursuit once more. Arrows flashed through the air, but in ones and twos rather than the concentrated volleys of before.

Scattered and disorganised, the Laithu warriors were easy prey for the Glade Riders, amongst the finest mounted warriors in Athel Loren. Leofric felt the blood surge through his veins as he slew another enemy warrior, remembering the savage joy of bloody combat and the thrill of riding down a defeated enemy.

Whooping riders rode hither and thither through the trees, hunting down their enemies with savage fury. None of the Glade Riders were in any mood to offer mercy towards the Laithu kinband and the snow-bound forest echoed to the sounds of their screams.

He watched as an enemy archer took refuge behind the thick bole of an ancient oak, drawing and loosing a shaft in one swift motion. The Glade Rider next to Leofric tumbled from the saddle of his flame-maned elven steed and Leofric hauled Taschen's reins in the direction of his killer. No sooner had he done so than the elven archer loosed a shaft towards him.

But instead of aiming high, the archer sent his arrow low, the lethally sharp missile plunging so deeply into Taschen's chest that only the fletching was visible. Another arrow followed the first and the horse collapsed beneath him, foaming blood erupting from its screaming mouth.

Leofric kicked his feet from the stirrups as his horse died, leaping clear as it slammed into the snow in a tangle of broken limbs. He hit the ground hard, rolling and losing his grip on his sword as the breath was driven from him.

He shook his helmet free of snow as he pushed himself to one knee, and saw the archer who had felled his steed draw his bowstring back to send a shaft through his helmet's visor.

A blur of white leapt over Leofric and the flame-maned elven steed landed in front of the archer, its hooves smashing him from his feet. Leofric gathered up his sword and scrambled back towards his wounded mount.

Incredibly, Taschen still lived, but his every breath foamed red with blood and Leofric knew the horse was beyond saving. The horse's front legs were broken where it had fallen and it was in agony.

'You were a faithful steed, my friend,' said Leofric, drawing his blade across the horse's throat. Warm blood gushed from the wound and Taschen's eyes rolled back in their sockets as he died.

He would mourn the loss of the fine Bretonnian warhorse later, but for now there were still foes to hunt. He turned from the dead beast, seeing the elven steed that had saved his life sadly nuzzling its fallen rider. It looked up at him and Leofric was struck by the fierce intelligence he saw in the creature's eyes.

'What say you and I finish these murderers off?' said Leofric.

The horse seemed to consider his proposal for a moment then bobbed its head, reluctantly leaving its dead rider and cantering across to him. As it approached him, he sensed the steed's strength and loyalty in its every movement.

Clearly there would be no master in this arrangement, only two warriors fighting together. Just as Leofric was wondering how he was going to climb onto the back of a steed with no saddle, the horse dropped to its knees.

'I can see we are going to get along famously,' said Leofric as he climbed on and the horse rose up, seemingly unhindered by the weight of an armoured warrior on its back.

He gripped its coppery mane as the pale horse reared and with a wild, exultant yell, they rode off into the forest after the remaining enemy warriors.

KYARNO BLED FROM a score of shallow cuts, his endurance fading in the face of Sirda's overwhelming superiority with a blade. His every attack was batted aside with contemptuous ease, his every defence countered and defeated. He backed away through the press of combat that filled the hall, unable to tell which kinband held the upper hand.

'This is it, Kyarno,' laughed Sirda, twisting one of his blades around Kyarno's and sending it spinning through the air. 'Now you are going to die.'

Kyarno staggered back, desperate to put some distance between himself and Sirda, but each time his escape was blocked by his more nimble foe. He stumbled and fell back against a table, exhausted and defeated as Sirda closed in with a predatory smile.

Sirda raised his sword and shouted, 'This is for my brother!'

Kyarno closed his eyes and yelled defiantly as the sword slashed towards his throat.

But with a clash of steel and sparks, the blow never landed.

The frozen moment stretched and Kyarno looked up to see Cu-Sith standing on the table above him, the haft of his spear an inch before his neck where it had intercepted Sirda's blow.

'Red Wolf,' cried Sirda. 'This is not your concern. You swore to stay your hand.'

'Cu-Sith decides what is Cu-Sith's concern, and you should know better than to try and make deals with followers of the Trickster God,' said the wardancer, sweeping his spear up and effortlessly twisting Sirda's blade from his grip. Kyarno cried out in relief as the wardancer somersaulted backwards, the heel of his foot lashing out, catching Sirda under his chin and hurling him into the firepit.

The last son of Valas Laithu fell into the fire, the flames hungrily seizing his furs and tunic and he screamed as his hair and clothes caught light. Sirda rolled from the fire, ablaze from head to foot, his screams terrible to hear as his flesh began to burn.

Kyarno watched Sirda climb to his feet and stumble like a drunk as the flames devoured him, the sickening stench of cooked flesh filling the hall.

Gasps of horror at the fate of Sirda Laithu spread from his smoking corpse, but Kyarno felt no pity for him. In the lull of battle, Kyarno pulled himself to his feet and turned to Cu-Sith.

'Why?'

'Loec told me that he did not like that one,' said Cu-Sith, turning away.

'That's it?' asked Kyarno, retrieving his fallen sword. 'Loec didn't like him?'

'What more do you want?' shrugged Cu-Sith. 'You are alive are you not? Be thankful Loec likes you very much. Now begone, for Cu-Sith will dance the dance of war and it would be wise of you not to get too close.'

Kyarno nodded and staggered towards the dais as Cu-Sith shouted, 'Wardancers! Begin the storm of blades!'

NAIETH TRIED TO shut out the sounds of battle as she reached deep inside herself for the power needed to do what must be done. Her elven soul cried out to unleash the terrible energies of the forest against the betrayers, but she had foreseen this moment and knew she needed all her power for one thing.

She had not used magic this powerful in many decades and the thought of tapping into the vital heart of the forest both excited and terrified her.

Naieth knelt beside Lord Aldaeld, his chest a soaking mess of blood where Valas Laithu's dagger had pierced his heart. The elven lord's skin was ashen and his eyes unseeing, but she could sense that death had not yet claimed him, though its shadow hovered near.

Watching the unequal struggle unfold between Valas Laithu and the Hound of Winter, tears blurred her eyes as the blow she knew would end Tarean Stormcrow's life finally landed. Behind her, the battle in the hall raged with undiminished violence, vengeance driving the Laithu and betrayed fury filling the hearts of the Éadaoin.

'Please,' begged Morvhen, her hands stained with her father's blood. 'Save him!'

'I will try,' said Naieth, 'but it will be difficult. Take my hand, child.'

Morvhen reached over and Naieth took her slippery hand, placing it on the wound that still weakly pumped blood down Lord Aldaeld's robes. The heart had not yet stopped beating, which meant there was still a chance to save him.

'Focus all your thoughts on your love for your father, child,' ordered Naieth, pressing her own hand atop Morvhen's. 'Picture him in his prime, as a warrior of brave heart and noble aspect. Can you do that?'

'I will,' cried Morvhen. 'Just please save him.'

Naieth nodded and began speaking the words of power, feeling the ancient strength of Athel Loren's magic rush to fill her, breathing deeply and opening herself to the magic of the forest. She gasped as its power poured into her, the rampant need of the forest to grow and spread tempered by her desire to preserve the natural balance of the world.

She let the power flow from her, surging though her fingertips, through Morvhen and into the flesh of Lord Aldaeld. Her eyes shone with golden fire as she saw the terrible damage wreaked within his chest. She shaped the healing powers to her will, reknitting the torn muscle of his heart and forcing the sliced arteries to regrow.

Naieth felt the power of the Queen of the Forest working through her, warmth and healing compassion pouring from her in a wave of incredible strength. The flesh around Aldaeld's wound changed from angry red to pink, the skin sealing up over the wound and the bruising around it fading to nothing.

The power flowed through Aldaeld and into his throne, the wood cracking and splitting as new life and new ambition for growth seized it. Budding branches writhed from the back of the throne, bursting to verdant life and blossoming with snow-white flowers that curled and grew higher and higher. The throne writhed with power, growing into a tall tree with spreading branches and an intoxicating scent.

Aldaeld gasped and cried out as his chest hiked convulsively, his eyes snapping open in shock at the power within him.

Morvhen cried out in elation as her father's eyes opened and he gave vent to a cry of terrible rage.

KYARNO LEAPT TO the dais as a ferocious, ululating yell built from the throats of the wardancers and their battle dance began. Cu-Sith led his spinning, leaping warriors as they bounded through the hall, swords and spears stabbing and slashing at their foes as they wove through the battle with lethal grace. Screams and cries of pain followed in their wake as shrieking, laughing wardancers struck down warriors of the Laithu kinband and left those of the Éadaoin unscathed.

Valas Laithu and Cairbre fought behind Lord Aldaeld's strange, new throne, the Hound of Winter bleeding from deep wounds to his arm and leg. He fought with the Blades of Midnight clutched in one hand, his wounded arm held tight to his chest.

'Valas Laithu!' shouted Kyarno, leaping forward with his sword aimed at his foe's heart.

The lord of the Laithu kinband spun, smiling with malicious anticipation as he saw Kyarno coming. The Spear of Daith whipped around, deflecting Kyarno's attack, the haft coming round and thudding into Kyarno's stomach.

Kyarno doubled up, swaying aside as the spear point stabbed for his chest. The blade scored across his side and he leapt back as the magical weapon's return stroke slashed at his head.

'I will enjoy killing you, outlaw!' snarled Valas Laithu as he closed in.

Kyarno parried a thrust of the spear and circled left as the Hound of Winter flanked Valas from the right. The sounds of battle began to fade from the hall, the clash of weapons and the battle cries of the wardancers replaced with the moans of the injured and the weeping for the dead.

'It's over, Valas,' said Cairbre, pointing to the terrible aftermath of the battle for Coeth-Mara. 'Your warriors are defeated. Put up your weapon.'

Valas backed away from the Hound of Winter, his face ashen as he saw the blackened, burned form of Sirda lying sprawled across a table, the lust for battle draining from him in an instant.

'I cannot,' said Valas sadly. 'I am set upon this course and have sworn the oath of vengeance with the Kindred of Talu.'

Kyarno's blood chilled at the mention of the Talu, a dark and dangerous kindred of elves sworn to fulfil oaths of retribution for terrible wrongs done to them.

'You are a Mourn-singer?' asked Kyarno, lowering his weapon. 'Then there is no peace for you until you die or you slay me.'

'Even so,' agreed Valas Laithu as Lord Aldaeld climbed from his throne of blossoming life with Morvhen and Naieth's help to stand before him. Kyarno saw the anguished relief on Cairbre's face as he saw that his lord still lived, which was quickly replaced by simmering anger as he turned back to Valas Laithu.

'You will not leave this hall alive, Lord Valas,' promised the Hound of Winter.

'I know,' replied Valas, the imminence of his death granting him a dignity he had not possessed in life. 'What is left to me now anyway? The outlaw has seen to it that my sons are no more and that my line will vanish from the forest like the wythel trees. Death is all I have left.'

'It did not have to be this way, Valas,' said Lord Aldaeld, his palm pressed to his chest where he had been stabbed.

'No? What would you have done if he had been responsible for your daughter's death?' asked Valas, pointing at Kyarno. 'Could you have forgiven him?'

Lord Aldaeld shook his head and said, 'I suppose not, but it changes nothing, Valas. I cannot let you live.'

'No, you cannot,' agreed Valas. 'I would ask a boon of you before I die though.'

'Name it.'

'Allow those of my warriors who still live to return to their homes. They took no oath and have followed my lead in all things with honour and love. Let them live to bear my body back to the Vaults of Winter that it may lie beneath the moonlight.'

Aldaeld nodded and said, 'It shall be so, Valas, I swear by Isha's mercy that they will live.'

'Thank you,' said Valas, placing the Spear of Daith on the ground as Kyarno heard the sound of an armoured warrior approaching the dais.

He turned to see Leofric enter the hall, leading a pale, blood spattered elven steed with a coppery mane. A broken arrow jutted from the metal of his armour and his sword was blooded.

Aldaeld also faced Leofric, and said, 'Human, is my domain safe?'

Leofric looked surprised that Lord Aldaeld had deigned to speak to him, but nodded and said, 'It is, Lord Aldaeld. The enemy warriors have been driven off.'

'Very well,' said Aldaeld, turning and nodding to the Hound of Winter.

Cairbre brought the Blades of Midnight up and faced Valas Laithu.

'I will make it swift,' he promised.

'I am glad it is you, Hound of Winter,' said Valas.

Cairbre nodded and Kyarno winced as the Hound of Winter rammed the long blade of his spear into Valas Laithu's body. The powerful strike tore through his lungs and up into his heart, killing the lord of the Laithu kinband instantly. Valas sighed as his last breath left him and sagged against Cairbre, who gently lowered the elf lord to the floor.

Surprisingly, Kyarno felt nothing but immense sadness at Valas Laithu's death, his honourable end contrary to everything he had known of him. Only then did he see the lifeless body of Tarean Stormcrow. Giving a cry of loss, he dropped his sword and ran to Lord Aldaeld's fallen herald.

Blood pooled in a vast lake around Tarean's body and as he placed his palm against his chest, Kyarno knew that the Stormcrow had passed from Athel Loren. He felt a splinter of ice lodge in his heart at this great loss to Coeth-Mara, tears blinding him as he wept openly for Tarean Stormcrow, a friend he had never taken the time to know.

He heard footsteps behind him and looked up to see Lord Aldaeld's cold, unforgiving eyes staring down at him.

'Much blood has been shed this day and it is upon your hands, boy.'

'You think I don't know that?' wept Kyarno.

'I hope that you do,' said Aldaeld. 'For the knowledge of what you have brought upon my halls shall be your only companion henceforth.'

'Father–' began Morvhen, but Aldaeld cut her off with a look of cold fury.

'No. I will hear no more of this, my decision is made. A line of the Asrai is gone from the world and it is Kyarno's folly that has given rise to this dark day. It is time for him to face the consequences of his actions.'

Kyarno stood, facing the lord of the Éadaoin kinband, ready to face Aldaeld's judgement upon him.

'Leave,' said Aldaeld simply. 'You are a ghost in Coeth-Mara.'

BOOK THREE
Spring's Red Harvest

'A little madness in the spring,
is wholesome even for the King.'

CHAPTER FIFTEEN

THE BATTLE FOR Coeth-Mara had been won, but the first rays of morning revealed how terrible had been the cost. Twenty-one elves of the Éadaoin kinband were carried from the hall of battle and forty-nine of the Laithu kinband were dead.

Those followers of Valas Laithu that had not sworn vengeance oaths were allowed to leave Coeth-Mara with Lord Aldaeld's blessing, mournfully bearing the body of their lord and his son back to the Vaults of Winter.

As dusk fell the following day, Leofric joined the end of a torch-bearing procession of green-cloaked elves who marched solemnly through Coeth-Mara following the bodies of their dead. Each body was borne upon the shoulders of their kin and loved ones, wrapped in shrouds of leaves as they prepared to take their last journey.

Leofric had cleaned his armour of blood, but he was no smith and the holes punctured by enemy arrows remained. Now that the battle was won, a brooding melancholy settled upon him. Though it had begun as a prison, a hateful place that had taken Helene from him, he had come to regard Athel Loren and Coeth-Mara with a fondness he had not expected. Its golden light of autumn and crystalline splendour of winter were visions of unspoiled beauty, but now even they were tainted with blood.

Truly there was nowhere left in the world that the grim darkness of war and death could not reach. But looking around him as the funeral procession made its way along the snow-lined avenue of trees, Leofric knew that there were some things worth fighting for. Surrounded by such beauty, Leofric could understand the insular nature of the elves and their fierce desire to protect their forest kingdom.

With such a wondrous land of raptures to dwell within, who would not defend it as vigorously?

The procession passed through a dripping archway, the melting snow and ice falling on those who passed beneath it, as though the forest itself wept to see such bloodshed unleashed beneath its boughs. Leofric tilted his head back as he walked through the arch, the cold meltwater chilling him to the bone as it covered his face.

Naieth led the procession, Lord Aldaeld and the Hound of Winter following behind her carrying the body of Tarean Stormcrow. Morvhen walked beside her father with her head held high, Tiphaine bearing the long train of her dress. The Eternal Guard followed their master with their dead warriors borne upon their shoulders. The grey-feathered owl that was Naieth's companion flew overhead, even its hoots managing to convey boundless grief.

Kyarno was not part of the funeral procession, already gone from Coeth-Mara as if he had never existed. After his banishment by Lord Aldaeld, he had sheathed his sword before slowly marching from the hall and no one had seen him since. Morvhen had made to follow him, but Cairbre had held her back, knowing that her protestations would do no good. The lord of Coeth-Mara had spoken and no one but he could change his will.

The sad procession marched into the woods, passing through silent glades and along cold pathways, the trees sighing with soft songs of grief. The frozen bracken and thorny bushes parted for the elves, the forest mourning along with the elves who dwelt within it.

At length, the procession reached a wide glade of simple beauty, tall trees ringing its circumference like watchful sentinels and thin shoots of green pushing through the snow. Leofric saw that the glade was open to the heavens, the dusky sky shot through with vivid purples and reds. He did not know Tarean Stormcrow well, but had instinctively warmed to him upon their meeting and felt sure that he would have chosen something like this for his final resting place.

The procession circled the glade, now giving voice to a song of aching sadness that touched Leofric's heart, and he found himself unable to hold back tears at its sorrowful lament. He wanted to join in, but knew that his poor human voice would only do the dead a disservice.

As the column became a circle, Naieth walked into the centre of the glade and Leofric found himself standing next to Tiphaine and Morvhen. Cairbre and Aldaeld stood near and Leofric saw that the lord of the Éadaoin kinband looked tired and worn, still holding a hand to his heart. The normally stoic Cairbre looked ancient, even amongst a race for whom time passed much more slowly. Morvhen's features were regal and strong, though even she bore the hallmarks of great sorrow.

Naieth, slender and noble in a long gown of silver feathers, raised her staff of woven branches as her owl fluttered down to perch on her shoulder. Gemstones glittered on her belt of woven leaves and her golden tresses were woven with briar leaves. Her features were more careworn than he had ever seen them before.

Death ages people, realised Leofric, even the Asrai.

Having borne his share of sorrow, he wondered how his own features appeared.

The elves who bore the dead on their shoulders lifted them down and took a step forward in perfect unison, laying their kin gently onto the snow. At a signal from Naieth, they retreated, leaving the ring of the dead in the centre of the glade.

Naieth began to speak, her words hauntingly beautiful even though Leofric could not understand them, sounding more like song than speech. He felt a presence near him and turned to face Tiphaine, her smooth, oval face expressionless, yet also infinitely sad.

'The prophetess asks the forest to welcome the dead,' she whispered, answering Leofric's unasked question. He nodded as Naieth's song wove new heights of loss and the elves of Coeth-Mara joined her, adding their own words of loss to the song. The grief-song continued until the purple sky darkened to the black of night, the orange glow of flickering torches giving the glade a comforting warmth as night fell.

Her song concluded, Naieth walked from the centre of the glade, the circle of elves parting to allow her to leave. Lord Aldaeld and Cairbre followed her and the rest of his people slowly peeled from the circle and disappeared into the forest.

Leofric watched them go, wondering who would come to bury the dead, when Tiphaine said, 'Come, the duty to the dead is done and we must allow them their time beneath the stars.'

'They are to be left like this?'

'Of course,' said Tiphaine. 'What else would we do?'

'Bury them?' suggested Leofric. 'Erect grave markers to their memory? Something to ensure that they will not be forgotten.'

Tiphaine shook her head. 'No, Athel Loren claims back its own. They will become part of our woodland realm and live forever as they give life to the forest. The continued beauty of the forest is their legacy, and what better remembrance to a life is there than in the immortal soul of the forest?'

'I suppose,' said Leofric. 'What will become of them?'

'Let us not speak of it,' said Tiphaine, turning and gliding from the starlit glade. 'It is not seemly to discuss matters of the dead in their presence.'

Leofric followed her and said, 'It just feels wrong leaving them out in the open.'

'You would have us entomb the dead within a prison of stone as the dwarfs are wont to?' asked Tiphaine. 'No, to confine a soul thus is to deny it its final journey.'

'Journey?'

'To the immortality of memory. Those that loved them will remember them in song and tale, and they will pass these to their kin that come after them. In this way they will never die. Will you not remember your wife, Leofric? Will you not tell your son of her beauty and grace?'

'If I see him again, I will,' nodded Leofric sadly.

Tiphaine reached up and stroked Leofric's cheek with a smile of faint amusement creasing the corner of her mouth, the touch of her fingers light and smooth.

'You think you will not?'

'I don't know, I hope so. I don't even know if such a thing is possible.'

'This is Athel Loren,' Tiphaine reminded him. 'All things are possible.'

THE COLD DAYS following the funeral procession blurred into weeks; winter's grey despair reaching its peak then falling away as the world turned its face to the sun once more. Leofric passed much of his time resting to recover from his wounds or in prayer, strangely missing the company of Kyarno now that he had been banished from Coeth-Mara. The young elf – though Leofric knew that such a term was absurd in relation to a human – had become, if not a friend, then someone he could at least talk to.

Denied such distractions for the mind, the dark days passed slowly, and Leofric was now forced to endure the loneliness of a stranger in a strange land. The impish figures of his ever-present spites followed his every movement, and though he was glad of their presence, they were no substitute for real companionship. The halls of Lord Aldaeld were beautiful and majestic, but Leofric missed the warmth of human company, the energy of his race that, for all their beauty and grace, the elves could not match.

Most of all he missed Helene and Beren. Without the diversion of people around him he brooded more on her loss and his continued absence from his son. He dreamed of them more and more often, waking with a smile on his lips until he remembered that they were lost to him.

He wondered what Beren would know of his disappearance. Would those men-at-arms who fled the edge of the forest return to Castle Carrard or would the shame of their desertion cause them to flee to other lands?

Might his family and retainers not even be aware of the fate of their lord and lady?

Days passed, then weeks, and Leofric dared to spend more time in the forest around Coeth-Mara on the elven steed he had ridden into battle against the Laithu kinband. After the battle, he had attempted to return the horse to the riders of the Glade Guard, but their leader had shaken his head, saying, 'He is called Aeneor and he has chosen you, human. You are blooded together and bound to one another now.'

Pleased to have been so chosen, he and his new mount spent the last weeks of winter becoming used to one another. The beast was fast and bore his armoured weight without complaint, and though it had not the stamina or mass of a Bretonnian warhorse, its speed and agility were beyond compare.

The passing days also gave him time to think on the fate of the young boy-children taken by the elves and his decision not to seek out the one who may very well have been one of his ancestors. What would he say to him? What *could* he say to him?

As much as he wanted to see him with his own eyes, he feared to reopen old wounds and knew that there was nothing he could offer the boy. He could not take him from Athel Loren for fear he suffer a similar fate to the vanished Duke Melmon and, in truth, he did not believe the boy would want to leave.

Aidan had seemed content enough in Coeth-Mara, but was that true contentment or was it the result of the enchantments of Athel Loren? He had spoken briefly to Naieth of the children, but she had said simply, 'Would he have been happier back in your lands? Here they are happy. Here they will live forever.'

He had had no answer for her, knowing that the life of such fey children was the life of a pariah, shunned and feared for being different. Even so, he also knew that there was a terrible cruelty in denying a child whatever life they might have forged for themselves, to keep them forever young with no hope of ever attaining anything beyond service to the elves.

Of the rest of the inhabitants of Coeth-Mara, he saw little – Morvhen now directed her energies in ministering to her father, who, despite the prophetess's healing magic, was still much in need of care.

The wardancers of Cu-Sith remained in the forest around Coeth-Mara, much to Lord Aldaeld's annoyance, but there was little that could be done about their presence and so they were left to prowl the woodland in peace.

Often Leofric would think of both Naieth and the Lady's warning that days of blood and death were coming, wondering from whence the danger would come.

But the sun lingered a little longer each day and patches of green and colour appeared throughout the woodland as the tremors of coming spring rippled through the forest, and such dangers seemed far away.

LEOFRIC RODE CAREFULLY through the depths of the forest, the air crisp and the day clear. The snow was now in retreat from spring's advance, though the forest retained much of its white cloak. He felt a curious excitement, the same awareness of possibility that he sensed in the elves of Coeth-Mara as the thaw came. Perhaps the budding sense of anticipation that lingered on the air was being communicated to him with his every breath?

Whatever the reason, he was glad to be outside on this new day of sunlight, travelling the paths of the forest to find Kyarno.

Morvhen had come to his chambers the previous evening, entreating him to travel into the forest to find her lost lover. Since the attack of the Laithu kinband, the Hound of Winter had increased his watchfulness of her and there was no way she could go to him, but she had passed a leaf-wrapped scroll to Leofric.

'Talk to him,' urged Morvhen.

'I would not know where to find him,' said Leofric.

Morvhen smiled. 'He will remain close to Coeth-Mara for a time. Seek him out at the Crystal Mere, for it is there that he knew peace.'

As a tolerated guest of Lord Aldaeld, Leofric knew he ought to refuse Morvhen's request, but the guilt of having berated her in the forest before his vision of the Lady of the Lake still lingered in his memory.

'Very well, my lady,' said Leofric, taking the scroll.

'He loves me,' said Morvhen sadly.

'That is a good thing, surely?' said Leofric, seeing the sorrow on her face.

'Is it? Not for me.'

'Why not? Love is a gift that should be treasured.'

'Only if you can have it,' said Morvhen bitterly. 'Only if you can have it. He can never come back to Coeth-Mara. Not now. Our foolishness has cost me the one thing I wanted most in the world.'

'Lord Aldaeld may change his mind,' said Leofric. 'You told me Kyarno has been cast from his halls before.'

'By the Hound of Winter, yes, but never by my father. Isha's tears, I almost wish Cairbre had never brought him back to Coeth-Mara after his family was killed. Then I would never have known this pain for I would have known nothing of Kyarno Daelanu.'

Leofric wanted to reach out to Morvhen, to place a comforting hand on her shoulder, but felt that such a gesture would be inappropriate and that she would resent the pity of a human.

'I do not believe you mean that, Morvhen,' he said. 'It is always good to know love, even if it cannot be yours.'

'You really believe that?'

'I do,' replied Leofric, feeling the magic of Athel Loren flowing through him as he spoke. 'I loved Helene with all my heart and when she was taken from me I thought I would die. The pain of her loss is great... almost too great, but even if I could change things so that I had never met her and was spared this hurt, I would not.'

'You would not?' asked Morvhen.

'No,' said Leofric, shaking his head. 'I miss her so much, but I remember the golden time we shared and the son we conceived. If nothing else came of our union, then that is worth all the pain I suffer.'

'What will become of your son?'

'I don't know,' said Leofric. 'He will grow to be a fine man, of that I am sure. He will make me proud.'

'Will he become a knight like you?'

Leofric smiled. 'I hope so. Maixent, my chamberlain, will tutor him in the ways of a knight of Bretonnia and he will make his way in the world with courage and nobility.'

'I think that he shall,' agreed Morvhen.

LEOFRIC HAD RIDDEN out at first light, trusting that Aeneor could locate the Crystal Mere without running into the Wild Riders or anything else that might wish him harm.

The journey to the blessed pool was one of joy to Leofric, the scent of sweet sap heavy in his nostrils and the cold sunlight refreshing his skin as it dappled through the fractured canopy above him. Though the path he rode was unknown to him, he had a sudden skewed sense of déjà vu, as though he had come this way before... *or would come this way again...*

He shrugged off the unsettling sensation, seeing the sunlit glade through the trees ahead and hearing the growing thunder of the waterfall. The undergrowth and trees thinned and once more Leofric rode into the glade, its breathtaking beauty still with the power to render him speechless. He had thought its magic would have been spoiled for him by the touch of the creatures of Chaos, but as with all things natural, it had healed itself and the wonder of its magnificence was undimmed.

Sure enough, Kyarno was here, lounging atop the same rock from which he had watched Leofric when he had brought him here to bathe, his steed grazing at the edge of the glade. Dressed in the same clothes he had been wearing the last time Leofric had seen him, Kyarno looked sad and tired, his pale, narrow face turned towards the thundering waterfall.

Leofric sat for a moment to allow the calming presence of the glade's air to fill him, smiling and pleased to be back.

'Why are you here, Leofric?' asked Kyarno without turning.

Leofric did not reply immediately, sliding from the back of his horse and setting him loose in the glade to join Kyarno's.

'I came to see you.'

'Why?'

'To tell you that you are missed.'

Kyarno snorted in disbelief. 'By whom? Who misses the elf who leaves so many dead in his foolish wake? I do not deserve to be missed.'

'Morvhen misses you,' said Leofric, holding out the leaf-wrapped scroll.

Kyarno finally turned to face him and smiled wistfully. 'And she sent you to find me? No doubt because the Hound of Winter watches her like a hawk now.'

Leofric nodded. 'Yes, he does, and I should not have come here.'

'So why did you?'

'You should know by now it is never wise to refuse the requests of a woman.'

'There is truth in that,' agreed Kyarno, slipping from the rock and approaching Leofric to take the scroll.

Leofric turned to give Kyarno privacy to read Morvhen's words and walked to the edge of the crystal waters of the wide pool. Lights darted beneath the surface and glittering gems winked on the sandy bottom.

Kyarno joined him at the water's edge, a faraway look on his face as he watched the tumbling waterfall foam the water white.

'Thank you. I know you did not have to do this,' said Kyarno.

'You are welcome,' nodded Leofric, squatting down on his haunches and running a hand through the waters.

Kyarno tucked the message into his shirt and sat on the grass beside him and both man and elf shared a companionable silence, listening to the crash of the water and the sighing song of the trees.

'Tell me of your lands,' said Kyarno suddenly.

'I thought elves had no interest in what lay beyond Athel Loren?'

'Normally we do not, but I wish to hear you speak of them.'

Leofric thought of the world he knew, surprised to find that his memories of it were dim and hollow. He struggled to recall what he knew of the world, finding it difficult to think of the kingdoms beyond the forest.

'Bretonnia is a fine land, of honour and virtue,' said Leofric eventually, 'but it suffers as do all in these dark times. Orcs and undead raiders from across the seas attack our coasts, and our people live in squalor and poverty. For those lucky enough to be born to a noble family, it can be a fine place, but for all others it is a grim land.'

'And beyond Bretonnia?' asked Kyarno.

'To the north, across the Grey Mountains, lies the Empire, a grim and fearful place of sprawling, dark forests that are home to all manner of foul creatures – goblins, beastmen and worse. It is hardly a nation at all, riven with discord and its ruler barely able to keep his lands in order. Further east is the cold northern realm of Kislev, a land said to be locked in ice and snow.'

'Have you ever been there?'

'No,' said Leofric, 'I have never seen it, and nor do I wish to. It is a savage land, peopled by harsh men and women who fight a constant battle for survival against the northern tribes of the Dark Gods. It breeds them tough, but it breeds them dour. The closest I have come to Kislev is Middenheim, city of the White Wolf.'

'White Wolf? Who is that?'

'The city is named for the god of battles and winter, Ulric, and is a magnificent-looking place that sits atop a great crag of rock that rises from the forest like a mountain.'

'Why did you travel there?'

Leofric sighed, remembering the fierce battles fought around the northern city of the Empire, the death, the blood and, most of all, the hateful memory of their rout at the hands of the Swords of Chaos.

'The hordes of Chaos had poured southwards from the steppes, led by a powerful warlord named Archaon, burning and destroying everything in their path as they clove through Kislev towards the Empire. Though great victories were won at Mazhorod and Urszebya, nothing could halt the advance of the horde and they invaded the Empire in their thousands. They sought to destroy the city of the White Wolf and thence the world. My king declared an errantry war against Archaon and the knights of Bretonnia rode out to do battle.'

'I see by your eyes that it was a battle not easily won.'

'No,' said Leofric. 'It was not. We were victorious, but the cost was high. We fought to save the world and, though, in the end it is fruitless, Chaos must be fought at all times.'

'You have said that before,' said Kyarno. 'Why do you say that it is fruitless?'

Leofric hesitated before speaking again, unsure why he had made such a frank confession to Kyarno. Were the healing waters of the Crystal Mere working their enchantments on him once more? The thought of his sorrows being eased by the magic of the glade did not trouble him anymore; *this* pain he would be happy to be rid of.

'Each time the warriors of Chaos come, they come in greater numbers and reach further into the domains of men. In their wake comes death, famine, sickness and suffering. How long will it be until there is nothing left for them to destroy, until their armies reach the deserts of the far south?'

'But each time you have turned back the darkness,' pointed out Kyarno.

'We hold them back each time, but each time we are lessened.'

Kyarno shook his head. 'No, each time you hurl the forces of Chaos back you are strengthened. There is nothing fruitless about fighting Chaos, Leofric, nothing. Chaos *must* be opposed, for it is that fight that makes us strong. I have heard you speak of the lands of your race and one thing is clear.'

'And what is that?'

'That against all the odds they endure,' said Kyarno. 'For thousands of years – through plague, warriors of the north, dusty revenants of the southern deserts or foul orcs – these realms have survived.'

'For now,' said Leofric. 'It is only a matter of time before they are swept away in blood and war.'

'True, many kingdoms have arisen that their rulers thought would last forever, but are now nothing more than dust and legend, but they fought to preserve them for as long as they could.'

'What is the point if they are just going to fail?'

'I know you don't really believe that,' said Kyarno. 'You would not have become a warrior if you did.'

'What do you mean?'

'You know what I mean,' said Kyarno. 'A true warrior fights not because he wants to, but because he has to. To defend those who cannot defend themselves. To give hope to those around him who look to him to do what is right and to fight because that is what must be done.'

Kyarno's words spoke to Leofric of the last time he had entered the waters of the Crystal Mere, desperately scrambling for a weapon to fight the beasts of Chaos.

Though victory had seemed impossible he had fought anyway.

'Perhaps you are right, Kyarno,' said Leofric, rising to his feet and running his wet hands through his hair. 'I will think on what you have said.'

'You are returning to Coeth-Mara?' asked Kyarno with a disappointed sigh.

'Yes, is there a message you wish me to take to Morvhen?'

Kyarno said nothing, and Leofric saw the elf's attention was fixed on something over his shoulder. He turned to see the object of Kyarno's stare and his mouth fell open at the magnificent sight before him.

A great hart grazed with the horses at the edge of the glade, its furred hide a glorious, unblemished white, its mighty antlers curling above its head in a wide fan of bone. Leofric had hunted deer throughout his lands for years, but had never set eyes on a creature so fine and regal as this.

It stood amid a burst of yellow primrose, the scent of which was suddenly strong and intoxicating. The hart lifted its mighty head, as if sensing their scrutiny, and as its eyes met his, Leofric was humbled by the ancient wisdom and intelligence he saw there.

As he watched the wonderful animal feed, a tremor rippled through the earth, sending the imps that capered in the water scurrying into the undergrowth with wild squeals. A surging, powerful energy rose from the very ground and Leofric felt his heartbeat race with a nameless exhilaration. A breathless shiver of anticipation rushed along his spine, a primal energy filling his muscles with a wild urge to run, to fight and to hunt. He turned to ask Kyarno what was happening, the words dying in his throat as he saw golden wychfires blazing in the elf's eyes.

'Primrose…' breathed Kyarno, an ancient longing suffusing his voice as the echoing blast of a mighty hunting horn sounded from far away.

'What about them?' asked Leofric nervously, the distant skirl of the horn chilling him with its promise of blood.

'…the first flower of spring,' finished Kyarno.

CHAPTER SIXTEEN

DEEP IN ATHEL Loren, in a secret glade sacred to both forest and elf, a mighty oak tree trembled, its ancient surface gnarled and pitted with age. Five thousand and more summers had it seen, its roots stretching deep into the rock of the world. Known as the Oak of Ages, yellow blooming primrose flowered amid its thick, twisting roots and green, verdant grass bent and swayed in the gathering breeze.

A crack split the trunk from roots to branches and a gust of wind, like the first breath of the world, billowed from within. The deafening blast of a hunting horn echoed from deep inside the tree, as though a vast hall lay beneath the ground; the baying of hounds and the raucous cries of birds stirred from their eyries rising from the forest to accompany the exultant echo of the horn.

Sweet-smelling sap ran from the crack in the oak tree and the thunder of mighty hooves beat on the air as something ancient, terrifying and primal stirred from its slumbers and spread through the forest once more.

THE SOUND OF the hunting horn came again, Leofric could feel its power in the very depths of his soul. He trembled at its might, a fear deep in his bones screaming that he was this hunter's prey. His every sense told him to run, that nothing good could come of this sound.

He remembered a similar sensation when he had first ridden through the forest, when the wild riders of Kurnous had surrounded them. Kyarno had said that those warriors were the wild huntsmen who rode alongside the King of the Wood when he awoke in spring...

Leofric looked back towards the edge of the glade, seeing that the white hart had vanished into the forest at the sound of the horn and that the yellow of the flowers seemed much more vivid.

'We have to get out of here,' said Leofric.

'Yes,' agreed Kyarno, the gold fire still glittering in his wide eyes. 'We are in serious danger. The King of the Wood has awoken and is on the hunt...'

Every tale Leofric knew of the dangerous king of the faerie forest ended in blood. The same fear he had felt when confronted by the warriors who served him arose, but this was much worse: the paralysing dread felt by all hunted things.

Leofric and Kyarno ran for their steeds, climbing onto their backs and riding hard into the trees. As they plunged into the forest, Leofric saw that the bright feeling of vitality had vanished utterly, the beauty and grace changed to something far darker.

Where the sunlight had warmed his face, now it cast fearful shadows. Where the curve of branches had artfully shaped pleasant bowers, now they grasped for him and tore at his clothes as they rode headlong for Coeth-Mara.

Leofric saw the true face of the forest, ancient and powerful, its need to grow and spread manifest in the impossibly fecund hearts of the trees. Stark against the skies, the tall, clawed branches reached out for him as they rode and he cried out in terror as the rising horn-blast came again, louder and more powerful than before.

Kyarno rode beside him, his eyes alight with savage lust as the forest came alive around them. Shadows rushed alongside them, darting shapes and capering creatures with wings and branch-like limbs.

Faces leered from the trunks of gnarled trees and a shimmering mist gathered between them as the distant howls of hunting packs drew closer. Though it had been morning when he had set out for the Crystal Mere, the sky above swiftly changed from pale blue to an angry, bruised purple, dark clouds forming above the treetops and the first rumbles of thunder building.

'Kyarno!' shouted Leofric. 'What's happening?'

'The wild hunt is abroad! Hurry!'

Leofric urged his mount to greater speed as lightning split the sky and a rolling thunder tolled from the clouds. Ghostly shapes loomed in the mist, clawed hands of twigs reaching out to him with spiteful laughter. The horn came again and Leofric cried out, the wild blast sounding as though it came from right beside him.

Thunder came again and this time he realised that the sound came not from the clouds above, but was the hammering of hooves. He heard branches snapping aside, the barking of hounds and the caw of dark birds.

He looked up to see the sky alive with thousands of shapes, murders of ravens and crows swirling in huge numbers above as something massive thundered through the forest towards them. Rain, heavy spring rain, now fell from the skies as the full fury of the storm broke.

Dark light flared in the forest around him and he saw shrieking shapes in the mist either side of him, riders on dark steeds with eyes of golden fire. Whooping yells of fierce joy echoed from the forest and Leofric saw that cloaked riders surrounded them.

They rode with wild abandon, leaping and weaving in and out of the mist, brandishing long, thorn-looped spears above their heads. Skulls bounced from their belts and torques as they rode, and they had the look of a devil about them, their aspect no longer truly elven, but something far older and more powerful.

The wild riders of Kurnous unleashed...

Snapping hounds bounded alongside them, howling in praise of their king. Leofric gave his horse its head, knowing that it could better evade these riders and hounds than he. Something massive drew near from behind. He could hear the crash of its thunderous approach even over the booming storm that raged above, and Leofric felt a suffocating fear arise in his breast at the thought of laying eyes on this terrible, bloody king.

'Leofric!' shouted Kyarno. 'This way!'

He needed no further urging and yelled as his steed broke towards Kyarno. The beasts of the wild hunt howled and cried, the snapping crash of their king deafening as he charged towards them.

Leofric plunged after Kyarno, crouched over Aeneor's neck, his heart hammering in his chest as the undergrowth around them grew thinner. He heard Kyarno shouting something in the magical tongue of the elves and felt the forest shift in response to his words. Branches whipped past them, one laying open his cheek across the scar given to him by Cu-Sith, but Leofric ignored the stinging pain, too intent on the hunting packs behind them.

A sudden sense of vertigo seized him and the forest around him became blurred and ghostly, as though he looked at it through a fogged window. Lights streaked his vision and he fought to stay on the back of his horse as a wave of dizziness swamped him.

Sounds became muted and his every breath was like the bellowing of an angry god in his ears. He clapped his hands to his head in pain, tumbling from the back of his horse and landing heavily on the forest floor.

He lay still for several moments before he realised that the sounds of pursuit were no longer behind them and that the forest was no longer as hostile in appearance or deed. Kyarno lay across his horse's neck, his breathing shallow and his skin even paler than normal.

'What happened?' gasped Leofric, fighting to calm his rampant heartbeat as he climbed to his feet using the trunk of a nearby tree. 'Are we safe?'

'For the moment,' wheezed Kyarno. 'We have a brief respite. But we will need to ride again soon.'

'What did you do?'

'I spoke to the trees and asked them if we might pass along the secret paths that travel between worlds and link some of the glades of the forest. I told them of your service to the Éadaoin kinband and they were gracious enough to allow you to travel with me. We are some miles yet from Coeth-Mara, but if the Lady Ariel is with us we can still make it.'

Leofric rubbed his side where he had hit the ground, looking up into the sky where the thunder and lightning still seethed. Ghostly lights flickered above them and he knew that they were not yet safe.

'Coeth-Mara?' asked Leofric. 'Will you find welcome there?'

Kyarno shrugged. 'Let us worry about that if we get there. Can you ride?'

'I can,' said Leofric, climbing back onto his horse as he heard the far-off sound of the hunting horn once more.

'Then let us be away before the wild hunt catches up to us once again!'

LIKE A ROTTEN tooth expelled from a diseased gum, the waystone heaved from the blackened ground, its vast granite bulk swaying gently for a moment before it toppled to the earth with an almighty crash. The beastherd roared and bellowed in triumph as the stone fell, stamping the ground and locking horns with one another.

The shaman held himself upright with his staff. Its battle with the magic of the waystone had exhausted it to the point of collapse. The power of the gods had given it the strength it needed to drag the waystone down, but had left it precious little to sustain its life, and it knew that its last breath was upon it.

The Beastlord beat its chest with the flat of its mighty axe, the weapon ringing from its brazen hide as it sent the massive forms of its largest followers forward to gather up the waystone. A pack of hulking trolls, their massive muscles swollen by dark energies, grunted and roared as they lifted the enormous stone onto their backs.

Even the smallest of the trolls was twice the size of the Beastlord, their leathery skin a mottled green and brown. Their thick skulls and stupid features marked them as creatures of Chaos, but the shaman knew that they were not the chosen children of the Dark Gods; such a vaunted position was that of the beastmen.

The shaman turned a milky, distended eye back to the forest, grunting in satisfaction as it saw the raw wound in the ground where the waystone had once stood. The forest writhed as though in pain, roots and rapidly growing shoots of greenery bursting from the ground.

As though spilling outwards, the edge of the forest appeared to be drawing nearer, expanding beyond its previous boundary. The shaman slid down its staff as its life force faded, looking up as a wild horn blast echoed over the treetops.

The trolls bearing the waystone lurched back towards the mountains, their steps slow and ponderous, but they were easily outpacing the encroachments of the forest. Dark shapes moved within the forest's edge, wild, monstrous things and the shaman shuddered in fear as the horn blast sounded again and the breath of something impossibly ancient roared from the trees.

Like the last breath of winter, the wind gusted over the assembled beastmen, carrying with it the promise of death, blood and the huntsman's spear. A low bray of fear rose from the herd at the sound and sent many fleeing for the mountains.

The shaman's last sight was of the Beastlord standing firm against the power of the forest's magic, roaring its defiance and mastery. It had taken one of the fabled waystones of Athel Loren and no mere wind was going to frighten it.

It had taken what it had come for and with the way-stone well on its way towards the mountains, the Beastlord led its herd from Athel Loren.

LEOFRIC AND KYARNO rode off into the forest once more, willing their horses to greater speed as the charge of the wild hunt drew nearer with each passing second.

Leofric could feel the hot breath of the hunting hounds on his neck, the claws of the battle raven on his flesh and the gaze of the mighty King of the Wood upon his soul, but told himself they were but fearful illusions. They galloped a weaving course between the trees, the ghostly mists clawing from the trees once more as Leofric began to recognise parts of the forest from the times he had spent riding around Coeth-Mara.

Though in that recognition was strangeness, a sense that even though individual parts of the forest were familiar, they were gathered oddly, as though different parts of the forest had shifted and moved.

Nor were they challenged as they rode beneath the woven arch of leaves, branches and gem-encrusted belts of gold and silver that marked the edge of Lord Aldaeld's halls.

'Come on!' shouted Kyarno as Leofric heard the crash of something huge emerging from the trees and felt a lustful wave of aggression and power wash over him. Ahead he saw Kyarno stiffen in the grip of this power, his eyes alight with its energies.

He risked a glance over his shoulder and cried out in fear as he saw something huge and muscular, its antlered flesh green hued and daubed with runic symbols. Fiery-eyed riders surrounded it, whooping and yelling as scores of baying hounds loped through the thoroughfares and tree-lined avenues of Coeth-Mara.

Branches and leaves obscured Leofric's sight of the massive King of the Wood as he and Kyarno altered course and rode into the hall of Lord Aldaeld, passing into a high, vaulted chamber filled with the inhabitants of Coeth-Mara, their faces fearful and wary.

Shouts and cries of alarm followed them as they entered, warriors with spears and swords rushing to surround them. Leofric slumped across the neck of his horse, laughing and crying in relief to have escaped the charge of the wild hunt as it thundered past.

'You dare return in defiance of your banishment?' shouted a voice.

'Lord Aldaeld will have your head for this!' said another and Leofric looked up to see grey-cloaked warriors of the Eternal Guard drag Kyarno from his horse.

'Wait!' he shouted. 'No! Kyarno saved us both in the forest.'

The elven warriors ignored him and Leofric felt his fury build at them. Kyarno had saved his life. He dropped from Aeneor's back, lurching towards the struggling elves. A crowd gathered to watch the unfolding drama in their midst, grateful for the chance to take their minds from the danger beyond the hall.

'Release him!' shouted Leofric, his voice laden with anger and authority.

None of the Eternal Guard bothered to take notice of him, and he ran towards them, gripping the cloak of the nearest one and hauling him off Kyarno. Leofric hurled the warrior aside and reached for the next, but the fallen warrior was upon him a second later and, within moments, both he and Kyarno were held fast.

'Get off me!' yelled Leofric.

'Be silent!' shouted the Hound of Winter, emerging from the press of bodies surrounding them. Cairbre carried the Blades of Midnight in one hand and his helm in the other. Behind him came Lord Aldaeld, Morvhen and Naieth.

Cairbre marched towards them, his face an unreadable mask, though Leofric could see a flicker of emotion cross his stoic features as he spoke to Kyarno.

'You know you are forbidden to return to Coeth-Mara,' he said.

'I know,' replied his nephew.

'Then why are you here?'

'He saved my life!' shouted Leofric. 'Without Kyarno, the wild hunt would have caught me. He risked his own life to save mine. That is why he is here.'

Cairbre turned from Kyarno as Lord Aldaeld approached, his power and strength undeniable, though Leofric saw he still bore a faint white scar where Valas Laithu's dagger had pierced his heart. His cloak of leaves and his tattoos writhed with motion, and his face spoke of great anger, but also great regret.

'Is this true, Kyarno?' asked Lord Aldaeld.

Kyarno nodded, shrugging off the restraining arms of the Eternal Guard. Leofric felt the grip of the warriors holding him relax and threw them off angrily. In the silence that followed, he could clearly hear the howling hounds and the crash of the wild hunt as it passed through Coeth-Mara.

Behind Aldaeld, Morvhen looked on fearfully and Leofric's heart went out to her. Her lost love stood before her, yet she could not reach out and touch him for fear of her father's banishment, and the absurdity of this roused Leofric to speak out.

'Lord Aldaeld,' he said. 'May I speak?'

'I don't need you to speak for me,' snapped Kyarno.

'I do not speak for you, Kyarno,' said Leofric. 'I speak for the Lady Morvhen.'

Lord Aldaeld spun at the mention of Morvhen's name and his eyes narrowed. 'You speak for Morvhen? Why would you speak for her?'

'Because no one else will speak for her or Kyarno,' answered Leofric. 'She loves Kyarno, and he loves her. Why will you not allow them to be together?'

'Because he will lead her to ruin,' growled Aldaeld. 'Kyarno has had every chance to prove himself to me and each time he has thrown it away. I will tolerate him no more.'

'Then you are a fool!' said Leofric to a gasp of shock. 'For you do not see what you throw away for the sake of spite.'

Lord Aldaeld's face twisted in anger and his sword flashed into his hand as he stepped close to Leofric. 'I should kill you where you stand, human! You think to speak to me thus in my own halls!'

'I apologise for such harsh words, Lord Aldaeld, but I speak from the heart.'

'Your kind always thinks it knows better than any other,' sneered Aldaeld. 'You meddle and you throw your might around like children, heedless of the cultures of others, always thinking in your blinkered way that only you can know the will of the world.'

'What you say has truth to it, but give me a chance. That's all I ask.'

'Say what it is you want to say, but my course is set.'

Leofric stood before the lord of Coeth-Mara, but addressed his words to the assembled throng, raising his voice so that all could hear him over the howling and thunder of hooves from beyond the hall.

'I come from the land that borders Athel Loren. It is called Bretonnia and I am a knight of that realm. I serve my king and defend his lands when he calls me. I am a warrior and my path to earn my knighthood has been long and arduous.

'I began as a young man, what we Bretonnians call a knight errant. I was young, impetuous and ready to fight the world if it would mean I could become a knight of the realm. There are many young men of my land who aspire to this great height, but only a few who reach it. A knight errant is the very image of bravado – arrogant and haughty, brave to the point of recklessness. In battle they charge heedlessly towards the enemy, earning either great glory or a heroic death.'

'What has this to do with anything?' demanded Lord Aldaeld.

'Bear with me,' cautioned Leofric. 'Most of these knights errant do not survive and many a mother of Bretonnia has mourned a son before her time.'

'Then they are fools,' said Aldaeld. 'Recklessness has no place on the battlefield.'

'You are of course correct, Lord Aldaeld, but think on this – those who survive know that. While reckless bravery has its place, courage is at its best when tempered with duty. This is the lesson they learn.'

'You would throw the lives of your young away for this lesson?'

'To do otherwise would be to deny a young knight his destiny,' said Leofric. 'And by such means are the knights of Bretonnia kept mighty, for those who have not experienced such passions cannot truly understand the nobility of courage.'

'So what are you saying?'

'That Kyarno is young and has made many foolish choices, but that he is alive and he is brave. I believe he has learned the lesson of courage and duty and is fit to take his place within your halls.'

Aldaeld shook his head. 'His actions caused the death of many of my people. I have a responsibility to my kin-band and I cannot trust him.'

'I know that, and so does he,' said Leofric. 'He will carry the knowledge of what he has done to his dying day and no punishment of yours can make that any worse. All you will do is break your daughter's heart.'

'Do not think to manipulate me by recourse to my daughter,' warned Aldaeld.

'I do not, I swear. I am a knight of Bretonnia and I never lie. I speak only what I know to be true.'

Aldaeld did not reply, switching his gaze from Kyarno to Morvhen before turning to Cairbre and asking, 'What say you, Hound of Winter? Can your nephew be trusted?'

Cairbre took a step towards Kyarno and looked him square in the eye, daring him to look away. They stared deep into one another for long moments before Cairbre said, 'His heart is true, my lord. I have known that since he was born.'

'But can he be trusted?'

'I do not know, my lord,' confessed Cairbre. 'I want to believe he can, but I do not know for sure.'

'You have your answer, sir knight,' said Aldaeld, turning away from Leofric. 'Kyarno can stay until the wild hunt passes. Then I want him gone again.'

'No!' said Leofric. 'Did you hear nothing of what I said?'

'I heard, human,' snapped Aldaeld, turning and marching back towards him, 'but it changes nothing. I am lord of this domain, not you or your king, and I do what is necessary to protect it. I do not care for the traditions of your lands, for they are not mine. Did you think to come into my halls, make a pretty speech and return everything to normal? You should know your place, human, for life is not that simple in Athel Loren. For your kind it might be, but you are not among your kind now. Do not ever forget that.'

In the sudden silence that followed, Leofric became aware that the thunderous noise beyond the hall had vanished.

'Prophetess...' hissed Aldaeld, realising the same thing. 'The wild hunt... what has become of it?'

Naieth closed her eyes and Leofric watched as a dim glow built behind her eyelids, feeling the prickling sensation of magic nearby.

'It moves on,' said Naieth, her voice taking on the dreamlike quality of a sleepwalker.

'Where does it go?' demanded Aldaeld.

'It goes beyond,' cried Naieth, gasping and dropping to her knees. Cairbre rushed to help her and she sagged against him, opening her eyes and staring directly at Leofric.

'It goes beyond,' she repeated, tears streaming down her face. 'The waystones are breached!'

'Breached?' cried Aldaeld. 'How?'

'I do not know,' wept Naieth. 'I did not see. I did not see...'

'You said the wild hunt had gone beyond,' said Leofric, fearful of what the prophetess might say. 'Where do you mean?'

'I am so sorry...' whispered Naieth. 'It rides for your lands now.'

* * *

SATISFIED THAT HIS animals were bedded down for the night, Varus Martel closed the latch on the gate that separated the byre where he kept his three pigs from where he and his family slept. He circled the low-burning fire to reach his threadbare jerkin where it lay beside the simple pallet bed he shared with his wife and two children.

The hard-packed mud floor of their hovel was damp and cold, the thin soles of his boots keeping in not a shred of warmth. He lifted his jerkin from beside the fire, pulling out a carved wooden pipe from within, and began tamping what little weed he had left into the bowl. He jammed the pipe between his teeth and pulled on his leather skullcap, tying the thin cords beneath his chin before leaning in towards the fire and lifting out a lighted taper.

Varus lit the pipe and took a hefty drag before making his way outside.

The night was chill, but not cold, the winter having done its worst already. It had been hard on the villagers of Chabaon, many of the local families suffering sad losses amongst their children or elderly. Varus himself had lost a prime sow to the cold, and while it had meant they had had enough to eat for a few weeks, there would be no more piglets until he could afford to buy another at market.

The thought depressed him and he tried not to think about the future as he heard a distant rumble, like approaching thunder. He looked up into the sky, his brow wrinkling in puzzlement as he saw nothing but the pale face of Mannslieb as it shone down upon the little village.

The rumble grew louder and he saw several other doors open and inquisitive faces appear.

'Varus,' shouted Ballard from the hovel across the way. 'What d'you think that is?'

'Don't rightly know,' said Varus. 'Ain't likely thunder. Not a cloud in the sky.'

'Peculiar is what it is,' said Ballard, nodding sagely at his own pronouncement and taking out a pipe of his own.

'Aye, peculiar right enough,' agreed Varus, blowing a ragged smoke ring. He scanned the horizon, looking for any sign of horsemen, for the noise sounded a lot like riders. Lots of them too. The only riders round these parts were knights and suchlike from Castle Carrard and that was a good many miles away. Not like riders to be out this late so far from home...

Then he realised that the noise wasn't coming from the north, but the east. He looked up at the sky once more, the pipe falling from his hand as he saw spectral clouds slip across the face of the moon and heard an echoing horn blast carried on the wind.

'Oh no...' he whispered. 'Oh no, no, no...'

He saw the same realisation strike Ballard and hauled open the door to his hovel with a cry of alarm.

'Up! Up!' he cried. 'For the love of the Lady, up!'

His wife sat bolt upright, already frightened by his tone, his children still groggy with sleep. He shut the door behind him and threw the locking bar into place, hoping that it would be enough.

'What's the matter, Varus?' screamed his wife as he dropped to his knees before the badly painted statuette of the Lady that sat in a small alcove in the wall.

'Lady, please save us from the wrath of the faerie folk!' shouted Varus as the mounting wind rattled the ill-fitting door in its frame. The rumble of hooves beat the air, growing louder each second and the first peal of thunder shook the hovel with its booming violence.

His children screamed as a terrible, bloodcurdling horn echoed across the cold landscape. A shuddering tremor shook the hovel and the howls of wild hounds drifted across the bleak moorland. Plates and cups fell to the floor and the squeals of his pigs added to the din.

Varus rushed over to his family, holding them tightly as the terrible sound of the wild hunt closed in on the village of Chabaon. They huddled on the bed, weeping in terror at the sound of their approaching doom, praying to the Lady of the Lake that it would pass them by.

Howling winds tore through the village and Varus screamed as the roof of the hovel was ripped off, the lightning-streaked sky thick with shrieking ravens and ghostly riders on pale horses. Wild laughter and horns followed the charging huntsmen of the sky and thunder boomed in the wake of their charge.

The walls of his hovel blew inwards, but Varus Martel and his family had already been carried up into the sky by the wild hunt as it laid waste to the village of Chabaon.

CHAPTER SEVENTEEN

ANCIENT ANCESTRAL FEAR clutched at Leofric as he heard Naieth tell him that the wild hunt now wreaked havoc in Bretonnia. The dread of the howling gale of destruction and the terrible carnage it left in its wake surged through his body and he felt hollow, as though he had been winded by a fall from a horse.

'Are you sure?' he asked.

Naieth nodded sadly. 'Yes, I am sure. The King of the Wood has tasted blood already and he will not stop until much more has been shed.'

'Is there anything we can do?'

'No, Leofric, there is not. With the waystone barrier breached, the power of the king is free to reach beyond the borders of Athel Loren.'

'Then we must restore the barrier!' he cried. 'How can we do that?'

'Only by restoring the waystone to its former position, Leofric.'

Leofric turned to Lord Aldaeld and said, 'Please, my people are dying. Help me.'

'Help you?' said Aldaeld. 'What is it you think I can do?'

'I don't know,' said Leofric helplessly. 'Whatever you can.'

Aldaeld shook his head. 'The lives of humans are not worth the effort and risk to elven lives. The wild hunt will return to the forest once the king's lust for battle and destruction is sated. When he returns to Athel Loren, we will recover the waystone.'

'But my people are dying!' shouted Leofric. 'Your king is killing the people of Bretonnia and you will stand by while that happens?'

Aldaeld nodded and hissed, 'I would stand by while he wiped humans from the face of the world if that were his course. You bring nothing into this world and it is certain you will take nothing out of it. Why should I mourn your kind?'

Leofric stood speechless, shocked at this candid admission by Lord Aldaeld, who turned from him to address Naieth.

'How is it that the barrier has failed?' demanded the elven lord. 'Has the power of the enchantments wrought upon the waystone faded?'

'No,' whispered Naieth, closing her eyes once more and allowing her spirit to travel the mystic paths of the forest. 'The power of such ancient magic does not fade easily, some other power is at work here.'

'What other power? What could overcome the power of the elder magic?'

Suddenly Naieth cried out in horror and pain, and but for the support of the Hound of Winter, would have fallen. Blood ran from her nose and she wept tears of pain.

'No!' she wept, and Leofric was surprised to hear the venom of hatred in the prophetess's tone. 'It is the beast. It is Cyanathair! It has returned.'

A ripple of horror spread through the halls at the mention of this name, though Leofric did not understand what it meant. Swiftly the horror turned to anger and the mood of the hall changed to one of vengeful aggression. He saw the same golden fire he had seen in Kyarno's eyes at the waking of the King of the Wood reflected in every elf within the hall, a wild anger and lust for killing that sent a chill along his spine.

The elves of Coeth-Mara milled like caged wolves, the threat of violence in every face and every gesture as they clutched at sword hilts or gripped the hafts of spears.

Was this part of the King of the Wood's power? Did part of his anger and destructive nature pass to his people upon his waking?

'Who is this Cyanathair?' asked Leofric warily.

'Do not speak its name again!' gasped Naieth.

'It is the Corruptor,' said Cairbre. 'It is the enemy.'

'Your race knows it as the Shadow-Gave,' said Naieth. 'It is the bane of all things living, an abomination. It is the thing that should not be.'

The Shadow-Gave…

Legends spoke of such a creature, a fell monster too terrible to imagine, that had ripped its way into the world in a village near the Forest of Arden. A bestial creature of Chaos that warped everything around it into horrific new forms, it was a tale to frighten young children with. The myth of the creature was recorded in the Bretonnian lay 'Requiem', a tragic poem that spoke of men who crawled in the mud like beasts and animals that walked on their hind legs and babbled nonsensical doggerel as they feasted on one another.

'Surely such a creature must be dead?' said Leofric. 'Beastmen are no longer lived than humans. It must have died many hundreds of years ago.'

'How little you know, Leofric,' said Naieth, not unkindly. 'If only it were so. No, the Corruptor is a creature of Chaos Eternal. It has been slain many times in the secret war, but each time it is reborn anew to continue its destructive quest amongst the races of this world. The Lady Ariel seeks always to defeat it, but the power of the Dark Gods is strong and the beast lives still.'

Leofric struggled to understand Naieth's words, grasping at their meaning as a drowning man clutches for a lifeline. But amid the words of the prophetess, something stood out above all others.

'Who is the Lady Ariel?' asked Leofric.

'She is the voice and will of Isha,' said Naieth carefully and Leofric knew that she was not telling him the whole truth. He suspected he might not want to know the true answer to his question and decided to let Naieth's evasion go for the moment, the more pressing concern of his people uppermost in his mind.

'Well, human,' said Aldaeld. 'The Corruptor is a foe to all races, so it seems we will aid your people after all.'

'I welcome your help, Lord Aldaeld, however it is given,' said Leofric.

Lord Aldaeld shrugged and said, 'Circumstance makes strange bedfellows of us all,' as the elves of Coeth-Mara scattered throughout the hall, gathering up weapons and girding themselves for war.

Kyarno sidled close to him and whispered, 'Thank you for your words, even though they carried no weight with Aldaeld.'

Morvhen approached and Leofric said, 'My lady. I apologise if I spoke out of turn earlier, but I meant no disrespect in speaking for you.'

Lord Aldaeld's daughter smiled and gave Leofric a chaste kiss on the cheek. 'I was glad of your words, Leofric. They came from the heart and I felt that, even if my father did not.'

The Hound of Winter appeared at Morvhen's shoulder and said, 'Kyarno, I am sorry that I could not vouch for you.'

'It does not matter, uncle,' said Kyarno. 'I know your loyalty must be to your lord. It is as it should be. You would not be Lord Aldaeld's champion were it otherwise.'

'Will you fight alongside us against the Corruptor?'

'If Lord Aldaeld will allow me to, then yes, I shall,' nodded Kyarno, glancing in Leofric's direction. 'A true warrior fights not because he wants to, but because he has to.'

'He will be fortunate to have your blade,' said Cairbre, his eyes cast down.

'Uncle,' said Kyarno, gripping the Hound of Winter's sleeve. 'The bad blood between us is no more. The light of the Lady Ariel touched me and… well, I feel cleansed of the bitterness I carried. I tried to tell Tarean Stormcrow of this and I believe he and I might have been friends, but alas, that was not to be. I foolishly missed the chance to know his friendship, but I will not make that mistake again with my kin.'

Cairbre smiled and Leofric now saw the resemblance between the two elves as the barriers between them began to come down.

The reconciliation between uncle and nephew was interrupted by the raised voice of Lord Aldaeld as he shouted, 'To arms! The host of Lord Aldaeld Éadaoin goes to war! I will send word to the kindreds of the forest that Cyanathair has returned, and the blades of battle shall be wetted in blood, the fires of war fanned by hatred of the children of Chaos.'

Warlike cheering greeted Aldaeld's words, the wild exultation of the hall infectious as the elves of Coeth-Mara roared with the lust for battle. Leofric felt his heart quicken, caught up by the thought of taking the fight to the monsters of Chaos.

Kyarno was right: it was the fight that mattered, not the outcome. It did not matter whether they won or lost in the long war, it was that they fought at all that was the victory. So long as warriors of courage stood against the dark powers, evil could not triumph. So long as one blade was raised against evil then it could never win.

A flurry of swords, like a forest of glittering stars, flashed into the air as all the warriors in Coeth-Mara shouted their allegiance to their lord.

As the cheering died down, the Hound of Winter asked, 'If we take the fight to the Corruptor, how then are we to bring the waystone back to its home in the earth?'

Stony silence greeted his words, as the practicality of them sank in.

No one said anything until Kyarno hesitantly ventured, 'Beithir-Seun could do it.'

Morvhen said, 'No, he is surely gone from the world, is he not?'

Naieth took a step forward and said, 'No, he is not, but his chasm glade has been lost amidst the mountains for centuries. None now live who know of it.'

'I know of it,' said Kyarno slowly. 'I have walked in his glade and spied upon his mighty form. He lives still and if anyone could carry the waystone, then it is he.'

'Who is Beithir-Seun?' asked Leofric.

* * *

NAIETH LED THE way, following her owl companion through a part of the forest Leofric had not seen during his time in Athel Loren. The trees grew thickly here and a potent sensation of magic seeped into Leofric through the soles of his boots. Winged imps buzzed through the air, their bodies alight with faerie fire and the song of the trees was a gentle lilt on the air.

Despite the pastoral scene, Leofric was acutely aware of the ancient power behind this part of the forest's benign appearance. He followed Cairbre and Kyarno along the overgrown path, grateful for the chance to strike back at the creatures of Chaos that had unleashed the wild hunt on the world. Leofric still had no idea who this Beithir-Seun was, and no one seemed inclined to tell him.

Lord Aldaeld had reluctantly agreed that Kyarno should lead the Hound of Winter to the chasm glades of Beithir-Seun and entreat him to aid the recovery of the waystone.

'You have a chance to show me your worth, Kyarno,' Aldaeld had said. 'Live up to this human's faith in you.'

'I will not fail you, Lord Aldaeld. You will yet see my worth,' promised Kyarno.

Leofric had stepped forward, his sword drawn and said, 'I too will accompany you. For it is my people who are dying and the Shadow-Gave threatens us all.'

'Very well, human. May the blessing of Isha go with you all.'

Now the three of them followed the prophetess deep into the secret glades of the forest, though if what he understood of the chasm glades was true, then they were in for a long journey.

'Am I to understand the chasm glades are in the Grey Mountains?' asked Leofric.

'They are,' agreed Cairbre. 'If what Kyarno says is correct, then the cleft Beithir-Seun dwells within is in the Grey Mountains north of the river you call the Grismerie.'

'But that is what, two hundred miles away? Are we to walk all the way?'

Kyarno turned and said, 'Have you learned nothing from your time in Athel Loren, Leofric? There are many secret paths through the forest and time and distance may mean different things along different paths.'

The answer only served to confuse Leofric even more and he asked no further questions as they made their way deeper and deeper into the forest.

The trees grew thicker and darker the further they went, branches overhanging like creepers and the sounds of life and song growing fainter and fainter until they travelled in silence, the only noise the snap of twigs and the rustle of leaves beneath Leofric's feet.

Leofric's instinct for danger raised the hackles on the back of his neck as the light from above dimmed, obscured by the thickly growing branches of the leering hag trees. The scars on his cheek tingled and he reached up to touch one, his finger coming away bloody. He stopped in surprise and touched his other cheek, finding that it too wept a trickle of red.

The others had not waited for him and he quickened his pace, not wanting to be left alone in this dark part of the forest. He heard voices from ahead and emerged into a gloomy glade of mist and cold. Kyarno and Cairbre stood warily beside one another while the prophetess spoke to someone or something he could not yet see.

He moved to stand beside Kyarno and his heart skipped a beat as he saw Cu-Sith sitting cross-legged in the centre of the glade with Naieth's owl on his shoulder. The Red Wolf was just as Leofric had last seen him, his flesh painted in vivid colours, the tattoo on his chest regarding him with a terrible hunger. The wardancer held a pair of swords crossed on his lap and as Leofric entered, he rose smoothly to his feet.

'Cu-Sith wondered who would come,' he said.

'Why are you here, Cu-Sith?' asked Cairbre.

'Loec told me to come here,' answered the wardancer. 'Why are *you* here?'

'We travel the hidden path to the chasm glades.'

The wardancer nodded, moving gracefully towards Leofric and he felt a tightening in his groin at the memory of Cu-Sith's blade at his manhood. The wardancer raised his eyebrows and smiled crookedly at him.

'You bring Cu-Sith's pet with you,' he said, reaching up to dab his fingers in the blood on Leofric's cheek. 'His flesh remembers its place, even if he does not.'

'Why did Loec tell you to come here?' asked Cairbre.

'You should ask the prophetess. She told Cu-Sith that Loec speaks to her. Was that a lie?'

'No,' said Naieth, 'He does. But he does not tell me everything.'

The Red Wolf laughed, 'That is ever the Trickster's way. Cu-Sith cares not anyway, he is here and Loec tells him to offer you his blades and dances of war.'

'You are here to help us?' asked Kyarno.

Cu-Sith slid over to Kyarno and circled him with a nodding smile. 'Yes, Loec likes you very much, Kyarno of the Éadaoin kinband. You please him with your nature. Too bad for you.'

Leofric released a tense breath, glad that the Red Wolf did not appear to be here to kill him or otherwise maim him.

'Why should we need your help, Cu-Sith?' asked Naieth. 'I can open the paths that lead through the secret heart of the forest myself. I need no help for that.'

'No, but such paths can be dangerous. Does your band of heroes know the way?'

'We will find a way,' growled Cairbre.

'Spoken like a true warrior,' said Cu-Sith. 'Brave, but stupid. The paths between worlds are not to be travelled lightly, warrior. The dark fey and the spirit guardians of the forest do not take kindly to mortals entering their domain.'

'And you can show us the way?' asked Kyarno.

'Cu-Sith can show you the way,' agreed the wardancer.

Naieth said, 'Then you shall do so, Cu-Sith. Now stand back while I open the doorway to the path you must travel.'

The four warriors retreated from the prophetess as Othu flew from Cu-Sith's shoulder to return to Naieth. The prophetess raised her staff of woven branches and began a musical chant that spoke to Leofric's heart of yearning and powerful magic. The song of the trees echoed from the mists as though in answer to Naieth's, and Leofric heard a crack and creak of twisting wood.

He watched as the thick, gnarled trunk of a blackened tree at the edge of the glade groaned and twisted, its roots clawing the dark earth and reshaping itself into some new, unknown form.

Its bark split and the sweet smell of sap wafted out, together with a cold so intense, Leofric shivered as though pierced by a spear of ice. The tree twisted in the grip of its transformation, swelling and growing until a glowing, mist-wreathed portal was revealed. Hissing voices, spiteful laughter and wicked cries of malice gusted from within and Leofric wanted nothing more than to turn from this frightful thing, but knew with heavy heart that this was exactly where they had to go.

'The gateway is open,' breathed Naieth, 'but I cannot maintain it for long. Hurry.'

Leofric exchanged worried glances with Kyarno and Cairbre. They could all feel the malicious presences beyond the gateway and each felt some deep part of themselves recoil from them in terror.

Cu-Sith leapt towards the portal, grinning wildly. 'Come. Follow Cu-Sith's lead and do not stray from the silver path. The dark fey will try to beguile you, terrify you and attempt to claim you for their own. But believe them not, for they are lies designed to ensnare you in their world forever. You understand?'

'Yes,' said Cairbre, impatiently, 'we do.'

'They all say that,' laughed Cu-Sith, 'then they die. Do as Cu-Sith does and you will live. Do it not and every one of you will die.'

'We understand,' said Kyarno.

'We will see,' shrugged Cu-Sith, stepping into the glowing mist of the gateway and disappearing.

Cairbre followed him without another word and Kyarno stepped carefully after his uncle, both elves vanishing in the light.

'Go, Leofric,' said Naieth. 'I will see you on your return. And remember the words of the Red Wolf.'

Leofric nodded and, taking a deep breath, plunged into the gateway.

LIGHT BLINDED HIM and he cried out as his body told him that he was falling. He felt solid ground beneath his feet and dropped to his knees as the falling sensation seized him again. He opened his eyes slowly seeing the soft earth beneath him, veins of silver light threading the ground and casting a soft glow about him.

Leofric's breath came in short, panicked heaves, his body unable to shake the sensation of falling despite the evidence of his eyes. He tried to climb to his feet, but his terrified instinct for self-preservation kept him rooted to the spot.

'What is wrong with him?' he heard Kyarno ask.

'Humans were never meant to walk between worlds,' said Cu-Sith.

Leofric's resentment at Cu-Sith's easy condescension fanned a flame in his heart and he angrily climbed to his feet, fighting the nauseous vertigo his body felt.

'Maybe not,' he hissed, 'but I will be damned if I will be left behind.'

Cu-Sith bounded over to him and wrapped his hand around the back of his neck and pulled him close until their eyes were inches apart. 'You have spirit, human. It looks like Cu-Sith was right to let you keep your balls.'

The wardancer released him and set off along the silver-veined pathway. Leofric fought to calm his breathing and adjust to his surroundings.

The sky above was a ghostly grey colour, bleached of all life, and the landscape around them was one of glittering mist and twisted, dark trees as far as the eye could see. Laughter, cruel and hurtful, drifted from within the mists and a multitude of whispering voices chattered on the wind.

'Where are we?' asked Leofric.

'We can talk later,' warned Cairbre. 'Cu-Sith leads the way and we cannot linger here.'

Leofric nodded and followed the Hound of Winter as he and Kyarno set off after the wardancer. His senses rebelled against the enchantments of this place and though Cu-Sith's words had angered Leofric, he knew that the wardancer was right: humans were not meant to see such things.

Their course followed the ribbon of silver light as it wound a path through the dark forest. Blurred shapes shadowed their every movement and Leofric kept his gaze fixed on a point between Kyarno's shoulder blades for fear of the terrible things he might see if he allowed himself to look anywhere else. Whispered voices drifted to him, taunts and promises of wealth, flesh and peace, but he forced them from his head as he concentrated on putting one foot in front of the other.

He heard a cry of pain, a woman's, and his ingrained chivalric code turned his head before his body's warning could prevent him.

Leofric cried out as the mists parted and he saw Helene on her knees, wearing the same red dress she had worn the day the forest had taken her. She wept and pleaded with cackling creatures of branch and root, their whipping, thorny limbs and bark-formed faces mocking her helplessness. Was this where Helene had been taken? Had she been brought to this damnable otherworld to be tormented by these maniacal spirits for all eternity?

His hatred of these beasts knew no bounds and he drew his sword, the blade shining with silver fire, running towards her and shouting, 'Helene!'

No sooner had his feet left the silver pathway than the scene before him dissolved into a whirling blur of light and mist, and he heard a host of wickedly gleeful laughs surround him. Sinuous shadows flitted towards him from the darkness between the claw-branched trees and Leofric's heart chilled to see such primal, elemental spirits of the forest as they slipped through the air like liquid.

But he was a knight of Bretonnia and his courage was greater than his fear of these things. Leofric brought his sword to bear, its silver blade a shining beacon in the darkness as the shadows circled him like sharks with the taste of blood.

He backed away, casting darting glances around him as he sought the silver path once more, but all was darkness and shadow, the path lost to him.

'Lady protect me,' he whispered as a dark shadow darted towards him. He swung his sword, the blade passing clean through it without effect. Black, clawed arms slashed for him and slid through his armour without effort, reaching into his flesh with the chill of the grave.

Leofric cried out as the deathly touch of the spirit creature filled him with pain. He dropped to his knees as aching cold spread agonisingly through his body. His heart beat wildly in his chest as he fought the glacial chill. More of the shadow creatures slipped from the trees, their eyes pinpricks of yellow against the dark of their ghostly forms, and Leofric knew he was undone.

Then a howling shape spun through the air and a painted figure with twin swords of golden light landed before him.

Cu-Sith spun his swords before him in a dazzling circle and said, 'You cannot have him. This human belongs to Cu-Sith.'

The shadow beasts circled the wardancer, wary of his bright swords and hissed in anger at his interruption of their hunt.

'Human,' shouted Cu-Sith. 'Get up! Fight their touch!'

Leofric gritted his teeth, biting the inside of his cheek hard enough to draw blood, the warm liquid and pain forcing the chill of the shadow's touch from his flesh. As the dark touch left him, his strength returned and he stood beside the wardancer, silver and gold blades keeping the spirits at bay for the moment.

'Follow Cu-Sith,' said the wardancer. 'Walk where he walks.'

Leofric nodded as he once again saw Helene beyond the shadows, naked and bloody as the branch-creatures whipped the flesh from her bones.

'It is not real, human,' warned Cu-Sith. 'Whoever she is, she is not real.'

Leofric forced himself to look away, following the careful steps of the wardancer as they backed away from the dark fey of the forest. Sadness welled in his heart at the sight of Helene's tortured body, but he held to Cu-Sith's assertion that it was but an illusion.

Then there was silver light beneath his feet once more and the hissing curses that had followed them faded to a faint susurration.

'Foolish human!' snapped the wardancer. 'Did you hear nothing of Cu-Sith's warning? Cu-Sith told you to stay on the path.'

'I saw Helene!' shouted Leofric. 'I saw my wife.'

'Your wife is dead,' said Cu-Sith. 'That was not her. Now come, there is a long way to go yet.'

Leofric fought past the grief at having seen Helene so close once more and nodded, looking down at his shining sword.

'Why does my sword glow?' asked Leofric.

'The weapon is touched by magic,' said Cu-Sith. 'It fades, but there is still some power left to it.'

'Yes,' said Leofric proudly. 'It was blessed by the Lady of the Lake herself.'

Cu-Sith winked and turned away, but before Leofric could ask more, he saw the Hound of Winter emerge from the mist bearing a weeping Kyarno back onto the path.

Like Leofric's sword, the Blades of Midnight shone with a nimbus of light.

'I saw them,' cried Kyarno. 'My mother! My father! We have to go back.'

Cairbre dropped his nephew to the path and Leofric saw that the Hound of Winter's body was cut and bruised. He took a great breath as Cu-Sith shook his head and met Cairbre's gaze.

'Foolish youths,' said the wardancer and Cairbre nodded in agreement.

Kyarno blinked and let out a shuddering breath as the power of the dark fey faded from his mind. Leofric helped him up and the four warriors set off once again down the silver path.

Dreams and nightmares assailed them from every turn, scenes of horror and bliss paraded before them in equal measure. But their hearts were hardened to the glamours of the dark fey and though each blandishment was more outlandish or horrific than the one before, nothing could now tempt them from the path.

'We are here,' said Cu-Sith at last, and Leofric looked up to see a shining, mist-wreathed gateway hovering before them. Through it he could see craggy mountaintops and a pale sky of clear blue. Nothing had ever looked so welcoming and they hurried towards the gateway, stepping through with none of the reticence they had felt when entering this dark domain of the spirit.

LEOFRIC'S HEART SANG to be back in the real world, the rocks and trees and earth having a reassuring, familiar solidity to them that he had not realised was so necessary an anchor for the human soul. Stepping through the shimmering gateway, he had stepped onto bare rock high in the mountains, the air wondrously clear and refreshing.

He stood on the edge of the mountain, drawing great lungfuls of crisp air into his body and tilting his face towards the sun as it warmed his flesh. After the journey through the secret paths of the forest, to feel the sun on his skin was the most incredible sensation Leofric could remember.

'By the Lady, I never want to have to do that again,' he said.

'Nor I,' agreed Cairbre, shuddering at the memory of whatever visions had come to him within the spirit realm.

To have travelled so far in so short a time amazed Leofric. Such a journey would normally have taken well over a week, but, by the position of the sun, they had reached the mountains in a matter of hours.

Jagged crags of grey stone reared above them, cloaked in shawls of white and patches of fragrant pine, the highest peaks of the Grey Mountains lost in the clouds. Below them, the forest stretched out across the landscape, a massive swathe of green and red and gold and brown.

He could not see all the forest, wisps of cloud far below them conspiring to conceal some areas and shimmering heat hazes rippling the image of the far distant treetops. The sight of the forest laid out like this was truly magnificent and Leofric took a moment to drink in its savage beauty.

'What is that?' he asked, pointing to a cluster of distant golden spires that rose above the forest canopy.

'It is the Waterfall Palace of the Naiad Court,' replied Cairbre. 'It is a place of wonders and raptures.'

'Who lives there?'

'The naiads, beautiful nymphs of lakes, rivers, springs and fountains. They make their court amid a torrent of a hundred waterfalls. I have visited their court once before and it was... most pleasurable.'

Leofric raised an eyebrow, surprised at Cairbre – if he understood the Hound of Winter correctly. He was spared asking more by the arrival of Kyarno and Cu-Sith, who beckoned them over to the sheer cliff face behind them.

A thin, snaking crack split the cliff, barely wide enough for an elf, let alone a human in armour, and Kyarno nodded, saying, 'This is it, this is the way.'

'You are sure?' asked Cairbre, doubtfully.

'Yes, uncle, I'm sure,' said Kyarno. 'Remember I have been here before.'

Cairbre shrugged and followed Kyarno as he disappeared into the mountain. Cu-Sith indicated that Leofric should go next and he squeezed himself into the fissure with some difficulty as the wardancer slipped effortlessly between the rocks behind him.

After a while, the crack widened a little. Not by much, but enough so that every step was not an effort. Nor was it a simple path, branching off many times into a maze of thin cracks in the rock and low passages. Each path divided over and over again, and Leofric wondered how they were going to navigate their way back.

Their course carried them deep into the mountain, sheer rock rising on all sides and thickly growing pines fringing the top of the chasm. Oft times their route carried them along narrow paths with drops of thousands of feet to one side or over narrow bridges of rock that crossed yawning rents in the earth. A pungent, animal aroma permeated the chasms and the further they went, the easier became their passing as the chasm finally widened into a tall, steep sided valley.

Tall trees dotted the valley, the vertical sides of the chasm rearing hundreds of feet above them. A craggy cave entrance opened into the mountain on one side of the chasm, the ground before it strewn with boulders and the white gleam of bone.

'What manner of creature would live in such a remote place?' asked Leofric, seeing human skulls amongst the piles of bone. 'The only way you could get in without difficulty is…'

Leofric's words trailed off as a great shadow enveloped their group and a powerful downdraught of air threw up clouds of blinding dust with a deafening boom. The odour Leofric had smelled in the chasms was much stronger now. He shielded his eyes from the dust and heard something take a powerful intake of breath that echoed from the rocks.

He squinted through the slowly settling dust and saw a great form silhouetted against the sky, a massive, sinuous body with a long, muscular neck and a pair of slowly folding wings.

Leofric blinked away the last of the dust and gasped at the monstrous creature that perched on the rocks above them.

A dragon.

CHAPTER EIGHTEEN

A DRAGON. IT was a dragon. Leofric was looking at a dragon. It took several seconds for the reality of the sight to sink in, but when it did, his hand instinctively reached for his sword. As his hand grasped the hilt, Cairbre gripped his arm and shook his head.

A dragon… creatures of terrible aspect and fearsome reputation, it was the stuff of every knight's dream to slay a dragon. Of such things were the legends and tales of Bretonnia built.

The mighty creature regarded them quizzically, its huge, horned head leaning down into the chasm glade and its huge jaws opening to reveal row upon row of saw-like fangs. Its breath reeked of noxious gases, the blades of its teeth longer than Leofric's forearm.

It climbed head first down the vertical sides of the glade, its great claws gripping the rock as it descended to the dusty valley floor, its scaled green body rippling with massive slabs of muscle. Its huge, leathery wings were folded across its spined back, frills of tissue stretched between the sharp spines.

'A dragon...' breathed Leofric, straining to draw his sword despite Cairbre's restraining hand. 'It's a dragon.'

'I know,' hissed Cairbre. 'This is Beithir-Seun. This is who we have come to see.'

Leofric looked incredulously at the Hound of Winter. This terrifying beast was who they had risked travelling through the realm of the dark fey to find?

'Are you insane? It is a monster. It has to die!'

'Be silent!' warned Cairbre. 'Beithir-Seun is an ancient denizen for the forest and we are here for his help. Do not anger him.'

Leofric looked across to Kyarno and Cu-Sith to see if they were as deluded as the Hound of Winter in believing that this creature was anything other than a monster to be destroyed.

He saw tension on their features, even those of Cu-Sith, but nothing to show that they shared his intent. Slowly he released his grip on his sword hilt and though his knightly traditions screamed at him to charge the beast, he forced himself to wait.

The dragon approached them, towering above them as it reared up on its hind legs and let out a terrible roar that shook rocks from the sides of the glade. Leofric flinched, but followed the example of the elves and remained motionless. The creature sniffed the air, its jaws drawing open again to reveal its razor-sharp fangs, and lowered its head towards them. One of the dragon's eyes was a mass of poorly-healed scar tissue, the other a fierce yellow and slitted like a cat's. Leofric saw an ancient intelligence within that eye and knew that this was a creature not to be trifled with.

'I smell human,' snarled the dragon, its rumbling voice deep and laden with authority.

Leofric fought to control his mounting panic in the face of the dragon's pronouncement. The great wyrm's eyes narrowed and it cocked its vast head to one side, its breath sounding like the bellows of some mighty, piston-driven engine of the dwarfs.

'Beithir-Seun,' began Cairbre. 'We come as emissaries from–'

'I smell human,' repeated the dragon, thrusting its jaws towards Leofric. Its head was the size of a coach and though its enormous fangs were inches from his body, he held himself immobile before the monster's scrutiny.

'I know your kind,' said the dragon. 'Humans in armour slay my kind. Brave heroes out to make a name for themselves. Is that it, human, have you come to slay me?'

Leofric said nothing until nudged in the ribs by Kyarno, who gestured urgently that he should reply.

'Uh… no,' said Leofric. 'No. We… that is… no.'

'It is as well for you,' rumbled the dragon, 'for you would die if you tried. Beithir-Seun has eaten humans in armour before and one more would be of no consequence. The bones of a hundred men lie strewn before my cave. Yours may join them yet.'

The dragon drew back its head and Leofric let out the breath he had been holding. The creature scraped deep furrows in the rock with its claws and said, 'I smell elf as well as human. It has been long centuries since Beithir-Seun awoke and yet longer since he tasted warm flesh bitten from the bone.'

Its long tongue slid from its jaws and Leofric had a terrifying mental image of their bodies sliding down its throat to be digested in its stomach.

'Blood and meat,' hissed the dragon, taking a long step towards them. 'Yes… blood and meat and bone.'

'Beithir-Seun,' said Cairbre again. 'We come to you for help.'

'Help?' roared Beithir-Seun. 'What help can elves want from me?'

'We come with tidings from Aldaeld, Lord of a Hundred Battles and guardian of Coeth-Mara. He sends you greetings from the Asrai and bids you take heed of our words.'

'Beithir-Seun knows of Coeth-Mara,' nodded the dragon. 'A grove of saplings in the south of the forest.'

'It has grown since last you awoke, Beithir-Seun. Now it is a mighty hall of the Asrai and its beauty is beloved by all the forest kin.'

'Now I see why you bring armoured humans to my glade,' said the dragon, its mouth splitting in a grin of monstrous appetite. 'It is an offering to me to secure my aid. One of the armoured humans that put out my eye with a lance brought to me for a meal of flesh and bone.'

'No,' said Leofric. 'I am a friend to the Asrai. I have fought alongside the warriors of Coeth-Mara and do so again to save both our peoples.'

'A human fights with the Asrai?' asked Beithir-Seun.

'He does,' said Kyarno. 'He is a warrior of courage and has slain creatures of Chaos.'

'Mention not that word,' spat the dragon. 'For Beithir-Seun has feasted upon the flesh of the unclean and still I taste their rankness. If this human be not an offering to me, then what do you bring?'

'We bring only the chance to once again defend Athel Loren,' said Cairbre. 'For Cyanathair has returned to the forest.'

Beithir-Seun let out a terrible, echoing roar at the mention of the Corruptor, its bellow full of anger and loathing.

'Cyanathair walks the earth once more?'

'It does,' said Cairbre. 'Its minions have managed to topple one of the sacred waystones and we need your help to retrieve it, for we cannot bear it back to Athel Loren without your mighty strength.'

'Flatter me not, elf,' cautioned the dragon. 'Centuries have I slumbered in this deep mountain and many are the creatures of evil I have destroyed.'

Beithir-Seun shook its horned head and said, 'A human fights alongside the Asrai and the Corruptor walks the earth. Truly it is well that the forest wakes me that I might see such strange times.'

'Then you will aid us?'

The dragon nodded and bared its fangs. 'Yes, I will aid you, for I see that your cause is that of Athel Loren. Too long is it since Beithir-Seun slaughtered the children of Chaos.'

Leofric watched as the great dragon spread its wings, the enormous pinions almost scraping the sides of the valley as it reared up to its full height.

'Come!' bellowed Beithir-Seun. 'Climb upon my back and we will away. The call to war is upon us!'

Leofric's stomach lurched at the dragon's words and he grabbed Kyarno's arm as the young elf took a step towards the mighty creature.

'What does it mean?'

'By what?'

'By "climb upon my back".'

'Exactly what he says,' said Kyarno, looking oddly at Leofric and then chuckling to himself as he clapped Leofric on the shoulder. 'How did you think we were going to get back to Coeth-Mara?'

'I'm not sure,' said Leofric. 'I assumed the same way we got here.'

'You would rather travel the paths of the dark fey once more?'

'No,' said Leofric, 'But this…'

'You should relish this,' laughed Kyarno. 'After all, how many humans get the chance to soar through the sky on the back of a dragon?'

'Oh yes,' said Leofric sourly, 'I feel so privileged.'

RUSHING WIND WHIPPED past Leofric's head, but he kept his eyes tightly shut for fear of seeing what lay below him. Or, more accurately, what did not lie below him. He gripped the spine on the dragon's back as tight as he could, his arms wrapped around it and his fingers digging into a frill of skin with all his strength.

They had lifted from the chasm glade of Beithir-Seun in the beat of powerful wings nearly an hour ago, and Leofric had barely opened his eyes the entire time. To be carried on the back of a horse was the way for a knight to travel, not like this.

Man was not meant to fly, and though the king oft rode to battle on the back of his hippogryph, Beaquis, and some of the richer knights of Bretonnia boasted a trained battle pegasus, the saddle of a warhorse was as far as Leofric wanted to get from the ground.

He could feel the great creature's powerful heartbeat through its tough scales, a deep and slow thudding boom, and the motion of its muscles lifted him up and down as they bunched and relaxed to keep its wings moving.

'You are missing a spectacular view,' shouted Kyarno.

Leofric looked up to see Kyarno standing at the dragon's shoulders next to Cairbre, the wind rushing through his braided hair as he called back to Leofric.

Behind them, all he could see was sky, brilliant blue and cloudy.

'Do you have to do that?' asked Leofric. 'You are making me feel sick.'

Cu-Sith sat astride Beithir-Seun's neck, but Leofric kept his eyes focussed on the hard, scaled back of the dragon. The elves seemed completely at ease, their stance shifting in response to the creature's movements, looking for all the world like they were having the time of their lives.

The dragon dipped one of its wings, curling round in a slow bank and Leofric saw the green canopy of the forest speeding past, thousands of feet below him, and cried out, clutching onto the spine even tighter.

Far below he could see the snaking course of the Grismerie as it meandered through the forest, sparkling and clear as it flowed from the mountains towards Parravon, one of the frontier towns of Bretonnia, with its deep chasms, high walls and many towers.

Though it was a great distance away, Leofric could see a slender bridge crossing the river, a graceful structure of wood and crystal. Thousands of birds of many colours flocked around the bridge, the sound of their trilling song reaching Leofric even up here.

Soon the bridge was lost to sight, but hundreds of the birds flew up from their circling to join them, crying out in welcome to the dragon as though it were a long lost friend unexpectedly returned. The dragon slowed its flight to allow the birds to keep up with it, roaring in answer to their cries.

Leofric began anew his prayers to the Lady of the Lake as the tremors of the dragon's roars reached him, entreating her to keep him safe until he had solid ground beneath his feet.

'Lady watch over your humble servant,' whispered Leofric as the long flight continued. 'Keep my grip strong. And keep this beast from moving too suddenly!'

Soon Beithir-Seun angled his course to the west and as a thin line of green came into view above the blades of his muscular shoulders, Leofric could tell they were descending. He began to relax a little at the thought of being on the ground once more, opening his eyes and watching as the forest canopy rushed up to meet them.

Birds surrounded them, hundreds, if not thousands of them, and though he was utterly terrified to be travelling in this manner, he could not deny the magnificence of the sight.

The motion of the dragon's wings ceased as they flared outwards to slow his flight, the left wing dipping, and once again Beithir-Seun banked sharply as he descended in ever-tighter circles towards the ground. Leofric saw the River Brienne and realised they must be approaching Coeth-Mara.

'Hold on, Leofric!' shouted Kyarno from the dragon's shoulders. 'We will be on the ground in a moment!'

'Not a moment too soon!' shouted back Leofric as Beithir-Seun folded his wings in close to his body and dropped towards the forest floor. Leofric screamed in sudden alarm, fearing that some calamity had befallen the mighty creature, but at the last moment, the dragon's wings shot out and gave a powerful beat to flare outwards and control his descent into the elven halls.

Leofric felt the dragon's claws settle on the ground and let out a heartfelt sigh of relief as he released his death-grip on its spine. He slid down the dragon's haunches, landing on unsteady legs, supporting himself on the trunk of a silver-barked birch. Hundreds of birds fluttered and flapped through Coeth-Mara – white plumed doves, colourful finches, robins and sparrows, and their song filled the air with music.

Kyarno landed lightly beside him, his face alight with amusement, and Cairbre soon followed him, a youthful vigour creasing his features with a boyish grin. The Red Wolf somersaulted to the ground in front of Leofric and he could see that quite a crowd had gathered to greet them.

Elves stared at Beithir-Seun in fascination, thrilled to have one of the most ancient guardians of the forest in their midst. They came forward in great number, eager to meet this defender of Athel Loren, and the lack of fear they showed towards the powerful creature amazed Leofric.

As he regained his equilibrium, he saw that Coeth-Mara was thronged with elves, more than he had ever seen before. Elves of all different appearance and garb clustered around the dragon and Leofric saw a wide variety of runic symbols on furs, tunics, robes and cloaks, realising that these elves must belong to different kinbands.

The kindreds of Athel Loren had answered Lord Aldaeld's call.

NIGHT WAS DRAWING in and the torches had been lit by the time the last of the warrior kindreds that had answered Lord Aldaeld's summons arrived in Coeth-Mara. Not all had come, and many had not even acknowledged his call. But enough had come and at first light, the elves of Athel Loren would take the fight to the mountains and the children of Chaos.

Kyarno sat with his back to an ancient willow, feeling its connection to the earth in the rhythmic pulsing of its

sap. He had hoped Morvhen would have been waiting
for him upon their triumphant return on the back of
Beithir-Seun, but she was nowhere to be seen, no doubt
Aldaeld was keeping her safely ensconced from his
attentions.

The forest was alive with elves of many kinbands,
warhawk riders, waywatchers, glade riders, Eternal
Guard and the wardancers of Cu-Sith. Tomorrow they
would fight and Kyarno would go with them. What
awaited him, he did not know, but it had to be better
than the life of solitude that was his lot from now on.

What was left to him now? Was he to travel the lands
of humans as an itinerant adventurer, forced to seek his
fortune by grubbing through ancient ruins and dun-
geons for treasure?

He traced the rune of Vaul in the forest floor with a
twig, pondering on his uncertain future, when he heard
soft footfalls behind him. He recognised the tread and
said, 'You grow no stealthier with age, uncle.'

'No,' agreed Cairbre. 'I was never cut out to be a waywatcher, was I?'

Kyarno shook his head. 'No, you always were noisy.
It's the one thing I remember of you from when I was a
child.'

'You must remember more than that, surely?'

'Yes, uncle, I do,' whispered Kyarno. 'I remember the
flames and blood when the beastmen killed my mother
and father. I remember you carrying me clear of the
burning ruin of our halls. But most of all I remember
the loneliness.'

'I know, boy, I know,' said Cairbre, sitting on the other
side of the willow trunk with his back to Kyarno.
'There's not a day goes by I don't wish I could have
reached you sooner.'

Kyarno smiled, staring up at the pale glow of the moon. Flocks of birds still circled Coeth-Mara and he said, 'I never hated you, uncle. I want you to know that before tomorrow.'

'I never thought you did, Kyarno,' sighed Cairbre. 'And I always loved you and wanted the best for you.'

'Strange how such thoughts often come on the eve of battle,' said Kyarno.

'Yes,' agreed Cairbre. 'War makes philosophers of us all. I suppose the nearness of death brings home to us what matters most.'

'And what is that?'

'Kin,' said Cairbre simply.

THE NEXT DAY dawned bright and clear, the spring sun bathing the central glade of Coeth-Mara in warmth and light. Everywhere was bustling activity as the elves readied themselves for battle. Leofric watched as solitary individuals in hooded cloaks disappeared into the forest surrounding the elven halls to protect its borders while others took the fight to the mountains.

Warriors checked the keenness of blades and archers gauged the line of their arrows, smoothing the fletching and sharpening the points.

But of all those gathered beneath the boughs of Coeth-Mara, the most pleasing to Leofric's eyes were the giant hawks with long tails, hooked bills, strong talons and broad wings that would carry them into battle. He had hunted with falcons many times, and appreciated the grace and deadly beauty of such birds, but these were magnificent and regal, quite unlike anything he had seen before. The warhawk riders shared many similarities with their mounts, slender-limbed and agile, with quick, lethal-looking movements.

Though not nearly as huge as Beithir-Seun, who growled impatiently at the edge of the glade, Leofric had a more obvious connection to the warhawks than a beast he would normally have tried to slay. The flight on the dragon had been terrifying, but Leofric strangely relished the idea of riding into battle on a warhawk; the prospect filled him with a mixture of terror and excitement. Though saddened not to be able to ride into battle on Aeneor, there was no way a steed, even an elven one, could match the speed of the warhawks.

Leofric had tended to his sword and armour as best he could and though the impish spites that followed him around Coeth-Mara were helpful when it came to putting the armour on, without an actual squire to clean them properly, they looked far from their best.

He saw Kyarno and the Hound of Winter approaching, Kyarno with his sword strapped at his side and his bow slung over one shoulder, and Cairbre with the Blades of Midnight carried lightly in his right hand.

'Good morning,' said Leofric. 'It is a fine sight indeed to see so many magnificent warriors gathered together.'

Cairbre nodded and placed his hand on Kyarno's shoulder.

'Isha watch over you, boy,' said the Hound of Winter, 'and may Kurnous guide your hand this day.'

The two elves embraced one another, the gesture looking forced and awkward to Leofric's eyes. Cairbre and Kyarno may have made their peace, but there were still barriers between them. Eventually, the Hound of Winter released his nephew and, without another word spoken between them, turned and walked away.

'Ready?' asked Kyarno.

'Yes,' said Leofric. 'I am. It is time to hold back the darkness one more time. For we are warriors are we not?'

'That we are,' agreed Kyarno, as Leofric held out his hand to him.

Kyarno took the proffered hand and said, 'There is much I do not understand about humans, too much I think for us ever to be friends, but you and I may yet be brothers in battle.'

'That would sit well with me, Kyarno,' said Leofric. 'And who knows what the future holds. Perhaps one day our races may become friends.'

'I would not count on it, but it is a noble dream,' said Kyarno.

'Tell me one thing though,' said Leofric.

'What?'

'I know Éadaoin means Fleetmane in my language, but what does Daelanu mean?'

'It means Silvermorn, the promise of the new sun after the long night.'

'It is a good name,' said Leofric. 'I wanted to know so I could speak of you when I leave Athel Loren.'

'When you leave?'

'Yes,' said Leofric. 'If we win this day it will be to save the lives of the people of my lands. I will return to them soon, I can feel it.'

'I feel it too,' said Kyarno, falling silent as Lord Aldaeld and his warriors made their way to the centre of Coeth-Mara. Naieth walked with Lord Aldaeld, dressed as Leofric had first seen her, in a robe of gold and elven runes, her copper hair teased into braided tresses above her tapered ears with silver pins and garlanded with feathers and gemstones.

She carried her long staff of woven twigs with a carved eye at its top and Leofric saw she wore a secret smile, one of pride and love for those around her.

Lord Aldaeld wore a scarlet cloak of feathers and his body was adorned with many fresh tattoos and painted designs. Gleaming torques of gold and silver banded his arms and he wore a golden helm with the curling horns of a stag. His sword was scabbarded at his hip and he carried a silver lance with a spiral pattern carved on its blade.

Behind him came Morvhen, clad in simple brown leathers and furs, with a powerful recurved bow carried at her side and a pair of crossed quivers across her back. Leofric straightened as he saw that Tiphaine accompanied Morvhen.

Aldaeld crossed the glade towards Leofric and Kyarno, stopping just before them and fixing them with a stern gaze.

'Lord Aldaeld,' said Kyarno, giving a respectful nod to the lord of the Éadaoin kinband. Leofric followed suit, unsure as to why Lord Aldaeld felt the need to speak to them this morning of all mornings.

'Kyarno,' began Aldaeld. 'You have done my kinband a great service by bringing us the great Beithir-Seun. I thank you for that.'

'I was happy to do it,' said Kyarno. 'I may not be part of your kinband now, but I am glad to fight alongside it.'

For a moment neither said anything until Lord Aldaeld finally said, 'The Hound of Winter speaks highly of you, Kyarno Daelanu, and my daughter seems taken with you, though Isha alone knows why. I can see just by looking at you that you are no longer Kyarno the troublemaker. Only time will tell what you have become, but should you live through this day, we shall speak again.'

Kyarno struggled for words, but settled on saying, 'Thank you, Lord Aldaeld.'

Aldaeld nodded and turned away, moving to stand in the centre of the glade. As he left, Morvhen approached Kyarno and spoke softly to him in elvish as Tiphaine drew near Leofric.

She nodded in greeting, her almond eyes sad.

'Hello, Leofric,' she said, holding her hand out to him and Leofric saw she offered him a beautiful, faultless crystal, its surface smooth and unblemished.

'I cannot,' said Leofric. 'It is too beautiful.'

'I desire you to have it,' insisted Tiphaine. 'It is a moonstone from the Crystal Mere, like the one gifted to the warrior hero Naithal by a naiad of the Waterfall Court. It has great power and will protect you from harm.'

'It is beautiful,' said Leofric, pulling the blue silken scarf of Helene's from his gauntlet and wrapping the gemstone within. He returned the favours to his gauntlet and started to say more, but Tiphaine stopped him, placing her finger on his lips.

'I do not know if I will ever see you again, Leofric Carrard,' she said, 'so think on all we have spoken of and your time in our forest realm will have been well spent.'

'I will,' promised Leofric. 'For you have inspired me to great deeds and have always spoken to me with courtesy and grace. For that I thank you, my lady.'

Tiphaine did not reply, but stepped away from him, all activity in Coeth-Mara coming to a halt as Lord Aldaeld cast his head back and raised his lance to the sky. The sunlight reflected dazzlingly on the silver blade, the power of its magic clear for all to see.

For a moment all was silence until Leofric heard the faint beat of wings and looked up to see a gigantic eagle circling to land before the elven lord. A gasp of astonishment swept the glade as the powerful bird landed gracefully before Aldaeld, its feathers golden and its bearing both noble and fierce.

The magnificent creature took Leofric's breath away, his admiration for the warhawks swept away by the regal countenance of this noble bird of prey. From the looks of awed admiration of the assembled elves, it was clearly a sign of great favour to have such a beast consent to carry an elven lord into battle.

Aldaeld climbed swiftly onto the great eagle's back, the elves following his example and climbing to the backs of their warhawks. Leofric, Kyarno and Morvhen ran for the warhawks chosen to carry them as passengers and climbed onto their backs behind the elven riders.

The great eagle spread its graceful wings and leapt into the air, carrying Lord Aldaeld into the sky. The eagle gave a piercing cry and the warhawks also took flight, following the golden form of Lord Aldaeld's eagle.

Beithir-Seun took to the air immediately after, his bulk slower to gather speed, but soon catching up to his smaller, more nimble brethren.

Leofric felt a wild exhilaration as he was carried higher and higher above the trees, his earlier fear of the skies forgotten in the rush of adrenaline that surged around his body at the thought of battle.

He watched as the aerial armada climbed into the air, privileged to be in the company of these magnificent warriors. Scores of warhawks filled the sky, with Lord Aldaeld at their head atop his eagle and the terrible form of the great dragon, Beithir-Seun, flying above them.

Once again, hundreds of brightly coloured birds flew alongside them, their cries sounding as sweet as the call for battle from the silver trumpet of a Bretonnian clarion.

CHAPTER NINETEEN

WITH ITS HIGH walls of red stone, wide barbican and many towers, the strength of Castle Carrard never failed to impress Teoderic Lendast of Quenelles. Though ill-fortune had dogged the line of its lords, it remained a formidable bastion against any foe.

He rode his snorting steed through its thick gateway, hung with a banner of gold depicting a scarlet unicorn rampant below a bejewelled crown. Teoderic straightened his cloak over the rump of his horse then checked that his sword hung correctly at his side. A muster of levies and peasant men-at-arms were gathered outside the castle and a knight of Bretonnia did not appear before the lowborn looking less than his best. Behind him came Clovis and Theudegar, brothers-in-arms and virtuous knights of the realm both. Three score knights followed behind, resplendent in surcoats of many colours with guidons snapping from the ends of their lances and banners raised high.

Passing from the gateway and thumping across the wooden drawbridge, Teoderic watched as the peasants stood to attention at the sight of him, displaying the proper reverence to a knight of the realm such as he. He lifted the visor of his helmet and stared up into the darkening sky. Though the sun was barely past its zenith, the day was dim and had the purple cast of twilight. Dark thunderheads gathered on the eastern horizon, though Teoderic knew that they preceded no natural storm.

A shiver of anticipation ran down his spine at the thought of facing the might of the forest spirits. What did such creatures know of honour or chivalry? Was there glory to be earned in their destruction or would he feel no more than a woodsman might feel in hewing a tree?

'How many more men arrived this morning?' he asked, turning in the saddle to address the knights who rode after him.

'A goodly number,' answered Clovis, raising his visor and surveying the assembled peasantry. 'Perhaps a thousand men now muster at Castle Carrard in answer to their lord's summons: archers, yeomanry from nearby villages and the men-at-arms we brought with us.'

'Indeed,' said Theudegar, 'as well there might be. For it is their lands that are ravaged by the faerie king. It is only right and proper that they fight.'

Teoderic nodded his agreement, though he knew that to defeat the force arrayed against them, they would need a lot more. Fear was already rife in the peasants and he saw no need to add more with any pessimistic opinions just yet. He watched as a group of tired-looking peasants hammered sharpened stakes into the hillside before the river and others dragged a cart of boulders and rubble inside the castle for the trebuchet mounted on the walls. Teoderic disliked such weapons, but could nevertheless appreciate the strategic value of being able to drop large blocks of masonry on an enemy from far away.

'They say another village was destroyed last night,' added Theudegar. 'Orberese, I think. Not a soul lives there now, carried away to their deaths by the wild hunt.'

'Orberese?' said Clovis. 'That's a damn shame, they bred a fine pig there. Made some good sausage as I recall.'

'How many is that then?' asked Teoderic.

'Nine this past two weeks alone,' answered Clovis. 'The eastern parts of Quenelles and Carcassonne are virtually deserted. All have fled to the castles of their liege lords.'

Teoderic saw desperation on every face they passed, knowing that peasants expected the knights to save them and end the threat of the Green King. Mounted yeomen had brought word that the rampant forest creatures were heading towards Castle Carrard, covering all the land in a swathe of violent life. Battle was soon to be joined.

For nearly fourteen nights, the King of the Forest and his wild hunt had rampaged through the southern dukedoms of Bretonnia, destroying all those in their path, and now they rode out to stop them. It would be some time before a larger muster of knights could be gathered, and though Teoderic knew that it was folly to meet this threat with so few warriors, they had a duty to their people to protect them in times of trouble.

Teoderic relished the chance to ride out and face the enemy on the field of battle as much as the next knight, but knew that, if the scouts' reports were to be believed, they were likely to be outnumbered nearly four to one. Better that the enemy come to them and then the creatures of the wood would break themselves against walls of stone.

But as he turned to look at the silver-haired lord of Castle Carrard, who stood on the crenellated battlements of the tallest tower, Teoderic knew that nothing less than the glory of a bloody charge would satisfy the venerable lord's lust for vengeance.

THE FOREST SWEPT by beneath them as the warhawks carried them swiftly through the sky, the wind whipping past in a blur of cold air. Leofric clutched the bird's feathers tightly, gripping its body with his thighs as its powerful wings bore him and its elven rider towards the mountains.

The mighty bird carrying Kyarno flew alongside him, with Cairbre and Naieth carried on the backs of birds just behind Lord Aldaeld's great eagle. Morvhen rode atop a warhawk of her own, balancing easily on its back with her long hair cascading darkly behind her. Cu-Sith and his wardancers made their own way towards the Shadow-Gave, easily able to keep pace with the warhawks through secret paths of the forest that they alone knew or dared to travel.

The site of the breach in the waystone barrier was clearly visible from the air, a spreading patch of darkest green that spilled out from the forest's edge. Who knew how many had died in Bretonnia already and how many were yet to die? It seemed as though the undulating green swathe moved even as he watched, the speed of its growth swifter than he would have believed possible.

The mountains ahead reared up like grim, grey sentinels, towering peaks that marked the southern boundaries of Bretonnia and Athel Loren, and, beyond which lay the mercenary city-states of Tilea.

Their ultimate destination was easily visible, the corruption unleashed by the Shadow-Gave impossible to miss from the air, a spreading dark stain on the mountain that pulsed like a wound in the rock itself. A huge fire burned at the centre of the darkness that smothered the mountainside, circled by scores of howling beastmen. The host of monstrous, baying abominations waved spears and axes towards the massive form of the missing waystone, perched on a rocky plateau below a wide cave mouth.

Dark pinioned shapes wheeled in the air above the fire, their piercing cries carried on the cold wind and sending a jolt of loathing through Leofric.

'What are they?' he shouted, pointing to the shapes.

'Creatures of Chaos!' cried Kyarno in answer. 'Beasts of the air warped by the Corruptor's foulness and drawn to its fell powers.'

Leofric watched as the monstrous birds began climbing higher into the air, angling their flight towards them, and gripped the warhawk's flanks tighter as its rider coaxed it into a rapid descent. The elf looked over his shoulder at Leofric and said, 'I will need to set you down, human. I cannot carry you and fight.'

Leofric nodded as the warhawk riders that carried passengers dropped from the aerial armada, heading quickly for the ground to deposit their burdens before rejoining their comrades for battle.

The ground rushed up to meet Leofric as the warhawk rapidly lost altitude, dropping through the air until it was skimming the rocks, no more than a few feet above the mountainside.

He saw Kyarno and the Eternal Guard leap from the backs of the warhawks, landing easily on the jagged rocks as though such a feat of acrobatics was the most natural thing in the world.

Fortunately, he did not have to try and imitate the natural grace of the elves, as the warhawk he rode upon spread its wings and landed atop a flat slab of rock above them. Leofric slid from the back of the mighty bird and started to thank the rider for bearing him this far, but no sooner was he down than the bird leapt back into the sky to rejoin its fellows.

The ground underfoot was black and slick, as though the fabric of the rock itself softened and attempted to reshape itself under the malign influence of the Shadow-Gave. Leofric heard wild howls and brays from above and knew that the creatures of Chaos were ready for them now.

Behind him, he saw Kyarno and Cairbre, both with their weapons at the ready, bounding from rock to rock, heading uphill towards the Corruptor. Morvhen still rode upon the back of a warhawk, an arrow nocked to her bow, the dark shapes of the warped creatures of the air closing rapidly with her, and Leofric wished her safe in the battle she would fight.

Leofric drew his sword and began making his way uphill, unable to match the grace of the elves, but making up for it with sheer determination.

The route uphill was steep and treacherous, winding through a copse of dark trees whose branches twisted towards the sky as though clawing at the clouds in agony at the foul transformation wrought upon them.

Further on, the ground levelled off onto the rock-strewn plateau and Leofric saw the silhouettes of dozens upon dozens of bestial creatures appear at its edge.

With an echoing bellow, the monstrous creatures loped down the mountainside towards the mutated trees and Leofric felt his fury at such abominations spill out in a cry of purest rage.

'For Quenelles, the king and the Lady!' he cried as he ran towards the charging beastmen with the warriors of the Asrai beside him.

LIKE HARPIES OF their dark kin, the winged beasts of Chaos sped through the air towards them, their ungainly flight a crude mockery of the graceful movements of the warhawks and their riders. As the gap between the foes closed, Morvhen saw how badly they were outnumbered as yet more rose from dark eyries in the mountains.

She took aim at a creature with the head of a slavering wolf and the leathery wings of a bat. Its eyes were red and slitted, its mouth filled with long fangs. Her warhawk banked, instinctively swinging into a position that gave her a better shot. Between breaths she loosed her arrow, the shaft arcing through the air to pierce its skull and the monster tumbled from the air, clawing at its face.

A flurry of arrows flew from the warhawk riders and a dozen or more beasts fell from the sky, their foul flesh home to blue-fletched arrows. Morvhen bent her knees, leaning into the sharp turn of her bird as it banked again.

Then all semblance of formation was lost as the flying monsters were among them, the sky awash with spinning birds and creatures as each manoeuvred for position. She saw Beithir-Seun tear a Chaos beast in two with his claws as he bit another in half. Morvhen loosed a trio of arrows, one after another, as the white under-belly of a beast flashed overhead, swiftly drawing another arrow as she saw another beast slash at one of the warhawk riders and tear him from his mount's back.

'No!' she screamed as the elf fell from the warhawk. She spitted his killer on an arrow, ducking as long, yel-lowed claws snatched at her head. Her bird spun around and she sent an arrow into her attacker, a monstrous black-winged creature with the twisted body of a snarling lion, but the shaft passed through the thin membrane of its wing. It screeched in pain and looped around, turning with its clawed rear legs reaching for her.

She dropped to her knees, gripping her mount's feath-ers as it rolled to avoid the beast's claws, but as fast as it reacted, it wasn't quite quick enough and she felt the mighty bird shudder as the beast's jaws snapped and tore open its belly. Her warhawk screamed in pain and broke from the combat, desperately heading for the ground to save its rider before it expired, but Morvhen knew they were too high for such a manoeuvre.

Morvhen heard a screech of triumph behind her and risked a glance over her shoulder to see the same leo-nine beast closing for the kill. She slung her bow over her shoulder and leaned in close to the warhawk's head.

'Farewell, great heart, I will avenge you,' she said to the dying bird as she rose to her feet and leapt towards the diving monster.

It roared in anger, snapping at her as she flew towards it, but her unexpected jump had caught it by surprise and its wide jaws snapped empty air as she looped one arm around its neck and swung herself onto its furred back.

The creature bit and clawed at her, but could not reach her. It rolled and lowered itself into a dive, attempting to shake her from its back, but she wound her fingers into its mane and held on tightly. Morvhen's sword hissed from its sheath and she plunged the blade deep into the beast's back, pulling it clear and stabbing it in again and again. Blood gushed from the mortal wounds and the monster let out a piercing roar of agony as the elven blade ripped through its body.

Morvhen looked up as she heard the shrill cry of a warhawk and yelled in relief as she saw a riderless bird flying alongside her. Abandoning the dying monster, she leapt from its plummeting corpse, the ground rushing towards her until the warhawk slotted itself between her and the rocks and pulled into a shallow dive before climbing back to the battle.

'My thanks,' shouted Morvhen as she sheathed her sword and slung her bow from her shoulders. Climbing towards the furious aerial battle, she saw warhawk riders jink and roll in a deadly ballet with the black-winged creatures of Chaos. Many of the warhawks fought alone, too many of her fellows having been torn from the backs of their mounts by the flying beasts.

Above her, her father slew beast after beast with his unerringly accurate lance strikes, skewering their vile bodies upon the blade of his magical weapon while his noble eagle tore at them with claw and beak. Beithir-Seun roared and fought with all the fury and might of his kind, his jaws snapping at his enemies and his claws tearing them limb from limb as they swarmed him. Deadly accurate bowfire picked off the beasts that were able to evade his huge jaws and land on his massive body, but the dragon still bled from a score of wounds where his thick, scaled hide had been torn open by bestial claws.

The battle was far from over, the sky filled with spinning, looping combatants, arrows flashing through the air, claws and beaks tearing at flesh and screaming bodies falling to their doom.

She nocked another arrow to her bow and angled her bird's course back into the thick of the fighting.

A BOOMING PEAL of thunder sounded, though no rain fell and no storm broke upon the fields. A wild, exultant horn echoed from the mist that gathered on the darkened eastern horizon, and the distant howls of hunting packs drifted on the cold wind. Despite himself, Teoderic Lendast shivered at the sound of the horn, its skirl promising blood and death. He gripped his lance and cast an eye along the thousand men that awaited the wild hunt on the slopes before Castle Carrard.

Nervous bowmen were arrayed behind lines of defensive stakes and trembling men-at-arms stood ready with long, hooked polearms. The lord of this host, though Teoderic knew that to call such a paltry gathering of force a host was a joke, rode at the head of a group of twenty knights in the centre, his scarlet and gold banner snapping in the strong wind.

Teoderic commanded a score of knights, banners and lances held upright and ready for the charge, and at the far end of their battle line, Theudegar led another twenty armoured warriors. Clovis sat on his whinnying steed beside Teoderic, struggling to calm his mount as yet another blast of the horn sounded, much closer this time.

'Damn, but I loathe the sound of that horn,' swore Clovis. 'It chills my blood to hear it.'

'I know what you mean,' agreed Teoderic, rubbing his gauntlet over his own mount's neck as it stamped in fear at the sound.

'Never fear, though,' he said, with a confidence he did not feel. 'We'll soon put these things to flight and it will sound naught but their retreat.'

Clovis nodded, but Teoderic could see his eyes through the visor of his helmet and remained fearful. Teoderic did not blame him, Clovis had but recently been elevated to a knight of the realm and knew full well the bloodshed that awaited them in battle.

'Look!' cried Clovis, pointing to the eastern horizon. 'The mist parts!'

Teoderic followed Clovis's pointing finger and saw that he spoke true. The mist thinned as the crack and snap of branches sounded from within and the rustle of leaves, like malicious laughter came to the assembled Bretonnians.

'Stand firm!' shouted the lord of the host as a ripple of fear passed through the men. 'Not one man shall take a backward step or he shall have me to answer to!'

Teoderic heard that damnable horn again, accompanied by the wild baying of hounds and the shrieks of ravens and crows. The ground before the mist rippled with life and growth as shoots of plant and flower erupted from the ground and shifting forms of green light emerged.

Like packs of capering maidens of briar and thorn, the forest creatures threw off their concealing cloak of mist and stood revealed in all their terrible glory. Cries of alarm and fear sounded from the Bretonnian lines, yeomen and those of more stout heart steadying the ranks with clubs and stern words.

Packs of hunting hounds swarmed over the ridge, weaving in and out of the wraiths of branch and root as they flocked downhill in a tide of razor thorns and spiteful shrieks. Billowing clouds of black birds thronged the air and ghostly clouds spread across the face of the moons as a peal of thunder and a sheet of actinic lightning split the sky.

The terrible, brazen note of the hunting horn sounded once more and Teoderic felt a primal fear seize him as he saw the enormous horn blower emerge from the mist, tall and mighty, with a crown of antlers and a cloak of leaves and clutching a terrifying, many bladed spear. Crackling magical energies wreathed the awesome figure and there could be no doubt as to this mighty being's identity.

The King of the Forest...

Snapping hounds and fiery-eyed riders atop rearing black horses and bucks that snorted in fury surrounded the king, whose burning gaze swept across the pitiful army arrayed against the might of the forest.

Teoderic lowered his lance as the woodland king's booming laughter echoed in time with another rumble of thunder, nodding to Clovis as the giant figure unleashed another deafening blast of his hunting horn and led his wild riders in a furious charge towards them.

THE HAUNTED COPSE of dark trees beneath the plateau was a bloodbath as elf and man and beast clashed in furious combat. Leofric hacked his sword through a thickly furred limb and deflected an axe strike away from his body, turning and slashing his silver sword across his foe's back. A spear thudded into his breastplate, spinning him around and he backed into a tree as a bestial horror with monstrously wide jaws and a frill of reptilian skin around its neck lunged for him.

He roared and thrust his sword into its mouth, stabbing the point up into its brain. The monster bellowed in pain, its jaw snapping shut on the blade. Leofric wrenched it clear and beheaded the creature as Kyarno moved to stand beside him, firing arrow after arrow into the mass of beastmen.

The young elf was unbelievably swift with his bow, nocking and firing almost without pause and sending shafts into the eyes and vitals of every beast he shot at. The two forged a path through the beastmen, Kyarno loosing deadly accurate arrows and Leofric hacking them down with his brutal swordwork.

Cairbre fought like no one Leofric had ever seen before, twisting, stabbing and cutting with a skill unmatched by any other. He fought to protect Naieth, a wild wind of bright power weaving around her as she smote the beastmen with her magic. Though twisted into new and vile shapes, the trees of the copse arose to her bidding, a storm of razor-sharp missiles of jagged wood engulfing any beastmen who drew near her.

The venerable Cairbre was always in motion, never stopping or slowing as he slew the foul children of Chaos, the Blades of Midnight cleaving through unclean flesh with ease as he fought to protect the prophetess.

The elves of Coeth-Mara fought side by side, swords and spears cutting down beastmen by the score, but always there were more howling monstrosities to take their place. Bestial and elven blood mingled on the rocky ground as elf after elf was torn down by the brute savagery of the beasts and Leofric knew that such losses could not be maintained.

Even as he thought this, Leofric chopped his sword through the face of a baying monster with myriad eyes and mouths as a snapping, red-furred hound with two heads leapt upon him, its claws scraping down his pauldron and ripping it from his armour.

The hound bore him to the ground, one set of its bloody fangs closing on his visor and crushing it in its powerful jaws as the other sought his throat. Leofric cried out and slammed his armoured head into one of the hound's faces, rolling as he struggled to remove his helmet. A squeal of pain came from the hound and as he tore off his ruined helmet, he saw two of Kyarno's arrows buried in its ribs.

He clambered to his feet and drove his sword into its flank to finish it off as he heard a great clamour from the ridge above him and yet more beastmen came charging towards them.

'Kyarno!' he yelled. 'There are more!'

'I see them!' called back the elf as he retrieved arrows from the corpses of the dead.

'We must get past them,' said Cairbre, panting and out of breath from the exertions of the battle. The white blades of his spear were streaked with black blood and he bled from a number of minor wounds, but the Hound of Winter's courage was undimmed.

The charge of the monsters was almost upon them when Leofric saw a spectral mist of sparkling lights form around his feet. It oozed from the bark of the trees, a whisper of things unseen rustling nearby, and as he readied his weapon to fight once more, he shook his head to clear it of the ghostly apparitions he thought he saw. Had the two-headed monster's attack stunned him more seriously than he had thought?

A ululating war cry, wild and passionate, burst from the trees and, with a wild howl, the ghostly apparitions suddenly resolved themselves into solidity as Cu-Sith and his wardancers appeared from the mist.

The Red Wolf leapt amongst the beastmen, a sword and short-hafted spear cutting and stabbing. The painted wardancers smashed into the beastmen with weapons spinning around them in blindingly swift cuts – beheading, disembowelling and cleaving them with a speed and viciousness that was breathtaking.

No matter where the bestial monsters attacked, the wardancers evaded them, somersaulting and bounding aside from their clumsy attacks before darting in with a graceful pirouette to ram a blade into an exposed throat or eye socket.

While the monsters reeled from this unexpected attack, Leofric, Cairbre and Kyarno pushed on towards the plateau.

But before they could do more than gather their wits, they heard a monstrous bellow of rage and power that sent a wave of terror through every one of them.

Leofric looked up through the leaping wardancers to the plateau and saw the monolithic form of the way-stone towering above them. Crude symbols had been daubed upon it, blotting out the elven runes carved there. Before it stood a beastman of colossal proportions, its hide dark with blood and scaled in bronze. Its horned head was scarred and burned, but its flickering, multi-coloured eyes burned with purpose and power.

Thick, hooked chains looped across its chest and it wore spiked shoulder guards crudely fashioned from beaten breastplates. It carried a massive, double-headed axe, its blades rusted, but with a potent magical aura surrounding them.

In front of it thrashed a diabolical creature that defied any recognisable shape or form, its limbs a slashing web of thorned pseudopods, its fluid form shifting and roiling in constant motion. A cadre of similarly gigantic monsters surrounded the waystone, hulking bull-headed monsters, slavering wolf creatures and drooling, slack-jawed trolls with tough, warty hides and great stone clubs.

Naieth cried out in anger as some unseen force drained her skin of colour, and she cried, 'The Corruptor... it is here!'

'Where?' asked Cairbre, rushing to her side.

'Upon the mountain!' gasped Naieth, pointing to the cave mouth.

Leofric looked into the darkness of the cave, feeling an instinctual dread of the dark claw its way up his spine as he saw something lurch from the depths. A powerful beast with a dark miasma of power swirling around it like black mist emerged into the sunlight, though a shadow crept with it, as though unwilling to allow such an abomination to bask in its light. Gibbering, screeching wails accompanied the monster, skulls woven within its fur and horns screaming in anguish.

Leofric dropped to his knees in pain as a powerful nausea clamped his gut. All around him elves fell to the ground, assaulted by the dark forces surrounding this monster.

Naieth reached up to grip Cairbre's wrist and shouted, 'Quickly, now is your time! The white hound, the red wolf and the hawk, I see it now!'

'Prophetess,' said Cairbre. 'What–'

'No time!' cried Naieth. 'If the Corruptor reaches the waystone then all will have been for naught, the magic will be perverted to serve the Dark Gods and it will be lost to us. Go now! Destroy the beast!'

CHAPTER TWENTY

CAIRBRE RAN FROM the tearful prophetess and made his way uphill, gritting his teeth against the rising pain and dark energies he felt assail him. Behind him the elves of Coeth-Mara began climbing to their feet as they fought against the power of the Corruptor, but their advance was slower and more painful than his.

He felt his flesh answering the dark call of the Corruptor's foulness and exerted every last ounce of his will to resist its vile imprecations. Before him, the war-dancers carved apart the last of the beasts between them and the waystone, but rather than continue their bloody rampage up the mountainside, they gathered around their painted leader, the wolf tattoo on his chest writhing and snapping beneath his skin as it revelled in the bloodshed.

The corpses of beastmen surrounded the bloodied troupe, but their victory had not been won without loss, fully half of their number lay gored on the dark rocks. Cu-Sith met Cairbre's stare and the wardancer nodded, 'It is our time then? The white hound and the red wolf?'

The Hound of Winter frowned at the Red Wolf's familiar turn of phrase and nodded, saying, 'Yes, the prophetess–'

'Cu-Sith knows,' interrupted the wardancer with a wild grin of feral anticipation on his gory features. 'Loec knows all and Loec tells Cu-Sith what he must do.'

'But how did–'

'No time!' said Cu-Sith as more packs of wild beast-men charged towards them from the plateau above. Cairbre nodded again, glancing into the sky at the vicious battle being fought above them as winged mon-sters clashed with the warhawk riders and the mighty Beithir-Seun.

Arrows slashed past the Hound and the Wolf as the elves of Coeth-Mara and the human fought through the Corruptor's power to make for the waystone. The odds had been evened by Cu-Sith's arrival, but there were still many scores of beastmen to slay before victory could be won.

The Red Wolf set off up the mountain, his sword and spear spinning in his grip, but Cairbre could see that even the mighty Cu-Sith was in great pain from the touch of the Corruptor's dark magic.

Once again the beasts of Chaos and the Asrai clashed in the shadow of the waystone, but Cairbre did not stop to fight them, cutting himself a path through their mot-ley ranks to follow the Red Wolf towards the terrible beast that advanced from the mouth of the cave towards the waystone.

* * *

LEOFRIC COULD BARELY hold off the agonising pain wracking him as he fought to climb uphill. His flesh seethed with rebellion, and it took all his rage and anger to hold himself true to his form. He slew beasts without mercy, channelling all his emotion into each blow.

Axes struck him and his own blood ran from his body, but he cared not, striking down his foes with each sweep of his gleaming sword. Beside him Kyarno screamed with each arrow loosed, his movements supple and swift despite the battle he fought against his own unquiet flesh.

They fought their way alongside a score of elves, their blades and bows reaping a fearsome tally of their bestial foes. But each yard gained was paid for in blood and the dead were left to fall in their wake. Only victory would grant them eternal life in the funeral glades of the forest, and Leofric just hoped they could give them such a memory.

At last, awash with blood and death, they reached the plateau and the waystone.

Cairbre and Cu-Sith had already broken through the beastmen and were working their way up the steep rocks towards the cave mouth above them. Leofric wished them the blessing of the Lady, but could ill afford to spare them more than a glance as he took in the scale of the foes before them.

Surely this massive, bull-headed monster must be the leader of this herd, its terrible bulk greater than any beast they had slain thus far. As they stood before it, the monster gave out a deafening bellow and raised its massive axe in a defiant challenge.

An arrow from Kyarno's bow slashed towards it, but it batted it aside with its axe blade, the weapon moving impossibly swiftly for its bulk. Another arrow slashed towards the Beastlord – this time from above – thudding into the meat of its shoulder and Leofric looked up to see Morvhen circling above them, bloodied and riding a ragged, scarred warhawk.

Brutish trolls lumbered forward with the Beastlord and with another fearsome bellow, it released the chained spawn creature towards them. Faster than Leofric would have believed such a malformed abomination could move, it slithered and lurched towards them, howling and screeching in blind, lunatic hunger.

Its thorned limbs ended in snapping mouths of razored fangs and bladed hooks, and ripping claws seethed in its riotous flesh. Arrows hammered into the soft meat of its body, but if it felt any pain from them, it gave no sign.

Leofric charged to meet the beast headlong, his sword cleaving into its rippling body. The blade parted the skin easily, slicing through warped muscle and bone, but before he could bring his sword back for another blow, a fanged jaw surged from the spawn's flesh and snapped shut on his vambrace. He cried out as the metal compressed on his arm, stabbing his sword into the mouth and ripping his arm free as a club-like limb smashed him from his feet. A clutch of stabbing, blade-like appendages writhed from its body and reached for his face.

Another blade slashed above him and the creature screeched as Kyarno dragged him back, his sword stabbing at each of the beast's grasping limbs as they snatched at them. More arrows thudded into its flesh as the elves overcame their horror at the vile beast and rushed to aid them.

Leofric and Kyarno attacked together, their swords hacking great lumps of greasy fat and gristle from the heaving spawn's body. Its struggles grew weaker and weaker, but still it would not die until its flesh was carved to bloody chunks.

But by then it had served its purpose as the Beastlord and its monstrous acolytes smashed into the elves. Three were killed instantly as it clove its axe through their bodies with one mighty blow, another two smashed to bloody ruin by the return stroke.

It bellowed as it slew, red-flecked spittle flying from its jaws and a dark light flaring in its eyes. Yet another arrow thunked into the great, bull-headed monster, but it ignored the wound as it turned to face Leofric and Kyarno.

Perhaps a dozen elves still stood with them, and each loosed a shaft towards the mighty beastman as it hacked yet more of their number down in a welter of blood and bone. Leofric raised his sword and darted in to slash it across the Beastlord's side, his blade biting an inch before sliding clear.

Kyarno rolled beneath a scything blow of its axe and drove his sword into its gut with all his might. The blade penetrated a handspan before snapping off in his hand and Kyarno threw himself back as the huge axe swept towards him, the edge of the blade coming within an inch of gutting him.

Leofric took advantage of the Beastlord's distraction to chop at his foe's arm, his sword slicing into the meat and rebounding from the bone beneath. The Beastlord roared and its wounded arm slashed down to break him in two.

But instead of tearing him to pieces, a dazzling white light erupted from Leofric's gauntlet and the Beastlord's claws simply carved a series of parallel grooves diagonally down his breastplate and hurled him back across the rocks. The terrible creature's blood splashed his vambrace and cuirass, burning through them like engraver's acid.

He rolled to his knees as fragments of white crystal fell from his gauntlet, and he silently thanked Tiphaine for her favour, knowing it had just saved his life.

Despite their courage and Morvhen's arrows, Leofric saw that while the Beastlord lived, this fight could have but one outcome. The bull-creatures were killing them one by one and every elf slain brought them closer to defeat. The wardancers had joined the fight, cutting down the trolls with deadly grace, but it was slow, brutal work, their enemies able to withstand even the most terrible wounds before finally succumbing.

But such things did not matter any more. They had to fight and if that meant they had to die, then so be it. They fought because Chaos had to be opposed wherever it was found.

Leofric rose to his feet once more and charged back into the fray.

CAIRBRE STRUGGLED TO keep up with Cu-Sith as the more nimble wardancer bounded from rock to rock, climbing the slope towards the Corruptor as it closed on the waystone. He heard wild howls below him and saw that around forty of the more agile creatures were following them, rushing to defend their despicable leader.

Every step and every breath was pain, the dark power of the monstrous beastman above him threatening to change him into something vile and terrible. Only his indomitable will kept his form constant, though he knew that should he falter for an instant he would be lost.

'Come on!' shouted Cu-Sith from above as he vaulted onto the ledge in front of the cave mouth. Cairbre bit back an angry retort and forced himself to climb faster as the yelping howls of the creatures behind him intensified.

His breath came in sharp bursts, his muscles burning with fatigue and their continued resistance to the power at work on this mountain. His hand closed on the rock of the ledge and he hauled himself upwards, but as he pulled, the rock melted beneath his fingers and he felt himself falling backwards.

A hand shot out and gripped his wrist, pulling him onto the ledge as claws snatched at him from below. He had no time to thank Cu-Sith as a horned head appeared at the lip of the ledge and roared in fury at him. The Blades of Midnight flashed and the headless beastman spun through the air to dash itself on the rocks below.

Cairbre ran after the Red Wolf, glancing up to see more of the black-winged creatures dropping through the air to come to the defence of the Corruptor, which now halted its advance upon the waystone to face this new threat.

The terrifying creature turned its burning gaze upon them and both elves groaned in pain as they fought the full force of its corrupting powers. It threw back its head and let loose an ear-splitting roar of hate and bloodlust, the twisting staff it held rippling with smoky magic.

'Loec says they will talk of this battle for centuries,' said Cu-Sith, giving Cairbre a sly wink.

'I look forward to hearing it,' answered Cairbre, as they hurled themselves towards the howling beastman. Wardancer and Eternal Guard attacked the Corruptor from either side, flashing swords and spears stabbing for its unclean flesh. But for all its lumpen appearance, the Corruptor was a terrifyingly powerful beast and fought with all the ferocity and cunning its kind were famed for.

Its thick hide turned aside their every blow, its deadly staff turning in midair to intercept their attacks without apparent effort. Its claws smashed Cairbre from his feet, sending him skidding to the very lip of the ledge. The Hound of Winter grunted in pain and clutched his chest where he knew at least one rib was broken and his flesh burned with the touch of the beast.

He climbed painfully to his feet, seeing that they were now cut off from the rest of the elves, a mass of chanting, bellowing beastmen surrounding their struggle on the ledge. They knew better than to approach the Corruptor too closely and seemed content to let their master fight this battle alone.

Cairbre watched as Cu-Sith leapt and spun around the vile beastman, his sword and spear batted aside at every turn. No matter where his blades struck, its dark staff blocked his every attack. A shadow flashed overhead and Cairbre looked up to see one of the winged beastmen slash through the air towards the Red Wolf.

Cu-Sith swayed aside from its attack, hacking its head from its shoulders as it writhed with rampant mutation at its proximity to the Corruptor. But the momentary distraction was all the opening the beastman lord needed, its mighty staff hammering into Cu-Sith's temple and driving him to his knees.

The great wolf tattoo on his chest howled in anger and the wardancer looked in amazement at the red liquid pouring from his head.

'You made Cu-Sith bleed his own blood...' he said in shock.

Cairbre pushed himself forward, but he already knew he would be too late as the Corruptor's staff swung back around and smashed the Red Wolf's skull to splinters.

LEOFRIC SLICED HIS sword across the Beastlord's side, drawing a spray of dark blood, but not slowing the beast at all. Elves were dying every second; the monstrous beast's axe slaying them with an unnatural savagery. Dark magic pulsed in the blades and Leofric knew that with such power, even their skill and courage could not triumph.

Kyarno jumped back, barely avoiding a deadly stroke of the creature's axe as yet another arrow loosed by Morvhen thudded into its flesh. There seemed to be no stopping the monster, but Leofric attacked again regardless. Kyarno stumbled, his left leg bloody where it had been gashed from hip to knee by one of the Beastlord's followers.

Only Leofric stood before the terrifying creature, his silver sword glowing with a faint light as he faced the Beastlord. Its blood hissed and spat where it dripped from its body onto the rocks and its mighty chest heaved with exertion. It may have nearly defeated them, but it had not been an easy battle.

The two combatants circled one another as he heard a scream of rage from the ledge above, but Leofric dared not risk tearing his gaze from the monster before him. It growled and its chest hiked, giving voice to a low, growling bray. Leofric was confused for a moment before he realised that the creature was laughing at him. Laughing at him for daring to stand against such a monstrously powerful avatar of the Dark Gods.

Leofric's fury lent his tired limbs strength and he charged the monster with a cry of rage, 'Lady guide my hand!'

He swung his sword towards the beast's midriff, feeling the hilt of his weapon grow hot as the blade leapt with silver fire, outshining the sun with its brilliance. The Beastlord's axe came round to block the blow and the two weapons met in a shower of dazzling sparks and fire.

The gigantic axe exploded into fragments of dark iron and wood, a flaring after-image of some malevolent shadow erupting from the shattered weapon. Leofric fell back, reeling and numb from the impact, blinking to clear his vision from the glaring after-images of the explosion.

He dropped to one knee, still clutching his glowing sword, amazed and thankful for its hidden power when a shadow swept over him and a powerful voice shouted, 'Human! Down!'

Leofric threw himself flat as the golden form of Lord Aldaeld atop his magnificent eagle swooped low across the battlefield and streaked towards the stunned Beastlord. He looked up in time to see Lord Aldaeld ram the blade of his silver lance into the creature's chest, the shaft plunging deep into its body and ripping out through its back in a fountain of blood and fragmented bone. Lord Aldaeld angled the flight of his eagle back into the air and, skewered like an insect on the needle of an academic, the Beastlord was carried high above the battle.

It fought to drag the weapon from its body, its flesh smoking where the faerie lance of Athel Loren seared it with its purity, but it could not escape as Lord Aldaeld lifted it higher and higher.

Only when both figures were little more than dots of black against the sky, did Lord Aldaeld finally allow the creature to slide from his lance, the tumbling figure of the Beastlord falling thousands of feet to smash on the jagged rocks of the mountains.

Leofric bowed his head and gave thanks to the Lady of the Lake as clouds of dust were blown skyward and another huge shadow enveloped the plateau. He squinted through the clouds of swirling dust, seeing the mighty form of Beithir-Seun hovering just above the plateau, his green, scaled flesh torn and bloody, but triumphant. Warhawk riders circled him, their faces alight with the savage joy of victory.

The great dragon reached down with his claws and ripped the waystone from the pile of skulls, weapons and armour that surrounded it and slowly began to climb into the sky. Riderless warhawks set down on the bloody field of battle to collect the few surviving warriors of Coeth-Mara.

Kyarno limped over to a scarred bird and said, 'Come on. We have the stone, now let's get Cairbre and Cu-Sith and get out of here.'

Leofric nodded and breathlessly staggered over to Kyarno, climbing onto the back of the mighty bird.

'We won,' he said, hardly able to believe it.

'Oh, no...' gasped Kyarno, looking at something above them.

Leofric turned on the warhawk's back in time to see a battle he would remember to his dying day.

THE CORRUPTOR'S STAFF again thwarted Cairbre's every attempt to breach his defences and the Hound of Winter knew that he could not defeat this monster alone. The Red Wolf was dead, and as he watched Beithir-Seun lift into the sky with the waystone clutched in its claws, he smiled as he realised they had succeeded.

Blood ran from his mouth and his breath rasped in his throat. But he was the Hound of Winter and he never gave up, never stopped fighting and never took a backwards step in the face of the enemy.

'Come on then, you monster,' he snarled. 'Time for you to die.'

He lunged forward, the Blades of Midnight spinning in a whirling arc of white blades. Though pain stabbed through him with every movement, he shut himself off from it, focussing all his thoughts on slaying the monster before him.

The skulls woven into the fur of its back and horns screamed at him, promising death in all manner of uncounted ways, the dark miasma of change that surrounded the Corruptor straining at the bounds of his will to rupture his flesh with mutation.

'You shall not have me!' shouted Cairbre, swaying aside from a scything blow and spinning close to the stinking, shaggy monster. His left blade slashed across the beast's stomach, a spray of black blood gushing from the wound and ripping a bellowing roar of pain from its jaws.

Its writhing staff slashed down, hooking under Caibre's legs and sending him flying backwards to land atop the corpse of Cu-Sith. He rolled from the body of the Red Wolf and felt a fresh vigour course through him.

Loec is not done with Cu-Sith...

Cairbre cried out in amazement as the voice of the wardancer echoed in his head and he looked down to see that the great, snarling tattoo of the Red Wolf now adorned *his* chest, its fangs slavering for blood and vengeance.

He heard a bestial roar and looked up in time to see the Corruptor's staff arcing towards his head. He leapt into the air, somersaulting over its head with a maniacal laugh that was not his own.

As he leapt through the air, he twisted the haft of the Blades of Midnight, separating them into his twin swords and drove them straight down into the shoulders of the Corruptor.

The terrible beast shook the mountains with its roar of agony, its unclean flesh seething at the touch of faerie magic. Cairbre landed behind the beast, dropping lightly on the balls of his feet and pulled his swords clear with a wild yell of fierce anger. The Corruptor spun, its flesh burned, and its insane gaze settled on Cairbre once more.

The Hound of Winter felt his new found strength wither before its gaze, dropping to his knees as agonising pain returned to swamp him.

The Corruptor staggered away from him, blood flooding from its body and the dark, smoky trails of its vile, magical essence pouring into the air. It let out a howl of outrage and pain, before turning and limping back into its cave to recover its strength before the power that sustained it was undone forever.

Cairbre watched it go with a mixture of regret and exultation. Regret that he had not rid the world of its foulness, and exultation in the atavistic glory of victory.

He looked down and smiled weakly as the snarling tattoo of the red wolf on his chest began to fade and nodded in thanks to the departed Cu-Sith as the wardancer's voice echoed in his head one last time.

Not bad for an old man and a wild one, eh, Hound?

'No,' agreed Cairbre, watching as the vengeful followers of the Corruptor closed in on him now that the mutating influence of their master had withdrawn. 'Not bad at all.'

He counted at least forty, and while, in his prime, he could have taken them on with some chance of success, he was far from in his prime. Slotting the Blades of Midnight together again to form the twin-bladed spear, the Hound of Winter painfully pushed himself to his feet, watching as the warhawks took to the air alongside Beithir–Seun.

He smiled as he saw that Kyarno still lived, his nephew's bird racing towards him in a futile attempt to save him. No, the Hound of Winter's season had passed and with it his stewardship of the Blades of Midnight.

As the creatures of Chaos closed on him with axes and swords raised to cut him down, he shouted Kyarno's name, drew back his arm and hurled his spear into the clear blue of the sky.

'CAIRBRE, NO!' SCREAMED Kyarno as he saw what his uncle intended. But Cairbre's course was set and the white-bladed spear streaked into the air like a glittering comet. Its arcing course cut the air above them and Kyarno leapt onto the warhawk's back to catch the spinning spear as it began to curve downwards.

'Go back!' shouted Kyarno as the warhawk began to turn away from the mountain and back to Athel Loren, but the bird could see the outcome of the battle below, even if he would not.

Both he and Leofric could only watch helplessly as the beastmen surrounded Cairbre, clubbing him and stabbing him with their crude weapons. Though he fought bravely, killing over a dozen with a short sword taken from a dead foe, he could not defeat them all, and soon his body was lost to sight beneath a mound of thrashing, stabbing beasts.

Kyarno sobbed in loss as his uncle was finally overwhelmed, unable to believe that so mighty a warrior as the Hound of Winter could have been bested.

The warhawk dipped its wings in sadness at the passing of a great warrior and beneath the shadow of mourning they flew back to Athel Loren.

CHAPTER TWENTY-ONE

SADDENED BUT VICTORIOUS, the warriors of Coeth-Mara descended towards the forest in the wake of Beithir-Seun, welcomed home by the same host of birds that had seen them on their way. Too many had died and too much had been lost for there to be any kind of celebration at this battle's end, but it would be remembered in song and tale for centuries to come as one of the great battles against Cyanathair.

The waystone had been saved by the might and strength of the Hound of Winter and the Red Wolf, and their names would live forever in the glory of the forest, remembered by all the Asrai in their dreams and their songs.

THE MIGHTY DRAGON hovered above the ground, weeds and thorny branches reaching up to try and snag its limbs as it gently lowered the waystone back into its rightful place. Leofric and the survivors of the battle watched the dragon return the waystone to the ground from a rocky hillock, an island of grey amid a seething carpet of verdant greenery.

Leofric had taken it for beautiful from the air, but upon landing, he saw it for the wild, savage glory of nature unbound that it truly was. Everywhere the greenery smothered all other life, destroying it and replacing it with its own. Kyarno stood next to him, still clutching the Blades of Midnight, with Morvhen's arm around his shoulders as they wept for the lost Cairbre. Leofric had shed no tears for the old elf; after all, they were not friends, but even so, he was saddened to see such a noble warrior fall to such base creatures as beastmen.

Lord Aldaeld and Naieth stood before them, knee deep in the swaying undergrowth that swirled around them with questing fronds and curious flowers. The greenery parted before Naieth, her staff held before her and her owl once again perched on her shoulder now that she had returned to the forest.

'What are they doing?' asked Leofric. 'Is it over? Is the wild hunt over?'

'Not yet, no,' said Morvhen. 'Terrible violence was done here, dark magicks have been unleashed, and it has tainted the forest.'

'Tainted it?' said Leofric, horrified at the thought of all they had fought and bled for being snatched away and that his people might still be dying. 'No, that cannot be.'

He took a faltering step from the hillock, stepping through the rising greenery and calling out to Naieth. 'Prophetess! The waystone is returned. Why does the wild hunt still lay waste to my lands?'

Aldaeld and Naieth turned to face Leofric as the waving strands of growth slithered around him, curious and hostile to this human within their domain. As he drew nearer to them, his armoured boot crunched bone and he looked down to see the leather-wrapped skeleton of a beastman, its bony hands clutching a staff of dark wood. Not a scrap of flesh remained on its bones, but whether they had been picked clean by insects or the ravages of time and the elements, Leofric could not say.

'The healing magic will take time to undo the damage done here, Leofric,' said Naieth. 'You must be patient.'

'Patient?' he yelled, turning his attention to the lord of Coeth-Mara. 'My people may be dying even now! I beseech you, allow me to travel upon one of these mighty birds to my lands. I have fought beside your kinband and I ask this boon of you as one warrior to another.'

Lord Aldaeld nodded and said, 'So be it... Leofric. We have much to work against here, the foulness of the children of Chaos runs deep and I know what it is to lose those under your care. If there is a warhawk willing to bear you back to your lands, then you may go with my blessing.'

'Thank you, Lord Aldaeld,' said Leofric, bowing deeply before the elven lord.

'Go in peace, Leofric Carrard,' nodded Aldaeld slowly. He turned back to Naieth then said. 'You will be welcome in Coeth-Mara again, human.'

Leofric said, 'I would be glad to visit here again some day,' and turned back to the rocky hillock he had come from.

'I will come with you,' said Kyarno. 'I wish to see this land you call home.'

Leofric smiled, 'And I would be glad to show it to you.'

'I will come too,' added Morvhen. 'I may never have another chance.'

Leofric and Kyarno climbed atop the warhawk that had borne them from the battle, its proud head held high as they settled upon its back. Morvhen mounted the bird that had saved her life upon leaping from the winged beast she had killed, and together they leapt into the sky, both warhawks climbing rapidly into the west as they flew towards Bretonnia.

NAIETH WATCHED THE birds rise into the sky with a great sense of sadness for the armoured form carried on the back of the second warhawk. As they vanished over the treetops, Lord Aldaeld asked, 'Does he know?'

'No,' said Naieth quietly, 'but he will soon enough.'

'Do you have any regrets?'

'Regrets? No. I did what I had to do to guide my people, Aldaeld. You of all people should understand that.'

'I do,' nodded Aldaeld, 'but I thought that you had perhaps developed an affection for the human. Am I wrong?'

'No,' admitted Naieth. 'He has many admirable qualities, but in the end, he is still only human.'

'Very well,' said Aldaeld. 'I will accept that for now. But next time there is a threat to Athel Loren, speak to me of it first.'

'You know I could not,' cautioned Naieth as a shimmering white light built from within the trees and the waystone finally groaned into place.

She smiled in welcome and both she and Aldaeld dropped to their knees before the radiance of the goddess before them, her beauteous form indistinct in the haze of brilliant sunlight that enveloped her.

As the light spread before her, the dark greenery that reached beyond the forest's edge lightened, becoming thinner and more lush, the darkened branches and malignant mosses vanishing before the incredible power of her compassion and love.

Everywhere her light touched, the dark sorcery of the enemies of Athel Loren was undone, the foulness and corruption that had touched the land leeched from the ground in a dark mist that dissipated in the face of such radiance.

Naieth and Aldaeld watched in wonder as the balance of the world was restored and the beauty of the forest surged in their blood.

The light of Isha flowed through the Lady Ariel and both elves felt their hearts lifted as they heard her soft words in their heads.

The healing of Athel Loren must begin anew...

BLOOD AND SCREAMS filled the air. Men-at-arms fell like wheat before the scythe, unable to stand against the primal ferocity of the forest king. Arrows peppered his flesh and lances shattered upon his great muscles, but his mighty form was impervious to such things.

Teoderic raised his lance as his knights circled back to the fray after yet another desperate charge and shouted, 'Once more for the Lady! Once more for honour!'

Barely a handful of his knights still lived, the charge of the wild hunt crashing into their numbers like a thunderbolt. Each charge of the knights had smashed deep into the enemy lines, creatures of branch and thorn splintering and crumbling beneath their might. But each time the momentum of the charge had faltered, they had risen up once more, stinking of sap and fresh-cut wood as they tore warriors from the saddle.

Clovis still fought beside him, his lance splintered and useless, his sword clutched in his bloody gauntlet. Theudegar fought on the left flank, his knights surrounded by the whooping riders on the dark steeds who hung the skulls of those they had slain from their belts.

The forest king stood in the centre of the field, bellowing in fury and blowing deafening blasts of his hunting horn. Those who came near him died, and everywhere his long spear reached, blood was shed. There was no shape to the battle now, simply wild charges and furious combats as the muster of Bretonnia fought for honour.

Honour was all they had left, for victory was surely beyond their grasp now.

But the impossibility of victory was no reason for a knight of Bretonnia to give up and Teoderic punched the air as he saw the scarlet and gold banner of Castle Carrard's lord raised high in the gloom and charge towards the green-fleshed King of the Forest.

'With me!' he yelled, raking back his spurs and riding towards their commander's banner. Nine brave knights followed him as a thunderous impact slammed into the ground barely a dozen yards from his horse. A huge piece of rock, hurled from the trebuchet mounted on the walls of Castle Carrard, crashed through the encroaching forest creatures, smashing them to splinters and scattering them once more.

Teoderic lowered his lance as he saw Theudegar angle his charge towards the centre of the battlefield, having also seen the gold and scarlet unicorn banner raised high.

His charge thundered through the snapping hounds of the forest king, his thick-limbed steed trampling the howling animals beneath his iron-shod hooves as he closed on the faerie king.

Truly was he a terrifying sight, taller even than an ogre and with a fearsome aura of great power surrounding him. His cloak of leaves billowed in the storm winds and his curling antlers sprang directly from the brow of his savagely regal countenance. His giant spear dripped with blood and his eyes blazed with unimaginable power.

Theudegar reached the forest king first, his lance shattering on his iron-hard emerald flesh. Teoderic cried out as the immense spear slashed around and clove through Theudegar's breastplate, punching him from the back of his horse. The king swung his spear and hurled the brave knight's body across the battlefield before lunging towards the rest of Theudegar's warriors and slaughtering them in a frenzy.

Teoderic and the knights of the master of Castle Carrard charged at the same time, cries of vengeance spilling from their lips as they hit home. Teoderic was hurled from his horse by the thunderous impact, blood and screams of pain surrounding him as he fell. The shattered haft of his lance was all that was left of his weapon, and as he picked himself up, he threw aside the splintered wood and unsheathed his sword.

The lord of Castle Carrard stood before his enemy, his lance having pierced the forest king's flesh. White sap spilled from the wound and Teoderic quailed before the great and terrible anger of this monstrous god.

Man and god faced one another and, for a second, Teoderic felt the world hold its breath as a sudden sense of incredible peace fell upon the battlefield. The fury of battle fled from his body and he felt a wave of – something wonderful – pass through the land.

The forest king bellowed in anger and ripped the lance from his body, looming over the knight before him. His bloody spear was poised to strike, but for some unknown reason, the forest king held his blow.

Teoderic rose unsteadily to his feet and quickly moved to stand beside the lord of Castle Carrard, his sword held before him, though he knew it was scant defence against such a mighty being as towered above him. Clovis limped towards him, and the knights who still lived rallied to their commander's banner that fluttered in the breeze.

Shafts of sunlight broke through the clouds above and Teoderic saw that the forest king's army was melting away, the wild riders gathering to their liege lord while the creatures of branch and wood froze into immobility. The ghostly forms of withering hags faded like morning mist in the gathering sunlight and Teoderic watched as the spectral clouds dissipated into the brightening sky.

Deathly silence filled the field before the castle, broken only by the cries of dying men and the whinny of horses. The forest king put up his spear and hooked his mighty hunting horn to his belt of skulls.

'What's happening?' asked Teoderic of no one in particular.

No one answered, their eyes turned to the heavens as a pair of great, winged creatures swooped towards the motionless tableau in the centre of the battlefield.

As they drew near, Teoderic saw they were giant birds, hawks by the look of them, but hawks that carried riders. They circled the battlefield before landing some twenty yards away, one depositing an elf woman of startling grace and beauty, the other a male elf and a human warrior in the armour of a Bretonnian knight.

Teoderic thought there was something familiar about the knight, but could not say for sure what. But before he could question these new arrivals, the forest king leaned down to address the assembled knights.

'In all things must there be balance,' he said, his powerful voice redolent with age. 'My queen calls me home and the realm of the Asrai is restored. The world is now as it should be. But do not forget this lesson, for I will hunt again.'

And with that, the forest king turned away and thundered over the eastern horizon with his wild riders back towards the realm of Athel Loren.

LEOFRIC WATCHED THE King of the Wood go and felt a great surge of pride in the warriors who had so gallantly stood against him. Though the battlefield was littered with the bodies of the fallen, he knew a great victory had been won here. A low mist, the bodies of dead hounds and flocks of circling ravens were all that remained of the wild hunt, and Leofric smiled as he realised that he now set foot upon the soil of Bretonnia once more.

Sunlight filled the sky, the warmth of spring upon the air, and he looked up at the welcoming sight of Castle Carrard, its many towers and red stone walls a wondrously familiar and welcome sight to him after so long.

Kyarno and Morvhen stood behind him, wary and unsure of this new and unsettling place. Leofric pointed at the castle high upon the hill above the glittering waters of the Brienne.

'This is my castle,' he said with a wide smile. 'This is my domain. I am home.'

He turned as he heard the sound of armoured warriors approaching and saw a pair of blood-spattered knights. One wore a surcoat with heraldry he did not recognise, while the other…

The other…

The other knight wore heraldry that depicted a scarlet unicorn rampant beneath a jewelled crown against a golden field. Leofric started as he recognised the heraldry as his own and began to speak when the knight removed his helmet.

His hair was the colour of silver, his features regal and sculpted, with green eyes set in a face lined with sorrow. Leofric's skin crawled as he saw a dreadful familiarity in them.

'I would have your name, sir,' demanded the silver-haired knight. 'Who are you and what is your business in Carrard lands?'

'Carrard lands…' said Leofric, looking up at his castle and now seeing towers and hoardings where none had been before.

'Sir, I require an answer,' said the knight, a trace of recognition in his voice. 'And are these elves you consort with?'

'My name is… unimportant,' said Leofric, 'and, yes, these are elves. Kyarno Silvermorn and Morvhen Fleetmane of Coeth-Mara. Are you lord of these lands?'

'I am,' said the knight. 'I am Leofric Carrard, servant of the king and the Lady of the Lake.'

'Leofric Carrard…' said Leofric. 'How came you by that name?'

'It was my great grandfather's,' answered the knight. 'He was taken by the forest a hundred years ago and never seen again.'

Leofric dropped to his knees as the full weight of the knight's words sank in.

All that had passed within the forest had been but the turn of three seasons to him, but beyond the forest… a hundred years had gone by. Could it be true? Could this Leofric Carrard who stood before him truly be his descendant?

'Your grandfather,' said Leofric. 'He was called Beren?'

'He was,' nodded the silver-haired Leofric. 'A great and noble warrior.'

Leofric smiled at such an accolade given to the son he had never had the chance to know.

All that he knew had passed away and all that remained was… what?

He looked up at the castle on the hill once more as a strange lightness came upon him, a fugue-like dreaminess filling his mind with thoughts of faraway lands. The sun shone from behind the red towers of the fastness, blinding in its intensity. As he watched, the glow spread until it filled his vision and he saw again the same glorious brilliance he had seen in the forest many months ago.

At its centre he saw a slender pair of delicate hands cupping a silver chalice that overflowed with dazzling light, a light that spilled over the towers and walls of the castle and washed it away in a tide of wondrous radiance.

His eyes lit up as he recognised the chalice of the Lady of the Lake.

The grail itself…

He rose to his feet as the vision faded from his sight, the knights around him seeing the rapture in his eyes as he smiled at them. He drew his sword and knelt before his namesake.

'This belongs to you, Leofric Carrard,' he said, offering him the blade, hilt first.

The knight reached out hesitantly and took the sword, holding it before him as though it were the most ancient of relics.

'The Carrard blade!' breathed Leofric. 'Lost this last century!'

'Indeed it is. Do it honour, for it is yours to bear now.'

The knight nodded, stepping back as Leofric rose and turned back to Morvhen and Kyarno, not surprised to see the prophetess standing beside them. How she had come to be here, he did not know, but her presence was the final piece of the puzzle before him.

'You knew this would happen?' he asked her.

'Yes, Leofric, I did,' agreed Naieth. 'I am sorry I could not tell you before, but there was much at stake.'

'For you,' snapped Leofric. 'What is there left to me?'

'You heard the words of the Lady,' said Naieth. 'You know what is left to you.'

Leofric wanted to feel anger towards Naieth, but the vision of the grail had purged him of such petty considerations. The Lady had indeed told him what was left to him and he nodded, dropping to one knee and pulling Helene's favour from his gauntlet. He wrapped the blue silk scarf around his hands as he recited a vow he had learned from childhood and had hoped always to some day pledge.

'I set down my lance, symbol of duty. I spurn those whom I love. I relinquish all, and take up the tools of my quest. No obstacle will stand before me. No plea for help shall find me wanting. No moon will look upon me twice lest I be judged idle. I give my body, heart and soul to the Lady whom I seek…'

He rose as Kyarno stood before him.

'What do those words mean?' asked Kyarno.

'That I am sworn to the quest for the grail,' said Leofric, bending to pick up a fallen helmet. Its shape was of a design unfamiliar to him, but it was not displeasing to the eye and he placed it over his head, raising the visor as he saw a flame-maned elven steed come galloping over the eastern horizon.

'Aeneor,' he said, recognising the beast as it cantered towards him.

'Would I be right in thinking that these are dangerous lands?' asked Kyarno.

'All lands are dangerous, Kyarno, you should know that.'

'Then you will need a weapon,' said the elf, twisting the haft of the Blades of Midnight and separating them into a pair of white-bladed swords. He offered one of the weapons to Leofric, who smiled and took up the weapon.

'It is light,' he said, spinning the blade.

'I believe the Hound of Winter would not have been displeased to know you bear it,' said Kyarno. 'May it keep you safe in your quest.'

'I will return it to Coeth-Mara when it is at an end,' swore Leofric.

Leofric turned back to Naieth and asked, 'I will return to these lands?'

'You shall, Leofric,' nodded Naieth. 'Many times.'

'Good,' said Leofric, nodding towards the assembled knights who watched their discourse fearfully, 'then I will say no goodbyes.'

Leofric climbed onto the back of his elven steed and snapped down the visor as he considered what lay before him. He was now sworn to the quest for the grail and his entire body sang with the glory and yearning of such a venture. Leofric took a last look at the castle that had once been his as his namesake approached him, the Carrard blade held before him.

'You never told me your name,' said the knight.

'These are your lands now,' replied Leofric. 'I charge you to keep them safe in the name of the king and the Lady.'

'Please, sir knight, I beg of you,' said the silver-haired knight. 'Your name?'

'You know my name,' said Leofric, before turning and riding into the west in search of the grail.

'There was a knight came riding by,
in early spring when the roads were dry,
And he heard that Lady sing at the noon,
Two red roses across the moon.'

EPILOGUE
Season of the Knight

LEOFRIC CARRARD TRAVELLED far and wide on his quest for the grail, journeying to lost lands and encountering many strange and wondrous things before its completion. In distant Cathay, he slew the Jade Dragon of the Emerald River and saved the wives of Emperor Zhang-Jimou from decapitation by the Executioner Cult of the Jade Pearl.

The mysteries of far-off Ind were laid before him as he quested for the grail in the Caves of Fire and learned the secrets of the ancient stylites who dwelt there.

His quest drove him ever onwards until, at last, in the darkest place of the world, Leofric discovered the grail and supped from its radiant waters as a hunter's moon arose over the forest of the Asrai.

Leofric was to return to Athel Loren many times over the years, each time travelling its secret paths and hoping to reach a young knight searching for his lost wife before it was too late.

...time is a winding river beneath the boughs of Athel Loren, and many things are possible there that some would think hopeless. Paths once trod may be trod again and their ends woven anew...